UNRAVEL

ALSO AVAILABLE FROM
KAITLYN DEANN

The Witches' Sleep Duology
The Witches' Sleep
World of the Beasts

Short Stories
On the Day of Silence

THE
FORGOTTEN
COUNTRYMEN

UNRAVEL

KAITLYN DEANN

THE FORGOTTEN COUNTRYMEN
UNRAVEL
Hardback edition ISBN: 978-1-915129-13-0
Paperback edition ISBN: 978-1-915129-15-4
Trade paperback edition: 978-1-915129-55-0
e-Book edition ISBN: 978-1-915129-14-7

Published by Two Trees Books, an imprint of Chartus.X LTD
www.chartusx.org

First Chartus.X edition: October, 2023
This version was published simultaneously in
Great Britain and the USA.

This book is an updated compilation of the first three books in *The
Chronicles of the Forgotten Countrymen* novella series.

Map by Andrés Aguirre Jurado
Cover designed by GetCovers
Character illustrations by Chicklen Doodle

www.authorkaitlyndeann.com

This one is for my husband, Chris,
who always believes I can do it.

PART 1

THE BRAND OF
ANEM

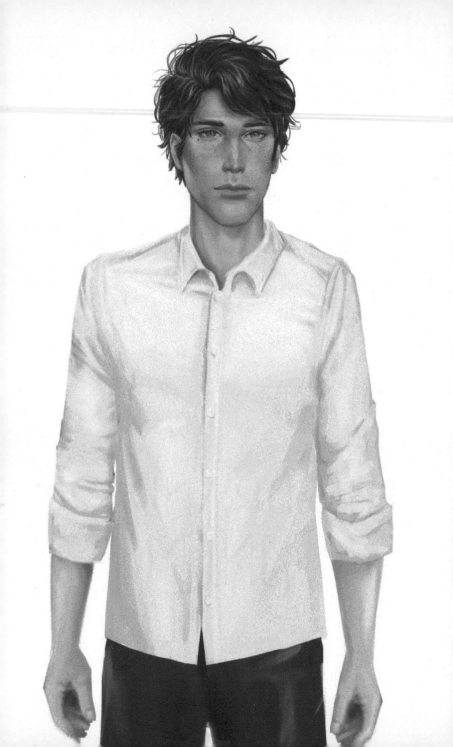

The weather mirrored Carson's mood: morose and cantankerous and bleak.

The coastal breeze cut through his finely-tailored evening suit like a frozen knife, straight through to his shivering bones. Beside him, his younger sister, Casey, squeezed his bare hand with her gloved one. Her scarf had unwound itself and hung freely around her shoulders. Carson paused to wrap her scarf back around her neck to protect it from the harsh wind and tug her hand-knit hat over her frozen ears. Casey was six years younger than he was, and that made her his responsibility, though Carson would have cared for the eleven-year-old even if she wasn't.

They resumed their hand-in-hand walk to the temple, where their parents waited for them at the city's engagement celebration of the year. The worst of winter had passed, thankfully, and spring was slow to wake from its hibernation. The northern breezes that carried the chill of winter still cut sharply through the city, but the warm sun kept the ground free of ice and snow.

Carson told himself not to show how he felt, and as he walked to the temple with his sister in tow, he practiced an expressionless mien. It took less effort than he had expected, even though he'd been in the business of hiding his emotions to the outside world since he was twelve.

"Carson?" rasped Casey. She sounded like she was possibly getting sick, and that worried him a tad.

Carson reached over with his free hand and pulled the scarf up over her mouth and nose. Perhaps that would help some, but he wasn't all that confident. "What is it?" he replied, voice low.

"You're very quiet." There was no question. Just the statement.

"And you look very cold."

She shivered in agreement.

"Don't worry," he said. "We're nearly to the temple. Just a few more minutes."

Thankfully, the goddess was looking down on their shivering bodies and had mercy. She stopped the wind for the rest of the walk, and the still cold air was not so unbearable. Carson quickly sent a thank-you prayer to her as they trotted up the marble steps of the temple.

Once inside the warm sanctuary, Casey let out an exasperated sigh of relief during the all-important moment of silence. Horrified, Carson covered her mouth halfway through the sigh, yet several people nearest them still turned to look in disappointment and some even in disgust.

He nodded his apologies at them and dragged Casey along the back wall, past the iron stools of burning incense, still covering her mouth. Glaring at him, she shook his hand off but remained silent as they made their way further into the candle-lit sanctuary to where their parents, Derek and Kayla, were seated.

They never sat anywhere else in the whole of the grand temple.

Red robes hissing with the movement, the prophet climbed the steps to the podium where a twelve-foot-tall white marble statue of a slender woman loomed, as she had for hundreds of years, her face veiled to represent modesty and her belly pregnant with the universe and all its inhabitants.

The prophet turned to the congregation, the hood of his robes shadowing his face from the afternoon sun streaming through the stained-glass windows behind him. He pushed back his hood, his gelled white hair remaining perfectly combed to one side. His booming voice carried through the whole sanctuary as he gestured to the statue behind him and said, "We thank Anem for blessing us with opportunities such as this. Today we have all gathered to celebrate the most recent engagement of our wonderful city. Ambassador Amaia James and Judge Mark James' daughter, Duchess Margaret James, to the chief officer, William Lach."

The words prodded at Carson's heart like a million tiny needles. Casually, he placed a hand over it, tenderly rubbing at the ache in his tightening chest as he fought back tears, fought back the lump that formed in his throat. Fought to keep his promise.

Margaret and William ascended the podium, William positioning himself on the prophet's left while Margaret took up her place on the prophet's right side, and Carson felt the leash on his emotions slip just a fraction. William's expressionless face had never been so punchable.

"Please help me welcome this soon-to-be wedded couple!"

Carson's throat squeezed, but he reeled himself back in time to clap along with everyone else in the room.

Margaret glanced at the congregation, smiling sheepishly, a smile that didn't meet her hazel eyes. A simpering smile she had learned to show the world. Not like the ones she revealed around him, the ones that lit up her entire face and set a hive of bees buzzing in his belly every time he looked into her eyes. Memories ricocheted in his mind, sending pain shooting down his spine and settling in his chest.

Kristina Margaret James...

Carson tried not to stare. It was no use. He couldn't look away. Couldn't look away from her auburn waves pinned atop her head; from her pink glossed lips, likely tasting of her cherry lip balm. Couldn't—

Margaret's wandering gaze swept over the sea of spectators to settle on him. Her eyes screamed at him that she was sorry and wished things were different. Carson looked away. He wished things were different too. None of it was her fault. She didn't pick this life, yet she was forced to live it. He could never fault her for what she couldn't control.

"After the service," began Prophet Theo when the applause died down, "there will be a dinner in the recreational hall provided by our Ambassador and the Judge. Everyone is encouraged to stop by for a plate and to congratulate Margaret and William."

The service was shorter than he had expected. The message was on marriage and the goddess's blessing of children, yada yada. Distracted by his own racing thoughts, Carson tuned most of it out, having heard it more times than he could recall. In the end, the prophet closed with a prayer and sent them on their way to the recreational hall.

"I don't feel well," Carson said quietly to his parents in an attempt to avoid going. "Can we leave already?"

His nurse-of-a-mother slapped her hand on his forehead seconds before declaring, "You don't feel warm."

"We won't stay long," his father added. "We'll say our due to the couple, grab food, and leave."

Resistance was futile.

Carson watched with resignation as his parents joined the crowd heading toward the hall that was connected to the sanctuary. The bottomless pit that she was, Casey was right on their heels, skipping gleefully at the smell of the food.

Dragging his feet, Carson integrated into the crowd, allowing people to pass him by as his family disappeared into the throng far ahead of him.

The overwhelming smell of mollusks and other seafoods from the Port of Kaitos wafting from the dishes to fill the air in the hall caused the pit in his stomach to toss. He wasn't sure he'd be able to eat anything, not even the slow-cooked lamb or chicken or beef. He *technically* wasn't lying when he said he didn't feel well.

After hugging the wall and following it to one of the corners, Carson searched for his family. Hopefully they'd said something to

Margaret and William so they could get out of there already.

"Carson."

His attention snapped to his left to find Bobby, an old school friend of his, also escaping the farce of this celebration. His discomfort mirrored in Bobby's incessant fidgeting with the cuffs of his own blue suit. Carson forced a grin.

Bobby's discomfort was not the same as his. He suffered from an anxiety disorder which rendered him useless in large crowds if he didn't take his medication properly. Carson wasn't supposed to know that—it was against the rules to know such personal details about anyone, really. He hadn't asked to know. Bobby volunteered the information one day after he'd broken down in front of Carson at school. Carson had never mentioned it to anyone. Perhaps it was the very reason Bobby had felt comfortable enough to tell him.

"Are you going to get food and leave too?" Bobby asked.

Carson simply nodded, looking over at the buffet. He caught sight of his mother handing Casey a plate with exotic meats, heavily doused in a honey glaze and a roll of bread shiny with a garlic-butter spread. He watched his sister's eyes widen as one of the six hired chefs standing on the opposite side of the buffet offered her a generous helping of creamy homemade pasta made from the eggs of cerulean owls—a rare bird only found in the District of Diphda. Their eggs were expensive to eat and required special permission to purchase since very few were sold every year.

Carson couldn't recall how long it had been since his family had eaten such rare and extravagant dishes. Five years ago, perhaps? At Margaret's Coming of Age dinner.

The line behind his parents grew longer.

Bobby heaved a sigh. "So many people came out for their engagement."

"Yeah," Carson agreed in a small voice. "She is the Duchess after all."

His friend nodded. "I miss when we were all in school."

Carson's eyes skimmed over the crowd, searching for the Duchess. He found her standing next to her betrothed, a line of people waiting to speak to them, to shake their hands, to congratulate them on their soon-to-be marriage.

Bobby elbowed him in the ribs.

"Ow!" Carson hissed. "What was that for, you jerk?"

Bobby whispered, "You were staring at her."

Scowling and rubbing his side, Carson looked away.

"I'm not going to say anything," Bobby added quickly. Carson groaned internally. "I've got your back." There was only a moment's lapse before he continued, "I know today's hard for you, but—"

Carson looked directly at him. "Shut up, Bobby. You know nothing."

Except he wasn't necessarily wrong. But Carson could never admit to such things. Admission would spell out certain punishments, and then everyone would know everything. He couldn't afford that.

He spotted his family eating at one of the many white silk-draped tables, clear globes of twinkling lights mimicking Anem's heavenly constellations in the center surrounded by lit plum-colored candlesticks each set in golden crescent moon dishes. Carson said bye to Bobby as he rushed over to his family. His mother was chatting with one of the older women sitting next to her while his father was speaking to Casey quietly.

"Carson," Kayla said when he walked up to the table. "Get some food. You should eat."

"No, thanks," he declined politely. "I would like to leave now, Mom."

"Oh, come now," the older lady sitting next to Kayla said. "Don't live your life in such a hurry, my dear! Sit and eat!"

"That's kind of you, Mrs. Clementine," said Kayla, "but I think Carson isn't feeling well."

"Oh," Mrs. Clementine crooned, looking over Carson for any signs of illness. Carson attempted to slacken his facial muscles—droop his eyelids and downturn his lips—in hopes of looking tired and hopefully even ill. "Poor boy! Take some food with you and rest."

Suddenly, somebody bumped into him hard, a yelp escaping them—feminine, he noted—and the clattering of a plate spilling its contents on the floor had many turning their heads. He quickly gathered his footing and turned to whoever knocked into him. Carson's eyes met with a pair of emerald green ones, and his breath hitched at the familiar sight. He knew those eyes anywhere, knew the girl they belonged to.

"Gina," he croaked, voice little more than a whisper.

The blonde girl did not hear him as she exclaimed, "Oh, stars!" and bent to clean up the salad and steak pieces scattered around them. "I'm so sorry, Carson," she blurted. "I wasn't looking where I was going."

Carson blinked, her words drowned out by the buzzing in his head. The room seemed to expand and contract all at once, and Carson wished the ground would open up to swallow him whole.

Not here. Not now. Not her.

He silently helped her pile the mess into her plate, the whole while wracking his brain to come up with something to say to her. But what could he say to Gina Blake? It was *Gina Blake*.

Gina rose, her disposable plate filled with the gathered meal, and Carson pursed his lips, jaw clamped tightly shut. They shared a long silent moment as she searched his face, waiting. Was she expecting him to say something? His palms began sweating, and he shoved them in his pockets.

A server dressed in all black with a white bow tie offered to take Gina's plate. She gracefully accepted, handing him the plate. The server scurried off with a promise to bring her a new meal.

Their eyes met again. She blinked once, softly, disrupting his gaze into her emerald eyes. Her plump lips pursed to the side of her mouth, and she looked down at the scuffed toes of her worn leather boots partially covered by her draping teal-blue skirt.

He needed to say something. *Anything*.

"*Itisgoodtoseeyou*," he stumbled, his words breathless and crashing into one another haphazardly. He cleared his throat, face crimsoning, and then whispered, "I hope you and your family are doing well, Ginevieve."

Was that awkward? Damn it. Why can't I be normal around her?
And *Ginevieve*? Had he *ever* called her by her given name?
This night truly can't get worse.

For a second, he wondered if he would feel awkward around Gina for the rest of his life. Would it always be so uncomfortable to see her and be reminded of all the empty promises they had made to each other? Perhaps it was only awkward because they hadn't been empty to him. Even after all this time, a part of him ached at the sight of her.

Perhaps he indeed deserved the misery of Margaret's engagement to another man.

Gina gave him a small smile. "We're getting by," she whispered, looking over her shoulder at a table a few rows down.

Her father was easy to spot; he was loud and large, and his presence demanded attention. Her four siblings were sitting down around him, plates of their own piled high with the delicious delicacies paid for by Judge and Ambassador James.

Carson was glad to see the young children smiling. It pleased him even more that Gina was smiling. He remembered wondering if she'd ever smile again. His heart swelled and ached at the same time. *Praise the goddess for her returned happiness.*

"Have you spoken with the Judge yet?" Gina asked, voice as light and airy as it always had been. Her green eyes sparkled when he met her gaze with his own.

He lost his breath for a moment. He opened his mouth to answer but no words came out. He wanted to ask what for, because he had no reason to speak to the Judge.

"Gina." Derek's voice interrupted Carson's thoughts. His father handed Gina a small plate with a large slice of vanilla cake and strawberry icing on it. "They gave me the last piece of cake. Did you get any?"

She smiled kindly at Derek. "No, sir. I was a tad too late."

"Please take mine. I'm too full to eat it."

She took it and bowed her head in gratitude. "Thank you, Mr. Owens. For everything your family does for mine." She gestured to the dessert. "And for the cake."

Derek waved his hand dismissively at her, though a small smile played on the corner of his lips. "Go on and eat, child." He motioned to Carson too. "You may go with her, if you'd like. Be home by seven-thirty."

Carson shook his head, glancing at Gina who had immediately blushed. His heart swelled further at the joy on her face, though confusion at her reaction quickly invaded the remaining space in his heart.

Gina said to Derek, "As much as I would like Carson's company, I have chores to finish once I get home."

Derek shrugged. "All the more reason for him to go along. Four hands are better than two."

She gazed sidelong at Carson and whispered, "If you want to come over for a little while, I know my father would be okay with it."

An iron cage clamped shut around his heart. Gina had been clear about what she wanted. "I'm afraid I really am ill. I would hate to get anyone sick."

Her smile faltered. "Oh. I understand. I hope you feel better."

As she turned away, Carson made a conscious effort to keep his eyes fixed on the polished floor until he was sure she was seated with her family, and he pushed Gina Blake from his thoughts, as he had done many times over the last year and a half.

Perhaps losing Margaret in this way had kicked up the dust that had settled on his past heartache. Heartache... his heart had ached for Gina too. But she had rejected him, just as society would surely have rejected a future with him and Margaret together.

Finally, his father stood and announced to the table that his family should be retiring home.

"I'll be outside waiting," Carson said the moment Derek had finished speaking. Perhaps he indeed deserved to suffer such heartache. Shoulders slumped, Carson headed out into the cold, cruel evening.

Carson had already been in bed for an hour before it came time for lights out. This only confirmed to his parents that he had actually been sick.

He spent his time in bed, thinking. That was nothing new. There were a lot of sleepless nights where all Carson did was think.

He recalled Bobby noticing he was staring at Margaret back at the temple. That unsettled Carson; he wasn't sure who else had seen him staring. And his friend was right: it was inappropriate for Carson's eyes to linger on anyone, let alone the Duchess.

After his Coming of Age Ceremony at twelve, he was considered old enough to be held accountable for his sins. He remembered one of the elite acolytes of Anem sitting him down in an office at the Courthouse of Polaris—the capital of the Province of Deneb, their home. Derek was on his right and Kayla on his left. The holy man had had his book of the law in front of him, and they'd spent several hours that day going over the rules and all the consequences if Carson broke a single one. He then had to sign a paper saying he understood the rules and that he would accept any punishment that he deserved if he dared break one.

That day was a drag for Carson, he recalled, mostly because he already knew all the rules. Derek was an officer in their city. He had his own special copy of the rulebook at home to study, and that was what

Carson learned to read with when he was a young boy. Not only that, but he had always wanted to be an officer just like his father, so he had studied the rules carefully before his Coming of Age Ceremony.

Carson wasn't so sure that was what he wanted anymore, though. It didn't matter what he wanted anyway. No one got to pick their careers. They were all assigned, and he was one of the last in his class to receive a letter from the Courthouse announcing his job title. Bobby Collins had already received his letter assigning him to blacksmithing.

Perhaps they are going in alphabetical order, Carson thought. He wasn't sure what the true hold up was though. All he knew was that he thought the Job Assignment Test was easy, and Carson didn't think it was meant to be, which made him think that he was deceived by the wording of the test's questions itself into thinking it was easy. Perhaps he scored terribly on it. Was it a test that could be scored? Some sections didn't feel academic at all. He wouldn't know until he got that letter.

"Carson?" It was his mother. He remained on his side, keeping his back to her. She touched his shoulder lightly and sat down on the edge of the bed. "Can I get anything for you? It's nearly lights out, and you haven't had dinner. I can heat something up for you quickly."

Her soft voice was usually warming to Carson, but right now he just wanted her to leave. She couldn't understand if she tried, so he didn't even attempt to explain to her his thoughts. He wouldn't dare anyway. Not in a million years.

"I'm fine, Mom," he said, turning over to her. "I'm just a little...off, I guess."

"Ah," Kayla said as if she really understood what was going on, though she could never. "You're worried you won't be assigned to the justice department like your dad?"

"Yeah," Carson sighed.

In truth, it had nothing to do with that. He didn't care about becoming an officer. Fortunate—or unfortunate—to be born into a Class Five family, he'd be fine with whatever Middle Class position he was assigned to. The Middle Classes, Four, Five and Six, consisted mainly of officers like his father, nurses like his mother, and teachers like their neighbor Patrick. Carson pinched his blanket between his index finger and thumb, kneading the fabric until his fingers ached. He'd be assigned a Middle Class job, and a Middle Class wife.

A part of him had once hoped that wife would be Gina. As a Class Four, she would have been allowed to marry him. And though she had made it perfectly clear where she stood on that matter, he found a small part of him still held out hope. Or perhaps watching Margaret stand next to another at her engagement celebration had left his broken heart pawing desperately at something—anything—to hold on to.

Margaret had been born out of his reach, though he had somehow managed to deceive himself otherwise. She was a Class Eight, and as the highest Class, it meant the lowest she could go was a Class Seven.

Carson always wondered why the rule forbidding the marriage of separate classes existed. He always wondered why most of their rules existed. He assumed it was an attempt at control, though he could not understand why or to what end.

"Oh, honey," his mother crooned. "The city will make sure you get the job you are best suited for, even if it's something surprising." She patted his shaggy black hair, the color being one of the features he had got from her, including her curls. It was a pity the women of Deneb had to wear their hair pulled back. All the women in the Province of Deneb wore their hair up on their head in some form or fashion. It was the only appropriate way to wear it.

The mattress groaned and shifted as she got to her feet. Carson turned back over, studying his ceiling, ready to be left alone with his thoughts once more.

"Carson?"

He turned his face to see his mother lingering in the doorway. "If you need me, you may wake me whenever."

He shook his head. "It's against the rules."

"Illness is an exception. You look a little pale, son."

13

"I am not that ill."

She sighed. "Okay. Sweet dreams." She shut the bedroom door.

Carson listened to her fading footfalls, counting each passing moment before the lights in the house went out, just as it did in the whole of the Province. It was almost time.

Almost.

Patiently, Carson waited until the coyotes started singing to each other and the cold winter breeze coming off the sea rustled the trees outside his window. He sat up quietly, throwing the covers off his body. He changed into a pair of comfortable jeans and pulled a blue long-sleeve shirt over his white undershirt. What he was doing was definitely rebellious, and he had done it many times before. It was an addiction, if he was being honest with himself. Every time he got away with breaking a rule, he wanted to do it more and more and push his limits. How far could he go before getting caught?

There were so many rules with so many consequences. It was caging, limiting. It only made him want to rebel even more.

He was a trapped animal, and as each day passed, the cage shrunk more and more, severely cramped, pushing at him from all sides. Something was bound to give eventually.

A part of Carson blamed his own father. He always seemed to think Carson would do something stupid. As if it were inevitable for him to break the rules. As if it was something he expected of his son. Perhaps his father knew things about Carson and chose not to say anything. Maybe he could see himself in the seventeen-year-old. Was it possible that he had done what Carson had done when he was an Immature, too?

Under the bed, Carson had stuffed a bag with things he'd need. He pulled out his black boots and laced them on his feet tightly, as quietly as he could manage. He wrestled with his hunter green pullover sweater for a few seconds to get it over his head without knocking things over in his cramped room. Carson added a hand-knit hat that

14

his mother had purchased a few weeks ago from the outdoor Uptown Marketplace, tucking his ears into the warmth it provided.

His breathing was heavier from the adrenaline pumping through him. His hands shook slightly and suddenly felt clammy. He focused on his breathing as he wiped his palms on his jeans.

The consequences for purposefully breaking curfew was ten lashes at the whipping post.

His hands trembled as he fumbled with the latch on the window. Windows were only ever opened during the fall, when the cool breezes were plentiful and filled the house with scents of coming winter. Even then, no one was allowed to keep them open at night. They were shut when the lights went out. Period. No exceptions.

Carson quietly lifted the window as far as it would go. The opening was almost too small for his body to fit through, but he managed the tight squeeze. The browning grass crunched faintly under his weight. The cold breeze hit him hard the moment the window was cracked open, and he shivered against it. He didn't slow down though, and he didn't make a sound. It was a game to Carson. Part of him was ashamed, and he supposed maybe he should've listened to that part, but he ignored the tiny voice as if it were simply nothing but an annoying prod at his heart.

He shut the window as quietly as possible before darting across the backyard, over the fence, and through the few acres of scattered trees and brush browned by the weather. He climbed over a barbed wire fence, trying to be careful not to rip his brand-new sweater on the rusted barbs. His mother would kill him and demand to know how he managed to damage it after only two days of wear.

Stopping as soon as his feet hit the ground on the other side of the fence, he took a moment to glance up at the starlit sky. The moon shone brightly in the inky darkness of the night. The stars blinked at him a warning. In the distance, the wild coyotes howled mournfully at the moon. He wanted to yowl along with them from the ache clutching his soul.

Carson began running again. He jumped multiple fences and trespassed several different properties. Eventually, he was running through the trees that glittered the Judge's property. He stopped short behind a fairly thick tree when the Judge's white house with navy-blue trimmings came into view. All the lights were off, of course, but if the Judge gandered out a window, the moon would surely give Carson away.

He tried getting as close to the back corner window as he could by moving from tree to tree. He couldn't be too careful.

Finally, he had made it, standing only a few feet from a window several times the size of his window back home. He crept up to the glass, straining his ears for any sounds inside, but it was deadly silent. A curtain hung on the inside of the window, blocking his view.

His heart hammered in his chest. What he was doing was always the scariest part. It was always kind of a gamble, but he took the risk every time. He waited a few more minutes, listening for any noise, before tapping once on the glass with the tip of his finger lightly. He repeated the knock a couple of seconds later, then knocked a third time a moment after that.

The curtain within flurried and shifted a little, and Margaret's unsurprised face appeared directly in front of his, framed by her long wavy auburn hair parted down the middle and hanging around her shoulders.

Margaret smiled at Carson through the glass between them. He returned the simple expression, such joy flooding through him at the sight of her. She glanced over her shoulder to scan the room before unlatching the window and heaving it upward.

It cracked open only just.

Carson chuckled to himself as he watched her struggle with it a little longer. Determination shone in her hazel eyes, the effort flushing her cheeks to match the silk nightdress she donned. Knowing she would not ask for help, Carson watched her a moment longer before breathing a small sigh and slipping his fingers into the opening and shimmying the window pane all the way up.

Margaret perched on the sill, her nightdress bunching under her. Carson carefully sat next to her. The sides of their bodies pressed together in the narrow opening. A heartbeat later, he leaned into her, his lips crashing against hers. She met his kiss with the same fiery desire. For several long moments, words were unnecessary and unwanted.

They broke off their greeting, both panting gently. Margaret shivered against the cool northern breeze, goosebumps rising on the exposed flesh of her arms.

"You'll catch a cold," rasped Carson.

She grabbed the blanket folded neatly on the ottoman next to the window. Wrapping it around her shoulders, she turned back to him with a coy smile.

He smiled back, helping her adjust the lavender blanket to fit snugly around her frame.

She mumbled a thanks as he finished bundling her in the blanket, eyeing him carefully. "You shouldn't have been there today, Carson," she whispered. "You shouldn't have had to see any of that."

He gathered her into an embrace as he asked, "Any of what, exactly?"

"You know what," she grumbled, nuzzling her nose into his neck. When he did not respond, she heaved a sorrowful sigh, then whispered, "Why did you go? I told you not to."

He kissed her ear, the cold of her skin chilling his lips. "I can't avoid reality forever, now can I?"

"Yet here you are."

He supposed that was a fair observation. When he pulled away, she clung to him, a refusal to release him, and sniffled. She was crying. He didn't think he'd ever known the Duchess of Deneb to cry.

He squeezed Margaret to him tighter, and she melted into him. For several minutes, he didn't say a word or move a muscle as she shook with silent sobs.

Once she'd calmed and pulled away, he finally suggested what had been on his mind all evening: "Let's get out of here."

She cleaned the wetness from her face with her blanket as she nodded. "The neighbor's stable?"

He glanced over at the neighbor's property before responding with a curt nod. Over the treetops he could barely make out the top of the dilapidated horse's stable—an all too familiar place for Margaret and him.

Taking her to the neighbor's old stable was easy. No one would see them. For one, the neighbor was a crippled old man—a million and a half years old, Carson figured—and his house was positioned a good quarter mile away from the stable. Not to mention, the old man was blind in his left eye, and his right eye wasn't of much use either.

On top of that, the stable had been empty for many years, the occasional visitor being a small wild animal. It was the perfect place for Carson and Margaret to be alone, to hide from the harsh world that would see them destroyed if ever caught.

"We shouldn't stay here long," said Margaret as she climbed the ladder to the mostly bare loft. All that remained in the loft were a bunch of feed sacks that overtime the two of them had spread out to make a place to lie. That was the only place they could talk normally, not forced to be quieter than death.

To the side of the feed sacks, they sat on a pile of hay under a dirt-caked window that had a crack running through it from top to bottom. They wrapped themselves together in Margaret's blanket, the very same one they'd been bringing with them for as long as they had been going there.

Carson placed his forehead against hers and closed his eyes. After several long silent moments, holding her tightly in his arms and occasionally kissing her, Margaret asked, "What's wrong, Carson?"

He hesitated, exhaling softly a moment later. "Been a long day," he whispered, brushing his lips across her jawline.

"You mean it's been a long two months."

That was true. Ever since Margaret had told him her father had pledged her to William Lach, it had felt like time was moving slowly and in the wrong direction.

But that wasn't really what Carson had meant. He was trying not to think about Gina Blake. And he was failing miserably. The iron cage around his heart had not been effective enough to protect him from her. Their encounter earlier that day had stuck to him like tar, and he had difficulty pushing thoughts of her from his mind. Enough of Gina had entered his heart that it ached for her like a beached whale aches for the sea, for its home, for where it belongs.

His chest twinged under the ache in his heart, and for a moment, he wished—horrid, heartless, awful as he was—that Margaret was Gina instead.

Carson clenched his teeth, burying his face in Margaret's hair to hide the strain in his jaw from her. *I love Maggie,* he chided himself. *I do. I swear I do. I swear it!*

He clutched Margaret closer to him, squeezing his longings for Gina away and banishing the warring thoughts of the two women from his mind. But it didn't matter, he realized, relenting, his muscles releasing a second later with the truth that was now so glaringly obvious: He couldn't truly have either of them.

Tears dripped onto Carson's hand, which brought his attention back to the moment, to the fact Margaret was crying again. "I never wanted to hurt you," she whispered, words straining through her tight throat.

"You didn't," Carson told her in the same moment, hugging her tighter to himself. "It's not your fault. Your father forced this on you."

Sobs escaped her throat suddenly, despite her attempt to hamper them. Carson thought it was good he took her away from her house when he did. He would never tell her not to cry, but she couldn't relieve herself of everything she kept cooped inside her while near anyone else. She needed a place to allow herself the freedom of mourning, and that old rundown stable was just that place for her.

Carson ran his fingers over the series of scars on her left shoulder that made up the brand of Anem, the very brand that linked them together. He leaned down and kissed it softly. Another sob left Margaret. "It's not fair," she rasped between sobs.

He kissed the brand again, then whispered against her skin, "We can't change it."

After several minutes, she was able to calm herself down again. She hugged herself to Carson and warmed her icy hands under his shirt, pressing against his body. "Carson," she whispered finally, "about William…"

He shook his head, lips brushing against her neck. He kissed her once before saying, "I don't want to talk about him."

"You've been saying that for two months. When will you?"

"Not ever." He gave her neck another soft kiss.

She sighed, defeated. "Thought you weren't avoiding reality anymore."

She got him there. Carson gazed up at her, into her hazel eyes illuminated in the moonlight streaking through the cracked, dirty window. "I'm not avoiding it," he defended. "You think that I haven't thought about your engagement to him these past two months? As if I could get it out of my brain." He paused to swallow a rising lump of emotions. "For instance, what's going to happen when you marry him and he sees that stupid brand on your shoulder?"

"Don't call it that," she said, breathless. "It's the gift Anem gave us."

"Gift?" Carson huffed. "More like a curse, Margaret. It'll ruin you."

She shook her head vigorously. Quite obviously, she didn't like that he'd called something from Anem such a horrible thing. "She's bound our souls together, Carson. That's what it symbolizes. That you and I are forever linked."

"No one cares." Carson's throat tightened, making it harder to get the words out. "They just see the sin." That was the most disappointing part to Carson. They couldn't see past the sin and appreciate their love for each other. Couples rarely loved each other, and those who did were envied.

She was quiet for a few moments before whispering, "It will be our downfall."

"Inevitably," he agreed in a low voice.

She stood up then, disrupting the comfort of their body heat under the blanket. She took the blanket off Carson as well and spread it across the old feed sacks. "One hour," she said. She began undressing for him. She shivered slightly though it wasn't nearly as cold inside the barn as it was outside in the coastal breeze.

"An hour is more than I ever ask for," he said, following her to the makeshift bed.

Carson kissed her lips hard. They were salty from her tears and also sweet from her cherry-flavored lip balm. Her hands found their way around his clothing easily. There was a hunger in her Carson hadn't seen before, and he liked it far more than he should've. In general, he liked the way she felt against him, and he should not like such sinful things.

But why? What was wrong? Carson wasn't hurting her, and she wasn't hurting him. The only thing that separated them from loving each other properly were the rules, based on the principles and commandments outlined by the goddess in the Eight Star Scrolls, which forbade those in different Classes from marrying. No one had a good reason why it was that way, why it had been that way for thousands of years. It was an ancient and severely outdated law that should've been done away with but probably wouldn't as long as the law reflected the teachings of Anem.

That old stable wasn't the first place they were ever intimate with each other. Since they were sixteen they had been breaking that rule, and for nearly a year, no one had ever caught onto them.

It was strange too, Carson had thought, how no one had yet discovered them. After the first time they shared themselves with each other, they both received the brand of Anem on their left shoulders—two matching brands unique from the rest of mankind. The lines and symbols etched deep into the dermis could only be read by the goddess herself. Specialists speculated that the symbols spelled out the two names of the lovers, but it was code that couldn't be cracked.

Carson and Margaret were frightened that someone would see the brands, and then everyone would know they had broken such a sacred rule. So they were careful—so very, very careful. They hid their shoulders from every eye. No one had ever caught even a glimpse of their unique, matching scars.

C arson had seemed off. He was quieter than normal, and that was saying something. If his body mass was sixty percent water, then Margaret considered the other forty percent was simply made up of quietness and deep thought—the deep thought usually being the cause of his silence.

Yet, Margaret hadn't wanted to ask what he was thinking, because, if she were honest with herself, she knew exactly what thoughts churned in the mill of his mind. After all, it was only hours prior when they had been in the same room, pretending to not know each other while she stood next to her fiancé. She was sure he had watched her thank every person that congratulated her and William on their soon-to-be marriage.

It had to have bothered him, and for that she felt a tremendous amount of guilt. He had to know it wasn't what she wanted, though. She didn't pick William. Her father picked him, which was not an abnormal practice.

Every marriage was arranged, and in a lot of cases, people were paired together without any request to marry given. One could write a formal marriage request to the Judge, but it didn't mean he would honor the request. It was just the way it had been done for thousands of years. These traditions ensured a successful generation would follow.

If she could pick, she would've picked Carson a hundred times over. That was, if they were even in the same Social Class... Which, of course, they weren't.

If it wasn't one thing, it was another.

Margaret didn't like William, and she was sure it was solely due to the fact that he was not Carson. Part of her felt bad about disliking William even though he had not done anything wrong, but she couldn't help or change how she felt.

And despite having had several partially chaperoned meals with him, in an attempt to better know one another, she barely knew a thing about her fiancé. He had seemed quite content with sitting in silence as they ate. She felt awkward in the quiet, but he acted like it was no problem or concern. Perhaps he even preferred it, she had thought.

As she laid in her bed struggling to get comfortable, knowing a sleepless night lay before her, she recalled the day she met William Lach.

It happened only two months ago. Her father had just barely told her he had made an agreement with the chief officer of the central precinct in Polaris—the capital of the Province of Deneb. She was confused why it concerned her, until he'd said the word marriage. That was the last thing she'd heard, though his mouth kept moving. She'd assumed he was defending himself on why he had picked William, and why he hadn't consulted with her first before signing a contract with the officer.

Then, only an hour later, William Lach had stopped by the house through an invite extended by her father. He had bowed his head to her and smiled. She remembered thinking he wasn't too horrible before he'd even introduced himself.

But he wasn't Carson. He could never measure up to Carson, she was sure of it. And what would happen when he saw the brand on her shoulder? He wouldn't want her. He would have grounds to divorce her. She would be shamed, and there would be no place in this world for one Duchess Margaret James any longer.

But she'd never apologize for loving Carson. They couldn't make her. If there was ever one thing she got right, it was loving Carson, even if they insisted it was wrong.

"And to think you'll be having your very own Ritual in a little less than a year," said Carson's mother, clapping her hands together as if she were ecstatic, except her eyes were drawn and her tone fell flat. Tired. She yawned as if to confirm his thoughts.

Carson wasn't sure he was looking forward to his Ritual. Everyone that had their Ritual changed. They were never themselves again. Like with Fiona Lancaster; her personality—who she was—seemed gone completely and replaced with a more stoic, quiet, serious, daunting Fiona.

Carson didn't understand what it really was, let alone how to explain it. He supposed it was just a part of growing up. It scared him, if he was being honest. It wasn't the growing up part. It was the change, the Ritual of an Immature transcending to a Mature. He didn't understand how it happened because it was such a private ordeal, and perhaps it was the unknown that made him nervous.

"What would you like your color theme to be, Carson?" his mother asked, reaching her hand up to his forehead to move his black hair that fell over his eyebrows to the side. "We need to start planning it out. Also, you need a haircut this week."

"I don't care about the colors," he told her softly, shrugging. He wished she wouldn't pester him about his Ritual until later. He was preoccupied with his thoughts, and she kept interrupting them.

Regarding the haircut she mentioned, he said, "If I get a haircut, I was thinking about doing something wild. Maybe shave the sides and braid the top. I heard that's the style in the Port of Kaitos right now." One eyebrow raised on his mother's face. He just smiled crookedly. "Just kidding, Mom. I'll be tame, I swear it."

She rolled her eyes. "You are a handful, Jerry Carson. A handful, I tell you." Then she puckered her lips in thought and her piercing sky-blue eyes wandered away from his face. He let his stare wander from her too, looking around the room at the people crowding into the recreational hall at the temple for Samuel's Ritual.

Samuel Vickers moved to their city only a year before, halfway through their last year of schooling. He was quiet like Carson. He could count on one hand how many conversations they'd actually had, one of them being that very day, just a few moments before Samuel was escorted into a private room by multiple people of different occupations—three officers, a physician, a nurse, the Prophet, and the Judge—to perform the Ritual.

He had left with brown eyes, and Carson knew he would emerge with piercing, electric-blue irises. Everyone did when the Ritual was completed. The bright blue represented the Mature. Any other color represented the Immature, even the regular shades of blue some Immatures had. Carson's question of what the Ritual actually was burned in the back of his mind. No one was ever allowed to ask, and it drove him to the brink of insanity not knowing.

"What about green and black?" Carson's mother ripped him from his thoughts once again. "You like those two colors, right?"

Suddenly, Carson's eyes caught sight of auburn hair pulled back into a tight bun and the laugh of one Miss Margaret James.

He'd forgotten his mother had spoken to him.

"Carson," she addressed, snapping her fingers in front of his face, making him start slightly.

He looked at her. "Yeah," he said, nodding quickly, glancing over at Margaret who had gathered a few people around her—old schoolmates that Carson recognized. "Sounds good, Mom. I'm going to go talk to some friends." He gave her a quick side-peck on her temple so she couldn't complain later about him just leaving her hanging. Kisses and hugs always worked with his mother.

As he approached the group, Carson overheard Margaret talking to Fiona Lancaster, her old friend that she had been closest to in school.

"I know!" Margaret exclaimed excitedly. "It feels just like yesterday we were graduating school. Look at us now. Everyone's getting their job assignments and Rituals are happening back-to-back." She sighed and then smiled.

"When is yours?" Fiona asked, voice low. It was strange to hear Fiona so mild-tempered.

"Yeah, Mags," commented Bobby who stood a good two feet from the women. "I forget how old you are."

"I just turned seventeen, so a little less than a year away. I've always been the youngest of the Immatures in our class. You know that, Fiona."

"Yeah, Fifi," Kelly commented while elbowing Fiona jokingly. In Carson's opinion, Kelly always seemed a bit disheveled, but he would not speculate.

Fiona smiled at the two girls weakly. Her electric-blue irises shimmered in the fluorescent light. "Of course. It slipped my mind. Growing up is definitely something to be excited about."

Fiona used to be giddy and always bubbling with joy. Where was that Fiona now? He supposed after her Ritual a month ago that she thought it was time to grow up. But Carson didn't see anything wrong with who she was before—besides being obnoxious eighty percent of the time. She didn't have to change because of the Ritual, even if she was one of the Matures now.

Fiona turned her head toward him. "Carson," she addressed, her flat voice once again taking him by surprise. "Glad you made it. I was concerned for your wellbeing considering how quickly you left

Margaret and William's engagement party. Bobby said you were sick."

Carson glanced at Bobby. He couldn't recall telling Bobby he felt ill, but perhaps he did and forgot. He simply shrugged at Fiona's comment. "I just needed to sleep it off."

Kelly smiled widely at Carson and blushed as she said, "Glad you're feeling better." Her messy bun flopped to the side when she glanced down at her shuffling feet. It wasn't anything new, but... Was she dancing?

What a strange girl, that Kelly. Thank Anem she's pledged. Now there's no chance I'd get stuck with her. Carson internally shuddered at the thought of Kelly being his wife. She would actually drive him insane, and then they would be a perfect match.

"Hopefully you didn't infect anyone," Margaret said.

Carson smiled at her, but was consciously making an effort not to let his eyes linger on her. He looked from her to Fiona to Kelly to Bobby, then back to Margaret as he spoke, "No promises. Misery likes company, you know."

Margaret and Kelly both giggled, but Fiona didn't find Carson amusing. Bobby just smirked and said, "So you always like company then?"

"You saying I'm always miserable, Collins?"

Bobby threw up his hands in surrender. "I'm not saying you're not always miserable."

The three young women snickered, but Margaret was the one that responded. "You two haven't changed a bit," she said. "That's nice."

Both boys smiled at her. Carson thought in that moment that it was almost like they were schoolmates again, talking together at lunchtime about stupid, meaningless stuff. He missed those days when life was simpler. Classroom shenanigans with Bobby, and the girls would giggle as they were scolded for disrupting the class—which only encouraged them to do it again the next time. Covertly shooting spitballs at each other through the hollow cylinder of a disassembled pen as they passed one another in the hall. Carson would always aim for Margaret's ear, and half of the time he'd get it right inside. She hated it, and that was exactly what made it great. Those days now felt like ages ago.

"What's going on over here?" William stepped up next to Margaret, half an inch from touching her. His smile was more of a smirk than a grin.

What William didn't know, though—and it made Carson repulsively pleased to think about—was that on the night of their engagement celebration, *he* had held Margaret in a carnal embrace.

Carson had to fight a mirroring smirk that wanted to escape, but he forced it back which resulted in the corner of his mouth twitching a couple of times.

"Catching up with old friends from school is all," Margaret said, gesturing to the group. She smiled at her soon-to-be husband, but Carson knew that fake smile anywhere. It was one she wore around people, being that she was expected to always be smiling. People were always watching the Duchess of Deneb, after all. But Carson had seen her real smile enough times to know the subtle differences.

Suddenly, Bobby slammed his elbow into Carson's bicep. "Ow!" Carson spit through his teeth, gripping his arm. "I swear, Bobby. Do that one more..." he began, but stopped himself short of the threat.

Bobby's eyes widened in that same way that said what it had always said: *Quit staring at her.*

William interrupted their exchange. "Boys, is there a problem?" He used his typical officer voice with them, and it pissed Carson off even more.

Boys? As if we're twelve?

They both looked at William immediately. Bobby was much more nervous than Carson. He stammered, "Oh, uh... No, sir. No problems here. Nope. Why would there be a problem?"

Apparently, we are twelve.

William glanced suspiciously between the two of them. Carson just rolled his eyes at Bobby. "It was nothing, sir," he mumbled at William.

"Yeah," Bobby said. "It was nothing. An inside joke. You wouldn't get it. Ahaha. Funny, huh, Carson?" He nudged Carson with his elbow lightly.

Carson ground his teeth and glared at Bobby. He clipped, "Shut up, Bobby."

Bobby sucked his lips in and nodded at Carson as he wrung his hands roughly behind his back.

"Well," William said, shifting his weight a bit closer to Margaret. Carson was all too happy to notice her shift her weight away from him. "That's a bit harsh, don't you think?"

Bobby answered for Carson, and Carson just stared at him the whole time he spoke, fighting the urge to tell him again to shut up. "No, not harsh. You see, it's just our friendship dynamic. Don't worry about us, officer. We're a-okay! Ha, ha! All good, sir." He saluted him, to top it off.

William hesitated before saying to Bobby, "You don't seem okay, kid."

"He isn't," Carson remarked. The difference in demeanor between Bobby and Carson was palpable. "But it's not really of concern. Right now, he's just wound up. Too much cake."

Bobby bit his lip hard and mumbled out an "mm-hmm" while nodding at the officer.

William looked suspicious of them still, but he didn't seem to care enough to pursue their case. He looked away from them to Margaret, and said, "I have to leave now. I'll be seeing you later." He took too many seconds to look over her petite frame.

Heat shot through Carson. He wished Bobby would elbow the officer who was sizing up Margaret, quite inappropriate for an officer of the law to do.

Margaret smiled her people-pleasing smile again. "Have a good evening, William."

He grinned widely. He was too happy. Carson despised it. "You, too, my lady." He bowed his head to the Duchess, and then—*finally*—he walked away from the group.

Bobby let out a heavy exhale, and Fiona gave him a stern look before asking, "What was that, Robert Collins? Are you hiding something?"

Robert? Since when does she ever call him Robert?

"Oh, good point, Fifi," Kelly joined. "I guess he was kind of acting weird."

Everyone ignored Kelly. Bobby looked just as confused to hear Fiona call him by his real name as Carson had been, but he managed to answer anyway. "I've done nothing wrong. Officers just make me nervous."

It wasn't a bad answer, so Carson nodded his agreement at Fiona. "Oh, yeah. You don't remember? Bobby's always had a problem around officers." He was making things up now. "It's strange, seeing as we've always been friends and my father's an officer."

"Yep. Real weird," agreed Bobby with an over-the-top enthusiastic nod.

Carson wished he would stop trying.

Fiona rolled her eyes at them. "You know what, I don't actually want to know what the two of you are hiding."

"Fiona," someone said from a table near them, a man who Carson vaguely recognized as her father. Without a departing word, she turned and left. Kelly followed Fiona with a skip in her step and a quick wave goodbye.

Within a few short minutes, Bobby's mother interrupted them and insisted on introducing him to a "really nice young lady" that had just moved to their city from a small town in the Province of Kaitos. She thought the young lady would "make a great match" for Bobby. As she dragged him away by his shirt collar, he grumbled about her not understanding what his type was at all and how she had horrible taste in women with the potential to be his wife.

"Should I walk away, too?" asked Carson. They were out of earshot of anyone that wanted to eavesdrop.

"In one minute, yes," Margaret said, nodding and glancing around the room just the same as he. They played the part of inconspicuous lovers well. It was the only way they'd gotten away with what they had done for so long.

"Sixty seconds and counting."

"Tonight." It was all she said, but Carson didn't need much information to know what she meant.

He whispered, "If that's what you want."

Their eyes met for only a couple of seconds. "Just one more night," she said. Then she bowed her head in the way that said goodbye, and Carson returned it with an even more respectful bow fit for the Duchess.

He said quietly while bowing his head to her, "As my lady wishes."

Without another glance, they walked away from each other.

There was hardly any breeze that night, of which Carson was extremely grateful. Part of him thought that maybe that meant Anem wasn't angry at him for his sins. Perhaps everything they knew as sin was not sin at all—at least not to the extent it was taught.

Carson was sure there were things that were wrong, but he wondered how it measured against other sins to Anem. Surely, carnal relations with another outside of marriage was not as wrong as, say, murder to the goddess of childbearing.

Not two seconds after rapping slightly on her window did Margaret swing back the curtains and undo the latch. "Finally," she breathed, swinging her legs over the windowsill, fully dressed, burgundy cloak and all. She gestured for Carson to assist her out of the window, which without half a second of hesitation, he did. "C'mon." She grabbed his hand and started pulling him southeast, not at all in the direction of the neighbor's stable.

Carson was puzzled for only a moment concerning Margaret's behavior. She wasn't always one for leading the way, nor for planning much of anything. She always left that to Carson. Sure, it was true she had kissed him first, but even then, she had allowed him to take the lead when he showed interest in doing so.

Margaret was a curious girl, Carson thought about a year ago when they first started being so secretive with each other. She had been confident enough to express how she felt without much talk between them prior, and had later risked rejection by initiating a kiss. She preferred not being in control, he had quickly realized. Margaret was always more than willing to hand the reins over to him, but if she wanted things a certain way, she had no qualms about yanking them back.

And for the first time in a very long time, Margaret had snatched the reins out of Carson's hands.

He gripped her hand tightly as he rasped under his breath, "Where are we going, Margaret? The stable—"

"Not the stable," she rasped back, jerking his arm as she pointed toward the cliffs hanging on the edge of the ocean.

"The beach?" Carson was surprised. They'd never gone to the beach together. Not once and especially not at night. With good reason: Margaret was afraid of the dark and unpredictable waters.

She didn't answer Carson. She simply continued to aggressively pull him through the trees that glittered the many acres they still had to trespass before reaching the cliff edge. Carson had an uneasy feeling deep in his gut. He dug his heels into the ground, pulling Margaret back. She stumbled with the abrupt stop.

"Margaret," he warned, "what are you doing?"

She looked over at the dark sea. They could already hear the rustling of the water and the crashing of the waves against the rocks at the bottom of the cliffs. It sounded peaceful. To him, that was.

"I just want to go one time," she whispered. Then she looked back at him. "I want to go with you. You've always said the water was beautiful."

"It's dark, Margaret," he reminded her. "The night doesn't do it justice."

"But to be able to see it with you..." She shook her head. "I can only see it tonight if I want to do it with you at all."

He closed his eyes. *Be strong for her. If she wants to see the ocean, take her to see it. Do this one last thing for her.* "All right, Margaret," he whispered, opening his eyes. "I know a place we can sit and look out over the water while still being concealed."

Her eyes twinkled, and she stepped up against him. "Really?" She smiled, wrapping her arms around his waist.

He nodded once. The reins had been handed back to him. "I'll take you to it." And he gave her a small kiss on her lips before taking her hand and leading her along the appropriate path.

It wasn't the darkness of the water that frightened Margaret, nor was it the *whooshing* of the waves, the gritty sand, or the creatures that possibly lurked beneath the surface of the sea. And yet, the closer she got to the cliff—the saltier the air, the thinner the trees, the sandier the ground, the louder the waves—her heart hammered harder and she was tempted to tell Carson to stop. She bit her tongue, though, because she wanted to see the water she had never been brave enough to see herself. And if she was to ever see the ocean, it would be with the only person she trusted, the only person she knew would save her if she was lost to it.

Though she was only four years old when it happened, she recalled, even if only vaguely, the many weeks Deneb had spent searching high and low for the ten-year-old Ariana Cynthia James. Cynthia had been a sleepwalker, and from what Margaret could remember, Cynthia had been found asleep on the beach twice before the morning she went missing. It was Margaret who had found the door ajar that morning, and from the cliff edge, Cynthia's stuffed toy animal was recovered alone.

But Cynthia herself was never found—not a shred of clothing or a drop of blood. There wasn't a single inkling left of Margaret's beloved older sister.

She would've turned twenty-three last month. Margaret had always kept up with Cynthia's birthday. She swore to never, ever forget, despite the rules that said to leave the past in the past. She wasn't even allowed to properly mourn her sister.

Except she could mourn with Carson. Carson was always ready to listen. He let her mourn, and he never told her to forget the past. She hadn't told him about Cynthia until she'd already confessed her attraction to him.

Margaret was unsure who else knew about Cynthia, but she assumed only those older than she was would remember her sister. If they cared to at all. That bothered Margaret. It was as if her sister never even existed. Why weren't they allowed to remember lost loved ones?

Damn this place that had buried all the precious memories of Cynthia.

Margaret thought Carson would take her to the very edge of the highest cliff, so she could look out over the ocean. But he didn't. He led her down a steep pathway that must be frequently used during the day due to the lack of foliage. Then, he took her off the path and up onto the rocks and boulders littering the base of the cliffs. They climbed over them together, Carson never releasing her hand except to grab her waist to hoist her over a particularly large boulder. Margaret had a bit of difficulty with the climbing due to the dress she wore.

If only girls were allowed to wear slacks like the boys, tasks such as these would be easier! Then again, tasks like those were illegal. They were not supposed to be climbing in that area. It was restricted. Deemed dangerous.

So dangerous.

The water was loud in her ears.

Very, very dangerous.

The water mocked her.

Extremely dangerous.

The water was darker than sin.

This is Cynthia's grave.

Carson's arms were suddenly around Margaret as he spun her around to face him and squeezed her tightly against his chest. "It's okay, Margaret," he whispered in her ringing ear. He was a warm breath of relief. "Just breathe," he told her gently, still holding her tightly. "I've got you. As long as I'm here, nothing bad will happen. I swear it."

Margaret had not even realized she'd been hyperventilating. She closed her eyes and focused on steadying her breathing. Carson didn't let go for several minutes, even after she'd calmed down. Finally, he asked, his grip unchanged on her, "Would you like to go back? It's okay if you do."

She shook her head against his chest. "No. Let's continue on our way."

He slowly released her. "As long as you're sure."

"Positive." He took a full two seconds to stare into her eyes, and she could only assume it was to make sure she was truly okay. "So," she whispered. "Where are we going?"

He gazed over his shoulder at the base of the cliff only a few yards from them now. "Almost there now. It's just around the side."

"What is it?"

His eyes found hers again, a small smile playing on his lips. Around others, that grin was the most anyone would ever get out of him—if they were lucky enough. She always thought his genuine smile, the one he let loose when they were alone, was such a handsome one. He simply whispered, "You'll see," and grabbed her hand to take her there.

When they rounded the side of the cliff, climbing over another boulder weathered by the tides, Margaret noted how dark it was on that side. She couldn't see a thing. The cliff blocked the moonlight, leaving everything in unadulterated darkness.

Though she was frozen with fear of the unknown, Carson was not afraid. In fact, she'd never known him to be inclined to fear. Perhaps there was something different inside of him? Was he truly never afraid? Or was he just so brave that he faced his fears without a moment's hesitation? Did he have any fears at all?

Carson assisted Margaret over many more boulders, and Margaret wondered if he'd been there during the day before. How else did he know his way in the utter darkness so well? Finally, he pulled her to a stop.

"Here," he whispered. He planted himself on the rock they were currently standing on, heaving a satisfactory sigh as his rump hit the stone.

Margaret slowly sat down next to him, as closely as she could in the pitch black. She blinked several times, but she could only see the stirring water that the moon illuminated far away from them. Everything else nearest to her was shadowless. She could make out a bit of Carson, but not as well as she'd like.

She wished she could see him. It was their last night together, and she didn't want to experience it blind.

He wrapped his arms around her and pulled her even closer to him, resting his mouth against her ear. "What do you think?" he whispered, then gave her earlobe a soft kiss.

She leaned into his kiss while looking out over the water. Margaret couldn't decide if the fluttering in her chest was due to fright or awe of the sea. One side of her thought it was incredibly beautiful, but the other part of her kept repeating the same thing over and over in her head: this is her grave, this is her grave, this is her grave. And it was unfortunate that was the loudest part.

Margaret closed her eyes to stop the fear that screamed at her. She clutched Carson closer to her, and he welcomed it. He pulled her up onto his lap carefully and held her there, her head tucked into his neck.

"I thought you wanted to see the water?" he questioned after a few moments. "You aren't looking at anything."

"It's dark; I can't see you."

He chuckled. "You said you wanted to see the water. You didn't mention being able to see me."

"Thought that was a given," she mumbled, playing with the first button on his shirt.

"I apologize," he said, though she could hear the amusement in his voice. "Shall I show you the rest?"

She raised her head. She could sort of make out a general outline of his face, but it still irked her that she couldn't fully appreciate how handsome he was. "The rest? I thought this was the place."

"It is, but there's more to it." He motioned, but Margaret had no idea where and couldn't see what he could possibly be gesturing toward. She wondered if he could see better in the dark than she could. "It's behind us," he said. "C'mon."

It was only a few more steps when Carson brought them to a halt. Then, there was suddenly a spark of light coming from Carson. He was smiling and held a small lighter in his free hand. She was glad to be able to see his face. She took in every feature quickly, and hoped she'd have more time to admire him. "See?" He motioned to their surroundings.

Margaret dared look away from Carson at the narrow entrance to what she assumed was a cave. She glanced behind them and realized they'd been sitting right outside of it the whole time.

"How did you find this place?" she asked, breathless.

"Long time ago, during the day." He pulled her through the narrow passage and into a strangely shaped opening. It wasn't a deep cave, she realized, but it was concealed—like Carson had said. He let go of her then, and he made his way over to a corner of the cave where he began to light eight different candles, casting the grotto in a warm glow. Had Carson put those candles there?

Carson continued answering her from before, "I was a kid when I first discovered it. It's actually incredible I didn't get caught. Didn't tell many people about it, of course. I thought it would be cool to have a secret hideout."

"You come here often?" She motioned to the candles.

He snickered. "No. I've only been here a couple of times. If you're asking about the candles, I didn't put them there. They've been in that very spot since I found this place." He shrugged his shoulders, placing his hands on his hips coolly. "I have no idea who they belonged to. Obviously, they still work just fine. They never get wet and are out of direct light."

He glanced back at Margaret and took a moment to assess her entirety. Quite a few men had often given Margaret that same look, though they always tried hiding it. It never failed to make her uncomfortable. But Carson was different. She always welcomed his lingering eyes, and she gave him an assessment of her own.

It took less than a few heartbeats for them to embrace and their lips to find each other. Heat spread from where their mouths interlocked throughout Margaret's entire body. She was sure that the hottest star spoken of by Anem in the Star Scrolls was not near as hot as they were pressed together in that moment. Carson was quick to remove his clothing and assist Margaret with removing hers.

Margaret recalled, though, when Carson was not always so hasty and was, in fact, hesitant about everything. During their first kiss, he had pulled away from her, having not kissed her back at all like she had expected, and he ducked out from behind the mathematics building without a word spoken to her.

She had never been denied before.

He didn't speak to her for several days following—out of guilt, he later confessed, because he enjoyed the kiss, and kissing her was wrong. Despite his convictions, they had kissed again—and again and again and again—until they were doing much more than just kissing. But with every new step they took, he always questioned the step beforehand. That was, until their first tryst, of course.

It happened too suddenly for Carson to think rationally about it, and by the time he took a moment to pause in the midst of their sin, they both had already been bound.

Margaret had felt guilty about it—still did—because she was the one that led him into that situation. She was the reason he had felt such guilt. Over a short amount of time, though, Carson seemed to let that guilt go, because he never stopped seeing Margaret, and he was, from then on, insistent that what was between them was not wrong.

How can it be wrong? Margaret constantly wondered. She was certain they were destined to be together. She was sure that there was no other man on earth or in heaven that could be what Carson was to her.

They lay tangled together on the floor near those old candles. The warm light the flames cast on the uneven, jagged walls flickered soothingly. The breeze wafting in from the ocean whistled through the cave's narrow entry. Though it wasn't necessarily cold inside the cave, they would've been chilled if it weren't for Margaret's burgundy cloak they nestled under.

Margaret curled herself into Carson's shoulder and threaded her legs through his. Carson lightly glided his fingers over her arm. Neither spoke, though Carson thought that maybe they had the same thing on their minds, which would explain the uneasiness silently shared between them.

This was their last night together. In just a few days, Margaret would be married to William Lach. And eventually, within the next few years—if he were lucky to be given that much time alone—the Judge would pick someone for him to marry. He would eventually have children with another woman that wasn't her, and she would have children with another man that wasn't him.

"This is my fault, Carson," Margaret said, "I'm the reason we've wasted so much time pretending."

"What are you going on about?" he asked, genuinely confused.

Sighing, she squeezed him to her lovingly. "I always knew this day would come. Our last day. I just didn't want to believe it, so I didn't. I was pretending, and I made you pretend with me."

Carson laid his cheek against the crown of her head and whispered, "I wasn't pretending."

Margaret raised her head off his shoulder, which forced Carson to look into her eyes. They twinkled with the dancing flames of the candles. "I didn't mean that what we have isn't real. I wasn't pretending to love you, Carson. If anything, you're the only thing real in my life." She paused as if to consider how to word her next sentence.

Carson took the moment to move strands of hair stuck to the side of her face behind her cold ear. He pulled the corner of her cloak higher up on her body, tucking it under her sides to keep the warmth between them. He took an extra moment before she spoke again to admire how beautiful her auburn hair framed her olive-toned face. Her complexion was smooth and tawny, the fire-gold amber glow of dawn.

Margaret exhaled in a puff of air. "It's only a matter of time, Carson. They'll soon know everything." She paused for a long second before adding, her voice a whisper, "If I could take it all back, I would."

Carson's eyebrows fell heavily over his eyes, and a twang of pain stabbed his heart. "You regret this?"

"I regret putting you in this situation." She refused to make eye contact with him. "I'm the reason we bound ourselves in the first place. I made you do this."

To that, he laughed. Loud and boisterous. "Whatever," he said through another laugh. He pulled her closer and squeezed her once with a hug. After half a moment, he said, "Margaret, you didn't make me do anything I didn't want to do. Trust me." He hoped that would make her feel better.

Carson wondered where all this guilt was coming from suddenly. Had she been shouldering it all this time and never told him? Or was it now, that the end was so near, she felt responsible for the impending punishment they'd no doubt receive once the brands were discovered?

Margaret exhaled again, exhausted. She whispered, "I realize that, Carson. I'm not saying I literally forced you to love me. I'm saying if I hadn't been so pushy... If I had just listened to you when you tried talking sense into me that first time I tried kissing you, our lives wouldn't—"

Feeling quite perturbed, he interrupted her, his tone only slightly acidic from the irritation rising inside him. "I wouldn't change a damn thing, Margaret." And that was all he said. It was all he felt he had to say.

She was quiet for an entire minute. Perhaps she was surprised at the tone he took with her, considering he never took a tone with her—or really anyone, for that matter. Finally, she whispered, "I guess I wouldn't actually change anything either, Carson. But I'm sure that's selfish."

"How?" He was still irritated, but he controlled it well enough.

She answered, "Because I'd risk your dignity just to have loved you for a short time, and that's not right."

He couldn't respond immediately from the sudden shame that washed over him. After a short moment, he had built up enough courage to confess to Margaret in a low voice, "I understand what you mean. I'd risk your dignity, too, and I know it has to be a sin. Anem must be severely disappointed in me."

Margaret nestled herself back into Carson's neck. She sighed against his skin, "Me, too."

"No, it's not the same," he insisted.

"How can you say that? Of course it's the same. Same sin, same punishment."

"No, Margaret... You're the Duchess. People watch you. They look up to you. They expect you to be perfect. When that brand is discovered, they'll never forget or forgive you. You'll always be the Duchess that fell to the flesh. Shamed. Then there's me: Everyone always expected me to be a troublemaker. When I'm found out, by the next day, it'll be old news." He turned his head slightly down at her and she lifted hers to lock eyes with him. "You know I'm right," he whispered, his throat getting tighter as he fought the tears that choked him. "Yet, I wouldn't change a thing, and I hate myself for being so selfish."

Margaret caressed his face and pressed her lips against his. He absorbed every millisecond of her presence and of how soft her pink lips felt against his. She pulled away after a moment and whispered just a centimeter from his mouth, "This isn't how I want our last night together to be. No more negativity, okay?"

He gave her a soft nod and tilted his head just enough to touch his lips to hers again.

L ight filtered through Carson's eyelids. He groaned and turned his back to the light. His body pressed against another body, which surprised him, because—

Carson sat up. For a moment, he just stared at Margaret's half-naked body on the cave floor. Early morning light shone through the narrow cave entrance, showering the two of them in bright rays of sudden horror.

Anem's burning stars!

He shook Margaret to wake her, more aggressively than he meant. He grabbed his clothing and began dressing haphazardly, his foot annoyingly getting caught in his trousers for two seconds too long. "Margaret!" He shook her again.

She moaned once, as if she wasn't concerned about the time. Then, abruptly, with a gasp, she bolted upright. "Stars!" she exclaimed. "What time is it?" She dressed herself more quickly than Carson had ever thought possible.

"It's a bit after sunrise," he said. His hands shook with adrenaline as he laced his boots. "I think we can get home in time. We just have to leave now."

"I'm ready," she said, pulling her cloak over her shoulders and clasping it. He noted the slight tremor in her fingers.

Carson finished knotting his boot laces. "Let's go."

Maneuvering over the boulders was easier with the bit of light rising in the east. Carson hoped the sunlight would work in their favor and not against them. Already, they were able to move quicker thanks to the light—and the adrenaline pumping through their veins. Thankfully, curfew wouldn't be down for an hour more; no one should be out yet, save the night shift officers they dodged.

They ran, and though Carson could outrun Margaret ten times over, he slowed himself and kept a tight hold on her elbow, pulling her along.

While they raced through the various parks and neighborhoods, Carson kept an eye out. It would be just their luck that an early riser would peek through their curtains right as they passed through.

Despite the sickening fear churning Carson's gut, they made it to the James' house unnoticed. They stopped running only when they made it to Margaret's bedroom window. Margaret was breathing heavily, but she still managed to say, "Go, Carson. Don't worry about me. My father lets me sleep in. He doesn't check—"

Carson didn't wait for her to finish. He opened her window and then heaved her inside without much help from her. Once she was safely in her room, he shut the window carefully, no farewell words exchanged. Carson immediately bolted for the trees, and he didn't glance back at her.

As he raced home, he prayed Anem would show him mercy and slow down the sun's expeditious progress across the pink-and-orange tinted sky. He contemplated the last year and all the time Margaret and him had wasted pretending—just as she had solemnly put it—as he sprinted across a bare pasture.

As Carson hastily crossed the last barbed-wire fence, he got his sweater caught in one of the barbs, snagging a hole in the sleeve. He huffed, already hearing his mother's inescapable lecture after seeing the damage.

When Carson arrived at his window, the red emergency light suddenly switched on inside his room. His stomach flipped sideways and upside down before planting itself in his throat. He dove for the shadow casted under the window.

He clutched at his chest, balling up the sweater in his fist. His ribcage ached as his heart pounded against it. The thumping of his heart migrated into his ears, the blood rushing drowning the rest of the world out for a moment, even his own heavy breathing. He waited until the gushing sound in his ears died down before forcing himself onto his knees, swallowing the fist-sized lump caught in his throat.

He knew he was caught already, but he found it difficult to conjure an ounce of courage to step up and face the consequences.

If only he had been a few minutes earlier.

Carson could hear his parents talking in the room to each other. His mother started crying, and that made it even harder for Carson to step forward and admit his wrongdoing. There was no way he'd be able to look into her eyes just to see the disappointment that was undoubtedly there.

"Why would he do this?" cried Kayla. "I don't understand."

"Yeah," breathed his father, but he didn't sound like he was on the same page as his wife. "I have to radio it—"

"No, Derek!" she interrupted quite loudly. "He's a good kid!" There was a crack in her voice with the rise of pitch.

"Kayla... Sweetheart, you know I have to call it in. He's broken a rule. He knew what he was doing, and he will be punished accordingly."

Only three heartbeats passed before his mother said in response, "He'll be flogged, Derek."

Carson inhaled deeply and closed his eyes. Something struck him in that moment, and it struck him hard in his gut, knotting into a million tangled clusters of angst.

They would see his brand. He would not be able to hide it if he tried. The whipping post required a shirtless victim. When they would arrest him, they'd no doubt strip-search him and have him change into a prisoner uniform. The brand that tied Carson's soul to Margaret's would be revealed.

They would label him a licentious backslider instantly, and he'd be issued an additional twenty lashes for his debauchery. Then they'd search high and low for his matching pair.

Fear seized Carson abruptly with cold, dead hands. *What would happen if I just ran far away?* He shook the thought from his head instantaneously. *Jerry Carson Owens, executed for running away* would be engraved on his tombstone. That was one rule he would never dare break.

Then that was it. The night on the beach... That really was the last time he'd ever hold Margaret in his arms, run his fingers through her silky hair, kiss her soft lips, or hold her tightly. It was the last time he'd ever share his love with her.

He didn't even say goodbye.

Carson could live with the punishment of his brand, he didn't doubt that. What about Margaret though? Had their secret affair ruined her life? Carson prayed his predictions were wrong about her future. He thought again about when William would find her brand and what he might do about it. She couldn't have a normal life anymore because of Carson, that was certain. William would never forgive her. She'd end up a divorcee. She'd be labeled a harlot. She'd be put through hell.

What have I done?

Carson really doubted their engagement would last much longer, though, now that they were going to be looking everywhere for a matching brand to his own. Eventually someone would check her shoulder, and as the daughter of Polaris's Ambassador and Judge, she would reap more consequences than Carson. She was someone born into a position of leadership and guidance for the rest of the Province.

People didn't expect much from Carson. They did not really know him at all, and what they did know was he belonged to the Owens family, who were rumored to be notorious for raising hellions. But those were just rumors that Carson had overheard one or two—or maybe twenty—times. He'd seen no proof of the Owens bloodline constantly creating trouble in their community. Although, according to Derek, his relatives had left Polaris several decades ago and never kept in touch, including his parents and siblings. Carson wondered if those were the Owens that older generations still whispered about.

But everyone knew Margaret. Everyone expected the absolute best from her. The guilt of that gripped Carson's heart. He hoped nobody would find the brand. He prayed diligently for Anem to take it away from her for the sake of her future. For the sake of her dignity. He'd take the inevitable punishment and shame for her, and then he'd multiply it by ten if Anem would only answer his prayers.

Slowly, Carson stood from where he was crouched. He couldn't stay hidden in the shadows forever. *Be brave,* he told himself. *Don't show your fear. Be blank. Don't give away what you know. If they find the brand, let it be as it must. If, by some miracle of Anem, they do not see it, praise the goddess for the undeserved blessing.* In the meantime, Carson would continue to send a thousand prayers to the heavens.

He peeked in his bedroom window. His parents still stood there, but they weren't talking. Kayla sobbed into Derek's chest, and he held her lovingly, trying his best to comfort her. Carson's heart clenched under the pressure of her sorrow and the knowledge that his actions were the cause.

He steadied his breathing with minimal effort. His heart, though, he could not control. He gripped the latch to the window, preparing himself for the consequences that awaited him, that would stick with him for the rest of his life.

If you're listening, don't let Margaret suffer the same fate as me. I'll take it all. Spare her.

BEING HANDCUFFED BY one's own father was the worst feeling in the world, in Carson's opinion. And as a parent, he didn't imagine it felt too great for his father either. The worst part of it all was the look in Derek's eyes when they made eye contact as he told Carson to turn around and put his hands behind his back. Carson would never forget that heavy, aged look. Not if he lived a million years.

He had Carson sit down on the edge of his bed while they waited for William and his team to arrive. Carson's stomach knotted a thousand times and continued to twist with each moment that passed. But he showed nothing.

Carson's younger sister opened his bedroom door a few minutes after he'd been handcuffed. Did the noise wake her? Or was it the red emergency light shining into the hall from under the door? She was already in tears. Had she been eavesdropping, then?

"Casey," said Derek gently. He was always gentle with her, as if she'd break with any kind of force. Carson appreciated that he didn't treat her as strictly as he had been treated at her age. "Go back to your room, honey. When the officers get here—"

"No!" Her voice was a screech. She ran at Carson and threw her small body onto him, curling herself into his lap and hugging herself tightly to him. "Don't do this, Daddy!" she yelled. "Don't get him in trouble! He's good!"

Derek squatted down next to where Carson sat handcuffed on the bed, where Casey was latched onto him. He pet her hair lightly in an attempt to soothe the child. "I know, honey. You're right. He is good."

Carson shut his eyes. *Anem, please...*

She jerked her reddened, wet face toward their father. "Then why would you do this?!"

He hesitated at the raw sight of her. But after a short second, he replied to her, saying, "It's what's expected of me, my dear child. I have to do my job."

"He's your son!" she yelled at him.

Kayla attempted to wrap her arms around Casey and pry her off of

Carson, but she knocked her arms away. "No! If they take him, they have to take me too!"

"You are not of age to be held accountable," her mother whispered to her. "They cannot punish you."

"They will lecture you firmly, though," Derek said in a stricter tone, his patience thinning. Still, it wasn't nearly as bad as how Carson had been scolded as a young boy. "And, Cassandra" —Derek used her real name and that always meant business with him— "you should know that the other officers are not like me. Because I'm your father, I love you, and I don't want to scare you or be mean to you in any way. But the others may have no such whims."

Casey's grip tightened on her brother.

Their parents sighed together, defeated. Carson looked down at Casey and her vice grip on his sweater. He would not let his eleven-year-old sister get in trouble simply because she loved him dearly.

"Casey," he whispered. Everyone's attention was on him in that second. After all, it was the first thing he had said since climbing back through the window.

She sniffled. "Yes?"

"You are growing into an amazing young woman. You are a better person than me." He paused for only a second to allow her to process. She sobbed a couple of times into his sweater. "Can you continue being good? For me?"

She sniffled, gripping him tighter. "I can try."

"Thank you. But first, I need a favor. Just one."

She looked up at Carson for the first time since he started talking to her. "What—what is it?" she said between sobs.

"I need you not to get in trouble. Not for me. Go back to your room and shut the door. Don't come out for any reason."

She stared at him for a few moments before saying, "But, you—"

"I'll be okay, squirt," he said to her, and then gave her a peck on her hairline. "Let Mom put you back to bed now." On cue, their mother stepped up and held out her arms for Casey. "Go on," Carson encouraged with a smile. She needed to see her brother smile. She needed to know he was going to be okay. "Everything will be all right."

"You promise, big brother?"

"I promise, little sister."

She stared at him for another second or two before giving him one last tight hug and taking her mother's hand to be led back to her room. If any officer had caught her out of her room, they would've chosen to lecture her strongly about breaking the rules of leaving one's room without good reason. Though Carson was unsure if she'd actually get in trouble since the situation at hand could have technically been considered a good reason. Even Derek was unsure on how they would react to her. Neither of them wanted to take that chance.

"Thank you," his father whispered, sitting on the bed right next to him.

"I don't want her to get in trouble because of me."

Derek huffed before he responded, his tone shifting to vexed. "But you want to get into trouble, is that right?"

Carson shook his head, fighting the urge to roll his eyes like a child. "No," he said quietly. "Of course I didn't plan on getting into trouble."

"Then what was that stunt, huh? Sneaking outside? What if someone else had seen you? What if someone else had caught you besides me?"

"Never happened before," mumbled Carson.

"What was that?"

Carson quickly changed course. "What does it matter if you caught me anyway? You still turned me in. Nothing was different."

He shook his head disapprovingly. "There's still so much you don't know." He cut his eyes at him from the corner. "Where could you even go?"

Carson shrugged, looking down at the wood floor. "I just walked around. I like nighttime. It's beautiful. All the stars—"

"It's dangerous," he interrupted. "There are reasons we have rules,

Carson." He shifted his body to face him better. "Hell, you know this! You know this better than anyone. What's going on, Carson, that you feel the need to break the rules? You're behaving like—" He stopped himself short, closing his eyes and taking a deep, deep breath.

"I'm acting like...?" questioned Carson.

He sighed. "Never mind."

I knew it, Carson thought, though he didn't dare confront his father in that moment. *I'm acting like him, aren't I? That's what he was going to say.* Carson would bet money on it, in fact. *He used to break the rules when he was my age. I must be more like him than he likes.*

A loud knock on the front door alerted them. It echoed eerily through the silent house. Derek sighed and said to Carson under his breath, "Let's go, son." And he stood Carson up from the bed, one hand lightly gripping the boy's bicep, only a few inches below the edge of his secret brand. He led his son to the on-duty officers standing on their front porch, ready to deliver his well-deserved punishment.

9

Carson leaned back on the cinderblock wall his lumpy cot sat against. Eyes heavy, he drifted for a moment, though the anxiety wrapped around his chest would not let him rest.

Jingling of keys and heavy footfalls alerted Carson, and he sat up straight, heart racing as he searched for the clock's time. *Too early. It's too early.* He tried to relax but found it difficult with the adrenaline suddenly pumping through him.

A large officer whose gut hung over his belt buckle stopped at Carson's cell and motioned for him to stand as he unlocked the door. "The chief wants you to watch today's execution with him," the officer explained, his gray beard unable to hide the disapproving downward twist of his mouth.

Carson's stomach tightened. *An execution? A real one?*

He'd never seen anyone die before. He'd never even seen a flogging, sinner parade, or attended any Quarterly Confessions where sinners convicted of crimes were forced to pray at the feet of Anem's statue for hours without break. His parents never allowed him or his sister to attend any public trials or punishments. They hadn't been too hard to avoid. The justice department only scheduled them during certain hours of the day and only on certain days of the week. Plus, Derek kept tabs on punishments, considering his main position was the investigation of crimes.

Even so, it wasn't like in the District of Diphda. The public there never knew when their guillotine would be in use.

The District left the method of execution up to the Judges of each Province to decide, and while the Elders in the District had gone down a more gory path, the three Provinces under them had chosen more subtle or humane ways to murder their people. Kaitos used electrocution, the Port used the gallows, and Deneb used lethal injection.

Whichever method was chosen, the abrupt end of a life was horrifying.

He steeled his mind as the cold metal handcuffs clamped about his wrist.

"Follow me, Owens."

Carson's heart thudded in his chest. *Move*, he thought as his legs seized up. *Move, now*. His knees threatened to buckle, and it took all of his willpower to get his legs to cooperate.

The officer led him down the gray-painted corridor. Swaying yellow bulbs hung interspaced along the length of the hallway every few paces. The clinking of his cuffs and the hollow thud of their footfalls echoed off the cement walls, an eerie tune their shadows danced to.

They reached a pair of locked doors which the officer had to swipe his plastic ID card to open. The large operating room was full of officers. A few Matures stood in the corner with their Courthouse politician badges pinned to their lapels. Carson recognized the Judge standing among them, arms crossed as he spoke with another man, one that wore a lawyer's pin on his lapel. A redheaded councilwoman glanced their way and scowled at the sight of Carson, but said nothing to protest the presence of a prisoner.

The room was set up simply: only a few officers sat in chairs at a control panel under a large window on the far wall while the others stood and observed.

The fat officer gently nudged him forward and directed him across the room, toward William. The chief faced a large window above the control panel, standing with his booted feet shoulder's width apart and arms clasped at his mid-back. He turned when the officer escorting Carson addressed him.

"Good," William said, tilting his head toward the officer. "Thank you, Tony." As Tony left their sides, William said to Carson, "Pay attention, Owens. Don't make the same mistakes as your friend here."

"Friend?" Carson's voice trembled on the whispered word, and he cursed himself for sounding so weak in front of William. His mind raced through his short list of friends, but he couldn't imagine any of them would do anything to warrant a sentence to the afterlife.

William nodded toward the window. Carson's eyes followed his direction. On the other side, two officers entered the room, dragging along a thrashing boy, a muzzle strapped across his face. Carson couldn't make out who it was for a moment until the boy was forced into the metal chair bolted to the floor and the caramel brown shag of his hair matted with mud, twigs, and leaves sent a jolt of revelation through Carson's entire being.

"Sam," breathed Carson. His stomach plummeted to his feet, a new sheen of sweat covering his palms. He took a step toward the window but William's outstretched arm shoved him back.

Why...?

Samuel Vickers, the quiet, well-behaved boy who had just had his Ritual the day prior, after turning eighteen only a week before that. Carson hadn't necessarily considered Sam a friend, but maybe an acquaintance.

But this was not the Sam that Carson recognized. His eyes—still their Immature brown despite having had his Ritual—were wild and afraid, and though his muzzle muffled any noises he made, he tried his best to shout at the two officers strapping him to the chair.

Carson's breathing grew labored. He could hear everything over the speakers in the room. Everything.

"They reversed the Ritual an hour ago," whispered William, "after his sentencing. That's why he's so..."

"Insane?" suggested Carson.

"No," breathed William. "He's well in his right mind."

Carson wanted to ask what Sam did within the first twelve hours of being a Mature that would sentence him to an early grave, but the question was lost in his lungs at the sight of one of the two officers pinning Sam's head against the backboard of the chair as the second officer tightened a strap around his forehead and another one around his neck to keep him sitting upright. All the while, Sam flailed and shouted muffled protests.

"Are you going to ask what he did?"

Carson glanced at the chief officer through the side of his eye, finding William also looking at him from the corner of his own eye. They looked away from each other in the same second.

When William didn't offer a further explanation, Carson managed through his tight throat, "What did he do?"

William answered immediately, almost like he couldn't wait to tell Carson, as if he was excited to gossip with him. "Ran away. Toward the Red Desert." He paused before adding in barely a whisper, "Bloody idiot. I mean, why would you choose to run to the Red Desert, of all places? The Wastelands may be in ruins, but at least a runaway would be able to find temporary shelter while waiting for the Provinces to call off their search parties." He chuckled and elbowed Carson's bicep. As if they were friends. "They caught him pretty quickly after sunset. He's been fighting ever since. He spouted nonsense about freedom from the slavery in the Provinces."

Carson whipped his face to the chief, but William remained facing forward, expression impossible to read.

Freedom? Slavery?

These were not words associated with the Provinces or the District, and by the hushed tone William used, perhaps he was not supposed to be repeating such things from a runaway to an Immature. Yet, the chief officer had said it to him, and he kept his attention forward on Sam as if he hadn't been gossiping about slavery in the Provinces at all.

The cogs in Carson's brain began churning from suspicion.

"Randall," addressed William calmly yet firmly.

One of the two officers that had strapped Sam into the chair now stood near the door. He replied to William, saying, "Yes, sir, I see him," as he opened the door to enter with the second officer right behind him.

Sam had somehow managed to unstrap the muzzle around his jaw and shook it half off before he belted out, "If you all would just stop listening to those damn Elders, they would be entirely powerless! *You* give them their power! You, their *slaves*, have allowed them to continue enslaving you, millennia after millennia."

Calm despite Sam's serious accusations, William ordered a man at the control panel, "Cut the sound. There's an Immature observing."

Before the speakers cut him off, Carson clearly heard Sam say, "Your cowardice is hurting the rest of us. Hypocrites, the bloody lot of you! The Elders don't control you; your *fear* controls you!"

Officer Randall and his partner were wrestling the muzzle back on him in the same moment the speakers were silenced. Sam, now feral with whatever the hell had happened during his Ritual, snapped his teeth at the officers' fingers, spittle flying from his mouth as he shouted and nipped at them repeatedly.

Part of Carson wished to hear what else he had to say. What had Sam found out that caused him to behave in such a way? What had happened to him? Carson would've thought he had gone insane, but William had just finished assuring him that Sam was in his right mind—if he could trust that. The chief's words almost sounded like nonsense as he watched Sam's wild behavior.

Finally, the two officers were able to secure the muzzle back around Sam's face with all their fingers intact.

William turned to his left, away from Carson, and spoke to a man wearing a lab coat. "We're ready when you are, doctor."

The doctor gave William a curt nod before motioning to the two medical assistants, one with a rolling tray of supplies and the other with a clipboard. Carson's stomach bubbled with acid as he watched them enter the execution chamber. They wasted no time as one of the medical assistants jabbed Sam with a needle and attached it to a primed bag of fluids hanging from a pole next to the chair.

The doctor pulled up a full syringe of a clear liquid from one vial, lips moving but the speakers were still turned off. The assistant with the clipboard jotted down notes as he spoke.

William stepped closer to Carson, brushing his shoulder. The chief's hovering presence kept the hair on Carson's neck raised. He wished to step away but thought he might look weak in doing so.

"He's giving him a relaxant first," William whispered. "It'll make the... transition easier on the kid."

Carson didn't think about the words before they slipped from his tongue, only a breath but still audible for William, "He's only a year younger than you."

William only chuckled at that, as if a man wasn't about to be killed in front of them, but he didn't respond or reprimand Carson for back-talking.

As the doctor slowly inserted the needle of the syringe into a port on the intravenous tubing, injecting the liquid slowly as he watched the time on his watch, Carson thought over William's statement.

"Transition," he whispered half a moment later. "You mean his transition to..."

"Anem's everlasting stars, of course. Or hell. Wherever the goddess sends his soul. What else would I mean?"

Sam closed his eyes as the doctor finished injecting the full dose of relaxant, his arms and legs loosening, tense muscles unwinding. Slowly, he blinked his eyes open and closed them again a few moments later. Tears escaped his eyes, leaving trails down his cheeks through the thin layer of dirt coating his skin.

Carson's heart broke in half for Sam. He tried to reason that Sam probably deserved this death sentence, but nothing inside him, in any crevice of his soul, truly believed that. Not even a little.

The doctor discarded the used syringe into a biohazard case attached to the side of the rolling tray before grabbing a fresh syringe, one much larger than the small one preceding it. The medical assistant continued her documenting as he drew up the contents of the large vial on the tray. The liquid inside of it was not quite clear like the relaxant. Instead, it was tainted an ugly yellowish-orange.

Whispering again, William said, and Carson wondered why he kept talking to him, "It's a shame, really. If only he had brains to go with that fighting spirit, he may have never been caught."

Carson wouldn't acknowledge William's statement. Surely the officer was baiting him somehow, for some reason. What was he trying to do? What was his point?

The bastard officer was likely trying to trap him into saying something incriminating. Perhaps he wanted Carson to agree with Sam so they could send him to Anem's everlasting stars too.

The doctor stuck the tubing port with the new syringe, the swirling poison inside causing the bile in Carson's stomach to inch up his throat.

To secure his place in Anem's good graces—and William's for the time being—Carson said clearly to the chief officer, "It's good he was caught. An uncaptured runaway doesn't reflect well on the Province."

At a slow rate, the doctor began injecting the lethal liquid into the tubing, but Sam didn't react to it immediately. He just blinked and blinked as he stared at the tiled floor, the tears cascading in rivers down his face and dripping onto his lap.

"I thought this boy was your friend," said William.

The doctor had injected only half of the poison before Sam began convulsing, his eyes rolling into the back of his head. Yet, the doctor didn't stop. He finished giving Sam the rest of the dose, and once the syringe was removed finally, Sam's convulsions slowed, and all his muscles went limp. From under the muzzle foam leaked out and dripped onto his shirt.

Carson swallowed the lump rising in his throat. "Not really," he carefully answered, keeping his face clean of emotion as he forced himself not to look away from the horror of death. "Even if he was, he still deserves this." His very heart and soul burned with the lie, and he silently begged Sam for forgiveness.

William didn't say anything in response, only *hmm'd*, as if disappointed in Carson's answer. Which only confirmed to Carson he'd been trying to bait him all along. That was why he'd brought him here. The chief thought watching his friend die before his eyes and hearing his blasphemous statements would break him.

William would have to do much more than that to break him.

And though Carson was confused at why the goddess would call for such harsh punishment, he still prayed she'd have mercy on his soul and allow Sam to join her among the everlasting stars above.

10

Carson was held in a cell and booked for a noon flogging at the whipping post. Made to sound and feel like a confirmation of his attendance to a picnic, he was not strip-searched or watched as he changed into the yellow uniform he had been handed by an unknown officer. Only one camera's red light blinked from a wall in the cell, and even that was easy to avoid. Almost too easy.

So far, he'd been blessed that his brand had remained a secret, but he was unsure how Anem could save him from the next obstacle—taking off his shirt for the whipping.

As noon approached, his stomach tangled into knots again. They gave him some oatmeal for breakfast at eight and then some toast at eight thirty when he didn't touch the first option, but he couldn't eat. He was on edge. The faintest voices down the hall made him tense. Yet, he practiced not showing his discomfort.

"Owens," a voice said from the cell door. A gentle bang on the bars meant to grab his attention sounded softly through the cell. Consciously ridding his face of any expression, Carson looked over to William Lach from where he sat on the bed.

"It's only nine," stated Carson, glancing at the clock on the wall.

William unlocked the cell door and let himself in before responding. "Yes, but you have visitors."

Carson's stomach flipped.

"It's your family."

Standing, Carson said, "All right."

The chief officer nodded curtly and retrieved a pair of handcuffs from his utility belt. Carson detachedly gave him his wrists. He placed them on Carson, careful to make sure they weren't too tight. "I do feel for you, you know. Sure, breaking curfew is a crime, but I'm sure you aren't a bad man." He patted Carson's shoulder, patted the brand. Carson's shoulder grew hot. "You're just a man, after all, and that can't be helped." He motioned Carson out of the cell then.

I'm just a man, and that can't be helped. Carson had never heard that before. That's not what they were taught in school or at home or at the temple. Who taught him that? Was it not blasphemy to blame one's sin on simply *being*?

William took Carson to the private lounge where his mother and sister sat patiently on a white couch, sipping on something steaming in teacups. The walls were painted the color of lavender and decorated in vibrant paintings of beautiful landscapes—the mountain range of Kaitos, the forests of Deneb, the beaches of the Port. Potted plants were scattered throughout the room, and the soft scent of pine tickled Carson's nose.

"Carson!" yelled Casey excitedly when they walked in. She set her teacup down in such haste that the contents splashed onto the table. She ran around it, not caring about the spillage, and plowed into Carson. Her arms wrapped around him tightly, squeezing.

She let go a hot second later when she remembered where they were. Her face reddened as she looked at William, curtseying. "I apologize for my outburst, officer."

William smiled at her sweetly, and Carson was thankful that he was treating her kindly. But his friendliness to Carson's little sister wasn't going to fool him. He was still a prick, no matter what kind things he did or said. Carson was sure he would always feel a twinge of animosity toward Lach in his gut. "Don't worry about it," William said. "I'm sure your brother appreciates having such a loving sister. Especially right now."

Carson bent a knee to get on eye level with Casey, a full foot and a half shorter than him. "Thanks for coming to see me, squirt." He pinched her chin gently as he smiled warmly at her.

She returned the smile with one of her own. "I asked Dad to come, too, but he said he'd have to come by later. He said he needed to run an errand."

Carson nodded. "I'll see Dad whenever he can come by."

She agreed with a nod that matched his. "Yeah, I'm sure he has a good reason."

He forced a grin but he could feel it faltering. "I'm sure you're right." Actually, Carson was sure she wasn't. What errand could possibly be more important than this?

His mother lowered herself onto the couch like it were a bed of jagged stones and not plush cushions. Her hands fidgeting in her lap as she chewed her bottom lip. The moment Carson made eye contact with her, she quickly stood and adjusted her ankle-length navy-blue dress, smoothing it several times. Carson noted the puffiness around her bloodshot eyes. Had she been crying non-stop since early that morning? The whole thing was surely taking a great toll on his dear mother.

"I'm so sorry, Mom," Carson whispered as he closed the space between them.

She didn't say a word to him. She caressed his face in the palms of her hands and tried to smile at him, though it faltered.

"Don't do that," he told her. "Don't try to make me feel better. I don't deserve that."

She shook her head, suddenly pulling him into a tight hug. They embraced for only a few heartbeats. When she pulled away, her hands found his face again. She whispered through a throat squeezed tight with sorrow, "Don't think about the pain. It'll only hurt for a moment." She shook her head again, as if trying to shake an image away, and tears trailed down her cheeks. "If only I could take the punishment for you."

"No," he said, taking her hands into his. "We reap what we sow, and you've done no wrong."

Her bottom lip trembled. "Still..."

Carson patted her hands, attempting to comfort her. "I'll be okay. No need to worry."

"They assured me right afterward you'd be seen by a physician."

He nodded. "That's what I heard too."

"Your father will make sure it happens immediately. He'll be right there with you the whole time."

Carson didn't reply. Her lips continued to tremble, and more tears escaped her eyes. "You won't be there, right? When it happens?"

She shrugged. "I don't know."

"Don't be. Take Casey home when you leave here, and don't leave the house today, if you can help it. Do this for me." He pumped her hands once with a gentle squeeze. "Promise me."

She was silent for a long moment.

"Mom," he whispered so only she could hear. "Do it for Casey, then. She shouldn't see such a horrible shaming."

She closed her eyes and another tear fell. "It's such an awful punishment. Meant to shame everyone into submission."

Carson glanced back at William, but the officer was speaking with Casey about the hot chocolate she spilled on the table, giving her a napkin to wipe it up. He hadn't heard Kayla's disapproval of the law, thank Anem.

Carson turned his attention back to his mother. "Go home, Mom. Please."

She simply nodded after a moment of consideration. She removed her hands from his face and wiped away the streams on her cheeks, then she called for Casey to prepare to leave.

"Already?!" exclaimed Casey.

"Hey, now," Carson said playfully, tapping her nose. "Do as you're told, little sister. I'll be home soon enough. Enjoy having the house free of me in the meantime." He winked obnoxiously at her.

She rolled her eyes, crossing her arms over her chest. Their mother draped Casey's white cloak over the young girl's shoulders and fastened it over her dress as she replied to Carson in a sassy tone, "That's not a good reason at all. The house is much more interesting when you're there. You make funny noises and jokes, and you tell really cool stories."

"And I will be right back to my usual gags as soon as I can, okay? For now, do as Mom says."

She pinched her lips in disagreement but continued to take her gloves from Kayla and pulled them on her hands. "See you soon, little sister."

She smiled at him and then poked his nose gently with her gloved finger, which Carson knew was always her way of saying she loved him. "See you soon, big brother."

They were gone moments later.

☽ ✳ ☾

TIME PASSED FAR too quickly. By half past eleven Carson's nerves were already eating away at his sanity.

There was a light rattling at the cell door. "All right, Carson."

Him again? Great. Go die in a hole, would you?

"Time to prep you for the post," William said.

Carson's stomach pitched uneasily. "Prep?"

William unlocked the cell door and propped it open. "Yeah, you have to wear a specific outfit. You'll probably feel uncomfortable in it, but I guess that's the point."

"Shame," stated Carson. It was all about the shame. The whipping didn't really have much to do with the punishment. It was only a small fear-factor compared to public shame.

William shrugged. "Enough chit-chat. Gotta pay your due."

Screw you, Carson thought, yet he complied with the officer's orders without any delay.

The halls of the corridor shrunk in on Carson as Officer Prick—as he had dubbed the bastard—led him with a tight grip on his elbow. Carson rubbed the wrist of the same arm where his brand laid just beneath the yellow button up shirt. The handcuffs jingled with the motion. Their footsteps echoed in the otherwise quiet hall. William's black boots drowned out the plastic sandals they'd given Carson to wear.

Occasionally, Carson glanced over at Lach with a wary eye. *What will happen once he realizes Margaret has a brand identical to mine?* Considering the thought made him sick.

They entered a sizable room at the end of the corridor where four other officers stood ready against the walls and—surprisingly enough to Carson—the Judge himself sat at an oak desk, engrossed in whatever paperwork was in front of him. He lowered the spectacles on his nose as he tilted his head down to look at Carson. The Judge's expression caused his stomach to toss, and it had everything to do with the fact that the Judge was about to see the brand that Carson shared with his daughter.

Judge James sat down his paperwork and removed the spectacles from his long, pointed nose. "Jerry Carson Owens, you have been charged with deliberately breaking curfew for which the punishment is ten lashes at the whipping post. How do you plea?"

Carson's voice was stuck in his throat. William nudged him with his elbow after a few short seconds. "Guilty," he choked out.

Judge James folded his hands on his desk in front of him and leaned forward. "How often did you break curfew? Was it just once? Or perhaps you've gotten away with it for a while?" A couple of seconds passed, but he continued before Carson could consider an answer, "I recall when you were a tyke and your teachers at school made comments on how you would probably grow up into a mischievous man if your parents continued to allow you to be a mischievous boy. Tell me: Did you grow into a mischievous man as predicted? Or was this simply a one-time offense?"

Carson waited half a moment before responding. He made sure to tread lightly. "Would my answer change anything?"

"No," the Judge stated matter-of-factly. "I will only charge you for the one misdemeanor. So I assume this means you've done it several times, then?"

Carson paused, leery of the Judge. There were only a handful of people in the room, but Judge James took up the most space despite his leanness. He was one of the thirty-two Judges on the entire planet, and Judges were the most important political figures in their cities.

Eventually, Carson nodded once, a small nod that the Judge could have easily missed if he hadn't been watching Carson's body language so carefully. Carson shifted his weight to distract himself from all the eyes bearing down on him.

"How many?" the Judge questioned. He tapped his index finger on the desk in front of him, impatient, but he never looked away from Carson. The tapping echoed loudly in the boy's ears.

"Is it important?" asked Carson quietly. The last thing he wanted was to get on the Judge's bad side, but he couldn't remember the number of times he'd broken curfew. Anything Judge Mark James said went with hardly any question.

He stared at Carson for a couple of heartbeats and then said, "Not really, but I'd like to know. How many times, Carson Owens?"

Carson glanced over at William who promptly motioned him to get out with it. Carson's eyes pierced him, but he didn't seem bothered in the least. Carson swallowed a hard knot in his throat. He wondered if his voice would betray him the moment his lips parted. As he gazed back at the Judge, he kept his voice low. "A few times. It was only ever for an hour. Never longer."

"What would you do?" the Judge questioned.

An image of Margaret undressing flashed through his mind, and he forcefully blinked it away. He fought the redness creeping up his neck to settle in his cheeks.

"Walk around," he lied. "Nothing special, really. I like the night air."

Judge James picked up the papers on his desk and glanced over them again before scribbling a few notes here and there on multiple pages. "All right," he said, motioning to the other five officers in the room. "Proceed."

One of the officers handed Carson a strange piece of cloth as William began removing the handcuffs. Carson held up the cloth to examine it, wondering what it was.

"It's a loincloth," the Judge said, obviously noting the curious expression on his face.

Carson's eyebrows raised. "But," he protested, "I'll be indecent in front of people. Isn't that against the rules?"

William mumbled next to him, "Have you never seen a flogging before?"

He hadn't. Carson's parents had always sheltered him from it, telling him to stay away from Central Square at certain times of the day. Derek usually knew when floggings were scheduled and made sure his household was far away from the whipping post spectacles.

Judge James stood from his chair to lean across the desk. Carson took it as a threat and heat shot through him. "The rules state not to be indecent in front of any person with the exception of criminals who must pay for their crimes," stated the Judge. "Just so happens this crime requires a shame-inducing punishment."

"Put it on," ordered Officer Prick, voice a bit colder than previously. The dagger Carson had shot him prior got under his skin after all.

Carson took a deep breath. He knew what was coming, and there was no avoiding it. He must pay for his transgressions. He first kicked off the plastic sandals. Then, in one swift motion, he removed the yellow inmate trousers along with his undergarments. Quickly, he slipped the loincloth onto his body to cover the nakedness. The loincloth was long enough in the front and back to cover everything. Still, he felt exposed and vulnerable. But, his shirt he left buttoned. He would buy his time and wait to remove it until ordered to do so.

"Do you feel uncomfortable?" the Judge asked.

Carson thought it was a strange question. "Yes," he answered, glancing around the room at the five men other than the Judge that just saw his nether region. Yes, one could make a case for Carson's discomfort.

"Good," said Judge James. "That's the point of this exercise."

Lach probed Carson suddenly with his baton, motioning to the yellow uniform shirt he still wore. "The shirt, Owens. Off with it. Then it's straight to the whipping post."

Carson was frozen solid in that moment. *Maggie*. Her name was a heavy whisper in his brain. How could he protect her now? How could he have ever protected her? The events unfolding before him were always inevitable. How could he have ever imagined differently? What an idiot he had been.

"Carson," the Judge warned. His heart leaped uncontrollably at the idea of what would happen to Margaret. "Your discomfort is normal," he said, "and expected. Do as you're told."

Carson's stomach twisted and turned and lurched and pitched as he bided his time unbuttoning the first button, then the second, then the third, hands shaking all the while. He told himself once again to not show anything.

Be brave. Be blank. Don't let your face tell what's on your mind. Damn you, Carson, if you give anything away that could hurt Margaret. Damn you to hell.

Once he completely unbuttoned his shirt, he locked his eyes on the ground and clenched his jaw shut tight. Just do it, he told himself. Get it over with. Let them see the sin Anem carved on you. He finally removed the shirt with a moderate amount of grace and tossed it in the pile with his trousers and sandals.

It was silent for a very long time, and Carson didn't dare look up at anyone. He remained fixated on the tiled flooring. He could feel the brand warming under the hefty gazes of the six pairs of Mature eyes in the room. It burned like the very sin it illustrated.

Finally, Judge James spoke, a sigh on the edge of his words, "You've indeed grown into a mischievous man, Carson Owens."

11

Carson wouldn't lift his eyes from the ground, and he swore to not speak one word more. He knew every question here on out would be geared toward finding his bed companion, and he couldn't risk any slip up of information that could lead them to Margaret.

"Get the camera and document the brand," the Judge ordered, motioning to the officer closest to the door. "William," he then addressed, "how is it that he's been in your custody for several hours and you didn't know about that brand?" He jabbed his index finger at Carson's left shoulder, at the abominable tell-all curving up his shoulder blade and over onto the head of his shoulder, continuing only an inch down his arm.

William cleared his throat. Carson wondered if the Judge made the officer nervous. Perhaps—Carson hoped—he would be reprimanded quite sternly. "I apologize for the oversight, sir. Officer Derek had already handcuffed him when we arrived this morning, and using my judgment, I had assumed it wasn't necessary to strip-search him. I see now that was a mistake."

Carson swallowed hard. His eyes never wandered from the tiled floor. He pinched the skin on his bare thigh, channeling away his anxiety.

"Yes, it was a mistake to assume," the Judge stated. Carson noted the annoyance that coated his voice. He exhaled in a frustrated puff of air. "Postpone the flogging for tomorrow morning. Eight o'clock sharp. There's much more paperwork that has to get done." Under his breath, he repeated, "So much more bloody paperwork."

William then ordered one of the officers on standby to inform the Correctional Lieutenant of the postponement, which he promptly left the room to do.

"What a shame," sighed Judge James. "I was hoping you'd be the one that broke the curse of the Owens family." Carson swallowed hard as the Judge shook his head, disappointed. "I suppose you can't completely fix innate behavior." He stood up straighter. "But we can most definitely modify it. Like we did with your father and with his father before him."

Carson's stomach pitched uneasily.

So he was right after all. Derek had been referring to himself earlier. And, all those years of Derek adamantly shoving the rules down Carson's throat, teaching him day in and day out what was right and wrong, punishing him strictly no matter the tiniest sin—so much more punishment than necessary—were all in an attempt to break the so-called curse of the Owens family.

The officer that had gone to retrieve the camera returned seconds later, and he didn't waste any time. "Turn your head to the right," he commanded as he switched the camera on. Carson obeyed, but kept his eyes downcast and jaw clenched.

Judge James strode around his desk, arms clasped behind his back. The slow, rhythmic clomping of his boots echoed in Carson's head louder and louder. As the Judge closed the gap between them, his heart banged against his ribcage harder and faster, and he wondered if anyone could hear it like he could. It was thunder in his ears, drowning out all other sounds.

Carson clenched his fists, skin stretched white over his knuckles, nails digging crescent moons into his palms. His lips pursed and mouth dried up.

Judge James studied Carson's brand as the officer continued taking pictures from different angles. After the officer's job was complete, he left the room to print them according to the Judge's directive. The Judge scratched his clean-shaven chin, perplexed, as if he thought he could read the writing of the goddess herself.

"Sir," addressed William after a moment, "would you have me return Owens to his cell?"

"Not yet," he answered quickly, still studying the scars that made up the unique, mystifying symbols of the brand. Carson focused on keeping his breathing even. "Set him up in the interrogation room. I have a few questions."

William nodded as Carson's stomach plummeted through the earth. "Yes, sir." He grabbed Carson's elbow firmly and twisted him around so roughly that he nearly tripped over his own bare feet.

Carson wondered if they weren't going to allow him to at least put his clothes back on in the meantime. *They have to feel some sort of discomfort as well at seeing me mostly naked,* Carson thought.

Once they got to the interrogation room, William gave him another set of clothes to change into, but this time, he didn't leave Carson alone to change. He crossed his arms over his chest and waited on him. Carson changed as quickly as he could, and relief flooded him once he was completely clothed again, even if it was another awful yellow uniform.

"Sit," commanded William, gesturing to one of the two metal chairs. A matching metal table sat in between the two chairs, empty of contents. A camera was installed in the corner of the room on the same wall that had one-way glass installed. Carson sat in the chair facing his reflection, the soft curls of his shaggy jet-black hair disheveled.

William left the room the moment Carson sat down on the ice-cold chair. The door locked with a distinctive click when it swung shut.

Carson twiddled his thumbs for the better part of half an hour, handcuffs clinking. William had slapped them back on him after dressing. He exhaled in a puff, impatient. He just wanted all of it to be over. He wanted to curl up in his bed and sleep for days.

Carson glanced up at the mirror only a few times during those long moments, but he always quickly looked back down at his hands laying in his lap. He didn't know if they could tell anything from the look in his eyes, but he sure as hell didn't want to risk it. Besides, mirrors represented vanity, and he wasn't all that used to staring at himself in the mirror—if you didn't count shaving, that was.

Most homes didn't have but a couple of mirrors. It was meant to simply check oneself quickly to ensure decency prior to leaving the home. If a home had more than three mirrors, usually found in the bathroom, it was questionable whether the occupants were vain or not. That was not a label anyone in the Provinces wanted attached to them.

His family's house had only two mirrors: one hung by the front door and the other was in his parents' bathroom. Carson found this annoying, though, once he started growing facial hair and was forced to shave daily by the school's dress code policy. Since graduating, he'd been able to get away with going a few days without shaving before his father would make a comment about how he shouldn't try to grow a beard until he could actually grow one. Carson only lacked a few patches of hair here and there. Otherwise, the hair on his face was thicker and coarser than many of his former schoolmates.

He started when the door clicked open and the Judge stepped inside. The door closed behind him, locking itself again. Carson's heart raced, and he fought the urge to rub his hands on his trousers. Judge James carried a folder under his arm and a glass of water in his hand, which he set in front of Carson, motioning him to take it.

Though Carson felt a twinge of thirst, he refused to take the water. Not because he thought it was tampered with, but simply because he was expected to drink it.

But the Judge couldn't care less if Carson drank the water. "Jerry Carson Owens," the Judge formally addressed as he set the folder down on the table and took the seat across from Carson. "What's home life been like for you?"

Carson stared at his clammy hands.

The Judge sighed. "Look, we don't want any trouble, Carson. It's unfortunate, but I have to do my job. I know you understand that, what with Derek being an officer. You should know very well how the system works."

Carson picked at his fingernails. The Judge gave him more than enough time to consider replying. When he didn't, the man huffed and crossed his arms over his chest, leaning back in his chair.

"Fine, then. Don't talk. Gives me a chance to play with some of my toys." Judge James glanced over his shoulder and made a motion with his hand at the glass.

The door opened a few moments later. Carson dared to glance up when he heard more than just footsteps. The officer who took the pictures of Carson's brand wheeled in a machine and parked it next to him. Carson's heart felt like it was going to pound its way out of his chest.

"What is that?" escaped Carson's lips without thought. He clenched his jaw tight, grinding his teeth. He accidentally caught his tongue between two molars and tasted blood.

"Ah, he speaks." The Judge sported a victory grin. The officer began wrapping sensors around Carson's fingers and slapping sticky electrodes to his face while Judge James answered Carson's question. "This, here, is a very special machine that we don't really get to use all that often. It's my favorite toy."

The officer strapped what reminded Carson of a harness to his torso, and he plugged it into the machine before turning it on. The machine's screen blinked.

"You see," Judge James said then, "most people cooperate once they've been caught. You, for whatever reason, won't. Why, Carson? We already know your bedding habits. What are you hiding?"

Carson stared at the machine as it was booting.

"Carson," the Judge said to get his attention.

Carson refused to grace him with a glance. He continued staring at the machine, clenching his jaw tighter.

The Judge continued anyway, "The machine will tell us whatever you don't. It doesn't matter if you talk or not."

Carson's heart skipped, and suddenly the machine made a muted beeping noise and an image of a line with a spike in it was shown.

Judge James snorted gleefully at the evidence. "Don't like that, do you? If it makes you too uncomfortable, you could just talk to us."

Carson thought for a moment before responding, voice straining as he tried not to give away anything more than his words. "If I agree to talk, will you take this off of me?"

Judge James was quiet for a couple of moments. Finally, he answered, "I will turn it off, but if you start to avoid questions—or if I think you're lying to me—it goes back on and it will not be turned off again."

Carson closed his eyes. He really had no choice. The machine could tell when he was lying. That was what it was designed to do. Even if he doesn't talk at all, the questions alone will get a physiological reaction out of him which can then be reported to the Judge.

"Okay," Carson whispered, looking directly at the Judge. "Deal."

The Judge nodded once and reached over to the machine, unplugging the wires that connected Carson. The lines and spikes disappeared, and an error message popped up on the screen of the machine. "Are you ready to cooperate?"

Carson inhaled deeply and nodded his agreement, though he wanted to smack himself for such a horrible betrayal—to not only Margaret but to himself as well.

I deserve to burn.

As he placed the round spectacles back on his face, Judge James said, "Let's start with an easy one." He flipped open the folder and took a pen out of his shirt pocket. "How is your home life?"

Carson shrugged. "Um, okay, I suppose. I don't really understand what you're asking of me, though."

The Judge started jotting down a few notes on a blank piece of paper. "Your family unit. Start with your parents. Do they fight? Are they attentive to you and your needs?"

Carson's eyebrows pulled down over his eyes. "My parents?" He shook his head. "I've never seen them fight with each other. They don't ever seem bothered by one another."

"And they've always treated you well?"

"As every parent should."

"You have a younger sister, correct?"

Quietly, he responded, "Yes."

"What's her name again?"

"Cassandra. We call her Casey." His voice wavered. He cleared his throat in an attempt to even it back out.

Judge James pulled some papers out of the folder that had information typed on it. He glanced over it for a moment. "She's eleven?"

"Yes." Carson wondered what any of that had to do with the brand. His family was not a factor, as far as he was concerned.

"And does she seem to be a bit..." the Judge paused, searching for the most appropriate word to describe his little sister, "...mischievous as well?"

"No," Carson answered quickly. "She's a good kid."

The Judge glanced up at him from over his spectacles for a few moments before returning to the papers. "So it's just you?"

"Yes."

He didn't want to mention what he suspected of Derek, that he had also broken the rules once upon a time. But, the Judge knew that, didn't he? He had said as much earlier.

Carson couldn't believe he had never heard about Derek's disobedient past. Although, he shouldn't have been surprised. The rules insisted that what happened in the past always remained in the past, never to be dredged up again. Especially if it happened when one was still an Immature.

"Okay, let's move on." The Judge shuffled through the stack of papers until he found what he was searching for.

He laid out images in front of Carson that had just been taken of his brand. It was the first time Carson had ever had a good look at his own brand, but the design itself wasn't foreign to him at all. He'd spent a decent amount of time admiring its match on Margaret's body.

"Start here," he commanded. "Tell me about your brand."

Carson swallowed. He stared at the pictures. "Well," he whispered, mouth drier than the Red Desert. He glanced at the water but thought he'd better wait until he finished answering before taking a sip of it. "It's the divine marking of the goddess Anem. She grants the brand to those who are...uh...intimate." His nails dug into his clammy palms painfully.

"And you have one." It wasn't a question.

Carson reached for the glass of water. The Judge promptly moved it away. "Don't avoid my questions by any means." It was a warning that he'd hook Carson back up to that machine.

"Yes," Carson complied, placing his hands back in his lap, handcuffs rattling. He licked his lips, looking back down at the pictures.

"You aren't wedded to anyone." That statement was not a question either.

"No."

"When were you branded?"

Carson considered the question for a moment. But a moment was too long for the Judge to wait. Judge James reached over to the machine to plug the wires back in.

Carson's heart raced. He blurted, "One!"

The Judge was frozen for a moment. He looked over Carson slowly, his thoughts not easily decipherable on his blank face. "One what?" His hand moved away from the wires gradually, and he clasped both of them in front of him, resting them on the table. "One day ago? Week? Month?"

Carson hesitated, but answered in a timely manner, "Year."

The Judge's face crinkled then, his nose upturned. "A whole year? You were able to keep a secret like that for a year?" He exhaled, disappointed. "For the record, state your age at the time you received the brand."

Carson removed his eyes from the Judge. Whispering, he simply said, "Sixteen."

"Practically a baby," the Judge muttered, shaking his head in disapproval as he jotted notes down on Carson's record.

Why is he acting like he can't imagine anyone would do such a thing? It's not as if I'm the only unwedded person ever caught with a brand. The whipping post's most frequent victims were those charged with adultery, many of them teenagers like himself.

The Judge asked another question after he finished writing a paragraph of dialogue, and Carson wondered if he would ever run out of questions. "Who is it, then? The one that has the matching brand?"

Carson's heart pounded hard. His palms began sweating. He was glad the machine was not on for that question.

"Girl? Boy?"

Carson found it difficult to swallow. He felt like his throat was collapsing.

"You have two seconds to give me an answer, Carson," the Judge stated. Carson thought he saw his fingers twitch, ready. "Girl or boy?"

"Girl," Carson choked out. Did he give too much information away? He should've lied. He should've let the Judge think it was a guy, though Carson wasn't sure that he'd been able to lie that well.

"I need a name."

No, Carson would never say her name. Even if he were about to die, it would not even be the last thing he ever said. He'd take her name to his grave, if it came down to it. Judge James could plug the wires back into the machine if he wanted, but not even the machine could tell the Judge the name of his lover.

"Her name, Owens. Two seconds."

Carson stared harder at the pictures and didn't flinch when the Judge's twitchy fingers snatched up the wires and jammed them into the lie detector. Immediately, it began beeping and spiking, showing how nervous he truly was.

Anem, I only ask that you spare her from the hell of our world.

12

Obviously, Judge James was not impressed with the results. "For Anem's sake..." he cursed. "You are really on edge about this girl." He paused for a moment to mute the beeping of the machine. "You only have the one brand, so I know there's only one name floating around in that head of yours."

Carson squeezed his eyes shut for half a second and focused on his breathing. He had to try his hardest to control his nerves.

"Carson," Judge James addressed. "Don't think I don't get it. You love her, so you want to protect her. Is that right?"

He didn't respond in any way. His breathing evened out, yet his heart still bounded in his chest. He thought it would explode if it continued to hammer so roughly against his sternum.

Judge James exhaled, frustrated. "Okay, let's take a few steps back. Let's talk about you. Forget the girl for a moment. You said you received the brand when you were sixteen." Judge James paused.

Carson realized he wanted confirmation, so he nodded, not once looking away from the pictures of his brand.

The Judge continued, "How often have you been having relations since? Was it just that one time? Was it maybe once every now and then? Be specific."

Carson whispered after a second and a half, "It varied."

"Varied how?"

He shrugged. How was he supposed to answer that? It was complicated. "Dunno. Life, I guess."

The Judge smirked. "It's not easy sneaking around, huh?" Again, Carson just shrugged. "What about recently?"

Carson just nodded once—a minute confirmatory nod. He didn't feel like that was too risky of a question to answer.

"How recent?"

Carson didn't want to answer that one. He thought maybe answering could give a lot away about Margaret. It was possible it wouldn't, but he couldn't be too careful around the same man that fathered her.

In response to Carson's absence of speech, the machine spiked only a little, and the Judge breathed out a heavy huff. "A month? A week? A day? C'mon, Owens, work with me."

The machine spiked harder the longer Carson remained silent.

"Hmm, interesting," the Judge mumbled, jotting down more notes. "Very recent then. Probably within the last week." Carson's heart and stomach both dropped through the floor. Could the Judge really tell that much from the machine?

The machine was suddenly spiking crazier than before. It started beeping again, wild warnings sounding in the small room despite it having been muted earlier. It must have exceeded certain parameters that it was muted for.

Carson understood at that moment. No, the Judge couldn't tell it was within the last week from the machine alone. He was calling Carson's bluff, and it worked. How could he have been such a fool? The Judge was able to get a reaction out of him that confirmed his statement. Without Carson saying a word, he had narrowed down a timeframe for the last time he had seen his lover.

"Hmm." Judge James wrote an entire paragraph before looking back at Carson and asking, "Is that why you were breaking curfew? Going to see the girl? Meet up with her? Did you have relations with her last night?"

Carson clenched his jaw and rubbed his palms subconsciously on his trousers, careful of the sensors taped to his fingertips. He was having extreme difficulty controlling his body's natural reactions. And, of course, they caused the machine to react.

"You know," said the Judge, setting his pen down on the table gently, a sigh on the edge of his words. "If you and this girl really want to be together, why haven't you talked to her father about sending in an engagement request?" Carson remained silent. He most definitely couldn't answer that one. "Perhaps he doesn't like you and would say no," assumed the Judge. "Or perhaps he knows nothing of you." Long pause. "Maybe you don't actually want to marry her."

Carson didn't even think before idiotically snarling, "That's not true."

Again, he cursed himself.

Judge James allowed a few moments to pass before he said, "Well, all I know really is that she can't be a married woman since her husband would know if she'd been unfaithful. It's the beauty of Anem's brand. Is she close to your age, then? It's unheard of for a woman—or man—over twenty years of age to not be married. It's not impossible, though."

Carson didn't respond. He bit his tongue to remind himself how dangerous his words could be to Margaret.

"I'm going to assume that's a yes."

The machine spiked. *To hell with you.*

"A definite yes," he whispered, picking up the pen and jotting more notes down. "I don't think you're going to give me much more information about her, so I won't ask who she is. We'll find her regardless. I've already ordered my men to start setting up checkpoints around the city to check every shoulder of every woman between the ages of thirteen and twenty-five."

Beads of sweat formed on Carson's forehead. *'We'll find her regardless,'* he had said. Those words echoed in Carson's head. He shut his eyes tightly, trying to squeeze the words and the worry out, but the machine told all. The only thing Carson could do was trust in Anem and hope she would answer his desperate prayers.

13

After spending the better part of the morning completing her daily household duties, Margaret had sat down at her desk to write up the essay required by her mentor, Mr. Gibson, on the rules of the land and how they positively affect society. It was a tough assignment for Margaret since she didn't have very many positive things to say about the topic, but she knew what she was supposed to say, so that's what she wrote. She was sure her mentor—who worked at the Courthouse—would appreciate the essay.

She'd been an apprentice for nearly a year, and though she was assigned a job earlier than most of her peers—before graduating, even!—she didn't necessarily hate it. It was her father that pulled the strings to get her in the system early, hoping his daughter would climb the ladder to Ambassador of the Province of Deneb faster than her own mother did. She supposed he trusted her judgment quite a bit.

She doubted he'd trust her much longer, though. Once she married William, he'd see that she'd already been bound to someone else. He'd hate her. Probably lock her up and divorce her on the grounds of sensual immorality. She'd lose her title of Duchess and any chance of becoming Ambassador.

Oddly enough, though, Margaret smiled at the thought. She cared not about her title or politics, and would honestly prefer to move down in station, if they'd allow her. If she moved down a few Classes, her and Carson would actually be allowed to marry. She'd receive a simpler life, and how could that be something to frown over?

But it was a silly thought. She would never be Carson's wife.

Margaret folded the two-page essay and placed it in her clutch purse. It was due that evening by five, but she intended to have it in Mr. Gibson's hands before one. Not because she wanted to be an overachiever, but because the Courthouse was close to the farmers' market that Carson was occasionally found in, either helping a few farmers unload their product for a few silver dollars, or shopping around himself with his sister in tow. She never stopped to speak to him, but she liked to see him in everyday life.

She missed the school days they used to share. It was where they first met, after all. Nowadays, they hardly saw each other outside of the temple, ceremonies, and committing hell-bound acts after curfew.

There was a knock on the front door then. Margaret glanced at the clock on the wall. She had forgotten about her appointment with her novice seamstress—and good friend—Gina Blake. She was too young to be a professional seamstress, but after her mother's passing two years prior, her father—a Class Four who tilled the ground every day from sunup to sundown—struggled to provide basic necessities for his five children. Being the oldest of the five, Gina took it upon herself to at least provide for herself if she couldn't provide for anyone else. But Margaret knew Gina skipped meals to feed her siblings a little more. So, when she came over to do her seamstress duties, Margaret always made sure she left with a full belly.

Gina was all smiles when Margaret opened the door to let her in. Margaret couldn't help but note how beautiful and truly genuine her smile always was.

"You're cutting this kind of close, Margaret, but I'm so excited you asked me to make your wedding dress," gushed Gina. She wrestled with the three bags she toted all the way from her home to give Margaret a hug.

Gina didn't start hugging Margaret until Margaret first hugged her several months ago. After all, it could be considered inappropriate if either girl were not for it. But the two girls were now friends, and neither were uncomfortable with the other in the least.

Margaret replied to Gina's comment with a smile, saying, "I know it's last minute! I'm so sorry for that, but time got away from me, and there's no one I trust more than you with a needle and thread. You've been making my clothing for two years now, haven't you?"

Gina shrugged gently. Everything she did was gentle. "That sounds about right. I'm very grateful that you and your father have such big hearts and have allowed me to—"

Margaret shook her head and took one of the bags from her. She noted how hefty it was. "Don't say it again, Gina. I swear, you express your gratitude toward us every time I see you. It's unnecessary."

Gina blushed. Her emerald eyes fluttered to the ground for a moment. She was such a shy girl with such a big heart. There wasn't a mean bone in her petite body. "I can't help it," Gina whispered, voice like a small bell. "I thank Anem every day for your family."

"I am the one grateful to you, Gina," Margaret said. She motioned for Gina to follow her to the living room where Gina would have space to work her magic. "First thing's first," declared Margaret as she set the bag she carried down on the couch. "Let's have a snack. I'm starved."

Gina set the two other bags with the other on the couch as well, nodding. "Sure." She never turned Margaret down when offered food. Not anymore, at least. Gina must've known if she did refuse, Margaret would've continued insisting until she had shoved food into Gina's mouth. It actually had happened once before. Since then, Gina always agreed to a snack.

After warming it, Margaret handed Gina a plate of spaghetti left over from the night before. Gina used to ask why their snacks seemed like full meals, but over time, she stopped questioning it and always finished her serving.

"Would you like more?" Margaret asked her timid friend who would never, ever dare ask for seconds.

Gina shook her head no even though Margaret was already putting more on her plate. "I'm stuffed, but thank you, Maggie."

Gina was one of the few people that called her by her name and not her title alone. Margaret liked that quite a bit.

"Let's get started," Gina suggested. "I have samples of the different fabrics I thought would look so beautiful on you." She clasped her hands together and smiled excitedly.

Margaret set the plate back down in front of Gina. "We have time. Finish your food first, would you?"

Gina slumped and gazed down at the food. "I really am full, though."

"Fine, then." Margaret shrugged. "I'll pack it for you to take home."

Gina opened her mouth to protest, but must have thought better of it after Margaret gave her a stern look. After packing three servings of spaghetti into a sealed container and putting it with Gina's things so she wouldn't leave it behind, Margaret announced to Gina she was finally ready to see the samples.

Gina laid out five different fabric squares, all white, all very delicate and beautiful. Margaret picked one that she thought she'd feel the most comfortable in: thick breathable cotton with a lace overlay.

"How much will it cost for you to purchase this fabric?" inquired Margaret.

Gina checked her notebook she had pulled out with the fabric samples. Margaret noted how organized and neat Gina's daily notes were compared to her own. She even color coordinated. Margaret tended to be envious of people who seemed to have their inner selves in such order. That was far more than she could ever hope for herself. "For all the material I'll need, it'll end up being about fifteen silver pieces."

Margaret nodded. "One moment." She grabbed her coin purse from her room and hurried back to Gina. She counted out twenty-five pieces and placed them in Gina's hand.

"Twenty-five is too much," said Gina, though she didn't seem surprised. She attempted to give Margaret back ten of those silver dollars.

Margaret grabbed Gina's hands and closed them over the coins. "Consider it a tip for stopping by today. Also, you never know if the price will go up! And what if you need any other tools? I want to invest in your craft so that my dress is as beautiful as it can be."

That wasn't really why Margaret gave Gina ten more pieces than required, and Gina wasn't naive. But, it was the reason Margaret stated, and Gina would never call anyone a liar.

Gina nodded and carefully dropped the pieces into her coin purse tucked secretly away in her skirt. "I'll head over to the Marketplace as soon as I leave here. Hopefully the vendor will have as much as I need for your dress." Then she grinned the smallest of smiles and grasped the necklace tied around her throat that she always wore.

Margaret wondered what the significance of the beaded necklace was to Gina. The letters on the beads were obviously carved by hand and definitely not by a professional. To Margaret, it looked like a homemade gift from someone that cared a lot about her, a gift that she treasured greatly.

As she rolled one of the beads that spelled *angel* between two fingers, she said lowly, "I may even buy fabric for my own dress while I'm there." She glanced at Margaret quickly. "Not with the silver pieces you've given me, of course. I've been saving for my own dress for a few weeks now as the Judge looks for me a husband."

Margaret was surprised to be hearing that news for the first time. "My father is looking for a husband for you? But you're under the age of consent. And you don't finish school for another half year."

She nodded. "Yes, but it's possible under Deneb's law for anyone older than fourteen to marry if the parents write a formal letter to the Judge and he agrees that it's beneficial. It's not a common practice, I'll admit, but it's legal. My husband would have to be able to provide, of

93

course, which means he'll most definitely be at least a year older than me."

Margaret was quiet for a moment. She knew about that rule, but it had slipped her mind. She thought it was one of those rules no one really took seriously. Outdated.

Gina shrugged when Margaret didn't respond. She pinched her plump lips to the corner of her mouth. "It's been two weeks since the Judge approved of my father's request, but we've heard no word from him since."

"Would you like me to ask him about—?"

"No!" opposed Gina, throwing up her hands. "Please don't bother your father with such a silly thing, Margaret. I'm sure he has bigger things to work on. And maybe he's having a difficult time with my case. From what I understand, there's a whole lot to take into account. It's a time-consuming process, I'm sure."

Margaret nodded, recalling all the different rules required for two people to marry. She listed them out loud: "Class, age appropriateness, non-familial check, blood type..." There were more, but those were the few Margaret could name off the top of her head, the ones that were most important to the Province.

Gina nodded and began packing her bags. "Yes, your father must be very busy."

Margaret helped Gina with packing as she asked, "Did Mr. Blake request you to be married because of...?" She didn't dare finish her illegal question. She was prying too far into Gina's private life.

Gina didn't seem bothered though. She simply nodded without any hesitation. "It was my request, really. I suggested it to my father, and he drafted the letter. He doesn't necessarily want it, but he knows it's the right thing to do. With me out of his household, he'll be able to care for my four younger siblings better." She smiled at Margaret. Margaret didn't think anyone could find joy where joy didn't exist except for Gina. She wished she was more content with life as Gina seemed to be with hers. "Everything will be so much better for my family when I marry. I look forward to relieving my father of the burden I am to him."

A heavy weight of sorrow befell Margaret in that moment. Gina considered herself a burden to her father, and since her mother's passing during childbirth, she had worked so hard to relieve her father of that burden.

In addition to her normal duties as a young teenage girl, she took care of the baby her mother died giving life to, cooked and cleaned, assisted her siblings with their daily chores and schoolwork, as well as started making clothing for Margaret and her family. Getting married early in life was Gina's last-ditch effort to completely and fully relieve her father of herself, now that some of the other children were old enough to take over the household and family duties in her stead.

Margaret wondered how Timothy Blake felt about his daughter getting married while in school and working so hard to just make a little difference in their household finances. She imagined he didn't like it. He was a good man, kind and loving. Margaret remembered when his wife died, and how he mourned her passing so roughly. Yet he never turned his attention away from his children. You could see the love he had for each of them in his eyes any time he simply looked at them. But with Gina...

Parents weren't supposed to have favorites, but Margaret thought he looked at her with more appreciation, adoration, and respect than any of his other children. Who could blame him? Gina wasn't one to complain about anything and was more than willing to give everything she had and everything she was to make someone's life better.

She was a true angel that Anem had handpicked and sent down to bless the people whose lives she touched. Of that, Margaret was convinced.

"Well, anyway," breathed Gina, picking up the bags again. "I'm off to the market." She smiled so lovingly at Margaret. "I'll be putting my heart and soul into this dress for you."

"You can have it done in time for the wedding? It's only four days away. I can always go by the Adler's Bridal Shoppe if you can't—"

"Don't do that!" She looked offended Margaret had suggested such a thing. "I can and I will have it done in time for your wedding."

Margaret frowned. "How?"

"This week is a holiday, so no school, which means I can dedicate every waking moment to this project. Besides, the pattern you chose is a very simple one." She smiled at Margaret proudly. "I'm very excited."

Margaret returned the smile with a small grin. "Make sure to rest and eat every now and then, Gina. Please."

Gina giggled at Margaret, waving her hand nonchalantly at her. "You worry about me unnecessarily."

Margaret saw Gina to the door and helped her put on her mother's gray cloak that she wore everywhere, though it was coming unraveled in some places. She watched her walk swiftly down the steps and onto the cobblestone road before closing the door.

She sighed, heart heavy. Her father was searching for a husband fit for Gina. Would he pick a good man? Or would the Judge think any man would suffice for the angel-incarnate young girl? The benefit of Gina getting married had nothing to do with the marriage itself but everything to do with the outcome of removing a mouth to feed from Timothy Blake's household.

Yet, a husband was still an important factor and not one to take lightly. Not just any man would do for Gina. She deserved a good man. Better than good. She deserved a great man—gentle, kind, soft-spoken. Not easily prone to anger let alone outbursts. Perhaps that's why her father was taking so long to match Gina to someone.

Margaret resolved that when her father returned from work that day, she would ask him about the status of the husband-search he headed for her dearest friend.

Until then, she had work to do herself.

Clutch in hand, she draped her burgundy cloak over her floral print long-sleeved blouse that climbed to a halt at the base of her neck.

She wrapped a gray scarf that she'd bought in the Marketplace earlier that week from an older woman around her throat. Pulling the hood of the cloak up over her braided bun updo, she set out for the Courthouse.

It wasn't a long walk, but Margaret wouldn't have minded even if it was. It would only take her thirty minutes to walk there, and what was thirty minutes during such a lovely day as that one? A tramcar driver stopped his vehicle half-full of passengers in the middle of the road to offer her a ride, but she declined it with a slight wave of her wrist. He tilted his uniform hat to her, said, "Have a good day, Duchess James," and he continued on his way to the next stop.

Margaret was careful not to drag her blush-colored skirt through any dirt or mud. She hoisted it as she walked through the wide cobblestoned streets of Uptown Polaris. Businesses lined the cobblestone. Smaller paths broke away from the main road and led to other shops.

Several people stopped what they were doing, whether buying or selling, just to greet her.

"How do you do, my lady?"

"Good afternoon, Miss James."

"Let us know if you need anything, Duchess."

And for some reason that day she felt guilty every time someone said something nice to her. They all held her in such high regard. What would they say to her once they learned about the brand she shared with Carson?

Harlot, she convinced herself they'd say. *Give her to the devils of the Red Desert. Throw her to the serpent in the Glassy Sea.*

Having the brand of Anem wouldn't kill her, she knew that much, but she would never be looked at the same again. A beloved daughter of a grand Ambassador and a mighty Judge, defamed in the most vile way by the likes of a Middle Class hellion.

Margaret knew the things people said about the Owens family. School teachers had warned the girls to stay away from Carson. They called him a mischievous boy, though he'd done nothing to deserve the title. She didn't see a mischievous boy in Carson at all. To her, he was funny, carefree, and jovial. And, if anyone was dedicated to following the rules, it was Carson Owens—though that didn't seem to matter to the adults. He was an Owens, and the Owens produced mischievous boys—period.

As Margaret passed the Marketplace on her way to the Courthouse, she noticed a large crowd gathered outside of it. Officers had set up a barrier with only one way into the outdoor market. The men and older women were allowed to go in unchecked, but they stopped every young woman and had her step into a privacy tent. A few moments later, they were released and allowed inside. She didn't see Gina in the crowd, so she assumed she'd already passed through the checkpoint.

What's going on? What a strange sight.

She scanned the crowd for Carson, but he was not there. Perhaps he was inside the market at one of the vendors' booths she couldn't see. She promised herself she'd swing by after dropping off her essay, if the line inside wasn't too bad, that was. It had been at least a week since she'd shopped there. Vendors would have brand new products to showcase at their stands.

She passed a bakery and coffee shop as she neared the corner of the street. The wafting scents tempted her to stop, but she hadn't brought but two silver dollars, and that she was saving for something special at the Marketplace. Perhaps another scarf from the old woman who knit the one she wore.

The Courthouse was right around the corner of the bakery, and as she rounded it, to her surprise, officers were also set up at the entrance there. Awkwardly, Margaret noted William was one of them, and she groaned internally.

There wasn't a crowd like at the Marketplace, but a few people trickled into the Courthouse—for what reason was unimportant and didn't tickle Margaret's interest. Margaret plastered a smile on her face and gracefully strode up to William.

He smiled back at her. "Miss Margaret, it's a pleasure to see you today. Are you well?"

"Very. Thank you, William."

He relaxed his stiff stance, and took a full gander at Margaret, which made her a bit uncomfortable seeing as she didn't necessarily like the fellow all too well. He'd never done wrong that she'd seen or heard, but she couldn't help how she felt. In Margaret's opinion, it was questionable whether or not they were a good match. And yet, they were to be husband and wife in only four days.

"What brings you to the Courthouse this afternoon?" questioned William, smiling at her sweetly. It wasn't a warm, heart-melting smile like Carson's, but it was one she could learn to like... If she tried really hard. Even then, she doubted it would ever trump Carson's genuine, butterfly-inducing smile.

"I have an assignment to turn into Mr. Gibson," she replied.

"Oh, that's right," he stated, losing the grin. "I'd forgotten you had an internship here. Forgive me. It's been a long day."

Margaret glanced over at the other officers requesting a young woman to step inside a privacy tent for a moment. She couldn't have been but fifteen years old. Perhaps fourteen, even. "I can see that. What's going on?"

He exhaled in a huff. "Well, this morning we arrested a young man for deliberately breaking curfew, and then we found out he had a brand. And get this: he's unwedded."

Margaret's heart stopped. "What?" she whispered.

"It's true."

She swallowed the knot rising in her throat and thanked Anem William had glanced away from her in that moment. "So I assume you're searching for his...partner?" she asked calmly.

He nodded once, glancing again over at the woman exiting the tent, allowed to enter the Courthouse. Innocent.

Margaret thought if he had continued looking at the woman for a second longer, it would be inappropriate. "No luck yet. He's tough to crack, too. He won't give up anything. Barely even said whether it was a girl or not. If we didn't at least have that information, we'd be searching everyone."

Oh, no, Carson. Please tell me it's not you. Please.

But what were the odds that a young man with a brand and missing partner had also broken curfew the night before? The same night they had.

Oh, Anem, let it not be true!

Margaret focused on keeping her voice calm. "Who was the boy?"

"Officer Owens' kid. It's odd, though; no one seems surprised." William looked at her then, just as her heart fell through the earth. She was glad she didn't stop to get that bagel and coffee, because she was sure she was about to vomit. "I heard some things about that Owens family. I won't repeat them, of course, since we shouldn't gossip. But, I must say, I'm surprised they assigned one of them to be an officer. Anyway... Go on in." William motioned with his head at the entrance, a smile suddenly crawling onto his face. "I won't keep you any longer from your duties. Have a good day, my lady."

She forced a grin in return. "Have a good day, William."

She started up the Courthouse steps when one of the officers stopped her. She didn't recognize the man. "Hold on, ma'am. We have to—"

"Randall," William called out, and the officer's attention diverted to him. "Let her go. That's the Judge's daughter and my fiancé. She has clearance." William then looked at her. "You'll have to excuse the rookie, Miss Margaret. He just transferred here a week ago. Good news is I'm no longer the new guy."

Randall bowed his head to Margaret. "Apologies, my lady."

"No need to apologize for doing your job," she said, feeling her throat starting to close. "Have a good day, Officer Randall." She tilted her head down at him, then quickly turned and continued into the Courthouse.

She didn't realize how quickened her pulse and breathing were until she hesitated outside Mr. Gibson's office door. She squeezed her eyes shut and focused on taking deep breaths. She was able to calm herself after a couple of moments, but she visibly shook for several more minutes, unable to control the violent tremors.

She considered how blessed she'd been to be engaged to William that day. Surely, if he had not have let her slip by, she would have been carted off to the justice department. Detained and charged for extramarital relations. She would've been stripped down and whipped at the post, publicly shamed for her sin.

She knew the shame was coming eventually. She wasn't ignoring the inevitability of the defamation, but she was grateful to be given another hour without slander to her integrity.

Her heart hurt so deeply. If only she hadn't have been so selfish to ask for one more night, he would've never been caught breaking curfew and his brand would not have been discovered.

Forgive me, Carson. This is all my fault.

14

Waiting for his punishment was worse than the actual punishment. *Agony. That's what this is,* Carson thought solemnly as he twiddled his thumbs and chewed on his bottom lip. He had been sitting in that dimly lit cell for only two hours since the Judge had exhausted all of his questions. He looked up at the clock at least every five or ten minutes, hoping an hour or two more had passed, but that was never the case. Time moved much more slowly than ever before.

He prayed so many prayers that Margaret would be okay. But no matter how hard he prayed, he doubted they wouldn't find her brand. Even if she was the Duchess of Deneb, she couldn't pass through a checkpoint without being cleared first. It was just the rules, and no officer would dare break them and allow someone through unchecked, even if that someone was the Judge's own daughter.

Carson wrung his clammy hands repeatedly. He knew Margaret would receive the same punishment as him: stripped and whipped. A very public shaming. It wasn't as humiliating for someone like Carson who was sure his sin would come as no surprise to anyone. But Margaret... She was expected to follow the rules without fail.

Carson's head fell into his hands. Defeat and guilt bubbled in his stomach, making him sick.

"Carson."

He didn't have to look up to know who it was. "Now you come to see me," he whispered, "when I'm already beaten down?"

"You're oddly pessimistic," his father stated. Carson couldn't hear sadness in his voice, and that bothered him. Did Derek not care that his own son would be flogged in the morning? That the flesh on his back would be shredded?

Carson raised his head to gaze over at his father who leaned on the bars of the cell door. "You think it's odd that I'm feeling a bit nervous?"

"I didn't say nervous," responded Derek. Carson noted there was nothing in his eyes to suggest sorrow either. "I said pessimistic. You made the comment that you've been beaten down. The facts are, you haven't been. Not physically or mentally. If you think the Judge's interrogation today qualifies you to claim that you were beaten down, then Anem truly has blessed you with an unburdened life."

Carson stood and strode over to his father. "I didn't mean I'd been beaten literally nor did I mean to imply the Judge or any of his officers could beat me down mentally."

Derek cocked back his head. "Then what did you mean?"

Carson was quiet for a moment. It wasn't necessarily that he didn't want to tell Derek the truth of what he was thinking. Then again, perhaps it was partly that. Regardless, Carson said, "I beat myself down."

Derek took several moments to think about his statement before replying. "Why would you do that?"

"I'm a sinner. I deserve it, don't I?"

Carson hoped his father would say he was wrong and didn't deserve it, though he knew those words would never leave Derek's lips. He was an officer, after all. He'd sworn years ago to uphold the rules mandated by the District of Diphda, and that included ensuring criminals knew they deserved the punishment they were to receive. It shouldn't matter whether Carson was his son or not. A criminal was a criminal to an officer of the Province.

"Humph," breathed Derek. He adjusted his trousers and glanced down the hall. There wasn't a soul anywhere to be found. Before looking back at his son, he said, "Perhaps you do deserve what's coming, but that's not for you to decide, now is it? Nor is it your job to punish yourself unjustly."

Carson's scalp prickled. *Did he just say...?* A moment and a half passed before he replied to Derek. "I suppose you would have a bit more sympathy for me than the average person."

"Of course," said Derek. "You're my son."

"I meant because you've been where I am now. Soon, my back will be whipped just like yours was years ago."

His father's eyebrows slowly lowered over his eyes. He asked, "What are you going on about?"

"The Judge said that the Owens family has..." He paused to find the best words. "A curse, whatever that means. Behavioral issues, I suppose. Issues that have had to be modified every generation. Like my father and his father before him—that's what he said."

Derek was quiet for several long moments as he stared at Carson. Finally, he grunted his disapproval and looked down at the ground. "If that's what he said to you, his memory is failing him. I was never disobedient, and I definitely was never punished for anything. The most severe thing I'd ever done was throw a baseball through a window when I was twelve. Even then, it wasn't on purpose, and I told on myself."

Carson studied his father's face, but he didn't see any dishonesty. Yet, he had a difficult time believing him. After a moment, Carson asked, "Then what did the Judge mean?"

Derek didn't respond immediately. In fact, Carson wasn't sure he was going to say anything more to him at all. But, finally, his father reached through the bars and grabbed his elbow. He squeezed it once then released it. "It will only last a short while, son."

Carson's eyebrows furrowed over his dark chocolate eyes. "What will?"

Derek turned away from him and started back down the hall. His answer echoed in the empty corridor, "The pain... Or so I've heard."

15

*P*hineas, perhaps?

Margaret shook her head once as she opened the oven and put the chicken casserole she'd just finished preparing inside to cook. She wasn't too impressive a chef, but Margaret was the only one who could make anything halfway decent in the James' household. She did so even when her mother came home to visit. Margaret was sure the woman had never touched a skillet in her life. It was probably what had driven her father to dismiss the handful of help they'd had and insisted she learned life skills like cooking and cleaning. That, coupled with Cynthia's disappearance and the Ambassador's self-assigned business in the district.

She shook the memories from her mind and focused on more pertinent matters.

No, Phineas won't do. She clicked her tongue. *He has a bit of a temper.*

As Margaret lounged in a dining room chair, she pondered all of the possible matches for Gina. If she could help her father find someone good for her friend, she would feel much better about Gina's situation.

Ryan? No, his eyes linger on other women too much. Scott? Eh, he's okay except he's very loud and obnoxious. David? She crinkled her nose and sighed. David was a known criminal, having been arrested for different things multiple times since he was twelve.

She allowed her forehead to hit the table a bit harder than she meant. Margaret was positive that no man in Polaris, the Highest City in Deneb, was good enough for Gina Blake. None. Zero. Zilch.

Her head popped up off the table then with revelation.

There was one good man that deserved a good wife.

The front door opened, startling Margaret slightly, and the sound of the Judge's boots on the marble floor echoed from the foyer into the dining room. "I'm home, Margaret," he called, heaving a sigh of relief.

Her stomach tossed. She took a deep breath to calm herself and said, "In here, Father!" She adjusted herself in the chair to how she thought she normally sat. Or did she usually sit differently? She didn't want to look too stiff.

Anem's stars! Get a hold of yourself, Margaret!

Mark James entered the dining room a moment later carrying a few files under his arm. He smiled at his daughter. "How was your day?" He set the files on the table and gave Margaret a peck on her forehead.

Margaret stood and followed her father into the kitchen. She answered while he poured himself a glass of milk, "Typical, I suppose. Gina came over this morning. I picked out the fabric for my wedding dress. It's really pretty, Father. I can't wait to wear it."

"Now, Margaret, don't overwork that poor girl."

"I'm not, I swear! She wants to make my dress. I'm paying her very well for it too."

"Make sure you give her extra."

"Double."

"Did you send food with her today?"

"Of course."

He nodded in approval. "She's so thin. I worry about her a lot. Tim refuses government assistance, stubborn fool."

Margaret smiled at him even though he complained about Mr. Blake.

"What?" he said, shrugging. "I'm the Judge, Margaret. It's my job to concern myself with the people of my city."

She continued smiling widely. "I was hoping you would say something like that. Now I know for sure you aren't going to pick just anyone to be her husband."

"Hmm." He took another sip from his glass. "She told you about that?"

Margaret nodded. "And I have a suggestion."

Her father's eyebrows raised. "You want to suggest a man for her to marry?"

Margaret shrugged. "I know of someone that I think would be a good husband for her."

He chuckled. "Is that so? Well, perhaps I haven't yet looked into this man you've considered for Gina. I'll hear you out."

Margaret was about to say his name, but it caught in her throat. Her palms were suddenly clammy. She shook her head and then said, "How rude of me. How was your day, Father?"

He gave her a curious look but answered her regardless, "Busy." He sighed, setting the now-empty glass in the sink.

"The checkpoints," said Margaret carefully. She paused for a moment to double check that she would remain calm. "William told me why you set them up."

Mark James gave her a disapproving look. "William?"

"He was at the Courthouse today," she defended. "He was overseeing the checkpoints there."

He rolled his eyes. "William isn't supposed to talk about an ongoing case."

"Don't be mad at him," she pleaded. "I'm sure he didn't intend to break those rules. I think he's just comfortable talking to me," she lied. It was what he'd want from her and her soon-to-be husband, after all. Nausea washed over her, but she schooled her face into a smile.

"I suppose," he mumbled, though his tone didn't match his words. "So what all do you know about the case?"

Margaret hesitated. He raised an eyebrow at her. She shrugged, looking over at the stove. "He said it was a kid called Owens." She opened the oven door and pretended to check on the casserole, though she knew it wasn't close to being done. "I assume he means Carson Owens?" She was careful to tread lightly.

He was silent long enough to make Margaret's stomach twist. Finally, half a moment later, he asked, "Do you know Carson Owens?"

She closed the oven door as she spoke, her stomach tangling itself into tighter knots, "We were schoolmates. He's of the quiet kind."

"Guess nothing's changed there," her father muttered under his breath, not necessarily at her. She thought that maybe he was annoyed at Carson for being so quiet, despite it otherwise being seen as an asset in a citizen of the Province. Mark James looked back at his daughter. "I hope you've told no one else of this."

"Of course not," she quickly answered. "I wouldn't dare, Father."

He nodded curtly. "Good." A sigh left him. "Your curiosity must be piqued. Come with me." Margaret didn't say a word as she followed him back out of the kitchen and sat at the table with him. "Perhaps it'd be helpful for the case to brainstorm with someone who knew him from school." He nodded to himself whilst stroking the stubble on his chin. "Yes, yes. In fact, I have a few questions for you, darling." He thumbed through the files neatly placed on the table.

Margaret's stomach flipped. It was annoying how uncontrollable her innards were. She was afraid it would affect her demeanor.

In a timely manner, she replied, "Of course. Ask me anything."

Don't ask me anything. For the love of Anem, please don't figure out what I've been doing with Carson. She was certain her father would disown her.

Why did she still fight? It was inevitable. She was on a one-way path that she couldn't turn back on nor veer from. The destruction of Margaret James was inevitable.

The Judge began. He was casual and much less intimidating than how Margaret imagined he had probably been with Carson. "He said he'd had his brand for a year. That means he was in his early sixteenth year when he first received it."

He shook his head, and a lump rose in Margaret's throat. Such disappointment etched on his face, and he didn't even actually know Carson.

He continued, "It's extremely likely the woman was either his age, or a grade above or below him. I really doubt she was much younger than him, and considering he just turned seventeen, if she was more than a year older than him, she'd be a Mature already."

Margaret nodded slowly. "Right," she whispered. "A Mature would have come forward."

"Not just that," Mark James said, flicking his wrist as if the information she presented wasn't important. "He was with this woman last night."

Margaret's stomach fell through the floor. "He told you that?" Her voice was caught. She cleared her throat once when he looked at her. Quickly, she said, "It's just that I wouldn't have expected that of Carson. It's out of character. He's quiet... and private."

"And I'm very persuasive." Mark looked back down at the papers in the file. "Anyway, if she was a Mature, surely she wouldn't have snuck out with him."

Margaret nodded. "I imagine you're right," she calmly, carefully worded.

Judge James glanced sidelong at her for half a second before looking back at the file before him. "Do you have any idea who this girl could be, Margaret? She must have been in school with you. I don't think she's a traveler; although, I admit, he didn't give me much to work with regarding that." Mark set the papers down and folded his arms on the table as he looked over at her.

Margaret pretended to ponder the question, but she had difficulty thinking of anything except that she was sure her father was already suspicious that she knew something. So, before too much time passed, she shook her head and said, "I'll have to think more on it, but nobody in particular comes to mind immediately."

"Were you close to him?"

She leaned back in her chair. "I'm sorry?"

He gestured with his hand vaguely. "I remember seeing him with another boy and a couple of your girl friends hanging around each other a few times. Most recently, at that one Ritual. What was that kid's name? Vickers?"

Margaret touched her chin thoughtfully with her index finger. "Oh, yes. Fiona, Kelly, and Bobby are all cousins. Bobby and Carson were always really close, and you know how Fiona and I were. Naturally, we'd occasionally end up in a circle talking together."

The Judge nodded to himself. "Sure. That's logical." A pause and a skip of Margaret's heart passed before he spoke again, "Did he seem inclined to Kelly? She's not yet a Mature."

"She's engaged to Steven, Father." Margaret struggled to keep the irritation from her voice, jealousy swelling in her chest at the mere suggestion.

"That's not what I asked."

Margaret pretended to think again, but then said two seconds later, "Neither seemed too intrigued with the other, as I remember." Except that wasn't necessarily true. Kelly had always given Carson second and third and fourth glances, but Margaret knew Carson hadn't once given Kelly more than a platonic acknowledgement when she'd spoken to him.

Mark stroked his chin thoughtfully. "Hmm. What about Fiona?"

"But she's a Mature. I thought you said it couldn't have been a Mature."

He shrugged. "It could be, if you think Fiona would do something like that. Matures aren't prone to sin like Immatures, but that doesn't mean some of them don't struggle with the flesh. So then... Fiona?"

Margaret shook her head quickly. "Oh, no. Fiona has been very distant from everyone since she became a Mature. And even before, she and Carson didn't necessarily see eye-to-eye."

"What does that mean?" He was suddenly very curious about the relationship between Fiona and Carson.

Margaret simply said the truth. "Fiona has always been too loud for Carson's comfort, and Fiona always thought Carson was too quiet to be any fun."

"Ah, I see." It was silent for several long moments.

The oven's timer suddenly went off in the kitchen, and she excused herself to remove the casserole from the oven. When she returned to the table, her father had pulled out a different file and was jotting notes down on some papers inside it.

As she sat down, he began speaking again. "While I'm thinking about it, what was the name of the boy you wanted me to consider for Gina?" He paused what he was writing to look up at her.

"Is that her file?" Margaret questioned. She realized in that same second that she was stalling.

Mark nodded once. "It is."

Margaret inhaled and shrugged. "I don't know if you'll think it appropriate to speak about anymore."

His eyebrows furrowed. "Why would it be inappropriate?"

She was silent for only a moment, and then her answer was but a whisper. "I think it best to wait. Considering you have an ongoing case concerning him."

The Judge set down his pen. "Owens? You were going to suggest Carson Owens?"

She looked down at her hands in her lap. "He's a good guy, Father. He really is."

"You think Gina deserves the baggage he'd bring into their marriage?"

"That's not what I—"

"He loves someone else. Don't you think she deserves someone who can love her and only ever her?"

112

She suddenly had difficulty taking in a decent breath of air. "Of course I do," Margaret breathed out, but the Judge kept talking and didn't hear her.

"Even if I have to find someone outside of the Highest City, I will. But I won't pledge her to a man-whore, Margaret. No one wants to marry someone who's already given themselves intimately to another. What's gotten into you?"

She simply shrugged, still looking at her hands. *No one wants to marry someone who's already given themselves intimately to another.* Her heart shattered under the weight of those words, and she wondered how much truth there was in them.

She whispered, "I apologize. It was a silly thought. I do want the best for Gina, but I just can't think of anyone else that would do."

He sighed. "I understand you wanting to help your friend, but this is my job. I *will* find the best husband for Gina." He reached over and patted her cheek softly. "I promise, darling."

He closed Gina's file and set it aside. Before Margaret thought about the words, they spilled out of her mouth. "At least consider him, Father. He deserves to be happy too."

He paused for such a long moment, not looking at her, that Margaret thought perhaps he'd figured everything out from that sentence alone.

Quietly, he asked, "Why would Carson Owens deserve happiness?"

"You think he doesn't?" She was very careful to seem unbiased. "Doesn't everyone deserve—"

"Of course everyone deserves to be happy, Margaret, but why do you care about Owens' happiness?" He finally looked at her, and his stare was so intense, she couldn't stand matching it. Her eyes flickered back down to her lap.

Her voice was but a whisper, "We were friends. I told you that already."

"Why not suggest the other boy? His friend that you said was Fiona's cousin."

"I don't know if Gina would like him." She was frantic as she tried to find excuses. "I just feel like Carson and Gina would get along very well. Their personalities... you know."

Mark James was quiet for a moment. Finally, he pulled out a file he had yet to touch that evening and flipped it open. The tab read *'Checkpoint Clearances'*. He skimmed the first four pages, obviously searching for something in particular. He paused on the fourth page, finger lingering. "Didn't you say you were at the Courthouse today?"

Margaret nodded slowly. "Yes," she whispered.

"Were you cleared for entry?"

"Yes." She swallowed and it made a distinguishable noise. He glanced sidelong at her again.

Oh, stars. He knows.

"Were you actually searched and cleared, Margaret? Or did William allow you to pass through?"

She couldn't control the tears filling her eyes. "Daddy," she whispered, choking on a sob.

He sighed, leaning back in his chair. "Margaret," he whispered, sorrow coating his voice. "It's not you, is it? Please tell me it's not you."

16

She was tired of fighting the inevitable. She deserved what was coming. But she would never apologize for caring about Carson, nor for wanting him, or for dreaming all the impossible things she dreamed, and she would certainly not apologize for loving him with every ounce of life inside of her.

But she was still scared, and without thinking at all about what the consequences would be, her automatic response kicked in and she bolted for the front door. Where she would go once out the door was not a thought that had crossed her mind yet. Her father must have seen the attempt to escape coming though.

He was right on her heels. He grabbed her arm before she could get but a couple of yards away from the table and yanked her back with more force than intended. Margaret slammed into the wall by the kitchen door. Mark James was rough enough that what he did surprised and frightened her, and since her father was not inclined to violence, that fear was multiplied by the unknown of such aggression, even though she was not injured at all.

Margaret's biggest mistake came next, though. She wrestled against her father's grip, screaming and crying at him to let her go. All the while, he remained silent. She didn't dare look at his face. She was afraid of what she'd see there. Disappointment. Rage. Sadness. All of the above.

Then, he calmly told her, "Stop fighting me, Margaret. Let me see your shoulder."

Yet, she fought harder, yanking and tugging and pulling herself away from him. After several moments, the Judge had enough. His grip tightened on her, and he shoved her against the wall, his forearm firmly pressed against her upper back as she continued to squirm. He grabbed her left arm and yanked it away from the wall. A cry of discomfort mixed with her sobs and pleas. She continued her attempt to remove her left arm from his grip to no avail. He twisted her arm roughly, and it was more than Margaret could handle. She shouted out in pain and cried harder.

"Stop fighting me!" he rasped. His forehead crinkled, distraught, and pain could clearly be heard in his tone. Even so, she couldn't help feeling betrayed by him. Through his teeth, he spat at her, "Kristina Margaret James! Show me your shoulder, damn it." It was as if he was hurting too, except he wasn't the one whose arm was bent back and twisted.

He grabbed the collar of her blouse and yanked on it hard enough that the buttons on her front popped. The cloth gave way to reveal the brand of Anem etched on her left shoulder. Quickly, less than a second after confirming, he let go of her. She pulled her left arm to her chest and cradled it, but other than that, she didn't dare move. She kept herself pressed against the wall. Her back remained to him.

The sobs stopped being so insistent then, and the only noise she made were her body's attempts to steady her breathing. Her arm throbbed in three different places. Hot tears streamed down her cheeks, fresh ones quickly chasing the old.

She didn't dare turn to look at her father, but she listened as his boots carried him slowly away from her, back into the dining room. A chair scooted noisily across the tiled floor, and he produced a heavy, disappointed groan as he collapsed back into his seat.

Trembling, she pulled her blouse back over her shoulder to cover the sin illustrated on her body. A brand was supposed to be beautiful, but only in the context of marriage. Prior to that day, Margaret had seen her brand as beautiful because she shared it with Carson. But now her whole world was beginning to collapse, and her brand was an ugly, putrid curse. A reminder of the sinner and criminal she had become. Proof that she wasn't fit to be an Ambassador.

She wanted nothing more than for the brand to disappear.

Minutes passed. Neither of them moved. Neither of them spoke.

Her sobs began building once more, threatening to erupt. She slowly slid down the wall and sat, knees pulled up to her chest, her back still to the dining table, and she allowed herself to cry into her blush skirt that covered her knees. As much as she wanted to run to her room and sob into her pillow, she was afraid to move. She didn't think her father would allow her the privilege of weeping in private.

Several long moments passed. Margaret didn't move and she didn't dare look over her shoulder to see if her father was staring daggers at her. She imagined he probably was.

What was he waiting for? Wasn't he going to call the officers so they could drag her to the department to be processed and sentenced?

"Margaret," her father whispered, interrupting her racing thoughts. Even though it was barely a breath, it was loud in the silence and made Margaret tense. "I want to know how this happened."

She didn't move.

"Come sit at the table with me." A chair slightly screeched across the floor. He must have pulled out a chair to indicate where she should sit. "Margaret," he addressed again. "Please." He was so calm that it frightened her more than if he were angry. She had prepared herself for rage, not the placidity he portrayed.

His boots clomped across the tile suddenly. Margaret tensed, trying to prepare herself for the unexpected. But how does one prepare for something when they don't know what's coming? Would he hit her? She'd never experienced violence from her father. He'd always been loving and soft when handling her, his beloved daughter. But perhaps now he saw her differently and therefore would treat her how he saw her. As a criminal. Harlot. Was that all he saw when he looked at her now?

A hand gently laid on her shoulder, the one with the brand. "Margaret, darling," he whispered. She hugged her knees tighter. "Explain this to me, please. How did I miss this? How could I have not known?"

Margaret sniffled. She shrugged slightly, but she didn't speak.

"For the last year? Since you were sixteen? Is that true?"

She hesitated but nodded eventually. "Forgive me," she rasped right before a sob that had built itself up in her chest released from her body in shivers and gasps. "Please," she begged through the convulsions.

He was quiet for a long, long time. He didn't move his hand on her shoulder, and he didn't make her look at him. He heaved a few heavy sighs but was in no hurry to lock her away.

Margaret wondered why not. Was he contemplating what to do? Did he have a choice? He was the Judge of the Highest City in the Province of Deneb. He was expected, more so than any other person there, to follow the rules without fail. And the rules said that anyone who had extramarital relations were to be flogged. Twenty lashes.

Margaret felt nauseated just considering how painful it would be.

Then, under his breath, he said, "I can fix it," and he jumped up so abruptly that it startled Margaret. Paying no mind to her, he hurried away into the kitchen. Margaret remained where she was a crumpled mess on the floor, leaning against the wall. She wished it would swallow her up forever.

Her cheeks were wet and flushed. Using her skirt, she attempted to wipe her face of all the unbecoming evidence that said she was afraid of punishment, that she was disappointed in herself, and, worst of all, that she was suffering from a sharp pain every time her heart thumped inside her chest.

Mark James was not trying to be discreet in the kitchen. Items clanged together and cabinet doors opened and shut, opened and shut.

Margaret wondered what he was rummaging around for in there.

A minute or two later, the door to the kitchen swung open again. Curious, Margaret peeked over her shoulder to find her father placing several random items on the dining table. Then, he left the room again, rushing by her without a glance, and re-emerged seconds later with the first aid kit he kept stored under the communal bathroom sink. He also carried several towels and an old bed sheet, which he then draped over one half of the table.

Her stomach dropped through the floor when she realized what he must have been thinking about doing. "No," she choked out, turning away from the dining area and scrambling to her feet. She started for the stairs, though they would only lead her to her parent's bedroom which had no lock on the door. Mark's arms were around her before she could put a foot on the first step. She quickly and desperately grasped at the banister and refused to let go despite the ache in her left arm from their earlier scuffle.

Mark tugged her away from the banister only slightly, just enough to make her uncomfortable so she'd let go. "I just want to make everything right again," he told her. "Please, Margaret. Trust me."

"No," cried Margaret. "Let go of me. Please!" She kicked her leg in all directions, trying to make contact with any part of him that she could manage, but she could never win in a tussle with her father.

"I'm sorry, my child," he whispered sorrowfully. "But this is something I must do." He tugged her away from the banister again, a bit more forcefully, and her grip on the wood slipped. He carried her to the dining table as she continued wailing and kicking and thrashing in his arms.

"Father, please!" she exclaimed. "Please!" Margaret wondered if he felt any sense of guilt for even considering what he was about to do. Did her pleas fall on deaf ears or did they make him feel worse about it? Or was she just an annoyance to him now that he knew her sin?

Mark James shoved his loud flailing daughter onto the table and forced her so she'd be face down on the old bedsheet. He pinned her arms behind her back, and, using medical wrap from the first aid kit, he hogtied her so she was completely immobile. Margaret screeched her protest and pleaded louder for him to let her go. He sighed heavily, keeping his hand on her head, and leaned over to see her face. He brushed away the hair that had fallen out of her bun and had stuck to her wet skin now the shade of crimson. "Margaret, stop for a moment and take a breath. Inhale and exhale. Take a deep breath, darling."

Margaret was getting lightheaded. She hadn't realized she was hyperventilating. After protesting loudly a couple more times—her father silent through all of it—she finally obeyed and took a deep, shaky breath.

Mark broke his silence. "I know you're afraid, Margaret, but I promise I'm on your side. I'll always be on your side." He took a moment to allow her to process his words. After she inhaled deeply again, he asked, "Do you trust me?"

She didn't answer. Her eyes wandered away from him and caught a glimpse of the assorted array of serrated knives, a knife sharpener, multiple bowls and plates, a bundle of paper towels, and a cheese grater he'd gathered from the kitchen. Her breathing quickened again. "Don't. Please, please, Father. Don't do this to me. Don't do this." Her voice felt too small.

"Shh." He pet her hair. "Close your eyes. Don't think about it. I have some numbing medication in the kit. I'll use all of it, I promise. I will try my best to not hurt you. Honey, I don't want to hurt you."

"Then don't!" she howled at him, voice cracking. "You don't have to!" She tried to wrestle out of the medical tape that bound her four limbs together, but it was useless.

He pressed her a smidge harder against the table to discourage her from fighting, and it worked. She stopped only a few seconds after she'd started. She was starting to feel a wave of exhaustion overcome her.

He didn't argue with what she had said. He must've known she was right to some degree. He didn't have to do anything to Margaret.

But perhaps he believed what he was doing was the best option for his daughter. Margaret wondered as she laid there, cheek pressed firmly against the tear-soaked bedsheet, if that was what he was thinking as he prepared for such a deranged procedure.

He continued petting her hair for a couple of moments more before he reached for the first aid kit and pulled out the numbing ointment. Margaret closed her eyes, heeding her father's words for the first time that evening, and vowed to keep them shut as long as she possibly could.

Mark pulled her blouse down to reveal her shoulder once again. When the whole of her brand was exposed, he opened the medicinal tube. The ointment was cold on her skin. Mark was careful to rub every last bit of it into Margaret's shoulder. He continued until she answered his question of whether or not she could feel him touching the brand anymore with a small, broken "no."

Margaret dared to peek after he cautiously removed his hand from her head for the first time. He poured rubbing alcohol into one of the large bowls he had collected earlier. Then, using the towels, he laid them out around and on her. One smaller towel he let soak in the bowl of alcohol.

"One day you'll understand why," whispered Mark James as he reached for the cheese grater and pressed it firmly against the center of the brand.

With the very first scrape, it was evident that the numbing ointment was utterly useless. And even though Margaret screamed in agony and begged him to stop, he wouldn't allow her to move, and he continued his attempt to erase the sin his daughter committed.

PART
2

MERE
MORTALS

17

The echoes of Derek's boots rapidly crossing the marble flooring of the Courthouse caused by-passers and employees alike to glance warily in his direction, but he paid no mind to the eyes gathering on him, and instead, focused on maintaining his cool composure. He would not allow the Judge to get under his skin any more than he already had.

Boldly, and without knocking, he strode into the large office, where most of Judge Mark James' time was spent.

Judge James cut his eyes up at Derek from where he was reviewing paperwork at his desk. His round spectacles were low on his nose, and Derek considered how aged and tired he looked in that moment. The man was ten years older than he was, and he was only thirty-four.

"Derek," the Judge addressed in a less than friendly tone. "What's the meaning of this? Barging in unannounced, especially at this early hour?" Derek closed the office door, but the Judge continued, "If this is about Carson, I have nothing to say to you. The kid won't get off easy because we're friends." He lowered his eyes back to his paperwork.

Derek quietly walked over and sat down in one of the red leather chairs positioned across from Judge James' desk. He considered how to say what he desperately wanted without overstepping but also without understating how he felt.

The Judge huffed. He ripped the spectacles off his face and tossed them down in front of him with a clatter. "What is it? For Anem's sake, speak! You and Carson are driving me insane with all the silence."

"You told me to be quiet and teach Carson the same," he spat back. "Now you want the opposite?"

The Judge's right eye twitched, eyebrows falling heavily over his piercing Mature blue eyes. "When Carson was born, I told you to stay quiet and to keep the kid out of trouble. I didn't mean you had to take a damn oath of silence, Derek."

Yet, that's exactly what Derek had understood when he was only seventeen and asked to take on such a big responsibility. "I stay quiet not because you ordered me to, but because it's safer. For Carson."

The Judge shook his head. "Look how that worked out."

"He's a good kid, Mark."

"I didn't say he wasn't." The Judge eyed him suspiciously then. "You did come to plea for his sake, didn't you?"

"No." It was the truth. "He broke the rules. He will reap what he sowed."

"Then, please, for the love of the goddess, state your business. I'm quite swamped right now."

Derek took a couple of seconds to study the carpeted floor before making eye contact with Judge James again, more intensely and dripping with anger unlike before. "You had no right to say what you did to him."

The Judge's eyebrows pulled together into a line. "What are you talking about?"

Derek focused on keeping his voice level and calm. He would not be known as an angry person, lest Mark mistake him again for his brother. "I visited him yesterday evening. He made an odd comment about the Owens family being cursed. He told me you were the one that said it to him."

Judge James rolled his eyes. "All I had said was that I had been hoping he would be the Owens that broke the curse. Now, granted, I

126

shouldn't have used the word curse. *Cycle* would've been a better word."

"*Cycle* would've still been too much. You shouldn't have said anything at all. Now he wants to know what I did wrong."

The Judge tapped his desk with his index finger, lips pursed. Derek allowed him a moment to mull it over. He replied after consideration, "I see the problem, Derek, and I'm sorry I've placed you in this position."

"He's a clever kid, Mark. He's going to figure it out."

"I'm aware of how smart he is; I have his JAT scores."

It was Derek's turn to be confused. "Why do you have those? Is that why it's taking so long for him to be assigned a job?"

Judge James nodded, opening his desk drawer and pulling out a manila folder that had "JAT—Owens, Jerry Carson" stamped on the tab. "My staff handles the assignments unless they're... complicated, in which case they come to me." He handed it to Derek and invited him to peek inside. "I think you'll understand why I'm the one handling his job assignment once you see his scores."

Promptly, Derek flipped it open and scanned the contents of the pages. "What am I looking at exactly?" he asked, trying to make more sense of the graphs and charts that greeted him.

"That first bar graph measures what general field he would excel in." The Judge paused to allow Derek to study the bar graph.

Derek was still confused though. Several of the bars were much higher than the rest. He glanced up at Mark. "What does it mean?"

"He's exceptional in mathematics and the sciences. He would excel in any field related to those studies. That's not the most impressive part, though. Flip to the next page." Derek obeyed. "That line graph measures the average IQ level of all the students he graduated with. His line is the green one."

Derek's eyes widened a bit. "It's above the rest."

Mark nodded his agreement. "I had been having a bit of difficulty trying to figure out where he would best fit. I don't want to waste all that potential."

"Do you have something in mind at least?"

Judge James leaned back in his chair and tapped his finger on the armrest. "Medicine. I spoke with Dr. Johnson. Once Carson becomes a Mature, he'll be able to help the old doctor with finding a cure."

Derek rolled his eyes, but his words didn't match his outward reaction. "Hopefully." Dr. Johnson was pushing old age, and his research on Immatures was invaluable. If the old pediatrician was willing to take Carson on as an apprentice... "You'll be promoting Carson to a Class Seven?" asked Derek. "Doctors have to be Class Seven citizens, no less."

The Judge sighed. "That's why it's taking so long. I have to get approval from the District Elders to promote him, and they have yet to get back to me."

"I see."

A long moment passed between the two men.

Mostly to himself, Derek whispered, "Carson is very clever. Perhaps he really will be the one that finds the cure."

Judge James nodded. "He's not a child anymore, Derek. He doesn't have to be protected."

Derek closed the folder with a snap and handed it back to the Judge. "I don't want him to know the truth. Not back then, not now, and not ever. Make it right, Mark."

"You want me to lie to him?"

"I don't care how you do it, just fix what you've nearly broken."

Mark smirked. "I don't owe you anything, Owens." Derek stood, and Mark followed suit. They didn't look away from each other until Mark breathed out a small chuckle, seemingly a bit uncomfortable with the prolonged eye contact, and he said, "But you are my friend, and if you don't want your son knowing the truth, then I shall lead him astray."

Derek nodded once, satisfied, though still irked that this happened at all. "Thank you." He offered his hand and, like always, Judge James gladly shook it.

"And thank you, my friend. You've always done as you're told, no questions asked."

"I am not my brother," stated Derek stoically. "It seems you're picking up a habit of mistaking me for him."

The Judge raised a brow. "Careful, Derek. We don't speak of mistakes."

"I've not forgotten."

"Then you'd do well to not mention him again."

Derek's expression didn't change. He remained a statue, his stone mask impenetrable. "I didn't say his name."

Mark James waved his index finger in warning. Derek found it irritating. "What name?" asked Mark. "You don't even have a brother."

Pausing, Derek looked down at the carpet. "Right," he whispered, turning and starting out the office door. "I've not forgotten."

18

Fitting day to be flogged. Carson watched the gray clouds through the bars of his small cell window as they slowly progressed across the morning sky. Unable to sleep, he had watched the moon and stars all night. He was grateful that there was at least a window to the outside world even though his view was limited to the heavens.

The bowl of oatmeal an officer had brought him early that morning still sat on the floor by his bed. Carson had eaten only a few spoonfuls before putting it down. Though he was hungry, he was afraid his stomach would betray him when he was flogged.

Carson was watching two birds glide across the morning sky toward the beach when loud clanking on his cell bars made him jump.

"Good morning," Derek Owens said, leaning his right shoulder against the bars.

Carson stood. "It is a good morning." He forced an enthusiastic tone, his left eye twitching slightly.

"Someone's cheerful this morning."

With a calculated calm, Carson strode toward his cell door. His father would not get to see him worried, let alone afraid. Leaning his back against the bars to the side of where his father stood, Carson folded his arms and forced a smile as he said, "Negativity shortens lifespans."

"I suppose," said Derek. "But it's okay to be nervous. Scared, even, would be an appropriate—"

"I'm not scared." From the corner of his eye, Carson caught the wary look his father gave him. Even as the apples of his cheeks reddened, he refused to turn his attention away from the chip in the concrete wall he studied the imperfection with his chin held high.

His father was quiet for only a moment. "I see. Did you sleep any last night?" When Carson didn't answer, he concluded, "I guess not." His father exhaled in a puff. "Well, I came by to let you know your mother and sister are praying for you." He paused. "Mom also wanted me to tell you not to worry because she and Casey will stay indoors all day."

Carson nodded once, slowly. "Thank you."

"I want you to know, son, I will be there."

Carson's stomach clenched. Slowly letting his hands fall, he turned to face his father. Their eyes met and Carson held his father's gaze for only a second and a half before looking away again. "You don't have to be," he whispered. "It's not something you want to see."

"Of course it's not. But you're my son so I'm going to make sure they treat you right. By the rules and nothing more. Thirty lashes and then they'll have the physician tend you immediately." He reached through the bars and patted Carson's shoulder. Sighing, he squeezed it once before letting go. "I won't leave your side today, okay?"

For the first time, Carson saw sorrow in his father's eyes. "Thanks, Dad," he whispered, emotion tightening his throat.

With a sigh, Derek leaned his back against the wall facing the bars and lowered himself to the floor. Carson returned to his cot and sat too. He gazed out the window for some time, focused on calming his nerves.

Eventually, the sound of shuffling drew his attention back to his father. Derek was on his feet, his own attention diverted down the corridor. "Is it time?" asked Derek.

"It is." William Lach appeared before Carson's cell. "The Correctional Lieutenant has reviewed the case and given the go-ahead."

Carson's jaw clenched. He couldn't explain why exactly, but the officer gave him a sickening feeling deep in his gut. Sure, he reasoned that it could simply be jealousy since Lach was pledged to Margaret. He hoped jealousy was all it was—for Margaret's sake.

William unlocked the cell door and motioned to Carson's wrists. The man cuffed him—no words offered this time—and gestured down the hall. "You know where to go," he mumbled. Motioning to Derek, he added, "You can come along too, I suppose. And why aren't you in uniform, Officer Owens?"

"I'm off the clock today, sir," Derek said. "I requested it, remember?"

"You requested the day off to watch over Carson?"

"He's my son."

"So?"

Carson staggered forward, letting the two officers behind him snip at each other.

Derek said in a low tone, one Carson recognized as a warning from growing up under the man, "My reasons for my leave are my concern. I don't need to explain them to anyone."

"No one said you had to."

"Then why the interrogation?"

Lach huffed. "Actually, you know what, Derek. You can wait outside. Go back the way you came."

Carson looked back, but William grabbed his shoulder none-too-gently and pushed him forward. Derek didn't move as they continued down the hallway. William shoved Carson through the corridor and into the same room that he had been prepped in the day prior.

Judge James sat behind the large oak desk, his dark robes swimming about him as his hand hurriedly scratched a pen across the paper before him. Four other officers stood quietly in different corners of the room, still as statues, fingers looped through their utility belts. The Judge didn't so much as glance up at him before speaking.

"Jerry Carson Owens." The Judge's words, like his penmanship, seemed rushed. Carson wondered if he was overbooked that day, which would've explained yesterday's irritation about postponing the flogging. "You've been charged with deliberately breaking curfew and with extramarital relations. Your sentencing will be thirty lashes at the post: ten for breaking curfew and an additional twenty for sinful relations." The judge glared at him over his spectacles. Carson noted there was more in the man's Mature blue eyes than just the disgust and disappointment he had seen the day before.

Carson's stomach pitched uneasily. He swallowed and pulled his gaze from the Judge's cold glare.

Judge James resumed his writing—a chicken-scratch of carelessly penned words—and motioned after a few moments to the officers. "On with it. It's already nearly eight. I've got far more important things to take care of."

The officer closest to Carson tossed him a loincloth like the one he had to put on the day before. Carson stripped down completely before slipping on the brown one-piece. He didn't feel so awkward changing in front of the six others, and he wasn't sure why. Perhaps he didn't care anymore. All he wanted was to go home, and to do so, he had to hurry this part along.

Two officers, strangers to Carson, took him by his elbows and led him through the building and outside into a fenced area. A windless cold blanketed him, raising the hairs on his skin and causing him to shiver.

Spectators lined the main cobblestone road, their anticipation almost tangible in the morning air. Carson wondered how they knew someone was to be flogged. His answer came in the form of a large sign hanging on the twelve-foot chain link fence. He couldn't see the front of it, but knew it must have blasted his name.

Out of the corner of his eye, he caught someone subtly waving from behind the fence, trying to catch his attention. His father. Carson sighed and kept his face turned forward. His father simply wanted him to know he was there, as he promised he would be. Carson had to admit it comforted him more than a little.

"Stop dawdling," one of the officers said as he yanked Carson's elbow and dragged him to the middle of the fenced area where a six-foot-tall wood post stood proud.

Carson spotted bloodstains on the wood and splattered around the base of the post. Abruptly, he dug his bare heels into the gritty sand beneath him. His pulse quickened and his breathing followed along, shallow and raspy. But the officers didn't care about the anxiety that suddenly wracked his insides. They shoved him forward and attached his handcuffs to a chain screwed into the post.

His back faced the main road, his brand exposed to the world, ready for judgment.

They all know what I've done now.

Carson bit his lip hard and shut his eyes tightly. He might not have been able to squeeze out the anxiety, but he could pray. He could still do that, at least.

Anem, I don't deserve forgiveness, but I ask for it anyway. Please have mercy on me.

19

It was difficult for Derek to watch the spectacle before him.

The sign hanging on the fence above him stated, "Deliberately breaking curfew: Ten lashes; Extramarital relations: Twenty lashes" in bold red letters. He had hung that very sign in the past for other victims of the whipping post, but now that it referred to his son, he wanted nothing more than to rip it down. It was only attracting a crowd.

But that was the purpose, of course. What was the point in bringing Carson outside into the cold morning air if there were no spectators to witness the public shaming? Shame was the single most important factor in many of their punishments.

Officer Lach exited the building holding the whip in his hands. Derek's stomach churned uneasily. Was William going to be the one that delivered Carson's punishment? He had prayed to the goddess that William wouldn't be, that the Correctional Lieutenant would assign someone gentler and more empathetic, but the goddess must not have been listening.

As if she ever listened.

The crowd stood still as William made his way around Carson, readying himself to deliver Anem's wrath on her behalf. William wasn't going to hold back; Derek knew that beyond a shadow of a doubt. He had never held back previously, and that was a worrisome trait to the department. Reprimands were never given to William by his superiors despite the complaints filed by many officers in regard to his boorish behavior.

The first lash cracked in the cold air before popping Carson's back. His skin split open immediately where the whip made contact. Carson arched his back away from the pain and into the post. But, he didn't make a sound, and as soon as the blood began to slowly drip out of the wound, he straightened himself again and prepared for twenty-nine more.

Be brave, son. It'll only last a short while.

20

Margaret opened her sticky eyes, raw from crying herself to sleep the night before. She wanted to rub them, but if she moved, the pain from her left shoulder would shoot through her whole body again. So, she didn't move for what felt like hours.

She laid topless on her stomach over her periwinkle silk sheets imported from the District—a gift from her mother. She stared out the very window that she had escaped out of with Carson so many times. The trees were calm from the lack of wind, but she didn't have to feel the temperature to know the atmosphere outside was cold. Gray clouds scattered the sky, warning of rain soon to come. Her heart and body ached in unison with the dreariness outside.

She didn't have the energy left to cry any more tears or to even feel sorry for herself. All she did was lay there, unmoving. She stared at the trees and gloomy sky, trying to ignore the pain throbbing in her left shoulder and neck, threatening to worsen. Slowly, it spread across all the small muscles in her back. Everything ached.

Where was her father? He said he'd come back with medication soon. Perhaps he was taking his sweet time, she wondered, due to her sin. Perhaps he thought she deserved to suffer for a time. The shame she felt from her father's disappointment was nothing compared to the public humiliation she knew Carson would endure.

She hadn't eaten anything since lunch the day before when Gina had come over, and her stomach was beginning to eat itself. The weakness she had felt was also cause for concern. No water or food all that time. She should have eaten the breakfast her father offered earlier that morning.

Margaret craned her neck toward the end table on the other side of her bed. She was hoping her father might have left some food there—or maybe simply a glass of water, if nothing else.

Her stomach growled loudly when her eyes feasted upon a ceramic plate with two pieces of lightly buttered toast—probably very stale by that point—and a large glass of clear water next to a smaller glass of orange juice. She vaguely recalled her father saying something about her needing to keep her blood sugars regulated.

She wondered why her father was acting kindly. He was disappointed, but he didn't react at all how she assumed he would have once he discovered her brand. She thought that surely he would disown her, denounce her publicly as a candidate for Ambassador, and have her suffer the same consequences as dictated by the rules. After all, she deserved to be flogged for her sin—one she had committed multiple times.

Margaret slowly moved her right arm to reach for the toast—so incredibly slow in an effort to test how much she could move her right side without disturbing the left—and though there was a bit of strain in her back which made her wince, she was able to grab one of the slices. She nibbled at it for a good ten minutes, not caring that it was cold and stale and sort of tasted like cardboard. She took the second piece the moment she finished the first and ate that one faster than the other.

She wanted to drink the water and orange juice oh-so-badly, but she laid there and contemplated how she would accomplish such a feat without moving too much.

Suddenly, there was a knock on the front door. Margaret's heart skipped several beats. She froze and subconsciously held her breath.

She hoped it was her father, but she knew Mark James wouldn't have knocked on his own front door.

After a moment, there was another knock. Several minutes passed before the intermittent knocking discontinued.

Margaret returned her attention to the fluids she so desperately needed to ingest. She slowly scooted her body closer to the other side of the bed, closer to the end table. She used her right arm and both legs—though incredibly exhausted and weak—to drag herself across the sheets, now ruined by the blood that occasionally wept from her back despite her father having bandaged the large wound with a beige towel and medical tape.

She'd lost a lot of blood during the unwarranted procedure the night prior. Margaret had never felt so sick, so weak, and so vulnerable in her whole life.

"Oh, my everlasting stars! Maggie!"

The voice startled her, and pain shot excruciatingly through her left shoulder. She cried out in pain, tensing hard. She froze all movement to stop the pain. It pulsed in her shoulder like it was alive and torturing her purposefully.

Gina Blake was next to Margaret instantly, bent down by the end table to look into her eyes, her own eyes wide with fright. "What happened to you?" Concern painted her. Margaret's state of being was truly disturbing. Her eyes scanned Margaret several times over, trying to make sense of the scene.

"Gina," croaked Margaret. Her throat stuck. She motioned for the water. "Please, help me drink something."

"Of course!" stammered Gina, grabbing the glass of water. Her hands shook. "Can you sit up?"

"No," Margaret whispered. "It hurts too much to move."

Gina nodded curtly. "I'll get a straw. I know exactly where they are." She hesitated to leave the room, petting Margaret's hair once softly before rushing out the door. She returned much faster than Margaret expected and was holding a colorful bendy straw from the stash in the kitchen. She helped Margaret position her head just right to be able to swallow the water without spilling any on the bedding. All the while, Gina didn't say a word, but pure horror swam in her emerald eyes.

"Thank you," whispered Margaret. "I don't know what I would've done if you hadn't come by. Were you the one knocking?"

Gina nodded shyly. "I came to show you what I had accomplished so far with your dress, but no one answered the door. I was going to walk away, I swear, but I accidentally saw the mess on the kitchen table through the window, and I had a bad feeling. My gut wouldn't let me leave without checking to make sure nothing bad had happened. I didn't mean to be nosey, really. Forgive me; I was worried. And obviously, I was right to be!" She gestured vaguely to Margaret. "You look awful!" Gina leaned over to look closer at the towel that covered Margaret's shoulder.

Margaret tensed, holding her breath, her heart stumbling over itself in her chest. Would her purest friend figure out that the area injured was where a brand had lain? She prayed Gina would not judge her harshly, though she feared the prayer was useless.

"Why do you have that? Is it supposed to be a bandage?" Gina paused only half a second, clearly not expecting an actual answer. "There's blood soaking through." Her voice shook only a fraction, matching her trembling hands. "What happened to you, Maggie?"

"I'm okay." She reached out her hand, grimacing as the movement pulled slightly on the damaged nerves, and grabbed Gina's fingers. She squeezed them in reassurance. "Thank you for stopping by. My father should be coming back soon. He went to fetch medication from the doctor."

Gina's green stare was soul-capturing. Margaret knew immediately she wasn't going to let it go or leave anytime soon. "Were you in an accident?"

Margaret hesitated, but then nodded half a second later. "Yes, but I don't wish to talk about it. Please let it go."

Gina pursed her lips to the side of her mouth in thought. "At least allow me to change your dressing. It's doing no good soaked with blood."

Margaret hesitated, but then sighed, seeing no harm, and nodded into her feather pillow. "All right," she began, her voice muffled by the feathers. "I'll allow it. Just please be gentle."

She didn't have to tell Gina to be gentle, though. Naturally, Gina had the hands of a saint.

Thank you, Anem, prayed Margaret sincerely. She couldn't remember the last time she sent a genuine prayer to the stars. *Thank you for sending an angel to heal me.*

When Gina began peeling off the towel that her father had used as a dressing, it hurt severely. Margaret cried out into her pillow and clutched the bedsheets, knuckles white and aching. It felt as if Gina was peeling off her skin instead of a towel.

Gina froze. She scurried away for a few moments and returned with a bowl of clear liquid and a handcloth.

Margaret's heart sped up. She remembered the bowl of rubbing alcohol her father had soaked a towel in and laid over her freshly butchered shoulder so it wouldn't become infected.

That was the absolute worst part of all of it. The burning was excruciating. Every nerve, every particle, every last atom in her left shoulder was set on fire. She had passed out from the pain and had woken up in her bed later in the dead of night, her father silently changing the dressing on her wound.

Gina grew closer to the bed with the bowl of liquid, setting it on the nightstand carefully. Margaret rasped, voice cracking with desperation and fright, "No, no, no. Please. I can't—" She shook her head, inching away from the porcelain bowl. A single tear stung her eyes, but she was too dehydrated for more to form let alone for that one tear to fall.

Gina paused as she was wringing the excess fluid from the wet cloth. "I thought water would help loosen the fibers of the towel from the dried blood and skin. I'm just trying to make it easier to remove the towel without causing you any pain."

"Oh." Margaret relaxed, laying her head back down on her pillow. "Sorry. Carry on, please." Gina squeezed some water out of the rag onto Margaret's back to loosen the towel. It was cold water, which was actually quite relieving. "Thank you, Gina."

"Of course, my lady," Gina whispered.

Did she just say my lady? Gina hadn't called Margaret that in a long time. They weren't formal with each other anymore. Not since they became good friends a few months ago.

Not another word was spoken by either woman as Gina gently and slowly removed the poor attempt at a dressing. Occasionally, Margaret had to clutch at her bedding to channel away the pain, her teeth clenched so tightly they creaked. But for the most part, as expected, Gina was gentler than her father had been.

Once it was removed completely, Gina poured some of the excess water from her bowl over the wound. She excused herself from Margaret's presence, once again using distinctly formal language. It caused a pit in Margaret's stomach to form.

She had lost Carson as a lover.

She had surely lost the respect of her father.

She couldn't lose Gina's friendship along with everything else. She was the only person left in all the world that treated Margaret like a normal person and friend—not someone who was only Duchess Margaret and nothing more than her title.

Why is she acting so strange? Margaret was bothered to her core. *Is it because I won't tell her what happened to me? I can't tell her the truth. She thinks highly of Father.*

Margaret wrestled with her thoughts through the fogginess that threatened to envelop her. *If she needs an answer, I'll have to lie.* The mere thought of lying to her dearest friend made Margaret feel guilty. She was surely hell-bound.

But what would be believable? What accident could she have possibly endured to cause such a severe injury? She wracked her murky brain for a believable answer but came up empty-handed.

It was for the best anyway. Lying to Gina was reprehensible—at best. She would simply have to stay silent. Omission was her best option.

Gina returned, knocking on the door frame to announce her presence. She carried random supplies and set them in the chair by the window. "I hope you don't mind. I rummaged for anything useful. Please forgive me if I have overstepped, my lady."

A bit of anger surged through Margaret with a smudge of heartbreak. She stared daggers at Gina, but the blonde girl refused to make eye contact with her.

As Gina was preparing a new dressing, Margaret finally found words to say, and they weren't all that kind. "Don't you dare treat me like a stranger, Gina Blake. You are my friend, and I am yours. How dare you act like I mean nothing to you?" Her throat choked her with the threat of sobs. If she wasn't so dehydrated, she would have been crying ages ago.

When Gina looked at her, her bright eyes were much kinder than Margaret deserved. "Of course I'm your friend, Margaret. I'll always be. I'm here, aren't I? I didn't call for help. I didn't flip the emergency switch. I should, but I won't do it." She looked away from Margaret then, tending to the makeshift bandage, also made from a towel, though this one was neater than the one her father made.

Margaret forced more words through her tight throat. "Then don't call me by my title. Not you. And stop acting so... so..." Margaret was frustrated the fog in her brain wouldn't allow her to come up with a better word than the one she spoke. "*Stiff!*"

Gina didn't react to this accusation. She grabbed an extra handcloth from the chair as well as a fresh glass jar of water that looked cold from the concentration on it. She poured some of it directly onto Margaret's shoulder, and then she blotted at it with the handcloth.

"I'm sorry," Margaret whispered, eyes burning though the tears wouldn't come. "I truly am grateful you are here with me right now."

Several minutes passed. Gina cleaned the wound slowly and meticulously. The silence was deafening.

Then, taking Margaret aback, Gina asked, "Why did you try to remove it?"

Margaret's stomach lurched into her throat. She swallowed hard, her throat tight again. "Wh—" she stammered. "What do you mean?" Her mouth was suddenly drier than the Red Desert and the Wastelands combined.

"Your brand," said Gina carefully. "Why did you try to remove it? You only hurt yourself, and it does no good to attempt something so futile."

Margaret's stomach tossed, nausea striking her innards full force, but she was able to keep herself from throwing up the stale toast. She buried her face into her pillow as if it would help drive out the queasiness.

"I guess I understand why you'd want it gone. But it wasn't worth it, Margaret." Her tone was sorrowful. "Your reputation isn't worth this type of suffering. And I'm not just talking about the physical pain. I mean the pain in your heart, too."

Gina didn't say anything more as she placed her new dressing on the wound. Finally, she touched Margaret's hair softly and asked in the sweetest of tones, "Does your father know you did this?"

Margaret didn't reply. How could she tell her friend that it was her father that did this to her, not Margaret? She didn't have the gall to pull something off like self-mutilation.

When no answer came, Gina sighed and said, "You shouldn't lay in that. I'll help you move over to the chair so I can change the bedding."

Margaret allowed Gina to help her up, biting her bottom lip to keep from crying out in pain. Once she was in the chair by the window, she carefully positioned her body in a way so the pain in her shoulder would lessen. She realized a moment later her mouth was flooded with the taste of iron-rich blood now trickling from the laceration in her lip.

Gina stripped the bed and grabbed all the soiled linens and towels. Margaret's bloodied blouse and undergarments from yesterday's tragic happenings were lying in the corner of the room where Judge James must've tossed them.

Heat flooded Margaret's face as she realized her father had to have undressed her to put her on the bed so he could tend to her wound properly.

How embarrassing. She hated that she couldn't remember it, but she was also grateful for the absence of memory all the same.

Gina turned half her body to Margaret after picking up the bloody clothing too. "I'll be right back. I'm going to soak these. Perhaps I can remove the bloodstains." She scurried away, strands of her hair more gold than the wheat fields the girl's father tended falling out of her braided updo.

I don't deserve a friend like Gina.

Margaret sat there for a few moments, still as a statue, afraid to make the tiniest of movements. She held her arms against her naked chest and focused on her breathing. But when she attempted to take a deep breath, the movement caught a nerve, and pain shot through her shoulder. She cried out once, a small cry but an audible one.

She gripped the edge of the chair and held her breath as the pain pulsed through her for a few seconds before dying out. Then, the front door opened and shut, and heavy steps sounded on the marble floor. She could tell by the pattern of the walk that it was her father, undoubtedly.

"Judge James!"

Margaret's stomach rolled at the sound of Gina's voice carrying through the house. Thankfully, her voice wasn't one of surprise but of gleeful greeting. She could imagine her pauper friend attempting a curtsy even with her arms full of bloodied linens.

"I'm glad you're here, sir," Gina said.

Margaret wished she could see her father's face. Was he horrified that Gina was there? Would he say anything rude to the girl after how nice she had been to her? After she had cared so well and unconditionally for Margaret? Would he scare her away? If he dared try, she would yell profanities at him from where she sat without hesitation.

"If I may inquire, sir," she addressed the Judge formally, dignified, like a woman of high station with utmost respect for authority. It was a wonder that she was from the countryside of Polaris. "Did you bring any medication for the Duchess? She's in a lot of pain."

It was quiet for a few short seconds. Margaret held her breath, readying her vulgar word bank for an insulting response from her father.

Finally, he replied gently, "Why are you here, Miss Blake? Did Margaret let you in?"

Margaret exhaled, relieved that he didn't sound angry.

"N-no, sir," she stuttered. "I stopped by to show Margaret the skirt of her wedding dress, but something was wrong. I could feel it. I just wanted to check on her. I only stayed because she needed my help. I apologize for entering your home uninvited."

Her father was quiet again, but he replied to her after a moment's thought, "Thank you for caring for her while I've been gone, Gina. I can take over from here."

"Of course," said the girl respectfully. Margaret once again imagined her curtsying. "Before I leave, if it pleases you, allow me to finish soaking her linens. Also, she's indecent in her room. Perhaps she'd like my help with covering up before you enter."

"That's incredibly kind of you. I would appreciate that. Will you do that first before the linens? I need to speak with her."

"Of course, sir."

A few moments later, Gina re-entered Margaret's room. "Your father's here. He was carrying a bag from the pharmacy. I assume it's medication." As she spoke, she shuffled through one of Margaret's dresser drawers and pulled out a black spaghetti-strap nightgown. She held it up to inspect it before nodding her personal approval. "If you get blood on this, it won't ruin it. Also, it has a low back and thin straps. Should be more comfortable on your shoulder."

She pulled it over Margaret's head and gently helped her pull her left arm through. Margaret grimaced and a small yelp escaped her throat.

Gina stretched her mouth, the corners downturned, and sucked in a breath of sympathy through her teeth, as if she could feel the pain too. "Sorry, sorry!"

"Not at all," Margaret breathed. "I appreciate everything you've done for me." She grabbed her friend's hand and squeezed it. "You are such a good friend. Thank you."

Gina opened her mouth to respond but the Judge's voice echoed down the hall and interrupted her, "I don't have much time. Can I come in yet?"

Margaret called out, "I'm mostly decent, so I suppose it's okay."

Her father came into the room holding a small white paper bag with the pharmacy's logo on the side. He held it up to show her that he made good on his promise. "I got several different things for you." He glanced at Gina warily before opening the bag and dumping different bottles and tubes onto the naked mattress.

"I can stay and help apply the medication," offered Gina. She looked from the Judge to Margaret. "If you would like me to."

Margaret said, "Yes, please," just as her father replied with, "That won't be necessary." Margaret made unpleasant eye contact with her father, but he looked away after only a second.

"Very well," he whispered. "Gina, please help apply the medication. She's probably much more comfortable with you doing it."

Gina simply nodded and strode over to the bed. She examined the different medications laying there. "Which one?" she wondered.

Judge James picked a bottle up and handed it to her. "For the pain. I got two, so use it generously. I also got pain pills." He shook one of the smaller containers and it rattled. "It's heavy-duty, so be careful with these and only take them as the bottle directs." He then grabbed a large tube of ointment. "This is for healing. It's supposed to heal wounds a hundred times faster than anything else we have available."

"They sell those without a doctor's script?" Margaret wondered, her voice low.

"No, they don't," is all the Judge said in response before handing Gina another bottle. "This one is to prevent infection."

She nodded as she said, "Okay, got it. Did you happen to bring any supplies for a dressing? I changed it right now, but I used a towel like the one I assume you put on it before."

He huffed, frustrated, and pinched the skin between his eyebrows. "I didn't even think of that." He cursed, which surprised both Gina and Margaret. He wasn't a man that used foul language. "I'll go back." He turned swiftly to leave the room.

"No, wait," Gina said quickly, grabbing his sleeve.

He gave her a curious look, which was fitting for the situation, in all honesty. It was improper for Gina to do such a thing as grab the Judge's clothing, no matter how innocent.

"I should do it," she explained, quickly letting go of his clothing, her face reddening slightly. "If you go back for dressing supplies after getting all of this," —she motioned to the bed with the array of medication sprawled on it— "someone may become suspicious. I'll go and get some things. If anyone asks me what it's for, I'll tell them my father had an accident with some farming equipment. It's happened before."

He stared at her for a long time. So long that Gina glanced over at Margaret with a question if she overstepped in her eyes.

"Why?" Judge James finally asked.

"Well," she began, looking down at her feet and clasping her hands behind her back, "I don't want to see the Duchess flogged any more than you do."

"Flogged?"

Margaret realized he was playing dumb. She rolled her eyes and butted into the conversation. "She knows, Father."

He gave Margaret a dirty look that frightened her slightly. She couldn't remember the last time he'd looked at her in that way. Had he ever? "You told her? Why would you do that, Margaret?"

Gina was quick to answer for her friend. "Oh, no, sir, it wasn't like that. She wouldn't tell me anything, but I could tell she tried and failed to remove the brand from her shoulder."

The Judge's eyes widened in gradual horror. "What do you mean *failed*?"

Gina seemed surprised by his question. "Oh... Well... You can see it still. You didn't see it when you dressed it last?"

"No, no, no," he breathed out, panicky. He quickly made it to Margaret's side. "I triple checked last night to make sure..." He yanked the dressing down on her shoulder, which stung quite a lot. Margaret had to bite her bottom lip to keep from crying out, tasting more blood. Her father cursed several times before he placed the dressing back and stomped out of the room.

That was when what Gina had been saying all that time and what her father was upset about hit Margaret, like three tons of brick slamming into her, knocking the breath from her lungs.

The brand was still there. Despite all the suffering she went through the night before and would continue to go through until she completely healed, she would never be rid of it.

It was all for nothing. Futile, as Gina had accurately put it. She recalled her father checking multiple times to make sure he'd removed every part of each individual scar that made up each individual divine symbol placed on her shoulder by the goddess herself.

Oh, Anem's stars.

149

The brand was *rebuilding* itself.

Her father should've known better than to attempt what he did, and she should've known better than to believe what he did would work.

Mere mortals cannot erase sin.

21

Derek watched as Carson's legs gave out from under him, and he hit his head on the post hard enough to knock him out cold. Once the flogging was done, Derek demanded to be let in, which one of his officers promptly obliged. He held his son closely, trying to wake him, not paying any mind to all the blood that was transferring to his own clothing.

When they finally released the restraints on Carson, Derek and another officer carried him to the door where a gurney had been prepared. They were mindful of his wounds as they lifted him onto the gurney, laying him face down, and wheeled him inside to be seen by the trauma team. After a while, one of the nurses—a man Derek learned was named Jake—suggested it would be best for Carson if he didn't see his father in clothing dirtied with blood. He thoughtfully offered him clean scrubs to change into instead.

Derek couldn't argue with the man. He wouldn't want his wife and daughter seeing him with Carson's blood on his clothes either, so he took the hunter green scrubs from the nurse and changed into them, surprised at how comfortable they were.

The scrubs were similar to the navy-blue uniform he recalled his wife used to wear, except she wasn't allowed to wear split-legged trousers like the men. She had to wear an ankle length skirt with special stockings underneath. He thought it was ridiculous that the women couldn't wear slacks like men, but those were the rules.

Derek stood in a corner of the indistinct, windowless room at the justice department reserved specifically for the trauma team to care for victims of the whipping post. An operating table was the center focus of the room, and next to it sat a rolling table serving as a station for surgical tools and supplies. Dr. Griggs and her staff had stocked it that morning, anticipating Carson's injuries. He tried to make sense of the numbers and abbreviations on the screen displaying Carson's current vitals, and he wished his wife was there to interpret it for him.

Kayla had worked with Dr. Griggs for years before the Province transferred her to the school to teach a health class. Apparently, she would have excelled in education just as much as she would've in medicine. His wife loved working for Dr. Griggs, and she always sang praises about the woman's steady hand and vast array of knowledge.

He observed Dr. Griggs meticulously clean every wound made by the whip wielded against his son, occasionally glancing over to the bag of fluids that flowed through the tubing to the IV in his hand. Derek wasn't sure what jargon the team used was about, but he knew his son was in good hands. That calmed his nerves some.

"All right," said Dr. Griggs, nodding an approval as she gave Carson's freshly cleaned, medicated, and stitched back another complete look-over. "We're done here. Good work, team. Jake, Sheila." She pointed at the two nurses in the room. "Use wet-to-dry dressings for the first dressing. I'll write a script on what I recommend and place it in his chart. Jake, please type up education for him regarding my orders."

He nodded once. "Got it, boss."

She removed her gloves and then mask as Jake and Sheila got to work dressing Carson's wounds. Then she motioned toward Derek, her hand telling him to *'come here'* as she walked over to him. Derek took only a few steps forward before stopping.

"He'll be okay," the older woman said with a smile. Derek wondered how old she was. He guessed about sixty. Maybe fifty-five. No younger than fifty for sure.

Kayla would know.

"Thank you, Dr. Griggs," he said, voice low as he glanced over at his son who was still under sedation. "When will he wake up?"

"He'll start stirring in less than an hour, but be careful; he'll be quite loopy."

"Loopy?"

She shrugged. "He may say some funny things that don't make any sense. You'll have to disregard everything he says. Also, it's very likely he won't remember saying any of it."

Derek's stomach pitched slightly. He hoped against hope Carson wouldn't talk about his lover. She didn't deserve to be investigated and flogged for loving him.

She waved her hand to dismiss the topic. "Anyway, I will write a script for some pain medication as well as ointment to apply with every dressing change."

"Oh, um." Derek patted his pockets for his notebook and pen that he usually carried at work, but he forgot he wasn't in uniform. He wasn't even wearing his own clothing. "Damned stars," he cursed, then quickly apologized for his vulgarity before saying, "I would like to write down exactly what to do so that I can show my wife."

She smiled kindly at him. "No worries. I'll have Jake give you instructions that you can give Kayla. All I need you to do is pick up the medication from the pharmacy when you head home today."

He nodded once, slowly. "I can manage that."

"How is Kayla?" the trauma doctor asked. "Is she liking teaching?"

Derek shrugged. "I think part of her misses this." He gestured to the two nurses carefully dressing Carson's wounds still. "But she's good with the students. Cares about them."

Griggs nodded thoughtfully. "Yes, she was always so caring with our patients the twelve years she was with my team. I was very sad when the Province reassigned her. But, I can't complain, really. See a need, fill a need. And the school needed a nurse to teach health." She shrugged her bony shoulders. "People like you and Kayla and myself... We serve our community faithfully."

"Right." He simply nodded but didn't feel any emotion behind it. It was just for show. In fact, the only thing real in his life were his feelings about his wife and children. He had no obligation to the Province and wouldn't care if it burned. He might even help light the match if given the chance.

But that was a dream. The Provinces and District of Diphda hadn't fallen in thousands of years, despite the occasional small uprisings that sprung up, the last one being fifty-odd years ago in the Port of Kaitos. That uprising resulted in the separation of the Port from the Province of Kaitos, now operating under no law but the District's. Truly, the Port of Kaitos was its own Province in every sense and right except by name.

She pulled out a script pad from her lab coat pocket. She began scribbling on it as she spoke. "Tell Kayla I said hi, and make sure you give your little girl a sweet hug for me. How old is Cassandra now? Nine? Ten?"

"Eleven."

"Already?" She ripped the page off the pad and handed it to Derek. "She'll be twelve and accountable for her sins soon. And then, before you know what's hit you, she'll be married with her own children. Happened with my kids. Now my grandkids are getting married. It's strange how quickly time passes."

Derek forced a grin. "Truly." He loathed the idea that his daughter would one day be a woman that men would look at with less than innocent eyes.

Griggs smiled at him once more and said, "Have a great day, Officer Owens," and then dismissed herself from the room.

He folded up the script and put it in his wallet so he wouldn't lose it. Jake and Sheila were done dressing Carson's back as soon as the doctor left. Jake removed his gloves and mask as he told Derek that he could finally approach Carson. "I have to go tell the officers we're finished here. Sheila will stay here with the two of you to continue monitoring Carson's vitals."

Derek nodded at him. "Thanks," he mumbled. He bent down next to Carson and removed strands of his jet-black hair off his forehead. "You desperately need a haircut," he whispered as if Carson could hear him.

To his surprise, Carson mumbled back, "I like my hair like this," but he didn't move or open his eyes. He looked asleep.

Derek glanced over at Sheila who simply smiled at him as she cleaned up the workstation and said, "It's normal. He may even carry on full conversations with you, but he won't remember any of them."

Derek thought that would horrify Carson, so he refrained from talking anymore to his son, though he desperately wanted to just for his own amusement.

Three officers entered then, one being William, with Jake on their heels. They told Derek to step away from Carson. Derek obeyed, but he didn't understand why that was necessary. William shook Carson's shoulder roughly, and Carson groaned in response. "Wake up," he ordered the sedated man. "Let's move, Carson."

Sheila and Jake protested before Derek even had a chance to open his mouth.

"He's sedated, sir," said Jake, quickly stepping up to the officer, squeezing himself in between William and Carson. Derek watched William's reaction carefully considering how close Jake was standing to the man. "He's unable to comprehend orders right now, let alone obey them."

"Even if he seems awake," added Sheila quickly, also stepping up to William, defensive of Carson's state of being, "he is not capable of acting accordingly or appropriately. Anything he says or does cannot be held against him."

William snorted, and Derek noted the irritation in the chief officer's voice. "Is that so? I say what can and cannot be held against him."

Jake shook his head at William, not deterred in any way by the officer. "What you're saying is against the rules, chief. I suggest you study a bit more on the law concerning medicated patients before making any hasty decisions."

Derek decided he liked Jake.

"He's a criminal," said William, even more annoyed with the two nurses.

Derek had enough. "Come on, Lach. Back off. These two are just trying to do their jobs."

"And I'm just trying to do mine," snapped William.

Derek clipped right back, "If you actually knew the rules, you wouldn't be arguing with them. They're right, Lach. He is sedated and can't be accountable until the medication has completed its course. Have you never overseen a flogging before?"

William's jaw clenched. After a moment, the chief asked the nurses, "When will the medication wear off?"

Sheila answered, "Give him three hours minimum. Four hours to be safe."

William nodded once. "Fine. Can he stand at least?"

Jake shook his head. "He may try, but it's not wise to allow him to walk in this state."

"He needs to go back to his cell," stated William. "Let's get him in a wheelchair or something."

"How about you be patient?" snapped Derek again. He was losing control of his own patience with the young chief. "Let him lay there for a while until he opens his eyes, at least. Then we'll take him to his cell. Besides," Derek threw up his hand in a frustrated manner, "why are you locking him back up? He received his punishment already. I intend to take him home when he wakes."

"It's not on my order," Lach said. "The Judge told me not to release him until he said so." He gave Derek a dirty look. "I'm just following orders. Perhaps you should too."

Though he was unsure what possessed him to say it, Derek didn't hesitate to retort, "I didn't receive any."

"How's this for an order: Stand down, Officer Owens."

Derek ground his teeth together and clenched his jaw until it creaked with the pressure. He remained silent as William told the other two officers, Peter and Cody, to wait until Carson awoke and then to take him back to his cell. The officers mumbled, "Yes, sir," as he walked out of the room, but they looked to Derek for confirmation.

Derek waved his hand at them. "Do as he says."

They both nodded, repeating, "Yes, sir," more confidently and sat down in chairs against the wall.

Sheila took Carson's vitals again as Derek pulled a spare chair up next to him. He had made good on his promise to stay by Carson's side through all of it so far, and, by Anem's stars, that wasn't going to change now. He was going to be there when Carson opened his eyes— even if Carson would never remember it.

After fifteen minutes, Jake had completed readying instructions on how to change Carson's dressings as well as information on the medications. Derek thanked him for the packet of information.

Carson began stirring not ten minutes later. He moved his left arm up to his face and tried to scratch at the liquid stitches across his cheek.

Derek grabbed his wrist and pulled it away from the wound. "Don't touch it, Carson."

Carson didn't open his eyes as he mumbled, "It itches."

"Leave it alone."

Carson moved his other arm to reach for his cheek, but he was so disoriented, he couldn't figure out how to reach it. His facial expression changed to one of frustration. "Let go of me," he rasped, tugging his left hand that Derek still held away from his face. His pull was unimpressive.

"Stop trying to touch your face."

"Here." Jake reached over Carson's head from the other side of the table and patted his cheek with a damp gauze, pressing firmly. "Better?"

"Yeah," groaned Carson. He relaxed his left arm, and Derek put it back at his side on the table. The edge of Carson's brand peeked out from under one of the gauzes on the head of his shoulder.

Derek exhaled in a bit of relief. He was glad he had found out about Carson's brand before they set up the checkpoints. It gave him enough time to tell Timothy Blake about the brand and for both of them to agree to keep Gina indoors until everything passed.

She was too delicate to be flogged, both men agreed to that, and the punishment for their two children loving each other was far too harsh. Both were, obviously, disappointed in their children, but they also partly blamed themselves. As Derek discussed the matter with Tim, they both agreed they should've known it would happen, and they hadn't done much to prevent it. It was just as much their fault as parental failures as it was their children's fault for succumbing to their flesh.

But Derek couldn't wholly fault Carson in the end. She was a very attractive girl with a beautiful soul to match, and Carson had always loved her, even before he fully understood what love was. Derek wished he had known about the brand before turning Carson in for breaking curfew. He would never have done it otherwise.

A few minutes passed before Carson's eyes fluttered open. Carson stared at him for an uncomfortable amount of time before finally whispering, "Did it hurt?"

"Did what hurt?" Derek whispered back. He reminded himself of what Dr. Griggs had said about the sedation.

"Your heart, Dad." When he remained quiet, Carson explained, "You were watching. I saw you when I looked back. Did it hurt your heart?"

"Yeah," whispered Derek, "it hurt to see this happen to you." He reached over and patted Carson's shoulder gently, where there were no wounds to worry about.

Carson closed his eyes slowly and peeled them open again. "I'm sorry I did that to you."

There were tears forming in Carson's eyes. Derek was surprised by them. He hadn't seen Carson cry in ten years. Maybe more. Even as a tyke, Carson hated crying. Derek had never taught him not to cry, though. That was simply something he inherited from the Owens side of the family.

"Don't worry about it," whispered Derek, patting his shoulder again. Derek could feel emotion gathering in his own chest, climbing up his throat and choking him. He patted Carson's shoulder again but didn't dare speak lest his voice break.

"Sir?" It was one of the officers.

After clearing his throat, Derek replied without looking at the officer, "What is it, Cody?"

"He's awake. Should we take him to his cell now?"

"That's what the chief ordered, isn't it?"

"Yes, sir." Cody sounded doubtful.

If Derek chose to tell him to ignore William's orders, he would without question. And perhaps that was wrong, but Derek liked that there were men that listened to him more than the young chief.

Derek gestured with his hands at the man. "Then let's get him into a wheelchair and back to his cell."

"Yes, sir."

The nurses provided a wheelchair and helped Carson sit up. Once he was sitting up, he was suddenly far more aware. He looked around the room and at each person there. "Did I pass out?"

"You hit your head," Sheila told him.

He stared at her for a long moment. Derek was about to tell him to look away from her since his eyes were lingering on her face, but then Carson said, "You're David's mom, right?"

She smiled sweetly at him. "Why, yes, I am."

He nodded slowly as he closed his eyes, head bobbing up and down. "Sheila Adams, wife of Matthew Adams and mother of David, Marcy, and Kimmy Adams."

She was silent for a short moment. "Well, okay then," she laughed. "Were you close friends with David in school?"

"Hell no." Carson made a disgusted face. "That kid's weird. And inappropriate. I had to put him in place far more often than I should've."

Derek grimaced internally. "Carson, you're being rude."

Carson shook his head at Derek. "Why is the truth considered rude?"

Derek glanced at Sheila, but she didn't seem offended.

Carson shook his head again. "Such a weird kid. Oh! And one time, he said something about—" He paused, suddenly looking uncomfortable. Then he rephrased, saying, "He commented on a girl's chest once, and I had no choice but to sock him square in the face. Broke the twerp's nose." He held his hands up to his face, examining his ten digits, squinting. "Why are my fingers so long? Are fingers supposed to look like this?"

Derek was about to respond to Carson about the new information that he'd broken someone's nose, but Sheila had beat him to it. "You were the one that broke his nose? He told me a different friend did it, and that it was an accident." She ignored Carson's concern with his fingers.

Carson rolled his eyes, smirking. "Of course he'd say that. If they asked me why I hit him, I would tell the truth, and you don't want to know what he was saying about G—" He paused. Derek's stomach pitched slightly at Carson's near slip up. "You don't want to know what he was saying about her chest. He would've been in far worse trouble than I would've been in for hitting him."

"Well," she whispered, face warming from the information about her son's inappropriate behavior. "I'll have to take your word for it."

Derek was relieved Sheila didn't seem too offended by Carson's comments about her son. She looked more disappointed than anything. "Sit down in the wheelchair, Carson," she ordered, tone kind.

Carson made a face of disgust. "I don't need that stupid thing."

Derek grabbed his son's elbow. "Sit down, Carson. Now."

Carson jerked his elbow away from him. "I'm not crippled. I can walk just fine on my own."

Jake responded, "Carson, you're drugged. It's safer to sit down."

Carson's eyes widened gradually, and as he complied, he asked, voice shaky, "I'm drugged? Oh, *stars*. I haven't said anything, have I?" He looked at Derek, and Derek recognized true fear and horror laid within them. "I didn't say her name, right? *Right*?"

It had been a long time since Derek had seen Carson express such strong emotions. Carson was usually so stoic around him. Derek shook his head at him. "No, you haven't said anything like that. You've just been talking about David Adams and your fingers."

Derek really hoped his son wouldn't say Gina's name. He didn't want her to be punished in the same manner as Carson. There was no way that sweet girl deserved such a shameful punishment, and it was obvious Carson knew that. Derek could tell that by the way Carson put his hand over his mouth and shut his eyes tightly. He would do anything to keep himself from saying the name of his lover and dooming her to the same fate as he.

He should've watched Carson more carefully. He should've seen their relationship becoming what it had. He should've had more talks with him about her, no matter how uncomfortable it was for either of them. Carson's current suffering was his fault. He should've been a better father.

But Carson was only human. How dare they punish him for being exactly what they admire?

Once they got him into his cell, Carson immediately stood up from his cot and walked over toward the window. Derek was next to him

161

quickly, just to make sure he didn't stumble in the drugged state he was in. For several minutes, Carson just looked outside and watched the clouds and birds in the sky. Derek watched right along with him. The silence was comforting to both of them. Familiar.

"What does freedom feel like?" whispered Carson abruptly.

Derek looked at him, curious. "What do you mean?"

"Freedom," is all Carson said, as if that should be enough explanation.

Derek sighed and glanced back at the closed cell door. He had requested the officers allow him to stay with Carson, even if they had to lock him in there with him. Now, they were gone, and it was just him and Carson.

Derek contemplated Carson's question about freedom. Did Carson already feel trapped and enslaved even though he wasn't yet a Mature? What could he possibly feel enslaved to? Perhaps he was referring to his flesh. Or perhaps he meant the damn rules that Derek used to mostly respect.

Of course, he could never give such things away. If they knew the Ritual failed on him, they would try to fix it, and Derek himself would quite possibly be forever lost. And if they couldn't fix it, they'd execute him.

Who would care for his children if he were dead? He was convinced no one could ever take his place. He couldn't even risk telling Kayla, his own wife whom he loved with everything inside him. He so desperately wanted to tell her the truth, that he was still the same as before—but was she? It was too dangerous to risk.

"I don't know, son," is all he could think of as a reply.

"I think it feels like clean bed sheets."

Derek gave him another curious look, but Carson continued staring at the midday sky. *What a strange analogy.*

Carson continued after a few moments, "Or like the smell of the salt from the sea, or the earth after it rains. Maybe it feels like a calm whisper... Here." He placed his right hand over his heart. "And

162

positive silence... Here." He moved his hand from his heart to his stomach.

He wasn't sure exactly what Carson's *here* was referring to. Or what he meant by *positive silence*. "What's there?" Derek asked.

"My soul." He looked directly into Derek's eyes at that moment, his gaze intense and innocent all in one. "What if freedom simply feels like silence and calmness collectively in your body? What if freedom feels like a quiet mind?"

A quiet mind.

Derek took a moment before responding. When he asked his next question, it was more out of concern than curiosity. "Carson... Is your mind not quiet?"

"Never. I'm always thinking." Carson looked back out the window. "I never stop thinking."

"You would like to stop thinking?"

Carson pursed his lips in thought, squinting at the clouds traveling across the sky. "I'd welcome the break."

"What do you think about?"

Carson was quiet for a long moment. So long that Derek had already let the question drop by the time Carson whispered, "Everything. I think about everything. Problems that have no solutions. Questions that have no answers." He closed his eyes then and shook his head slightly. "No, there's always a solution, even if it seems like there isn't one. And every question has an answer. This universe is simply a calculation of events. Has to be."

Startling the two of them, there was a sudden banging on the bars of the cell door. "I thought Carson wasn't allowed to stand, Officer Owens."

Derek forced his urge to snap at William deep, deep down. He said as stoically as he possibly could, "He's standing still, and I'm standing next to him to make sure he doesn't fall. What do you need, Lach?"

William threaded his arms through the bars and smiled at Carson who looked far too angry for Derek's comfort. "I have a few questions for the man-whore."

"Screw you, prick," choked Carson, and he turned his back to the officer, gazing out the window again.

"Carson," warned Derek. "You shouldn't speak to him that way." Derek was relieved that Carson was excused from using such language with the chief due to being under the influence of drugs, but he still was uneasy about what William Lach would say or do to provoke him in that moment.

"It's fine, it's fine," William said, waving his hand nonchalantly. "He's drugged. Can't be held against him, right?" His smile chilled Derek to his bones. "I just want to know about his lover. Her name, specifically."

Derek gritted his teeth. So that was why William was there. He was going to use Carson being drugged as an advantage to find out the girl's name.

Carson immediately slapped his hand over his mouth as a physical reminder to himself to shut up. He remained facing the window.

"You don't have to tell him anything," whispered Derek.

"What was that?" taunted William. "What are you telling him, Drew? Are you telling him to not give up the girl's name? Because if that's so, you're interfering with justice, and I'll have to ask you to leave."

It was eerily silent for several long, long seconds as Derek stared a hole straight through William. "What did you just call me?" he growled at the young officer.

For a fleeting moment, Derek thought he saw horror cross William's expression, but it was gone so quickly he wasn't sure if he imagined it or not. He replied to Derek timely, saying, "I called you by your name, of course."

"You think I'm stupid, William?" He left Carson's side and quickly approached the cell bars, pressing up against them, inches from William's face.

Before William could step away, Derek reached through the cell bars and grabbed William's uniform coat, pulling him hard into the iron bars. The man was lucky there was a barrier separating them, or else he would have done far worse.

"I know you just called me Drew."

"Did I?" The officer smirked. "Now, why would I do that?"

"Don't lie to me, William," he snarled, bringing his face to the officer's. "Tell me now: Where have you heard that name? And why the hell would you mistake me for him, of all people?"

William gave him a once-over, shook Derek off him, and stepped away from the bars. "Mistake you for who? A brother of yours I've never met? One that's been missing for nearly two decades?"

Derek ground his teeth. "Who told you about Drew? He is supposed to be a secret. By the order of the Judge himself. If anyone has not only said his name to you but also told you what he was to me, they should be punished accordingly."

William shrugged. "Now why would I give up the names of my informants? You may have people loyal to you in this department, Derek Owens, but I, too, have a few people who do only as I say."

Lies.

It would be an understatement to say Derek was furious and nervous and confused. Something didn't add up, and Derek would rather die than let it go uncovered.

They glared at each other for a few more moments before Derek called him out. "How could someone who has never met my identical twin brother mistake me for him?"

Again, Derek thought he saw horror flash across William's face, but, Derek had to admit, the man was exceptional at hiding it. He made Derek consider the idea that it had never been there in the first place—though Derek wasn't so naive.

Just as William opened his mouth to respond, Derek added, "Have you met Drew? Does this mean he's still alive after all these years?"

William suddenly laughed, loud and boisterous. "Why the hell would I know your probably-long-dead brother?" He laughed again and said, "I did not call you Drew. It was all in your head. Perhaps he's been on your mind quite a bit recently, what with Carson being flogged. Reminiscent much of a time when you stood and watched your twin brother pay for the same sin, perhaps?"

Derek looked back at Carson, who still faced the window and visibly shook as he pressed his hand against his ears and face against the glass on the window. He was trying so hard to find inner peace in a moment when nothing being said made sense and anything he said could ruin the life of someone he loved dearly.

Derek was glad Carson wouldn't be able to remember the exchange that had happened between himself and William.

"I don't need you to tell me her name," spat Lach abruptly at Carson's general direction. "I already know your lover is Margaret James."

With that having finally been said, he turned on his heels and strode down the corridor until he was out of sight, his boots heavily clomping on the tiled floor.

Derek rolled his eyes as he watched him disappear, smirking a bit. *The Duchess. What a ridiculous assumption.* He then glanced back at Carson who had turned to face him, and in that singular moment, Derek could read everything on his face like an open book. It was the most disheartening story he had ever read, seen, heard, and witnessed—and Derek was not unfamiliar with unhappy tellings considering his own story was not one for the faint of heart.

There was horror in his son's eyes that said William was *right*. There was fear etched on his face of what would happen to the woman he loved now that she was caught.

Wait... The Duchess? Really, Carson? Since when?

The pit in Derek's stomach couldn't have been anything worse compared to what Carson must have been feeling in that moment.

What about Ginevieve? He had promised himself to her years ago. Derek thought it was her. *When did your feelings change, Carson? Or have they? Have you ruined what you had with her? She's been waiting for you. When did you decide to stop waiting for her?*

"Sit down," encouraged Derek gently. He motioned to the cot, and Carson allowed his father to help him down onto it.

Derek grabbed a towel from the bedside and, with a few simple swipes, used it to wipe Carson's face of the wetness that clung there. "There," he rasped, placing the towel in the hand Carson reluctantly removed from his mouth. There was blood on his hand and lips. Had he bit his tongue in addition to covering his mouth?

What does the Duchess mean to you compared to Tim's daughter, Carson? Derek was genuinely surprised at the absurd idea that Carson had ever even had a thought about anyone else besides Timothy's daughter.

Does Gina know about this? If not, how are you going to explain it to her? Damn it, Carson. I told you years ago to not hurt that little girl, and yet you've gone and betrayed her in the worst way possible.

He patted Carson's shoulder gently, careful of the dressings. "It'll be okay, son," he lied.

It most definitely was not going to be okay. Derek prayed Carson wouldn't remember how he was feeling in that moment or the conversation with William. If Margaret James was indeed his lover— and it seemed obvious that she was—then may Anem and the people of Deneb have mercy on her.

Though, truthfully, Derek was far more concerned with William's sudden knowledge of his brother—the wayward twin that had been missing for eighteen years. Derek had assumed he was dead since there was nowhere to run and nowhere to hide and definitely nowhere to live without them knowing. Derek had a sneaking suspicion that, somehow and in some capacity, William knew more truth than he did.

Despite his brother's utter betrayal, he missed Drew Owens terribly—though if he ever saw the bastard again, he'd surely give him a decent beating for what he did to not only him but to Kayla and Carson as well all those years ago. He never got a chance to give him what he deserved, and if Drew was still alive...

I'm counting on you to be alive so I can show you just how much pain you caused my family. You will wish you had died wandering the Wastelands like I thought you had.

22

Gina was sure of only one thing: Margaret didn't deserve to be flogged and disgraced. Sure, she made a mistake—a pretty major one, in Gina's personal opinion—but it wasn't so bad that she deserved to lose everything, including the respect of the Province.

Gina grabbed several boxes of gauze, saline, medical wrap, and tape. She threw them all in a small basket she carried. To make it less obvious that she was there only for wound dressing materials, she grabbed random things off shelves she passed: a package of colorful markers, a sketchbook, three different types of chocolate bars, a bottle of shampoo, two cans of soup, and a stuffed toy bear.

Suddenly, a hand grasped her elbow tightly and spun her around. She gasped, but it was only her father. "Dad," she said, breathless, "you frightened me!"

"Ginevieve," he rasped, eyes wide, almost as if he was horrified to see her there. Him using her real name and not her nickname made her stomach twist, and she wondered if she was in trouble. "I told you that, if you left the house, you were only allowed to go to Duchess James' house. Nowhere else. Didn't I say that?" He definitely sounded worried, even annoyed, which was a tone he never took with her.

"I apologize," she whispered. "I was just running errands for her, at the Judge's request. The Duchess isn't feeling well, so she can't do it herself."

It was a half-truth—which was a nice term to describe something that was still a lie—and she felt like maybe she sounded as if she was struggling to make it believable. She stared at the store's tiled floor all the while to avoid being caught in the lie.

He huffed. "Well, fine, but I will walk you back to their home."

She was still confused by his actions. "Why do I need your escort?"

He shushed her when a mother with a crying infant hurried past them, but the frazzled woman didn't seem to notice them at all, let alone care what they were talking about.

He said in a low voice, "I will discuss it with you when you come home, and you will come straight home after you finish up at the James' house. Do I make myself clear?"

She hesitated for half a second. "Y—yes, sir." Pause. "Um, Dad?"

He glanced around as he replied, "What is it?"

"Am I in trouble?"

His electric-blue eyes pierced her green ones. He looked disappointed, but she didn't understand why. What had she done wrong?

It took him too many seconds to consider a response. "I am trying my best to *keep you out* of trouble." He exhaled, frustrated, bothering her further. "We will discuss it fully when you come home this afternoon. I'm going to wait outside for you. Finish grabbing whatever the Judge asked you to fetch." And then he moseyed out the door, hands dug deep into his jean pockets dirtied with grime from a hard day's work.

She spent the next couple of minutes walking up and down three aisles, her mind pulled in multiple directions: Margaret and her mutilated branded shoulder, the fact that Judge James knew about it and chose to keep it a secret, and her own father's worry about her not holed up at home like he'd asked of her yesterday. Why was he in the store in the first place?

Finally, she decided it was time to leave after putting cough syrup in the basket. She could say Margaret had a cough if her father inquired about the Duchess any further, but she desperately hoped he wouldn't.

He was a man that had no qualms about sticking his nose where it didn't belong nor for beating around the bush—of which Gina was far more like him than she cared to admit. And while those were not favored traits of a citizen of the Provinces, he never crossed any lines publicly. Gina had learned early on in watching her father's behavior how to quell her nosiness and keep to herself. Sometimes that was easier said than done.

The cashier smiled at Gina and asked how things were, to which Gina replied vaguely, making sure her words weren't a lie. She wasn't a very good liar, but if he asked specifically what the medical supplies were for, she wouldn't hesitate to attempt one. But what would she say now? He wouldn't believe the lie that her father suffered an injury since he'd just walked in and out, if he even knew that had been her father. The Blakes were frequent customers to this particular pharmacy due to its close proximity to their farm.

Perhaps she would say something about her brother Jedidiah doing something stupid, like spraining his ankle and scraping his knees after falling out of a tree. Could that work? Would it be believable? But the cashier never questioned any of the items in her basket. He kept up unsuspicious small talk with her, rang up all her items, took the coins the Judge gave her, handed her the receipt, and told her to have a wonderful day.

"You, too," she replied, smiling at him.

He gave her a second-too-long of a look before turning red and looking away. That tended to happen often with Gina. Young boys and grown men alike were always removing their eyes from her—some embarrassed, some not so much. Some eyes didn't look away, venturing down her body before realizing what they were doing and finally turning their attention away from her.

She knew she was pretty, but she didn't think she was better looking than most girls. *I am just being vain.* She scolded herself for the sin and let it go.

"Before you leave, Miss Blake," the cashier quickly said as she was about to walk away. She paused and waited for him to state his business. He stumbled over his words, stuttering, "I heard a rumor that your father requested the Judge to marry you off before your graduation. Is that true?"

She nodded once, her stomach tossing slightly. "Yes," she whispered.

Please don't ask me to—

"Would you be okay with me turning in a request to marry you?" His face turned bright red. His brown eyes darted away from hers out of embarrassment.

He wasn't the first to ask her that question. He wasn't even the fourth or fifth. Gina took a few too many seconds to respond, but she finally told him the same thing she'd told the others, "I'm afraid it would be for nothing, sir." She didn't even know the boy's name, and calling him *sir* seemed out of place. He couldn't have been more than seventeen. He was still an Immature, after all. She continued, her face reddening to match his, "I have turned my own request in for the man I'd like to marry, and he, too, has turned a request in. I'm sure the Judge is working on the paperwork for the two of us already."

She wasn't sure about it, actually, but she hoped it was true.

"Oh," the boy stumbled, the redness in his cheeks lingering. "I understand." He bowed his head to her. "I apologize if I've overstepped. I didn't mean to come across as inappropriate."

"You did not," she responded kindly, smiling at him. She glanced down at his name badge quickly before looking back at his face. "Have a wonderful day, Jase."

"Same goes to you, Miss Blake," he whispered.

She hurried out of the store.

She was thankful the Judge trusted her enough to go to the

pharmacy corner store for Margaret's medical supplies. At first, he didn't seem to want her to leave the house once he realized she knew about Margaret's brand. He wanted Margaret's sin to remain a secret.

That was another thing Gina found interesting (and perhaps a bit disheartening). Out of all the people in the city, she would have thought the Judge to be of the highest moral standing—next to the Prophet, of course. But there he was, desperately keeping a dark secret from the world.

But Gina couldn't find it in herself to blame or disrespect Judge James for keeping his daughter's secret. She was no better. They were both protecting someone they loved from the unjust wrath of their world. If it came to light, Margaret's life would be ruined. *It must be hard to be the daughter of a Judge.* She was thankful she was not a part of the High Class elites.

When Gina exited the building, her father took the paper bags of goods and carried them as they walked together. She tried to make small talk to curb the anxiety tumbling through her insides. "What brought you to the pharmacy? Did you get what you needed?"

He responded with a *harumph* and a pat of his shirt pocket.

Gina waited for him to say something—anything—but he never did. Every now and then, she would catch him looking at her with what she thought was disappointment, and her heart crushed under that weight. What had she done that caused her father such dismay?

And though she wanted to confront him and ask what was on his mind, the words were caught in her throat. She was too afraid of what his answer would be. Perhaps she had done something—perhaps something a long time ago that he had just found out—and she had forgotten about it completely.

Once they made it to the James' house, she paused at the white gate that introduced the property line. Her father handed her all of the bags and gave her a peck on her hairline. "Come home immediately, Ginevieve," he ordered, a warning in his eyes for her not to disobey again.

"Yes, sir," she whispered, and he turned away from her, starting back down the cobblestone to the tramcar stop. "Wait!" she exclaimed without thought and regretted it immediately.

He turned to face her, a question in his eyes.

She quietly asked, "What have I done wrong? Please, tell me."

His eyebrows furrowed together in a sad display of anguish. He glanced around to make sure no one was around before stepping back up to her and whispering, "I won't ask questions, Gigi. I simply don't want to see my little girl flogged."

Her stomach dropped. *Flogged? Flogged! What did I do? Oh, Anem, help me remember!*

After half a moment, he put his hands on her shoulders and squeezed them lovingly. "I will do everything in my power to protect you. You can trust me with your secret."

Secret? Her eyebrows furrowed.

Her mouth gaped, but she didn't get a chance to speak. Her father continued talking, "And Derek will too, okay? He wants to protect you as much as I do, bless the man. He's the one that came to me and told me to keep you hidden since yesterday. 'Lock her in her room if you have to,' were his very words. That's why I asked you not to leave the house."

And yet she had left the house the day before—which apparently her father was still not aware of. In her defense, she thought he was only asking that of her because Lilli Ann, who was feeling unwell, but Jedidiah was old enough to babysit for a couple of hours at a time, and she had other things she needed to do.

She swallowed, and it was loud. "Father, I don't understand. Mr. Owens? Wh—?"

He patted her cheek and said in a low voice, as if he was trying to comfort her, "I don't blame you for succumbing to your flesh. I'm in no place to judge, after all. None of us are saints. Besides, Derek and I agree this is just as much our fault as parents as it is you and Carson's."

Gina was beyond confused at that point. "Carson? What about him? I don't... I'm sorry, Dad, but... What are you talking about?"

He stood up straight. "You don't have to keep pretending, Gigi. I'm on your side. Always and forever."

Frustrated, she held up her index finger even as both arms hugged the paper sacks, a gesture that commanded him to stop. "Father," she addressed with a bit of a tone that she hardly ever took with anyone. "I need you to come out and tell me what I've done wrong." She was tired of trying to guess. "Out with it."

He paused for a moment, searching her eyes, but then looked down at his dirty work boots and whispered, "I know what happened between you and Carson, Gina."

Gina's stomach pitched uneasily as the foggy memory resurfaced. *He can't know that. I never told anyone. Did Carson tell someone? His dad? That would explain Mr. Owens' part in this, but... Carson promised he never would tell a soul.*

Her father continued, reaching over and squeezing her arm gently, obviously seeing the horror in her eyes, "Don't worry, darling. I will keep it a secret."

She swallowed loudly again. She could feel the embarrassment creeping onto her face. "Who told you?" she whispered.

"I suspected it would happen," was his immediate reply. "But Derek is the one that told me yesterday about Carson's arrest."

Her eyes widened. She breathed, "Carson was arrested?"

They'd only be able to arrest him if he confessed, because there was no evidence of their sin.

He nodded once. "Yes. I didn't tell you because I didn't want to scare you. They're looking for you, Gigi, and I can't have you flogged right after he is. The punishment doesn't fit the crime. Some of our rules are too harsh, and this is one of them."

"Flogged?" Perhaps she was mistaken, but she could've sworn the punishment for a kiss—even one as less innocent as theirs—was only

175

a day in jail and a few months' worth of counseling. "He's going to be flogged?"

"Already has been. He should be recovering now. Don't worry. He's okay. He'll be home this evening."

She was very confused about the severity of the punishment. Surely, he must have done something else to warrant the flogging. "What did they charge him with?"

Her father looked at her curiously, as if she should know.

"What was his sentence, Dad?" She was embarrassed he knew of the kiss she had shared with Carson, but her father obviously wasn't too upset about it, so she didn't feel the need to look away from his stare.

He answered, "Breaking curfew and extramarital relations, of course. Thirty lashes total."

Gina's mind was suddenly blank as she tried processing what her father said. "Extramarital...?"

He continued looking at her curiously. "Relations," he finished. "Yes, Gigi. They found the brand."

She rocked back on her heels, dizzy. "Oh," she whispered, the color draining from her face. Her heart squeezed and gave a few hard thuds against her ribcage.

He took her hand and squeezed it. "I won't tell a soul. You can count on me, darling."

He didn't know of the kiss then. He knew only that Carson had a brand, and he assumed that meant it belonged to her, his daughter. It should've belonged to her. Why didn't it?

Not knowing what to say, and mostly wanting him to leave so she could process the heartbreak she'd just learned about Carson Owens, she whispered to her father, "Okay."

He gave her a peck on her hairline and once again reminded her to head home as soon as she finished what she had committed to doing at the James' house. She watched, stunned by the new information, as her father walked back down the cobblestone road and left the subdivision.

She would have to face him again later that evening and tell him the truth—that she was not Carson's lover. And why did he assume she was? Sure, Carson and Gina had always been close, but not for a little over a year now.

Gina let herself into the Judge's house, hands shaking, tears threatening her. She inhaled deeply and exhaled in a puff.

Shortly after her mother had died, they'd grown much closer, so close that he had kissed her and she had kissed him back. Their kiss had been intense, and it bothered her how willing she'd been to give him whatever he wanted. Lots of things happened around the same time, and she couldn't handle the temptation Carson presented along with everything else. So, she had asked Carson to back away for a while, which he respectfully obliged.

I didn't mean to back away from me and find another girl, Carson. Her heart shattered into a million pieces at the single thought that he had loved someone else like she had wanted him to love her. Her and only her.

She tried to push Carson out of her mind for the time being, and focused on her immediate task at hand: changing the dressing on Margaret's brand.

Oh. Gina paused after she shut the door, her hand still on the doorknob. *The Duchess. It's her, isn't it?*

That's why she was trying to remove it, because they are looking for her.

She shook her head. *Doesn't matter. It doesn't matter!*

She wanted to curse, but she wasn't one to even think such words. *Oh, stars! It does matter. Anem, why would he do this to me?*

Before she realized what she was doing, she had set down the bags and walked out of the house, quietly shutting the door behind her so as to not alert Margaret that she had been back.

She marched down the cobblestone road to the tramcar stop. Gina's mind repeated the same prayers over and over as she rode in silence the whole twelve minutes to Uptown Polaris. The tears fell, and though strangers gave her concerned looks, she didn't care.

How could he do this to me?

After requesting to see Carson Owens at the justice department's central precinct, they took her straight to a lounge area that was nicely decorated and felt calming. It didn't help ease her anxiety even a bit. An officer insisted on checking her left shoulder, despite her having been through a checkpoint the day before.

Was this a bad idea? It was the first time she wondered that after the officer had left. She resolved that it probably was, indeed, a bad idea. But she couldn't let it go. She had too many questions and choice words for Carson.

She paced the room for ten minutes before the door opened again. Carson stumbled inside, disheveled and handcuffed, wearing his jeans and a new-looking green sweater, though there was a snag in the threads on the shoulder. An officer pointed at the cameras in the two corners of the room and said to the two of them, "I'll be in the next room with another officer watching. Nothing inappropriate, Owens."

Carson saluted him, which Gina thought was odd.

The officer informed Gina when she gave Carson a curious look, "He's drugged, just so you know. Derek Owens insisted I tell you he more than likely won't remember this conversation." Then the officer turned his back and shut the door behind himself without a departing word.

Most of her didn't care that he wouldn't remember. As long as he explained himself, that was all that mattered. Another part of her hoped he'd never forget this conversation they were about to have.

Carson turned to Gina and examined her from head to toe. It was inappropriate, but he wasn't sizing her up, and it didn't make her uncomfortable. He looked concerned about her. Still, he was acting so strangely.

"Are you okay?" she whispered. He didn't seem hurt or as if he'd just been flogged, but that could have been the drugs.

He nodded three times too many. "I'm okay, G." Her stomach tossed. It had been a while since he'd called her that, and no one else called her G. Everyone else called her by her usual nicknames: Gina or Gigi. "Just a bit loopy, that's all. They said I won't remember anything, but what do they know? They underestimate me." He gave her another full look. "Are you okay? Are you eating enough? You're so thin. And so pale. Are you sick? Are you eating enough iron? You need iron, G." Short pause. His brow knotted. "Wait. Why are you here?"

She ignored every question except for the last. "I just found out about you and..." She was hesitant. Butterflies crowded her stomach. She couldn't finish the sentence.

Something clicked in his head, and horror overtook his gaze. "Oh," is all he had to say for himself.

Tears welled in her eyes. "Oh?" she breathed. "That's the only explanation I get?"

He stared at her, his own eyes whelming with tears. "You told me to leave you alone. So, I did," he whispered, voice cracking.

She clenched her fists. "'Leave me alone' is not congruent with 'find someone else,' Carson! I never said to find someone else. I didn't mean for you to *leave me*!" She hadn't meant to shout. She took a deep breath to calm herself.

His lips were pressed tightly together, and the tears that had gathered in his eyes had escaped down his face, one at a time. He said lowly, "You said to leave. You said that to me."

"My mother had just died, Carson," she cried. "I was overwhelmed with responsibilities that I never had before. A newborn baby. A two and a three-year-old. Not to mention school was much harder—still is. And I had to start spending all my free time sewing clothing for other people just to feed myself." She couldn't believe she had admitted that last part out loud. She had always been careful to keep her nutritional struggles a secret. She added quietly, "And my mental health took a big hit, Carson. I couldn't handle more than myself. I just needed some space. Just some, and not forever."

He didn't reply immediately. He just stared at her for the longest of moments. Finally, he whispered, his voice coated in sorrow, "Oh, Anem's stars. I didn't know, Gina. I thought you didn't want me anymore. I was trying to move on. I didn't realize you—" He paused, ducking his head as the tears streamed down his face.

She clenched her jaw and exhaled, frustrated. He was drugged, and he wouldn't remember any of what she was saying to him anyway. She was wasting her breath.

She reached around the back of her neck and unclasped the necklace she always wore. The hand-carved beads rattled together as she bundled it up in her hand and held it out to him. He might not remember their conversation, but she was going to make sure he knew she'd been there.

He didn't reach out his hand to take it though. He looked down at the ground. "I don't want that."

She stepped up closer to him and jabbed it at him.

He shook his head. "No, G. It's yours. If you don't want it, throw it away."

She grabbed his hand, which caught his attention, now completely undivided from her. He would hear whatever she had to say to him, especially if she held his hand while doing so. She pressed the necklace into his palm, forced his fingers over it and squeezed. "Put it in your pocket, and you'll understand later when you are yourself again."

He stared into her eyes for a long moment. "Gina..." He said her name with such delicacy and sorrow and heartbreak. But he couldn't seriously think he was hurting more than she was.

He stepped closer to her, and though she was tempted to not step away, she was reminded of the cameras—and the brand on his shoulder—and she took a step back.

He paused where he was, but continued speaking, "I'm so sorry if I hurt you. I swear I thought you didn't want me anymore. You said that much to me." He was quiet for a second before asking, "Have you changed your mind, then? Do you want me again? Can I come back to you?"

Come back?

Gina thought his chocolate eyes looked hopeful. Had he been waiting for her to tell him to come back to her all that time? For a year and a half? If so, he wasn't very good at the *waiting* part. He couldn't even keep it in his pants long enough to allow her time to readjust to a life without her mother.

"Carson," she breathed. She couldn't stop the tears cascading down her face. "I never stopped wanting you. I never actually wanted you to leave. I didn't actually think you had left at all, in fact. I just thought we were waiting until we could marry. That's how *I* saw it. Obviously, you saw things differently." She gestured to his left shoulder.

His eyes closed. "Please forgive me," he choked out. "*Please.* I didn't know. I swear it. I didn't know."

She choked on her own words. "You should've known, Carson. If you weren't sure, you should've asked me how I felt."

"I thought you were clear that you didn't want me. And I did try to talk to you. I swear, I tried! You didn't want to talk to me. Don't you remember?" He paused for half a second. "Gina," the pain in his eyes was unmistakable, "if I had known, I would've never done this to you. Please, forgive me. I wouldn't be able to live with myself if you hated me." Did he notice the tears falling in waterfalls from his eyes? He added, whispering, "You're everything to me."

Everything? How could he say something like that to her after the sin he had committed with another girl? With the Duchess, no less! A girl who was much prettier and far better off in every way than she was. She could never compete with Margaret James.

"I only did what I did because I couldn't stand the pain. It hurt too much to think I could never be with you—to think of you at all. I needed a distraction."

"This wasn't the plan," she said, barely whispering, her tears matching his. "I never said I didn't want you, Carson. I never said that."

His mouth gaped as if he wanted to say something else, but it closed a few moments later when he couldn't think of anything more to add. He simply stepped closer to her, and that time she didn't step away. He whispered, "Can things go back to how they were? I would like that, Gina. Very much so."

She shrugged, and once again gestured to the brand hiding under his sweater. "I don't know if things can ever go back to how they were. You gave your heart fully to someone else. Besides, what about the other girl?"

His eyes were unchanged at the mention of Margaret. "Who?"

Gina rolled her eyes, annoyance pricking at her heart. "You want things between us to go back to how they were, right?"

His eyes sparkled. "More than anything."

"But what about your lover?"

His eyebrows pulled down over his glistening eyes. "What about her? She has nothing to do with you and me."

Gina shook her head. "Carson... She is a part of your life now."

"No," he disagreed. "She's getting married to someone else. Besides, if you and I get married, she's irrelevant. What does she matter?"

Gina was quiet for a few moments, a bit unsettled by his answer, and then she whispered, "Do you think she feels that way about you? That you're irrelevant to her?"

His expression shifted, eyebrows pulling up in the middle and eyes fleeting to his feet. "No," he answered honestly, a sigh on the edge of the word. "I know she loves me like how I love you." He bit down on his lip, closing his eyes for a second. Then he said to her, "This is all my fault. If I could take it back—"

"But you can't," she interrupted. "What you've done with her will always be marked on your body. And marked on your heart."

He shook his head fervently, stepping up to her again, closer. "You have more of my heart than anyone could possibly have. I'd do anything for you, love."

She sighed and rolled her eyes at him, remembering he was drugged and wouldn't be able to recall their conversation. Part of her felt like they were going to have to have it again anyway in the near future.

She started to turn to leave, but her flesh made her pause, and she couldn't help take advantage that he was drugged. The question slipped off her tongue with too much ease: "Do you love her, Carson?"

He was quiet for a moment as he examined her face. After a second, he whispered to her, "Not like I love you." He ducked his head, ashamed. "I'm so sorry. I wish I could change what happened."

"Was she worth all of this?" Gina gestured vaguely, her throat threatening to collapse under the weight of her heartbreak.

He answered quickly, no hesitation, "There is nothing in this universe worth hurting you over."

They stared at each other for a few long seconds before he whispered, "You look so beautiful today. I like how you did your hair with the braid. It—" He stopped speaking when she turned away, her departing footsteps the only sound between them as she left the lounge and him alone in it.

She left him holding the necklace he made years ago as a promise that he would love her forever and that he would wait his whole lifetime for her. What a joke on her that had been.

23

"**M**argaret!" called Gina as she entered the James' house. "It's me. I got everything for your dressing." She picked up the bags she'd left by the door and made her way to the back of the house.

When she entered Margaret's bedroom, she froze, voice trapped in her throat. Her eyes fell upon William Lach. He sat on the edge of the bed in front of where Margaret was still sitting in the chair. Remnants of tears stained her red-flushed cheeks and fear swam in her puffy hazel eyes.

Officer Lach stood up from the bed and turned to Gina. Gina thought her heart would burst from beating so hard against her ribcage.

"Who are you?" he questioned, eyes narrowed.

"Leave her alone," rasped Margaret, clutching her left arm as if it pinched, fear swimming in her wet eyes. "She has nothing to do with this, William."

Had this man hurt her? Threatened to hurt her?

Officer Lach didn't look away from Gina. "Your name," he ordered, tone less than kind.

"Ginevieve," she choked out. Tears began streaming down her cheeks. Had the officer found out? What would become of her? She had kept a secret of Margaret's, even if for only a few hours. What was the punishment for that? Surely it wouldn't hurt. Maybe it was only a slap on the wrist. She could handle that. Or an order for community service.

Oh, Anem, she prayed earnestly. *Please, please, don't allow my father to be dishonored. Forgive me for keeping such a secret.*

"Ginevieve," he repeated, eyeing her carefully. "Pretty name for a pretty girl. Did you know about Margaret's sin with Carson Owens?"

Gina wanted to answer the officer—she honestly did—but her voice caught in her throat.

Her parents had known the Owens family since before her birth. Their families had been closer before her mother died. She recalled seeing them at Emma Blake's funeral two years ago; they had been so kind during that time, staying with her father and siblings on that day. It had been as if they, too, were family.

She remembered thinking Carson was handsome when they had made eye contact during the Prophet's sermon, and then she'd felt an enormous amount of guilt that she'd thought such a sinful thing at her mother's funeral and inside Anem's temple, no less!

He had looked at her with sadness in his eyes, and afterward, when she had snuck out of the temple to cry behind a pillar, he had followed her and not said a word. He had simply sat a few feet away from her on the marble steps, silently letting her know he was there for her. He hadn't moved for the entire half hour or so, even though it had started raining, and they both got soaked. He'd acted like it wasn't a big deal. He had just continued to sit there quietly as she mourned.

When her father had finally found them, he had thanked Carson for keeping an eye on her. Carson's response had been a nod and a whispered, "Of course."

Gina reached for the hand-carved wooden beads laced around her throat, but she had forgotten she'd given them back to Carson. She inhaled deeply to calm her nerves, but without the beads, it proved difficult. What a silly thing those beads had become to Gina—an object of comfort. Even now, she regretted giving them back to Carson, despite the pain they also reminded her of.

"She didn't know it was him." Margaret attempted to stand from the chair. It must have been painful, though, because she grimaced and groaned all the while. She leaned on the back of the chair for support, her grip white-knuckled. William turned to face her as she continued speaking to him, saying, "She only found out this morning about the brand when she stumbled upon me like this. I didn't tell her who, though."

"Yet, now she knows." William turned to Gina. "And you won't say a word to anyone, will you?"

Gina was silent as her mind reeled. Was he asking if she was going to tell the justice department? Was he telling her not to tell them? Was it a trick question? If he was ordering her not to tell anyone, what was the reasoning? Did he care about Margaret despite her being bound to Carson?

A pit formed in her stomach as she glanced at the bloodied brand rebuilding itself on Margaret's exposed shoulder. *Carson's bound to her. Their souls are bound forever.* She had never considered a future where either of them would be bound to anyone else besides one another. The reality of the situation hit her hard in her gut.

Yet despite their souls being bound by the goddess, Carson had made it clear that day, even if he was drugged, that he wanted Gina. Thing was, she wasn't so sure how she felt about him anymore.

"Will you?" repeated William, his tone sharper than a butcher's blade.

Her voice was lost somewhere in her chest, but she managed to breathe out, "No."

"Not a word to any soul?"

She shook her head.

"Any?" he emphasized.

She whispered, "I won't tell a soul, I promise."

He nodded once, giving her entire body a once-over, which left her fidgeting. "Very good. I don't want any trouble befalling Margaret." Then he looked at his fiancé and asked, "Who else knows of your sin?"

"My father," she whispered.

"Huh," the officer huffed. "That would explain the way he treated Carson this morning. Who else?"

Margaret glanced over at Gina. "Just Gina. No one else."

His gaze fell on Gina for a second before he looked back at the Duchess. "Derek Owens also knows. I'll talk to him. He won't say anything to tarnish your reputation." William reached his hand out and wiped the tears from Margaret's cheeks with his thumb. He let his hand linger there as he whispered to her, "I won't allow anyone to ruin you. I can promise you that. Do you trust me?"

Gina shifted her weight from one foot to the other awkwardly. She felt as if she was watching an intimate moment and considered backing out of the room. But she thought maybe Margaret would not appreciate being left alone with someone she wasn't yet wedded to, and, frankly, seemed quite uncomfortable around.

The Duchess stared into William's eyes, hesitating. A moment and a half later, she nodded her head once and whispered, "Thank you, William."

William smiled at Margaret. Gina thought it was half kind and half alarming, and she didn't know what to make of the latter observation. "Of course. After all, you're to be my wife. I will be vowing to protect you from all sorts of danger. Consider this a head start on keeping that vow."

In the end, there was no reason for Margaret to try to remove her brand, and Gina felt sorry for her in that regard. She now had to heal from something so horrendous and incredibly futile. Not only did William choose to protect her from the law regarding the brand, but the mutilation itself could not and would never be able to erase what the goddess herself had declared on her body.

Surprising both women, William leaned down and gave Margaret a kiss on her cheek. It was very much illegal, but he didn't seem to care in the least. And it wasn't like either of the two girls were innocent of such sin. The only difference was that no one knew of Gina's sin with Carson.

"I must excuse myself now," he whispered to the Duchess. Gina felt so out of place standing there.

"Okay," Margaret whispered back unenthusiastically. "Have a good day at work."

"I'll make sure of it," he said, smiling the same smile as before. He glanced over at Gina then, as if just remembering she was there. Her spine crawled when they made eye contact. "Thank you for taking care of her. How can I repay you for your friendship to the Duchess?"

Gina shook her head, feeling a bit woozy. She reminded herself to breathe.

"There's nothing you want? Nothing at all?" He took a step toward her.

She had to answer him. Shakily, she said as she looked down at her old boots, "I simply serve Margaret as my Duchess and as my friend." She dared to glance up at him.

He raised an eyebrow, and it made her stomach pitch. "Is that so? Well, it's always nice to have loyal friends." He tilted his head toward her in a manner that stated he was thankful. "Regardless, if you are in want of anything, please let us know. The world can be yours, Miss...?"

"Blake," she answered, voice small.

He glanced over her whole body again, then he smiled at her. "Miss Ginevieve Blake." Her spine crawled, and her scalp prickled. She never wished to hear her name on his tongue again.

He walked out of the room, shutting the bedroom door behind him. Neither of the two girls moved or made a sound until they heard the front door open and shut, indicating the officer had left the James' house. Margaret and Gina stared at each other the whole time, sharing silent words of concern and worry and fear.

The words tumbled from Gina's lips before she thought on them. "You can't marry that man. He's awful."

Margaret's eyes deadened. "I have no choice, Gina. I signed a contract with him." She blinked and life returned to her hazel gaze. "My father will assign a good man to you, trust me. The only reason he picked William was to keep me here in Deneb."

Gina's stomach tightened. "He said that to you?"

"He didn't have to." Margaret inhaled a deep breath and exhaled as she explained, "My mother mentioned a boy she liked for me in a letter, one living in the District—a Duke from the Port, I think she said. The very next week my father had me signing a contract with William. I'm certain it was just to spite her."

Gina's eyes fell to the floor. "Oh. I'm sorry about all of that."

"No," Margaret said, "I'm the one who should be apologizing. I'm sorry you were dragged into this, Gina. You don't deserve to have such a heavy burden placed on your shoulders."

Gina shook her head and forced her shaky legs to carry her over to Margaret. She motioned the Duchess to take off her black nightgown and lay on the bed she had freshly made before leaving for the pharmacy. "It's not a burden, Margaret. Don't worry about it."

"You can't tell me not to worry," she argued as she struggled to remove the gown, her elbow caught in the fabric. "I am the world's worst for allowing my innocent friend to know this horrible secret, and then dare ask you to keep it."

Gina assisted Margaret in removing the gown, carefully untwisting the black fabric from her limb. "You are my friend, Margaret, and I don't want to see your life ruined, just like your father and fiancé don't. And I'm sure Carson doesn't want that either." Margaret didn't respond. Gina said, despite the knot in her stomach, "He cares about you, I'm sure." It hurt to admit it.

Take away this pain in my heart, Anem. I beg of you.

Gina removed the homemade dressing. The room was silent for a long time as Gina applied the different medications the Judge had brought home. Margaret didn't flinch or tense much. She had taken a couple of the pain pills prior to Gina leaving the house, and they seemed to be working well. In addition to the pills, Gina sprayed the topical pain-relieving medication for extra comfort.

Margaret whispered after several minutes of silence passed between the girls, "I suggested Carson Owens to my father as a husband for you."

Gina hesitated for half a second as she dabbed the anti-infective ointment onto the wound, concern creeping into her heart. "You did?" Margaret told her father to pair her lover up with her best friend? That sounded like a recipe for disaster and drama, and Gina wanted to stay far away from such things.

"He's kind and thoughtful. He would be an amazing husband. I hope him having a past with me doesn't bother you." Margaret paused, but Gina didn't know how to respond, so she kept working, lips tightly pressed together. "He would treat you very well, Gina. I know he would. Trust me, please."

She wasn't yet brave enough to tell Margaret the truth that she knew Carson longer and probably better than Margaret did.

Better? How could Gina know Carson better than the woman he had taken to bed? She could no longer say she knew Carson better than any other woman.

She sighed, "I'm sure you're right. You love him, after all, and Margaret James is a great judge of character."

Margaret laughed once. "About Carson? Yes, I know he's a good man. I can't say the same about many others."

A few seconds of silence passed again. Gina exhaled softly, closing her eyes, gathering her bravery, and said, "Our families are friends. We used to all be closer before my mom died." That was the closest to the truth Gina could currently muster.

Margaret turned her head slightly to look back at her friend. "Really? I didn't know that. He never mentioned knowing your family."

Gina didn't make eye contact with her. She was worried the Duchess would see the hurt her words unknowingly inflicted. "Mrs.

Owens and my mom were very close. Both were nurses on the same trauma team. After Mom died, Mrs. Owens made us food every day for two months. Carson and Casey would occasionally drop the dishes off in the morning on their way to school."

That was mostly true, except Carson was always the one that dropped off the food whether Casey was with him or not, and he'd stay to watch Lilli Ann long enough for Gina to get ready for school.

"Sometimes we'd all walk together." They had always walked together. Why was she only telling half-truths? "Still, to this day, Mrs. Owens brings my family a homemade casserole or pie every now and then." Twice a month, at least.

"That's nice," whispered Margaret.

"And I've seen Mr. Owens leave silver dollars in my father's mailbox a few times." That was not a half-truth at all. Derek Owens was a very generous man, and she didn't want to undermine that. It would be disrespectful. "So I know the Owens are good people. They care deeply..." Gina paused, her thoughts trailing.

Margaret glanced back at her, catching Gina's hesitation. "But...?"

"But..." she began, whispering her words and choosing them carefully. "I don't want to marry Carson if that means losing you as my friend." That, too, was a half-truth—maybe even a quarter-truth. "Tell your father not Carson Owens." She placed her hand lovingly on Margaret's forearm. "Please," she whispered.

She was asking not to be paired with the only man she had ever trusted, ever loved, and ever wanted to be with. The request sent a pang through Gina's heart, injuring the broken thing even further. But how could she accept a marriage contract with Carson now? How could she marry him when he had loved another in her stead?

"You won't lose me as a friend, Gina," she said sternly. "I'm not a petty little girl. Besides, I want you to be his wife just as much as I want him to be your husband. He deserves a good wife, and I know you could make him happy."

Gina was surprised by Margaret's harsher tone. She didn't reply to her at all. What could she even say?

Margaret sighed heavily. "Sorry," she whispered. "I didn't mean to snap at you. I'm just saying... I have good reasons."

So do I. He betrayed me. Thinking the words sent another stabbing pain through her heart. Tears stung her eyes, and she fought them back.

Several long seconds passed. She was barely able to control her choking emotions without Margaret noticing.

Gina carefully thought about what she should say next. Though she wanted to tell Margaret the story of her and Carson, including the short portion that was romantic and the ending that was tragic, she thought it would only upset the Duchess more and decided against it. Margaret didn't ever have to know about how Carson and Gina used to be, and she never needed to know what Carson had said to her earlier that very day, that he had not-so-subtly begged Gina to take him back. He had even brushed Margaret off as if she meant nothing to him.

Finally, Gina simply whispered, "I want to protect you and our friendship, Margaret." Even if Gina wasn't sure they could be as close as before, she was not lying.

Margaret's response was not what Gina expected. "I do not matter in the long run. I have no place in Carson's future, and I've come to terms with that. Regardless, I would like him to have a good life with someone that could love him like I love him. Someone he could learn to love too. Someone that would make it easier to move on from me. Please, Gina, if my father agrees to pairing the two of you, sign the contract. Do it for me, if not for any other reason."

"Maggie, I..." Gina hesitated. She wanted to tell her the truth— some of it, anyway—so she could understand the circumstances, even if just a little.

But Margaret wasn't going to allow her to argue her case. "Gina, please."

She looked over Margaret's brand that was becoming more and more obvious the longer time passed. The brand was supposedly identical to the one Carson had. It was beautiful, and a small prick of jealousy struck her in the center of her shattered heart.

That brand rightfully belonged to her, yet there it laid on the Duchess, taunting her.

Oh, Anem, why does it hurt so much? This pain is unbearable. Should I marry him despite his sin? I still very much want to, yet I don't, which confuses me. Should I not want to marry him then? I'm so confused... What should I do?

24

Carson's head swam, and for stars-knew how long, he tried to make sense of direction. The faint scent of mildew and industrial cleaner tickled his nose. Somewhere nearby, water dripped unseen every two seconds, and the distant caws of crows through glass panes could just barely be made out.

Where am I?

Forcing his heavy eyelids open, Carson tried to make sense of the gray blur inches from his face. He slowly shimmied his body in a bid to reconnect to it. The lumpy mattress pressing against his chest was reassuring. He bent his fingers, then his toes. The skin on his back pulled in places, the pain abruptly sparking his memory. He had been flogged. And then...

A slight sting ran across his cheek, and he reached slowly to brush his fingertips across the glued laceration. His back ached beneath layers of gauze and medical tape. Groaning, he turned his head to the opposite side. It felt as though it weighed a hundred pounds. Carson let his head plop onto the pillow.

On the ground next to his cot, his father sat staring out the window at the dreary sky.

"Dad," he choked out. The words scratched against his sore throat.

Derek repositioned himself, turning to Carson and lounging against the wall under the window. He reached into his pocket for something as he spoke, "About time you woke up. I assume the drugs have worn off and you're oriented again? You've been asleep for nearly four and a half hours."

Carson stared at his father. *Four hours?* What had happened to him? And why was he back in his cell?

Derek held up the item he'd retrieved from his pocket, a familiar necklace with beads that spelled *angel* in less-than-perfect penmanship, and Carson's stomach tossed at the surprising sight of them. "Please tell me you remember what she said to you. I wasn't allowed to accompany you when she came asking to see you. When you came back, you wouldn't say much, just kept apologizing to her as if she could hear you."

Carson took the necklace from Derek and examined the beads. "Gi—Gina was... here?"

Not only had she been there, he had spoken to her. He desperately wished he could remember that encounter. It had been a long while since the last time he spoke to Gina Blake, though every time he saw her, he wanted nothing more than to approach her and ask how she was.

But she had told him to stay away from her. So, he stayed away.

"I only know it was her because you gave me that necklace when they brought you back. Lucky I know it's hers. You told me to hold on to it for you until you could give it back to her. Also, you were trying not to cry. Went straight to bed after that. Cried yourself to sleep, though you tried hiding it. Poorly, might I add."

Surely he is kidding. Surely I didn't cry in front of him. Part of Carson wanted to crawl into a hole and die. He cleared his throat of the embarrassment squeezing it. "I don't remember."

"Whatever she said, it really got to you."

Carson clutched the beads to his chest. There were numerous things that she could have said to him to cause him to have such a strong emotional reaction. No matter how hard he tried to forget about her—about what she had meant to him—she would always have a piece of his heart. "I didn't say anything about her?"

"Which girl are you referring to?" asked Derek. His voice took on a suddenly irked tone. "The one whose life and future you ruined or the one whose heart you broke?"

Carson buried his face in his pillow, sick to his stomach. His father was right. He had ruined Margaret's future, and without meaning to, he'd broken Gina Blake's heart. The beaded necklace in his hand was proof of that.

But she had told him to leave, to back off. She had told him she didn't want him around anymore. She had said those things to him, and when he tried to talk to her about it, she'd had a near emotional breakdown, yelling at him to get away from her. So he'd left her alone, just as she told him to. He wasn't sure what he had done wrong at the time. He was only trying to be there for her when she was suffering.

Carson gripped the necklace tighter.

She didn't mean it? She didn't actually want me gone? Why didn't she say that then? If I had known... Oh, Anem, if I had only known!

Carson could barely admit it to himself lest feeling like he was betraying Margaret, but he knew deep down in his heart that the only reason anything happened between himself and Margaret of them was solely because Gina had pushed him away, because his heart was broken. Margaret was the first person that offered a distraction.

And he had taken it.

And he had regretted it immediately. He'd used her to forget his own pain, and that was never, ever going to be okay.

But then he convinced himself of a different beginning than the truth. He convinced himself that he had fallen for her before they had bound themselves together. He had convinced himself that she was the one for him, that their love was written in the stars.

Did he not actually feel that way about Margaret James, then? Had everything he ever told her been a lie? One meant to fool himself into not feeling guilty for using someone as a distraction from his own broken heart?

The beads in his white-knuckle grip drudged up all the ugly truth he had hidden away. He understood why seeing Gina had made him cry. She made him face his demons, and they were truly horrendous. Because of his selfishness, he'd not only severely broken Gina's heart beyond repair, but if Margaret knew about his true feelings, her heart would surely be shattered as well.

Yet, he was still far more concerned about Gina's heart.

He would've never bound himself to Margaret if he knew Gina still cared for him. He would've been more persistent about her mental health, if he had known she had needed that—which it was now obvious to Carson that that was the issue at hand all along.

Gina was dealing with massive grief. In addition, the burden of suddenly taking on motherhood responsibilities at only fourteen had weighed heavily on her shoulders. Why hadn't he understood sooner that was the reason for her distance? After all, he had tried helping out when he could.

He'd take the younger boys, Asher and Sean, who were two and three at the time, out for pastries and playtime in the park. Sometimes they would spend all day with Carson, and occasionally his family would assist. None of them minded, of course. The Blakes were like family to the Owens, and Carson was more than happy to help where he could.

And then she told him to back off.

He thought he had been helping. He thought she was appreciative. He thought she wanted him there.

"She said she didn't want me around anymore," Carson mumbled into the pillow. "I didn't know... I didn't know she didn't mean it. Why would she say something she didn't mean?"

Derek sighed. "You still have a lot to learn about women."

Carson didn't respond. He kept his face buried in the flat pillow.

Several moments of silence passed before Derek said, "You're

197

probably starving. Here." He grabbed a glass container from a canvas bag that Carson recognized as Kayla's famous and handed it to him. The inside was packed with his mother's chicken salad, including the narrberries and ground tree nuts.

Carson's stomach growled as he took the container and sat up. His back pulled, but it wasn't too painful. "Mom brought this?" he asked.

Derek nodded. "She was here less than an hour ago. She was getting worried since they haven't released you yet. Don't worry; she didn't bring Casey." He handed Carson a fork wrapped in a cloth napkin, one from his mother's favorite stack of linens. He was surprised she had allowed the piece to leave the house at all.

Derek continued speaking as Carson dug into the food, but it wasn't about anything Carson was particularly interested in. His mind was still consumed by Gina Blake and the necklace she'd given back to him, the one he still clung to even while eating. "Peter, one of my officers, brought some soup. That's what I ate. Didn't think you'd mind at all, considering your mother's food is much better than anything available here."

Carson nodded, agreeing, mouth full. "Mmm-hmm."

Derek reached in the canvas bag again and pulled out a white paper bag with the logo of the bakery across the street stamped on it. "She picked this up for you, too. I didn't touch it. Promise. Though I was tempted." He gave the bag to Carson.

Inside was an assortment of different pastries—glazed, jelly-filled, sugar-coated, and even some with sprinkles. Carson commented around another bite of the chicken salad, "I think Mom feels really bad for me."

"Yeah," his father sighed. "That's an understatement. She feels...responsible in some small way, and I suppose I do too."

Carson looked at him. "Neither of you are at fault. This is all on me."

Derek met his eyes with his own. "You aren't a parent, Carson. You wouldn't understand. I pray one day you won't have to be placed in a situation where you feel like maybe you should've done something better—been around more, watched for signs more closely, scolded less, or even scolded more..." His sentence trailed as he picked at his short fingernails.

Carson finished the chicken salad and ate two pastries, both jelly-filled. His head was feeling a bit better with a full belly, and he could think more clearly.

He then remembered his question from before that his father never answered. He asked again, "Why am I here? Am I still in trouble?"

"I don't know," his father whispered, sighing loudly, eyebrows lowering on his downcast eyes. "But..." He hesitated and that made Carson nervous. He clutched the beads tighter, but they gave him no comfort. "I think it has something to do with the Duchess."

Carson's stomach flipped upside down, but he kept a cool composure. "The Duchess? What about her?"

"You... You really don't remember?" It was odd, but Carson thought Derek looked hopeful that Carson couldn't remember whatever it was his father was referring to.

Carson's eyebrows became a line over his eyes. "Remember what?"

"Nothing," he answered too quickly.

Carson was immediately suspicious. What was he hiding? And about Margaret? Carson loathed not knowing.

Derek shook his head and looked down at his hands. "It's just that... I'm pretty sure William Lach knows." He looked up at Carson. "I'm sorry, Carson. I don't know what's going to happen, but if her fiancé knows about her brand..." He didn't finish the sentence.

Carson felt sick.

Derek moved on with a small sigh on the edge of his words, saying, "There's nothing you can do to stop what's going to happen, son. If she's punished, then that's how it's supposed to be. Choices have consequences, after all."

Carson's head began swimming again.

It's not true. Can't be. He held his breath and shut his eyes tightly. *It is true. Has to be. Stop lying to yourself.* He cursed under his breath, and his father was surprisingly dispassionate about it, even though he'd never heard Carson say a foul word in his life.

It was all inevitable. Deep down, Carson always knew they'd get caught. He was a fool for holding out hope that he could take all the punishment and that she didn't have to suffer for a moment. They sinned together, and together they were to reap what they had sown.

Carson's heart became heavy with sorrow. *Even Gina is suffering from my sin with Margaret.*

Indeed, choices had consequences.

Heavy booted footsteps echoed down the corridor. Another pair of footsteps followed the first closely, slightly less fervid. Derek and Carson were silent as they waited to see who was coming and if it was to speak with them. Carson glanced at his father who simply shook his head at him and motioned him to stay quiet, an order Carson was used to receiving from Derek.

Carson quickly stuffed the necklace into his jean pocket. Judge James along with William Lach appeared, and Carson's stomach dropped through the earth.

They know, don't they? They know it's her. Has she already been arrested?

"Carson Owens," the Judge addressed. "Do you remember Gina Blake visiting you earlier?"

Carson was taken aback at the mention of Gina instead of Margaret, but he shook his head, a no.

The Judge nodded once, glancing down at his boots. "I figured. She gave you something. What was it?"

Carson glanced at Derek, but Derek simply motioned for him to show the Judge what was in his pocket. He whispered, "A necklace." He pulled it out of his pocket and showed it to them briefly before stuffing it right back in his jeans.

"Why?" asked William. "Seriously, Carson. How many women do you have lined up for you?"

Carson's face warmed with anger at William's bold and hardly appropriate question, but he would answer him honestly nonetheless. He had nothing to hide regarding Gina—except for the kiss they shared a year and a half ago. He wouldn't dare tell a soul about that. He promised her he wouldn't. "It's not like that. I made it for her many years ago. I assume that she doesn't want it anymore."

They were both eerily quiet as they stared at Carson, his stomach doing a hundred somersaults. Finally, the Judge asked, "Did you have a romantic relationship with her years ago, when you made her such a gift? I know she's not your lover, but perhaps you moved on from her because..." He hesitated, but Carson understood and despised the implication.

William finished the sentence for him, no qualms about making Carson uncomfortable. "Because she wouldn't put out?"

Carson was appalled at his boldness. It irritated him how flippantly they spoke about Gina. He snapped, "We were not romantic, not physically. Gina Blake is a respectable citizen. She would never break any rules." Though his first sentence was partially a lie because of their kiss, his last statement was more true than not.

"All right, all right," said William, his hands up as if he was trying to calm Carson down, though he had no idea how much Carson was already holding back. "What did she say to you then? We have cameras but no microphones."

Still irritated, Carson's tongue slipped, and he said, "I don't remember, you dimwit."

"Calm down, son," whispered Derek as he placed his hand on his shoulder and squeezed hard. "Don't make this worse for her."

The Judge chose to ignore Carson's name-calling, for which he was grateful, and said, "I'll talk to Miss Blake about the conversation, then. The officer should've stayed in the room with the two of you, especially since one of you was under the heavy influence of drugs.

Rest assured, he's been reprimanded. Anyway..." He exhaled, clasping his hands in front of him as William unlocked the cell door. "I'm sending you home now. I'm sure your mother and sister are worried about you and would love to have you back home."

William opened the door and gestured with his hand for them to exit. Derek helped Carson stand up from the cot, and the movement pulled achingly at his back. He grimaced and chewed on his tongue to keep from making a sound.

The Judge waited until Carson and Derek exited the cell before saying, "If you don't mind, perhaps William and I can escort you two home."

Confused, Carson looked at his father for an explanation, but Derek looked just as bewildered. "Escort?" questioned Derek. "Why would we need that?"

The Judge shrugged. "Just as a precaution. Please, Officer Owens."

Carson was beyond confused and he wondered if his father felt the same way.

Derek simply nodded and grumbled, "If you insist."

25

No one spoke the entire trip home. The group of them waited at the tramcar stop for the next trolley, and once on the tramcar, they stood a good distance from each other, spread evenly through the vacant car. Carson's back pulled achingly as he held onto one of the poles for stability. It was the longest twenty-minute ride to their subdivision Carson had ever taken.

Once at the door to their home, Derek turned to the Judge and William. He stuck out his hand to shake, but they both hesitated, glancing at each other. Derek dropped his hand slowly, watching the two men carefully with narrowed eyes. "What is this about?" he bluntly demanded. "You didn't just escort us home as a precaution, Mark."

The Judge shook his head. "No, we didn't." He glanced at William again before looking back at Derek. "Don't tell anyone. I need your word, Owens. You won't mention what you've learned about Margaret to a soul."

Carson's stomach heaved, and his throat burned with vomit. He forced it back down. He wasn't going to be known as a weak-stomached man at the mention of Margaret's name.

There was no question about it anymore to Carson; they knew Margaret was his lover. He was horrified, frozen solid in that moment.

Surprising Carson, Derek said, "You know I won't."

He knew it was Margaret, too.

Judge James nodded his head once at Derek, a thank-you. "That's why you're the one friend I can trust."

Friend? The Judge is friends with my father? Carson didn't believe that, really. Derek had a few friends, but the Judge wasn't one of them. In fact, Carson could only think of one man that Derek considered a friend: Gina's father, Timothy Blake. Carson had seen the way his father interacted with him many, many times while growing up. But Judge James? He was not even on the same playing field as Mr. Blake.

The door swung open in that second. "Carson!" Casey's spirited voice screeched. He turned to her just as she threw herself on him, hugging him tightly. He winced, but he didn't make a sound even though his eyes stung with the pain.

"Cassandra, he's wounded," said Derek, quickly grabbing the girl's arms and removing them from her brother. "You have to be more considerate, child," he whispered to her. "Now, please, go inside. We are speaking with the Judge."

She looked at Judge James then, her eyes growing into large chocolate discs. "Oh, I'm so sorry," she apologized to the Judge, bowing her head to him. "I didn't realize—"

"It's okay, Miss Cassandra," the Judge stated, a stiff smile on his face. "No need to apologize. We were finished talking."

Suddenly, Kayla stepped outside with Gina right next to her, surprising everyone standing there. The two women also looked very surprised to see the four men outside—especially Gina. The initial sight of her sent Carson's heart galloping into his throat. He couldn't help staring. He fought the urge to blatantly ask her about the conversation they'd had earlier that he'd forgotten.

Carson thought he was the most surprised by Gina's presence until William rudely said to her, "Ginevieve Blake, why are you here, of all places?"

Did he call her Ginevieve?

Carson gave the officer his strongest scowl, but William didn't even look at him. He glared at Gina, and that made Carson angrier. He wanted to sock him hard enough to make his small brain rattle in his skull.

Without thought, Carson spat at William, "Mind your tone when you speak to her."

Immediately, Derek said, "Step down, Carson," and even though Carson didn't want to, he thought it wise to heed his father's advice.

Carson wanted to know how William knew her. He called her by her full name, as if scolding her like a child. Carson didn't like that he knew who Gina was, and frankly, it pissed him off even more. She was the very last woman on the planet that deserved the punishment of William's attention.

Gina's face turned red when she saw William, and her eyes immediately found her worn boots, her right hand reaching around her throat as if for something, but her hand found nothing. Carson knew she had absently reached for the beads that were now in his pocket.

He pulled them out and clutched them, ready to give them back to her. He didn't want them. They were hers. If she didn't want them, she was free to toss them, but he didn't want to be the one she tossed them at.

The Judge looked at Carson and then at William. He said to the officer, "The Blakes and Owens are old family friends. I'm sure Gina has a good reason to have stopped by their home." He glanced over at Gina, giving her the opportunity to explain herself.

"I made lasagna for them," she said, breathless. "I was just dropping it off." She almost sounded like she was trying not to cry.

Lasagna? She's giving us food? Carson's eyes darted to his mother. Why would Mom accept it? The Blakes can barely feed themselves!

Before Carson could protest, Derek said in a kind voice that he only ever used with his own daughter, "That's very kind of you, Gina, but you didn't have to do that."

She waved her hand dismissively, attempting a smile, though it faltered. "Of course I did, Mr. Owens," she said shyly. "Your family has always been so kind to us when going through difficult times. It was honestly the least I could do."

Gina glanced over at Carson for less than a second, but it was all the time he needed to see the brokenness that resided there.

Anem's stars. What have I done? What did I say to her?

"I hope your recovery is quick," she said, breathless, refusing to make eye contact with him. Then she turned to Kayla, giving her a quick hug. "Please excuse me now. I must return to my family."

Carson stepped in front of her before she could step off the porch, forcing her to step back and meet his gaze. Immediately, Kayla and Derek unanimously scolded him, calling out his name.

He ignored their warning. He wasn't going to move until she took back the necklace.

He extended his hand that held the old hand-carved beads to her. "This belongs to you," he said as stoically as he could, but he could feel his throat tightening.

She glanced behind him at William, her face reddening again. He couldn't help but wonder again how William and Gina knew each other, and it bothered him not knowing the details. She quickly took the beads back—though it was obvious she did so simply to avoid being there any longer. He noted how careful she was not to touch his skin as she snatched them out of his palm.

"I'd like to leave now," she said quietly to him, looking away from his eyes and at the beads in her hand.

Carson hesitated—there was so much he wanted to talk about with her—but he stepped aside for her to pass. It was not the place nor time to talk to Gina, no matter how badly he wished it was.

As she passed him and started down the steps, he whispered to her, "I don't remember our conversation, but whatever it was about, I'm so sorry, G."

She hesitated on the bottom step, but she didn't respond. After half a second, she continued moving forward with no acknowledgement to Carson.

William stared at Gina as she walked down the steps and passed him. Carson watched him carefully the whole time. The officer kept his eyes locked on her as she walked away—her head ducked and face still red—and he continued watching her as she left the Owens' property, heading for the tramcar stop. No one was telling him to look away from her.

Every cell in Carson's body caught fire and boiled his blood hotter. He didn't think about what he was saying until it had already left his mouth. "Stop staring at her, pervert."

How many boys had Carson said the very same thing to about the very same girl, now a near-grown woman? Carson wasn't even sure of the number, and he knew for sure Gina wouldn't know. Many of them she hadn't even been aware of at all. They had been simple looks from across the schoolyard, comments made about her in earshot of Carson.

Everyone looked at Carson, but no one scolded him for saying something presumptuous to the officer. They had to have known Carson was the one in the right and that William was in the wrong. His eyes had lingered for far too many seconds.

Why hadn't anyone said anything? At least they were allowing Carson to say it without any consequence. Not even William defended himself.

The Judge nodded at Derek after a couple of awkward, silent moments. "Have a good evening with your family." He motioned to William who was staring daggers at Carson. Carson didn't hesitate to return them. "Let's go, Lach." He patted his shoulder once, then turned away from the lot of them and began his stroll down the stone path to the cobblestone road.

William said to Carson as he was about to turn his back and walk away, "I'm not a pervert. Watch what you accuse people of, Owens." Then he turned around and began following the Judge.

But Carson wasn't going to let him off that easily, nor was he going to allow William Lach to have the last word. "Your eyes linger on a woman you have no business looking at—let alone speaking to—and you argue that you aren't a pervert?"

William paused for a second but then continued walking, surprising Carson by not satisfying him with a response. At least he got the last word.

"Carson," warned Kayla. "You can't say things like that—"

"Let him be, Kayla," whispered his father. He put his hand on Carson's shoulder and gently encouraged him to turn his fire-hot attention away from William Lach's back. "He's had a long day."

Kayla inhaled and exhaled, eyes closed. A couple of seconds passed as she calmed herself. On the flip of a coin, she smiled at her son and wrapped her arms around him, squeezing him tightly to her by his neck, careful of the stitched stripes decorating his back.

She whispered, "I'm so glad you're home, son. Now," she pulled away from the embrace and shooed him off the porch, into the house, "let me have a look at your back. Your father gave me the prescription that Dr. Griggs had written for you when I dropped off your food earlier. She gave you some good pain killers. And the healing ointment is the best in the Province. I'm very grateful she was the attending physician."

Carson mindlessly followed his mother to his room, barely listening to her ramblings. He obeyed her orders to remove his shirt and lie face down on his bed as his mind raced with a million and one things. Primarily, what was going to happen to Margaret now that they knew about her brand? The Judge told Derek to keep his mouth shut, so did that mean they, too, were going to keep their mouths shut? Surely, that's what it meant. The idea eased his worry minutely.

And then thoughts of Gina hit him hard, like a ton of bricks, rattling the iron cage locked around his heart. So many questions, so many emotions that he had bottled up and convinced himself no longer existed.

It hurt. It all hurt so much.

"Why did you accept the food from Gina?" Carson whispered after a few moments. "That wasn't right, Mom."

"You're scolding me for accepting a gift?"

"They can barely afford to feed themselves." He turned his head slightly to look at her more clearly. "We know that better than anyone else."

She nodded. "Yes, I do know that better than anyone else, Carson, but she was insistent. Also, I managed to slip ten silver dollars into her coin purse when she was distracted. That's enough for her to make at least five more lasagnas. They'll be okay." She paused for a moment. Carson felt better about Gina's gift knowing his mother had given more to her.

"So..." started Kayla hesitantly. "It wasn't her after all?" Her voice was small, almost a whisper.

He looked sidelong at her curiously. "What?"

"Your father and I were positive that it was Gina. But she told me today she'd been to the Marketplace yesterday and again today. They have checkpoints set up there. So it's not the Blakes' little girl then? I can't imagine she was able to slip by unchecked by the officers—"

Horrified by what she was suggesting, Carson quickly turned around to look his mother in her eyes more clearly. Interrupting her, he said, his voice cracking on the word, "What?"

"We thought Gina was your—"

"Mom!" exclaimed Carson again. "You're talking about Gina Blake. She would never..." He buried his face in his pillow again. "Angels belong with others of the same kind, Mom. I am not of the same kind."

"On the contrary," she began, her voice low, but she didn't explain her thoughts any further. "You still care for her though, and she very obviously cares for you. How could you hurt her like that, Carson?"

He was silent. He didn't know how to reply. He already felt an enormous amount of guilt for what he had done to Gina—never mind the actual sin itself.

He suddenly understood why there were rules prohibiting relations before marriage: To prevent heartache, drama, and any misunderstandings.

Kayla sighed. "She doesn't deserve—"

"I know, Mom," snapped Carson. He reeled his tone back to a respectful degree and said, "I'm aware of the consequences of my sin. And I'm very aware of what she does not deserve."

Kayla was quiet for only a moment before asking, "So what are you going to do about it, son?"

He didn't respond. He didn't know how. He had already apologized. What more could he do?

The absence of a reply prompted Kayla to add, "She sent you a letter a couple of weeks ago. I don't mean to pry, but you never brought it up, and I feel like it's appropriate for me to ask now."

Carson glanced at her, confused. "What are you talking about? I didn't receive a letter from Gina."

"Of course you did," she said. "I placed it on your desk." She gestured to his clutter-filled desk that he hadn't sat at since before graduation let alone looked at. He had become blind to it. If she had been setting mail there for him, he would not have noticed it.

He jumped up, ignored Kayla's protests and shuffled around the clutter on the desk. Finally, the cursive handwriting of someone he had exchanged many secret notes with caught his eye. She had written his full name carefully across the center of the sealed envelope, addressing it formally.

For the immediate and urgent attention of
Mister Jerry Carson Owens
Sent with care by
Miss Moriah Ginevieve Blake

His stomach twisted. Immediate *and* urgent? He snatched it up, hands shaking. He couldn't open it fast enough. He was irked with his mother for not telling him about the letter sooner, and due to his frustration, he snapped at her a second time, saying, "It says immediate and urgent on it, Mom. Why would you just set it there and not tell me about it?"

She defended, "I thought you would see it."

"Well, I didn't! You didn't think to mention it at all? Is my job assignment somewhere in here too?"

"Jerry Carson," she warned, her face and neck growing hot. "Choose your next words carefully."

Kayla was like a hurricane when angry, and he was definitely pushing his limits with her. He looked back at her for a moment as he finally pulled the letter from the shredded envelope. "Sorry," he whispered, though it was a lie, and he quickly looked back at the parchment he held.

It was a formal letter, and that somehow made it much worse. Immediate, urgent, and formal. And he was reading it two weeks later than he was meant.

Dear Carson,

Recently my father wrote the Judge regarding my marital status. It is to my family's benefit, as well as my own personal benefit, for the Judge to find a husband for me to marry so I may finish my last year of school without the hardships I am currently enduring. The Judge approved of my father's request only today, so I am writing to inform you of the change.

Perhaps you would be interested in submitting your own request to marry soon. When you do, I hope you think of me.

Forever Yours,
Moriah Ginevieve Blake

Sickness settled uneasily in his stomach. He recalled on the night of Margaret's engagement party when Gina had asked him if he had spoken with the Judge yet, and he hadn't known what she had meant.

This. This is what she'd meant.

He cursed, and Kayla warned him to watch his tongue.

Ignoring her, he reached over to the shirt hanging on the back of the chair tucked under the desk.

"Where do you think you're going?" questioned Kayla, her tone still annoyed from Carson's daring approach to her moments ago.

Carson started to put the shirt on. "I have to talk to Gina."

"Not right now, Carson," she said firmly. "Your back doesn't even have any dressings on it."

He started buttoning the shirt. He could feel it sticking to his back where the medication his mother had been applying lingered. "I have to," he breathed. "It's important."

"I'm sure it is, but you really should wait until after I dress your back." She paused. He continued buttoning his shirt. "Please," she said, though she was annoyed. "You're incredibly unpresentable right now. The medication is soaking right through your shirt!" He left the room. She yelled after him, "Carson!"

Suddenly, rounding the corner, Derek was standing right in front of him, blocking him. "Oh, I know you aren't ignoring your mother, boy." His voice was low and warning, almost a growl. Derek was always very defensive of his wife when he felt she was being disrespected.

Kayla had followed him out of his room. "Jerry Carson Owens," she said through gritted teeth, the rage of a hurricane storming in her piercing-blue eyes. Subconsciously, he took a step away from her. "I don't care what you do after I dress your back, but don't you dare ignore me. It will be the very last thing you ever do."

Derek placed a hand gently—yet hesitantly—on his wife's shoulder. He said to Carson, tone much calmer than Kayla's had been, "You shouldn't wear a shirt without the dressings on your wounds.

Go back to your room and let your mother finish dressing them."

Carson exhaled—gently so he wouldn't upset his parents further—and turned back down the hall, fighting the urge to drag his feet like a child.

"Where are you going anyway?" asked Derek, following both of them back to the room.

Carson answered as he stripped the shirt off, peeling it from his sticky back, "I have to speak with Gina. It's very important."

Derek was quiet for a few short moments. Finally, he pressed, "About?"

Carson laid face down on the bed as he replied, "She sent me a letter two weeks ago that I barely just read. I need her to know I wasn't ignoring her." He buried his face in his pillow as his mother started putting more medication on his back. "Oh, stars," he cried, voice muffled. "She thinks I'm ignoring her, doesn't she? She hates me." His heart gave a hard, painful thud against his ribs, the iron cage all but rusted away.

Derek exhaled, as if exhausted. Perhaps he was. He had learned a lot of things about Carson during the last two days. A lot of disappointing things. "Son," he began, "Gina is probably the kindest and purest person I know."

He turned his head so his father could clearly hear him when he said, "If you are trying to make me feel better, you are doing an appalling job at it."

"Why would I try to make you feel better?" was Derek's response. "Do you want the truth? Or do you want to feel better? Unfortunately, you can't have both."

Carson couldn't argue with him. He turned his face back into his feather pillow.

"Carson, look. Gina is a good girl, and I honestly am surprised she's not your lover. I've watched you closely, and I never thought you looked at anyone else the way you looked at her. And she looks at you the same way."

His heart ached and squeezed. "I don't necessarily want to discuss it," said Carson carefully.

"Fine," replied Derek. "We don't have to discuss it. I'll talk, and you listen." Carson groaned internally. He should've seen that one coming, honestly. It was typical of Derek to say something like that. "What changed, Carson? You love that girl. Or at least I thought you did. You had told me you did a couple of years ago. Said you were even gonna marry her one day. You were very adamant."

Carson hesitated. Finally, he sighed into the pillow then turned his head to mumble, "We grew apart after Mrs. Blake died. That's all."

"Yet you two still give each other looks from across the room."

"That's not true," Carson quickly defended.

"It is," insisted Derek. "Just last week, during the moment of silence at the temple, you and Gina looked at each other for several moments before looking away. The way you two look at each other teeters on the edge of inappropriate, but it's not necessarily how long you look at her. It's what's in your eyes when you do."

Carson couldn't recall the time his father was speaking about, and he wondered if subconsciously he had been looking at Gina in the way his father was suggesting all the time they'd been separated.

Derek said quietly, "You look at her with this hope in your eyes that I don't get. Perhaps you wished you were closer to her again. But her life has been very rough since Emma's passing. You have to allow her time to adjust."

Carson squeezed his eyes shut. He hadn't given her any time to adjust to a life without her mother, and how incredibly selfish and heartless and inconsiderate was that? He had thought only of himself and his broken heart. He had forgotten how broken she had been.

"That's all I have to say to you right now," said Derek, and then he stood and left the room.

Carson waited for Kayla to say something more, but she didn't. She dropped the subject entirely, for which he was thankful.

Carson closed his eyes and prayed, though it felt awkward as he asked for grace that he didn't deserve.

I didn't mean to hurt her, truly. I am a horrible, selfish man-child. Please grant me forgiveness, Anem, even though I don't deserve it. And, if possible, please let her forgive me as well. But if she doesn't, I understand and will accept her choice.

I am undeserving of her grace.

26

Gina walked to the tramcar stop much quicker than usual. She had been successful in holding back her tears while on the Owens' property, but once she was several houses down, she could not hold them back anymore. They streamed down her crimsoned face like waterfalls and dampened her floral-print cotton blouse. The breeze chilled the wetness on her cheeks. She wished she had chosen to wear her mother's cloak to drop off the lasagna. It had been warmer an hour prior, but the temperature was starting to drop as the sun slowly set in the afternoon sky.

On the tramcar ride home, she thought over Carson telling someone about staring at her before he called them a pervert. She couldn't imagine he was speaking to anyone else except William Lach. She had pretended she hadn't heard Carson and simply picked up her pace. She had wanted to run, but that wouldn't have solved anything and would only make her look suspicious at worst and childish at best.

Gina paused on the porch to her family's home. She looked at the necklace she had been holding tightly in her hand since taking it back from Carson. Most of her was relieved to have it back, and that was the part that laced it around her throat. But a small part felt like it was choking her, squeezing her chest with heartache.

She opened the door to the house after drying her face and eyes. She was immediately greeted by Jedidiah, the twelve-year-old second born child of Emma and Timothy Blake. He held Lilli Ann, the youngest of them all, who was crying her eyes out. Snot ran down the toddler's face, and her bright green eyes glistened with the moisture pouring out of them.

"Thank Anem you're here, Gigi!" Jed exclaimed, acting breathless though Gina suspected it was all for show. He shoved Lilli Ann into Gina's arms. "She's been crying for nearly twenty minutes now, and I'm going crazy! I don't know what she wants!"

Gina kissed Lilli Ann's cheek and rocked her gently. She petted the little girl's silky golden curls and hummed. The toddler seemed slightly calmer with Gina's touch. But why wouldn't she? Gina was the only mother figure Lilli Ann had ever known. "What's wrong, Annie?" she crooned quietly in the two-year-old's ear. "Show me what you want."

Lilli Ann pointed toward the kitchen. Gina shot Jed a disappointed glare, but he was no longer paying any attention to them and was focused on a book as he lounged on the couch. She rolled her eyes. "Did you try giving her something to eat?"

"Yes," defended Jed, "but she chucked it at me. Guess she's not hungry enough."

"What did you give her?"

"An apple."

"A whole apple, Jed? You didn't cut it for her?"

He dropped the book slightly to match Gina's stare with his own green eyes. "I didn't know she couldn't eat an apple whole, Gigi. I promise I didn't know."

"She's only two, Jed. She can barely carry on a conversation with us."

He raised the book back to his face. He mumbled, "Yeah, that's the most frustrating part."

Gina sighed and took the upset toddler into the kitchen. Lilli Ann immediately began calming down as she anticipated what was going to happen next. Gina set her down on the ground and took an apple from the fruit bowl. She showed it to the toddler. "How about this one?"

Lilli Ann nodded excitedly. "Apple!" she exclaimed, her voice light and frilly like a morning bird's song.

Gina smiled at her. "Yes, that's right. It's an apple." She took a knife and cut the apple into easy-to-grab slices for her little sister who hugged her leg and impatiently grasped at her skirts, occasionally uttering one-word phrases to hurry Gina along. Gina put the apple slices in a wooden bowl and gave them to Lilli Ann. "How's that?"

She took a slice and bit into it. Then she rocked her hips side to side and smiled happily. Gina gave her a peck on her forehead and ushered her back into the living room with Jed.

"Where's Dad?" asked Gina.

"Not inside."

"Jed."

"He's milking the goats. Or something."

"Go help him."

"Aw, c'mon!" He slammed the book shut and exaggerated the effort it would take to stand from the old, lumpy couch. "Wouldn't he ask for help if he needed it?" He opened the book back up as he walked at an excruciatingly slow pace to the backdoor.

"You should still offer. It's the right thing to do." She glanced around the room, asking, "And where are the boys?" She was nervous to know the answer. It was far too quiet in the house.

"Um," Jed started, not looking up from the book. He turned the page. "Last I saw them, they were playing in their bedroom. Maybe they went outside with Dad."

Gina was getting irritated. "Jedidiah!" She stomped over to him and snatched the book out of his hands.

"Hey!" he protested, lunging for it.

She couldn't keep it away from him easily, and he would probably try wrestling her for it, so she allowed him to grab it out of her hands as she scolded him, "I left you in charge. Can't you be an adult for *one* day?"

"You were only gone forty minutes, Gina!" he defended, tucking his book under his arm. "I watched Lilli Ann closely. Asher and Sean are old enough to watch themselves."

"They are four and five, Jed." She turned away from him and marched down the hall to the two youngest boys' room.

She opened the door and froze solid at the horror presented before her. "Oh, my stars," she whispered, a headache starting to pulse in her forehead. "What have you two done?"

Asher and Sean sat there on the carpeted floor, wearing only their underpants and smearing peanut butter all over themselves. They stared at their sister for a long moment before five-year-old Sean finally pointed at Asher and said, "He did it first!"

Asher snarled at Sean, his freckled face scrunched angrily, "Liar! You are the one that grabbed the peanut butter when Jed wasn't watching."

"Nuh-uh!"

"Stop lying, Sean! Gigi will tell Dad!"

"I'm not lying!"

Gina grabbed the doorknob and shut the door. The two boys still argued on the other side. She laid her forehead against the door, trying not to let the tears escape her again. The last thing she ever wanted was for her brothers and sister to see her cry.

She wanted them to be able to look up to her and know they could trust her. She didn't want them to think she had no idea what she was doing half of the time, or that the other half, she really didn't want to do any of it—and for that she felt guilty. But it was a feeling she couldn't escape, and that was the real reason she begged her father to write the Judge regarding marriage for her, even though she was only sixteen.

She wanted to escape her childhood home. Yes, it would be a relief for her father in a small yet notable way, but the real relief would be for Gina, and she craved that more than anything. She was sure that her father knew that even though she did not admit to him the real reasoning. Otherwise, he would've never agreed to marry his daughter off so young *just* because finances were tight.

It almost didn't matter to Gina who she married. She just wanted out. Out of the responsibility of mothering four children when she wasn't their mother—let alone fit to be.

Several breathing exercises later, she opened the door again, her tears under control now. "Go get in the bath," she ordered drily. "Both of you. Give me that jar."

Asher and Sean quietly stood up from the mess on the carpet that Gina didn't even know how to start cleaning up. On their way to the bathroom, Asher handed Gina the brand-new jar of peanut butter that was now nearly empty and had germs from children's hands as well as a few hairs and grit from who-knows-where all in it.

Boys.

Gina helped her two brothers draw a warm bath and instructed them on how to wash the greasy mess off of themselves. Abruptly, mid-instruction, there was a knock on the bathroom door, and it cracked open.

"Gigi?" Gina suddenly wanted to burst into tears, but she held back, pinching her lips into a fine line, her eyes burning with the intense desire to cry. Her father stepped into the bathroom. He took in the sight of the two fair-haired boys covered in peanut butter and then Gina's face. "Why don't you go work on Margaret's wedding dress? I'll bathe the boys."

She closed her eyes and stood up. She couldn't speak or else the tears would gush from her. She just nodded and left the bathroom. Once she exited, she heard her father sigh and say to them, "Can't you two just behave for once? Your sister has a lot on her shoulders, especially right now. Please. Just... Just behave."

They echoed, "Yes, sir. Sorry, Dad."

Gina shut the door to her bedroom and sat down on the floor against it. There, she cried for a long while.

She thought about everything that had happened over the last two years, but mostly she thought about everything that had happened in that single day.

Despite what Margaret had said about not being petty, she was definitely a jealous person. Gina could tell those things about people. And jealousy would lead to pettiness, and pettiness would lead to hatred, and Margaret hating her was Gina's worst nightmare.

Gina did *not* want to marry Carson. Not anymore.

But it didn't have much to do with her friendship with Margaret, if she was being honest with herself.

A large part of her was confused about Carson and Margaret's relationship and how it happened. It didn't make sense to her. Did he really love her?

She touched the wooden beads tied against her throat. They gave her peace and comfort and a sense of safety—as they were intended— even though she knew they were just beads.

He promised me.

She recalled when she turned twelve, and Carson had given her those beads. He had also written her a letter, one that she had read a million and one times, one she had memorized, one that she now wished he'd never written at all.

Gina scrambled to her feet and hastily pulled out her dresser drawer that held her intimates. Hiding underneath a stack of underwear was a hand-decorated cardboard box Gina made years ago for small keepsakes.

She opened it and shuffled through the random knick-knacks for the letter Carson had written her four years earlier. Finally, she found it with several other letters he'd written her and, with shaky hands, she unfolded it.

It had been a little less than a year since she'd pulled out that letter to read it. The corner of her mouth twitched when she read the single letter that he used to call her, that he called her earlier that day, and she hated that it warmed her soul when he said it.

G,

Happy birthday! Now you're accountable for your sins, but I know you don't sin, so I guess for you it's just another year, huh? No big deal.

I made this necklace for you. It's not that impressive, I know, but I prayed over each bead as I carved the letters into them, so I like to think they are blessed. May they give you peace when you have none, and, when I'm not around, may they help you feel safe and secure. I hope you like it as much as I think you will.

Yours,
Carson

(P. S. If you lose it, it'll be okay. I'll just make you a new one and give it to you as a wedding gift when we get married after our Rituals. Please wear the necklace at least once for me to see. I think you'll make it look more beautiful.)

Gina gripped the beads on her throat and ducked her head as the tears fell quickly down her cheeks. She couldn't hold any more of them back if she tried.

She had written Carson back and asked what made him think they would get married. He told her in person the next day in the schoolyard that he knew she would be his wife because no one else would do.

Yet, he found someone else he thought would do just fine.

She folded up the letter and stuck it back in the box. She pulled the most familiar letter out, one that she read all the time. The one that hurt her the most to think about now. She couldn't help herself as she unfolded it and read it too.

Gina,

I know it's hard right now with your mom gone. I know it

hurts. I'm trying to understand, but it's hard. Just know I'm always here for you, okay? You'll always have somewhere and someone to go to when you can't go home.

One day, I'll be your home. I promise, G. One day I'll take you away from all the pain you're feeling. I wish I could now, but I can only do what I'm already doing in the meantime. I'll continue to be there every day. I'll make sure you have everything you need. I don't know anything about babies or kids, but I'll try my best to help you take care of your brothers and new sister.

Please talk to me... You're so quiet now. If you can't talk to me, then talk to someone who can help you. I shouldn't ask if you're depressed, so I won't, but you should know that I wonder about it. Don't you dare even consider compromising your life, Ginevieve Blake. I mean it. I am not saying you would. I'm just afraid... You're everything to me.

I just want you to feel better. Please feel better soon. I love you, G. I always have, and I always will. Don't ever forget that.

Trust what Anem has written in the Eighth Star Scroll: "Heed my words and never forget: Tomorrow will be kinder. There is a joy that awaits, and it is on the horizon. Be patient, young ones. You will reap good fruit if only you wait for the harvest."

I believe the truth in her words, and I hope you do too. I know you do. You must! You are one of her angels, after all.

Patiently yours forever,

Carson

She untied the necklace from around her neck and gave the beads another look before stuffing it in the box along with the stupid letter that obviously meant nothing to Carson. It was painstakingly obvious to Gina that he didn't actually mean anything he ever wrote or said to her. If he had, he wouldn't have committed such sin with the Duchess.

He had to have known his sin with Margaret would hurt her. Did he not care? Or did he think he could hide it from her forever?

She had been a fool all those years. She should've known better than to believe Carson. She should've listened to the whispers about the Owens family.

She recalled a particular older woman who had warned her about Carson when she had seen him talking to Gina randomly at a candlemaker's booth in the Uptown Marketplace right before her mother died. She had said to Gina, "Any boy born with the blood of an Owens man in their veins is bound to be mischievous. Mark my words, that Carson will grow up a troublemaker. Probably already is, and we just haven't caught him yet. He'll slip up one day. Sinners always do. Be a smart girl, and stay away from him. A girl like you can be friends with anyone."

She should have listened. She should have stayed away. If she had just stayed away, she wouldn't be hurting like she was. Her heart would still be whole.

She went to work on Margaret's wedding dress to clear her mind of Carson and the betrayal she held in her heart.

Gina sewed for a long while before a knock came at the door. "Come in," she said calmly. She had been mindlessly sewing for so long, any hint at emotional distress was already long gone from her face. She wasn't even sure how long it had been.

Her father opened the door. He held a plate with a sandwich on it. "Did you eat?" he asked her.

She smiled gratefully at him and took the plate he offered. "I forgot. Thanks, Dad."

He was quiet for a moment as he assessed her. Finally, he said, "You took off your necklace?"

She touched her throat where the beads had always laid. She had already forgotten she had taken it off—twice that day, in fact. She suddenly felt very naked without them, especially since someone noticed their absence.

But she couldn't possibly wear the beads anymore. They represented a promise from Carson that he didn't honor.

When Gina didn't reply, he asked quietly, "Did you two squabble when you brought them the lasagna, or...?"

She suddenly realized he still thought she was his lover. She quickly looked at him and straightened as she said, "I've been meaning to tell you, Dad. It's not me. I know you think it's me, but it's not. I'm not..." She closed her eyes and looked away from him, back at the stitching she was doing. She whispered, "I'm not his lover, Dad."

Timothy sighed and slowly sat down on the edge of her bed. "Why did you act like you were when I spoke to you earlier today?"

She shrugged and turned away from her father, taking a bite out of the ham sandwich. Mouth full, she replied, "I was shocked. I didn't know what else to say."

"You were hurt," he guessed.

She didn't reply. He watched her start sewing again, occasionally pausing to take a bite from the sandwich. She didn't say a word all the while and was pretending he wasn't even there.

She didn't want to talk about Carson. She didn't even want to think about him.

"Ginevieve," said her father. He hardly ever used her real name unless he wanted to have a serious talk with her.

She paused to look at him through her lashes. He patted the edge of the bed right next to him, a silent request to sit and listen. She slowly stood and made her way over to sit by her father.

"What he did was wrong," he said. "Especially to you. He broke your heart. I can see that."

Gina shook her head. "It wasn't like that."

"Yes, it was." He paused. "For one—and you may be angry at me for this—but I've read all the letters Carson has written to you. Also, you should know, he didn't just write to you."

Gina looked at him curiously. Butterflies crowded her abdomen.

"Carson wrote me a letter many years ago. I didn't tell you. You were too young. He had to have been eleven or twelve at the time. The letter simply said that he planned on marrying you one day, and he was asking me to protect and love you until he could take over that role."

Gina's heart skipped from her father's words. She hadn't known about that.

He chuckled once, amused. "It's supposed to be the other way around, but I didn't dare correct him. I've always liked his spunk. Besides, there was nothing but innocence between the two of you at the time." He shrugged, "Hell, you two were still just children. Marriage was a much less complicated concept then."

She looked away from him. "He changed his mind," she whispered. "And he's allowed to. Like you said, we were only kids, Dad. Innocent."

"He loved you, Gina, well into his teenage years. I know you know that. He wasn't shy about telling you so. And maybe he has forgotten how much he loves you, and maybe he fell in love with someone else. Doesn't mean he doesn't care." He paused for another long moment. "Doesn't mean he won't make a good husband for you."

Gina wouldn't look at him, though she really wanted to. She was surprised by his comment.

He added, "I just finished drafting a letter to the Judge. I won't send it if you don't want me to. Would you like to read it?"

She nodded but still wouldn't look at him. He reached in his shirt pocket and pulled out a piece of paper. Gina unfolded it and skimmed the formal letter addressed to *The Honorable and Just Judge Mark James of Polaris, the Capital of Deneb.*

Her hands shook and she fought tears again once she read the purpose of the letter.

Her father wrapped one arm around her shoulders and squeezed her with a small hug. "Is that a no? Just crumple it up and toss it if you don't want me to send it."

She didn't crumple it. "Why do you want Carson to be my husband?" she whispered, and was pleasantly surprised that she didn't sound like she was about to burst into sobs despite having that very feeling clutch at her chest.

"Because you love him, and he loves you—even if he has to be reminded of it. All I want for you is lifelong happiness, and I don't think anyone else can give you that. I don't care if he has a brand with another woman, and you shouldn't either, Gigi. Our past mistakes shouldn't define our future."

She thought for a couple of heartbeats about what he said, and then she asked Anem for forgiveness before she folded the letter back up as neatly as her father had given it to her. She handed it back to him and said lowly, "What if he loves her more?"

Forgive me for I am jealous of my friend.

He was quiet for a long moment after he slid the letter back into his shirt pocket. Finally, he replied confidently, "He doesn't."

"You can't know that, Dad." He couldn't; he wasn't Carson. Only Carson could give such a definite answer.

And in a way, she supposed he had when he said in the drugged state he was in that he didn't love Margaret like he loved Gina... Not like he *still* loved Gina. Those were his words. Drugged words, albeit, so she wasn't going to hold him accountable for them. She was going to have to ask him again.

She didn't believe that he still loved her. If he still loved her, he wouldn't have done what he did.

"I have a hunch."

Gina rolled her glistening eyes that threatened her with more tears. "A hunch, huh?"

He squeezed her shoulders with another hug and kissed her temple. "Yes, a hunch. A love like that... It doesn't just go away. You just have to give him time to remember." He patted her hair that she let loose from her bun a while ago. "So, can I send this letter?"

Gina thought for a moment, closing her eyes. A couple of tears fell down her face. She finally stood and walked over to her dresser drawer.

She pulled out the cardboard box and carefully took out the necklace. She stared at it for a long moment.

"No," she finally answered, whispering. She ran her fingers gently over the five beads that spelled out *angel*. "I don't even want to think about him, let alone marry him."

Even as Gina said those words, she knew she was lying to herself. She shouldn't still care so much about Carson Owens. But she did. She very, very much did.

27

Timothy Blake hesitantly requested Gina help him put Lilli Ann to bed. Gina never said no to her father when he asked her for help, and she was used to taking care of her sister.

Her father had fed all of his children beforehand, so she only gave Lilli Ann a small bit of milk in a sippy cup to help comfort her as she was rocking her. She fell asleep quickly that evening. Gina was grateful that she didn't have to spend more than twenty minutes rocking the little girl she loved very much and felt horrible for abandoning soon. But her therapist agreed that the sooner Gina was out of the house, the sooner and better she could heal mentally.

It wasn't as if she was truly abandoning her siblings and father. She would visit often—as often as she could. She'd make sure they were all taken care of. Jed had promised her that he would try to do better in her absence, and that gave her a little bit of comfort. Very little.

She stood up from the rocking chair in the living room and took the limp, snoozing toddler to the nursery where she gently laid her in her bed. Lilli Ann's mouth hung slightly open, her eyes darting under her gently shut eyelids.

As Gina slowly pulled the door closed, a gentle knock on the front door surprised her. Across the hall, Timothy Blake was reading a book to the boys. He motioned her to please get the door, and she nodded at him.

"Gina Blake." She was surprised to find Judge James on her porch so late in the evening. She hadn't looked at the clock in a while, but surely curfew was approaching.

"Judge James," she formally addressed, bowing her head to him. "How may I be of service to you this evening?" Her mother had always taught her that service was the greatest gift you could give someone you respected and admired.

He took his hands out of his coat pockets and wrung them together, indicating how cold he must have been. "I need to speak with you regarding your visit to the justice department earlier today. May I come in?"

"Of course," she whispered, the breath knocked from her lungs.

Her heart raced as she opened the door wider for him to step inside. She motioned to the living room where they could speak. She prayed she wasn't in trouble for visiting Carson.

"Would you like something warm to drink?" she offered. "Coffee? Tea? I can even warm some milk, if you'd like. It is goat milk, fresh from the day."

He shook his hands at her, declining, then motioned with them for her to sit across from him on her father's large, worn recliner. Slowly, she took the seat and folded her hands in her lap. She suddenly remembered her hair was down and quickly scrambled to pull it back up on her head. "I am so sorry," she rasped. "I am unpresentable."

"Gina," the Judge said gently, his eyes kind. "Your hair is fine. There is no need to be so stiff." Margaret had called her stiff earlier as well. Was she really?

Gina exhaled and nodded, letting go of her hair and allowing the natural curls to fall down her back. She didn't speak, and allowed the Judge to take the conversation away.

He leaned forward and rested his elbows on his knees. "Can you tell me why you visited the department today?"

She swallowed the hard knot forming in her throat. Gina would never lie, especially not to Judge James. "I went to see Carson," she whispered.

He was not surprised. Her answer was one he expected. "Why?"

She gently cleared her throat before replying, her face crimsoning, "I wanted to know the truth."

"About?"

"Him and..." She paused. She looked over at the hall, but her father was still reading to the boys. She looked back at the Judge and whispered, "I wanted to know about him and Margaret."

He was quiet for a long moment as he stared into her eyes, unblinking. "Why?"

She contemplated how to answer that question. After a few moments, she shrugged and looked down at her hands in her lap. "I suppose I'm just nosey. Forgive me."

"There is nothing to forgive," he whispered, reaching over and patting her cheek gently. "You are not in trouble, Gina. There is no need to feel guilty." He smiled weakly at her. "But you gave him something." He leaned back into the couch. "A necklace. What does it mean?"

"Oh, uh..." She reached up and touched her bare throat, but her necklace was buried deep in the back of her dresser drawer. "It says angel," she whispered, voice strained.

"That's not what I was asking, and I think you know that," he said, and though he was gentle in his approach, she thought perhaps he was a bit annoyed. "What does the necklace mean to you and Carson?"

She responded quietly and honestly, "Carson made it for me when I turned twelve. It was a birthday gift." She glanced away from his face then which had scrunched in disapproval. She continued through the nerves that wracked her, "I just wanted to give it back to him."

"You were angry with him? Because of what he did?"

She shrugged. "Not as angry as I was hurt."

"Why not just throw it away?"

231

She fought tears and ducked her head away from Judge James. She whispered, "I suppose I knew he wouldn't throw it away and would try to give it back, and I guess I didn't actually want to get rid of it."

"You love him." It wasn't a question.

She didn't look at him or respond.

"Does he know how you feel?"

She swallowed hard.

He sighed. "Gina, again... You aren't in trouble. It's not wrong to care about someone romantically." He was quiet for a few seconds to allow her to process before asking, "Did you two have a romantic relationship? I know you aren't his lover, obviously, but before all of that happened. When you two were younger. When he was making you jewelry by hand."

She glanced up at him and a couple of tears fell. Quickly, she wiped them away and sniffled. She wanted to answer him, to tell him the truth, but surely she would get in trouble. And Carson would be worse off than he was already.

He sighed and changed course, "I only just read your request to marry him that you sent a couple of weeks ago. Would you like to rescind it?"

"Judge James?" Her father walked into the living room then, and relief washed over Gina. "To what do we owe the pleasure?"

The Judge stood and shook hands with Timothy Blake. "I had a few questions for your daughter, that's all."

Tim shot Gina a glance from the side of his eye then quickly looked back at the Judge. "Whatever people are saying about Gina and Carson, it's not true."

Judge James shook his head. "I know she's not his lover, Mr. Blake. Although, I have to admit, it is a bit concerning how many tips we've received that point to her." Her face reddened a bright cherry color. "But she's been cleared more than once already. That's not why I'm here."

"Oh," he said, glancing over at his daughter again. "Are you okay? Why are you crying?"

She shook her head at him. "I'm fine."

"We were speaking about possible suitors for her," the Judge lied. It surprised Gina for a moment. She wondered why he didn't want her father knowing she visited Carson that day. She really wished he would tell the truth. She was uncomfortable with all these lies.

"Ah!" Tim exclaimed. He plopped himself down on the rocking chair and motioned for the Judge to continue. "Tell me some good news, then."

The Judge smiled at him, though it seemed disingenuous to Gina, and he sat back down on the couch. "First of all, you should know, I have requests from many of the eligible men in the Middle Class to marry your daughter. I could not possibly read through all of them. Over half of them I've left unopened."

Interrupting Judge James was a knock on the front door. Gina turned her head to the foyer, confused at who could possibly be at the door. Weeks could go by and they wouldn't have a visitor, but two in one night?

And all Gina wanted to do was go to bed. She was exhausted.

Timothy Blake stood from the rocking chair and politely excused himself to answer the door.

The Judge looked at Gina after her father left the room. "Expecting more company?"

She shook her head. "Not that I'm aware of, sir."

After a couple of long moments, her father re-entered the living room with Carson right behind him. "Look who showed up, Gigi!" her dad exclaimed, smiling. He patted him on the shoulder, and Carson winced slightly.

Gina stood up quickly, her stomach knotting tightly. She wanted to say something to Carson but felt awkward with her father and the Judge there in the same room.

"This is perfect, actually," Judge James said in her stead as he stood up and stuck out his hand to Carson. The look in his eyes was less kind than his gesture. "I was just about to talk about you with the Blakes."

Carson took his hand warily, his other dug deeply in his coat pocket. Coldly, he asked, "Why?"

Gina admired how brave and bold Carson was to speak to Judge James in that manner despite him being *the* Judge... But he wasn't just the Judge. He was also Margaret's father who knew about Carson, and Carson knew he knew.

He's truly fearless, thought Gina. She shook the warm feeling from her heart quickly, turning her attention away from him.

"What's in your pocket?" The Judge motioned to the hand that he refused to remove.

After hesitating for a couple of seconds, Carson looked over at Gina and removed his hand. In it was a sealed envelope. He handed it to her.

Her heart sped up as she took it and noted the formal writing on its front side. "What is it?" she asked, voice low and face crimsoning slightly.

He glanced at the two other men in the room and simply responded to her, "I wasn't ignoring you." He touched the envelope with his right index finger. "Throw it away, if that's what you want. But this," he tapped it, "is what I want."

He turned to the two men. "I should go home. Curfew is in an hour—"

"Nonsense," the Judge quickly said. He motioned to the couch. "Sit down. The four of us are going to have a nice chat. If we stay longer than an hour, I will write an excuse for you, though I doubt we will be here that long."

As Carson slowly made his way over to the old couch and took a seat as far away from Judge James as he could manage, the Judge's gaze fell on Gina. "Open the letter and read it out loud. I would like to know its contents." He shot a damning scowl at Carson. "Just want to make sure Carson Owens is behaving appropriately with you."

Timothy suddenly defended, "Judge James, with all due respect, Carson and Gina have exchanged letters with each other for years. I've read every single letter that's ever passed between the two of them, and nothing inappropriate has ever caught my eye. Perhaps having her read the letter out loud is...an invasion of her privacy."

Gina was thankful for her father's words.

The Judge sat back down on the couch, only one seat away from Carson. He stared at Tim for a long moment before saying, "Only this morning Carson Owens was flogged. Thirty lashes for breaking curfew and bedding an unknown woman."

Gina's stomach somersaulted, but she wasn't sure if it was because the woman was definitely *not* unknown to the Judge or because he so flippantly spoke about Carson bedding someone.

He continued, "I am the Judge, and it is up to my discretion whether or not to allow a simple letter that Carson has taken the time to write your daughter to pass between them unchecked." His eyes darted over to Gina then, and they no longer felt kind. "You may read it to yourself first, but then you must hand it over to me for review."

She inhaled deeply and exhaled as she looked over the letter.

For the immediate and urgent attention of
Miss Moriah Ginevieve Blake

Sent with care and affection from
Mister Jerry Carson Owens

Slowly, she popped the seal and pulled the parchment from the envelope. Her stomach twisted as she read the letter, and she fought tears all the while.

Dearest Ginevieve,
 Though this letter may be reaching you too late, I would be remiss if I didn't attempt to write it regardless. I received your

letter late by accident. If you had thought I was ignoring you, I was not. I would never do such a thing, no matter what. If anything, your letter meant a lot to me. I had thought your feelings for me were long gone. All this time, I had thought that. Please forgive me for any ill feelings or pain my recent actions might have caused you. If only I had known to wait on you, I would not have hesitated to do so.

You are everything to me, G. If it is still a wish of yours, giving the Judge a formal request to marry you would please me greatly. I cannot imagine a life without you by my side, for I have tried and I have failed miserably—though I have learned I'm pretty good at fooling myself into thinking otherwise.

I do not blame you if you hate me. For the record, I hate me, too. Yet, I pray you'll forgive me, even though I can't forgive myself for what I've done to Anem's angel. I know I am undeserving of the grace I ask of you, yet I ask it of you fervently, with a promise that I will never hurt you again. I swear it on my very life.

Until all the stars in the sky dim with the promise of the end of time, I am forever yours.

Hopefully,
Jerry Carson Owens

Gina handed it to the Judge as soon as she finished reading it, her heart tumbling in her chest, mind racing.

As the Judge began reading, Carson's face reddened, and he tried hiding half of his face by turning it away from them, propping it against his hand which rested on the arm of the couch. He glanced over at her then, and their eyes locked for a whole second. Her face crimsoned to match his as she looked down at her hands resting in her lap. Her heart continued pounding away in her chest.

Judge James read the letter carefully, and she thought he probably read it more than once. Maybe even more than twice.

Carson exhaled loudly after a few more moments and turned to the Judge, his face still red. "Would you stop analyzing every word and just speak your mind?" Gina had never heard Carson so frustrated before, and he was speaking to the Judge, of all people.

He was gutsy, and she liked that about him. She couldn't help feel that familiar pull of her heart toward him. She reeled herself away forcefully and looked down at the carpet to avert her eyes, lest lustful thoughts enter her mind.

But it was too late. Her mind was already full of Carson, every part of him, and she hated how much of her heart he would always hold in his grasp.

She was always going to love him, wasn't she?

The Judge looked at him as he slowly folded the letter back up. He didn't respond to Carson, just gave him a once-over glare which felt quite menacing, and Gina was glad it wasn't her that he gave that look to. He then looked at Gina, but his eyes had morphed and softened the moment they fell upon her. Sweetly, he said as he handed the letter back to her, "I am going to be quite frank with you, Gina, dear. I am going to allow you to pick who you want to marry out of the top five I've chosen."

Carson butted in, "Am I in the top five?"

The Judge ignored him, though Gina thought it was a fair question. Why else keep him there? The Judge pulled a small folded paper from his coat pocket and handed it to her. "Those are the best matches for you, in my unbiased opinion." He glanced at Carson then back to Gina. "You may look over it tonight, but I am going to have to ask you to choose by tomorrow afternoon. It is necessary to close your case as soon as possible."

Gina didn't open the note as he spoke, so her father reached for it, and she allowed him to take it. She replied to Judge James while her father studied the names of the only five suitors the Judge would approve of her to wed, "Why must you close it? Is it time sensitive?"

He nodded once. "Indeed, it is. According to Deneb's law, once a

Judge has approved of a request to waive the age of consent to marry and agreed to find a husband for the to-be-bride, the teen must be married by a maximum of twenty days. I approved your request eighteen days ago. You have two days to be married."

28

Margaret hoped her back had healed enough to handle the bath water she drew for herself. She couldn't go any longer without bathing. She felt grimy and sticky and smelled worse than simply stale, especially under her arms. She couldn't stand herself.

Slowly, she eased her body down into the tub. Her wound stung only a small fraction, but after a couple of moments, it felt nice immersed in the steaming water.

She sat there for several long minutes submerged in the clear bath water, only her nose and above peeking from the surface. Finally, she washed herself, scrubbing every inch of her body save the massacre on her left shoulder.

She was grateful it was her left side that was affected since she was right-handed, and everything she tried to do with her left arm hurt like hell. She had been babying her left arm ever since the night before, and she wondered if she would have permanent nerve damage there. Would she never be able to use her left arm comfortably again? She was pessimistically positive the answer was no.

Abruptly, the door opened, and William stepped into the bathroom. A shrill of surprise escaped her, and she curled herself into a ball, glancing at the towel she had set out on her vanity. It was too far for her to reach without standing up and exposing herself completely, and she was not that brave. "William!" she exclaimed, breathless. "What the hell are you—"

"Relax," he said calmly, pulling out the stool tucked under the vanity where the towel sat. He set a white paper sack on the glass tabletop and gestured to it as he sat down on the stool. "I brought treats. You like pastries, right? You ate some vanilla cream-filled ones at our engagement celebration, so I got you three of those."

She didn't know what to say or how to react to him and how casual he was acting in front of her while she sat stark naked in her bathtub. She gripped her left arm and pulled it tighter against her chest to cover herself. The static pain of the movement and position shot through her shoulder, but she tried not to show it.

He watched her face carefully. She had a difficult time reading him. He wasn't daring to explore the rest of her body with his eyes, which was strange, Margaret thought, because she expected that of him. He had no qualms about it when she was fully dressed, and there she was, completely exposed yet his eyes stayed on her face.

"How's your shoulder?" he whispered after a couple of seconds.

She shifted her body weight and the water swooshed with the movement. "It's healing," she whispered back.

What the actual hell? Get out, William. She wished she was brave enough to say those things out loud, but her courage had retreated.

"And the pain?" His voice was soft—perhaps even worried— which also surprised Margaret.

She swallowed a painful knot in her throat. "When I'm careful, it doesn't hurt at all." She paused, and he didn't respond, so she added quietly, "I'm worried that I may have permanent nerve damage. I don't know if my left arm will ever be the same."

He simply shrugged. "At least your profession doesn't require physical labor, and you're not left-handed, correct?" He searched her eyes for confirmation.

"Correct," she breathed. She wished so hopelessly that he would leave.

He picked up the towel from her vanity then. Her heart slightly sped up with hope that he would give it to her, but he laid it on his lap and said, "You shouldn't have done that to yourself, Margaret. It was stupid." The way he said stupid was harsh and critical and meant to hurt deeply. Even though she didn't even do it to herself, she felt the guilt as if she had, and the label of *stupid* stuck in her head.

Yes, she had been stupid. But she didn't butcher her brand. That was not a choice she made, but it was one she would have to live with for the rest of her life.

Margaret glanced at the towel. "William?" she dared. "Can I please have that?" She desperately wanted to be covered.

He picked up the beige towel and surprised Margaret by sniffing it. "Mmm," he approved. "Smells like you." A chill spider-crawled up her spine, her stomach somersaulting. "Daisies and cherries." He smiled at her, and it was full of perversion.

She swallowed hard. "Why are you here?"

He tossed the towel haphazardly behind him, discarding it to the floor in a crumpled mess. "I told you. I brought you pastries. Thought it would be a nice gesture. You don't appreciate it?"

She shook her head, and strands of her wet hair stuck to her cheek. "It's not that. It's just... You're in my bathroom while I'm bathing." She paused a moment, and he just stared at her. His eyes ventured for half a second to her chest that she had difficulty covering and then quickly back to her face. "Please leave," she choked out. "I'm very uncomfortable with your presence."

He stood up with a sigh. She dared release a breath in relief, but it was premature. He began unbuttoning his uniform shirt and stripping it off. He folded it as he said, "It bothers you that the man you'll be sharing a bed with in just a couple of days sits in the same room with you as you bathe, yet a man whom you have no ties to politically or otherwise, you have shared every inch of your body with." He laid his neatly folded shirt on the vanity stool and looked over at Margaret. "If

241

I were Carson instead, would you have invited me into the bath with you the moment I walked in?"

She was appalled at his nerve. "How dare you?!" she exclaimed. "I am the Duchess!"

He stripped his trousers and undergarments in one quick sweep. Margaret stared down at the bath water. Her heart raced wildly in her chest. She prayed earnestly that Anem would deliver her from William.

Abruptly, he grabbed her jaw and turned her face to his. He was bent down next to the bath, not a thread of clothing on him, their faces inches apart. "You may be the Duchess," he said quietly and calmly, his eyes boring into hers, "but you're also secretly a harlot."

Fearful tears whelmed in her eyes. "Please," she rasped. "Just let me be."

How was she supposed to marry this man? Be his wife? Have his children?

His Mature eyes didn't look angry, but they didn't look like much of anything to Margaret. She couldn't read him at all. He loosened his hold on her jaw, stroking it with his thumb. Quietly, he said, "It was your choice, Margaret. You knew what you were doing when you bound yourself to him."

The tears fell in streams and mixed with the water seamlessly.

He continued as he wiped the tears away, "We are products of our own choices, and you've made some less-than-forgivable ones."

Her stomach twisted into a knot. *Less than forgivable.*

"But," he added, leaning in closer to her face. He brushed his lips against hers. She tried to pull away but his right hand held the back of her head in place and his left still gripped her jaw. "I have chosen to forgive you, Margaret. Now, thank me by inviting me into the bath with you."

She didn't say a word. The tears continued to cascade down her face.

He pressed his thin and unskilled lips against hers. The kiss was hard and unromantic. She kept her lips tightly pressed together, refusing to kiss him back. When he pulled his lips away, he ordered, his breath hot and curdling against her face, "Invite me in. It is the only polite thing to do now."

She replied, "You are not my husband yet. I will not—"

His right hand suddenly moved from the back of her head and gripped her left shoulder hard, sending pain jolting through her body. She screamed out in agony and tried to move away from his grip. He didn't let go of her shoulder as he stepped into the warm water and sat down across from her. Finally, he removed his hands from her and lounged back. She cradled her throbbing arm, her whole body tense from the pain.

She sat there, unmoving, for several long moments. She refused to look at him and was terrified of what events could and probably would follow. Finally, she whispered, "My father still checks my shoulder to medicate it. He'll see if I have another brand—"

"I'm not going to rape you," he bluntly said, and he sounded slightly offended she would suggest such a thing.

She cut her eyes at him, but he still didn't have any expression on his face. It was frustrating for Margaret. How was she supposed to know what to expect from him if his face didn't tell her beforehand?

He rolled his eyes at her right before she looked away. "I know I'm not a saint, Margaret James, but I'm no devil. And you know something interesting?" He waded through the short distance between them, and their bodies touched but only barely. Margaret tried to move away, but he only moved closer and pressed his body further against hers. He moved her wet hair that stuck to her face out of the way and cradled her jaw gently as he continued speaking, "You and I are the same. We are the in-between. Those that are neither good nor bad. The gray area, if you will."

The in-between. The gray area.

He was right. She couldn't deny it, though she desperately wished she could. She knew, beyond a shadow of a doubt, that on a scale of angels and devils, Gina would be the epitome of good and Carson would follow closely in second, while she lagged behind them a good twenty paces. She knew she could never catch up.

They were naturally good, and she was naturally neutral.

She craved things neither had any inclination toward. She had no self-control regarding certain sins, while they did a damn good job resisting temptation, for which she was immensely jealous.

Carson—she knew for sure—gave her a run for her money when she tried so desperately to get him to love her. Plenty of other boys would've given her anything she asked for the moment she asked for it, which was probably why Carson interested her the most. He wasn't so inclined to give her anything her heart and body desired. Not at first, at least. Over time she was able to break his resolve down, though little by little, and she would always carry the weight of that sin on her shoulders.

She was going to hell. She had tempted a righteous man into sin, and he had been publicly shamed and flogged for it. All the while she had been protected by the same hands who punished him.

Marriage to William was exactly the hell she deserved.

A few moments passed. Neither spoke a word. William finally moved away from her and resumed his lounging with a sigh that mimicked relief. She looked at him with a strange sort of curiosity, and he smiled at her. He said calmly, "If you like, I could help wash your back. Probably hard to reach with that injury, huh?"

She looked away, over at the towel crumpled on the floor near the door. She would have to expose herself for several seconds before reaching it. She debated whether it was worth dodging for or not. "That won't be necessary," she stated lowly.

"You said it's difficult to move your arm."

"My left arm, yes, but my right arm works just fine."

"Surely you still have difficulty. Are you sure you were able to reach everything?"

All fear had vanished. What became of her due to her next outburst didn't matter anymore to her. She just wanted so badly to tell him off. She snapped her head to him and angrily spouted, "For the love of Anem, you are not going to help me bathe, William. For one, I've already bathed myself, thank you very much. For two, you are *not* my husband. I may have sinned with my body in the past, but that does not mean I want to continue walking that path." The acid dripping from her words could not be mistaken. "Remove yourself from my bathroom immediately, or else my father will hear of this extremely uncomfortable and inappropriate situation you've forced me into."

He sat there for several seconds, watching her with no expression of his own. She wondered if he thought her anger would fizzle out and she would submit to the fear he evoked. He was sorely mistaken, if that were the case. She would be angry for a long, long time—if not forever.

William smiled at her and stood, unashamed of his body in the least. She turned her attention away and listened as he stepped out of the bath. He dried himself with the towel she'd set out for herself and then redressed slowly. No words were exchanged the whole time.

She peeked at him when she knew he had his pants on. In the middle of his back, she was surprised to see a brand. The small divine symbols created a perfect diamond that laid across the whole of his small back. It was astoundingly beautiful. Dare she consider it more beautiful than her own?

Had he been flogged for extramarital relations in the past? Was he never caught? Perhaps he sympathized with her more than he let on. Perhaps he was only there to show her his own brand in a roundabout, confusing sort of way.

What was his point?

After tucking in his buttoned-up shirt and lacing his boots back on his feet, he bent down next to the bath again. "I hope you like the pastries," he whispered, his eyes focused intently on hers, sorrow suddenly creeping into his voice.

She was desperately confused.

He didn't venture a single look over her naked body as he stood and turned his back to her. He left the bathroom quietly without a second glance.

29

Two days. Only two. That was all the law would give Gina to be married.

Carson's mind raced with disapproval, his heart with pain from seeing her brokenhearted, and the fear of the three of them choosing someone besides himself for Gina Blake. He thought maybe Timothy Blake would pick him, but after finding out about his brand with another woman, he wasn't so sure anymore.

If Carson had only stayed away from Margaret James during that vulnerable time...

"I've chosen," said Timothy Blake not but two seconds after the Judge completed his sentence about how she had to be married in two days. He looked over at Gina. "If you care for my opinion, that is." He pulled a pen out of his shirt pocket and circled a name on the parchment. Carson itched to know not only who he picked, but if it was him. Was he even an option?

Mr. Blake handed the paper back to Gina, and she looked at it for a few seconds longer than Carson was comfortable with.

"It's your decision," the Judge reminded her.

"Yes," agreed Mr. Blake, motioning with his hands. "It's always up to you, darling."

She glanced up at her father and then at Carson for half a second before returning her eyes to the paper. She cleared her throat and said to the Judge, "I have chosen."

Mr. Blake smiled at Carson, and Carson wondered if that meant he had picked his name from the lot of suitors.

Gina handed the paper to the Judge. "Robert Collins."

Mr. Blake's smile disappeared instantly, and his eyebrows furrowed heavily over his eyes. "Gina?" It was only a whisper. Obviously she hadn't picked the same man that her father had chosen for her.

She made eye contact with him. "I've chosen," she repeated. "You must excuse me, I am terribly exhausted. Have a good night." And then she stood and left the room without another glance at Carson like he had been hoping.

Carson's heart shattered into a million pieces. The pieces settled uncomfortably and painfully in his stomach. He wondered if that was how it felt for Gina when she found out earlier that day that he had been arrested for extramarital relations. He had shared himself with someone other than her. He couldn't imagine if it were the other way around, how much it would hurt him knowing she had allowed and maybe enjoyed another man besides himself touching her.

What would he have done? Would he have been as calm as she was? His heart would surely ache forever.

An image of two unclothed figures wrapped around each other in a dark, secret place clawed its way into Carson's mind—unrelenting and unforgiving. It was everything he didn't want to imagine: eagerness, passion, insatiable hunger. Bare legs intertwined. Swollen lips trapped between teeth. Breath heavy and hot against skin. Gina's golden locks entangled in another man's ravenous clutch.

Carson's fists tightened into a ball, knuckles white. The mere thought... He couldn't stand it.

If she had been the one with a brand, he would replay that horrible scene, true or not, over and over and over until he'd go mad. He would never forget her sin, no matter how much forgiveness he would give. He would always remember.

Yet, that was not what happened. She was not the one who had sinned with her body. She was not the one in need of forgiveness.

From the other side of the couch, Carson caught a glimpse of the paper the Judge still held open right before he folded it, and he noted the name of the man Timothy Blake had chosen for his daughter, circled in black ink: *Jerry Carson Owens*. Right above his name, though, was the name *Daniel Robert Collins*.

Bobby. Carson ground his teeth together. Bobby and Gina knew each other, though not well, and Bobby wasn't a bad guy. That was at least comforting for Carson. He would never hurt Gina. But if he ever did, Carson would murder that son of a harlot.

But I hurt her. Carson's jaw relaxed ever so slightly. *She deserves better than me.*

"Well, then," Mr. Blake said, a sigh on the edge of his words. "I don't know about either of you, but that was quite surprising." He shook his head. Then he leaned toward Carson and mumbled, "He's your friend, right? Do you think he'd be a good match for her? I don't think so myself, but you must know him well."

"I—"

"Why do you ask him?" the Judge said sharply, interrupting Carson. Carson thought he was acting incredibly rude toward Mr. Blake, never mind himself. "He's going to say no to make himself look better."

Mr. Blake wrinkled his nose and shot back, "Mark, you saw the paper. Clearly, I think the best option for my daughter is Carson Owens."

Carson shifted awkwardly. They were acting as if he wasn't sitting right there, a few feet from each of them.

"And clearly your daughter disagrees," the Judge replied stoically.

"She's just angry," defended Mr. Blake, waving his hand. "Don't settle for Robert quite yet. She barely found out today about Carson having a lover. Let her mull it all over."

Judge James exhaled a puff of air and looked down at the ground. "She's overwhelmed."

"Exactly. She'll give you her final decision by tomorrow, as you said you needed. I bet it'll change from Robert to Carson once she's thought about it."

"Why?" squeaked Carson. He cleared his throat, redness returning to his face. He looked away from them as he said lowly, "Why would she change her mind? Bobby isn't a bad choice for a husband. He's a good guy."

Mr. Blake stared at Carson for a few moments, his graying eyebrows gathering over his eyes slowly as the seconds passed. Finally, he said, catching Carson by surprise, "He's gay, Carson."

The possibility of Bobby being gay wasn't foreign to Carson, but he hadn't realized anyone else had thought the same of his friend. He had considered briefly a few years ago that Bobby could be interested in boys and girls—if not only boys—but being they weren't allowed to ask questions and that being gay would label you the most unproductive and useless member of the community, Carson had ignored his curiosity. It hadn't mattered to him anyway. It was interesting to Carson that of all people, Mr. Blake had thought as much about Bobby as he had.

Carson shrugged. "At least you know he won't touch her."

The Judge exhaled loudly. "Apparently you aren't surprised about this assumption, Carson." There was a hidden question in his statement.

"I'm simply observant," he replied. "He never seems interested in girls. That's all." He looked down at his hand fisted in his lap.

"Do you know if he has a male lover? Because, if he does, he's automatically disqualified from this list." The Judge held up the paper with the five names on it.

"How would I know?" Carson rolled his shoulders, shrugging. "I imagine he does not, but only because he's an adamant rule follower." He looked at Judge James. "An outstanding citizen."

"Your father said the same thing about you, and look what happened."

Carson was silent as the Judge continued staring at him. Finally, Carson barked, "One rule, that was all. And I am repentant."

"Two rules. And are you really repentant, Owens?" It sounded more like a warning than a question. "You aren't going to see your lover again?"

Carson replied timely, "My past is behind me. The girl is part of my past."

He grunted, "How dismissive. As if she means nothing to you. As if you simply used her."

"You don't like that answer?" Carson was growing tired of the berating. "Would you like a different one? Would you like me to say I plan on seeing her continuously for the rest of my life? While she's single, while she's married, while she's pregnant with children from her husband? Shall I say that instead, Judge James? Would you prefer *that* answer?"

"I would not," he growled. "I want you to stay away from her."

Carson was amused at how easy it was to irritate him. He said calmly to the man, "What do you want me to say? I'll say it."

The Judge was quiet for a moment, the corners of his jaw pulsing with strain from clenching his teeth together. He said quietly, "The truth. That is the answer I want."

Honestly, Carson replied, "I will never touch her again, I swear it."

Mr. Blake suddenly cut in, "I feel that perhaps this conversation has become much more personal. Shall I leave?"

"This is your home," Carson said before the Judge could answer, and he stood up to dismiss himself. "I should leave. I apologize for intruding."

Judge James stood up too. He said to Mr. Blake, "Forgive me if I've overwhelmed Gina, Tim. Truly. I hadn't considered everything she's been through today."

"It's definitely been a long day for her," replied Mr. Blake softly, glancing back at the hall Gina had disappeared down. "I wish I could take away all the pain she's ever experienced. I love that little girl more than life itself." He looked at Carson then. "Do me a favor. Don't leave yet. You should speak to Gina, like you intended."

The Judge gave Carson a wary look, but Carson just shrugged and replied to Mr. Blake, "She said she was tired. I would rather not keep her awake."

"Please, Carson. You should have a chance to make your case."

"He did," the Judge replied. "In the letter."

"No, I didn't," he argued, crossing his arms over his chest. "I didn't even touch on an explanation for my behavior. The letter was only meant to be a reply to the one she sent me."

"An explanation for your behavior, huh?" The Judge motioned with his hands for Carson to sit back down as he took his own seat again. "Perhaps you'll give me this said explanation first. I'd love to hear your excuses."

Carson hesitated, glancing at Mr. Blake who also seemed hesitant. But, both of them sat down slowly. Mr. Blake said, "Gina should be here."

Carson shook his head. "It's okay, sir. Let her rest. I will come over first thing in the morning to speak with her. I promise."

The Judge waved his hand at Carson to hurry him along. "Enough chit-chat. We don't have all night."

Just as Carson opened his mouth to make a snide remark, Gina walked back into the room. He closed his mouth quickly, snapping it shut audibly. They stared at her as she just stood there glancing between the three of them.

"Gina, honey?" questioned Mr. Blake. "Is there something you want to say?"

She closed her puffy eyes and cleared her throat. Had she been crying? The sight gripped Carson's heart. Finally, she whispered, "I have some questions for Carson. I would prefer to ask him privately, but if that cannot happen, I will settle for asking him here and now."

The Judge and her father both gazed over at Carson before Tim said to Gina, "I am okay with stepping into the foyer for a few minutes. I can still see the two of you in here, but I won't be able to hear you. Is that private enough for you?"

The Judge protested immediately, "That is not appropriate, Tim." He shook his head. "It's a wonder that Gina wasn't his lover. Now I understand why we received so many tips pointing toward her."

Carson opened his mouth to defend Mr. Blake and Gina, but Mr. Blake could defend himself and his daughter without anyone's assistance. He clipped, "How inappropriate of a Judge to take a case so personally. Carson's, I mean. And why is that, Mark? Is it because he's Derek's son? Doubtful. Is it because his lover is someone you love more than life itself?"

There was a cold silence that suddenly swept the room. Carson's insides flipped every which way, and he wondered if Mr. Blake really knew it was Margaret. How could he know, though?

After several moments lapsed, Mr. Blake added lowly, "Don't you dare speak an ill word of my daughter again, Mark James, and I won't speak of yours."

The Judge hesitated and then glanced over at Gina. "Did you tell him?"

Carson blinked, confused. Needles of embarrassment and horror pricked his skin, traveling slowly up his back, over his neck, and onto his face.

"No," she breathed, "of course not."

Mr. Blake glanced at her. "You knew it was the Duchess?"

Carson couldn't stay quiet any longer. "Both of you know?" He was horrified.

Mr. Blake shook his head. "It was a wild guess, honestly, but all of you have confirmed it for me." He looked at his daughter then. "But I am surprised you know. Now I understand."

Pregnant silence filled the room. Carson thought it impossible to die of embarrassment, but if it were, he would've kilt over right then without a doubt.

Gina broke the silence and asked, "May I please have a moment with Carson? Five minutes will suffice."

Carson wanted more than anything to speak with Gina alone, especially now that she knew Margaret was his lover. That, horrifyingly, made everything so much worse. It would be easier to ask her to forget his sinful past if she couldn't put a face to the brand on his shoulder, but now she could. How could he ask her to forget something like that?

Mr. Blake looked at the Judge. "Five minutes won't hurt, Mark."

Judge James looked at Carson then Gina. "Fine," he grunted after a moment. "Five minutes." And the two men walked out of the living room and into the foyer where they stood too far away to hear a conversation whispered between the two Immatures, but they could clearly see them.

Gina sat down where Judge James had been sitting. Carson was very still, and though he finally could speak freely to Gina, he had no idea what to say or where to even begin.

She wouldn't make eye contact with him, and that bothered him, though he could understand her discomfort. She stared at the carpet as she whispered, "Why her?"

His heart squeezed painfully at her question, but he didn't hesitate to tell her anything she wanted to know. "She was the first person that gave me attention after you."

She was quiet for a few moments as she processed his answer. Finally, she asked her second question, "Do you love her?"

Somehow that question felt incredibly familiar, but he answered immediately anyway, pushing the feeling of *déjà vu* away, "I think so. But it's not the same as with you."

"What does that even mean?" she clipped.

"No one could replace you, Gina, no matter how hard I tried. I'll always love you unlike anyone else." It was the truest and most vulnerable thing he had said that evening, and he was nervous at her reaction to it.

She glanced over at him for a moment, and a tear escaped her eye. She quickly wiped it away as she looked back down at the carpet. "I didn't mean to hurt you, Carson. I know I did when I pushed you away. I had no idea at the time that you were hurt by my actions. In fact, that's what I was trying to prevent, believe it or not."

He was quiet for a moment, trying to make sense of what she was attempting to explain. Finally, it was his turn to ask a question. "Why did you push me away? I thought we were in a good place."

She nodded and more tears fell down her face. She wiped them with her sleeve as she whispered, "*We* were, Carson, but *I* wasn't."

"That makes no sense."

She glanced at the foyer. Her father made a hand motion as if asking if she needed him, but she waved at him to stay there. She turned her attention back to Carson then. "My father told me I should have told you a long time ago, and I think he was right."

Carson readjusted himself on the couch, nerves crawling.

"When my mother died, as you know, my whole world collapsed. Your family was the only reason my family didn't completely sink." She paused. Carson was patient though. "*You* were the only reason *I* didn't completely sink... Then we got closer. Really close." Her voice lowered. "Then you kissed me, and it was nice. But it was also not nice." His stomach turned. "My mental health couldn't handle everything."

He suddenly understood what she was trying to tell him, but he remained silent for her.

"I was skipping therapy—which was stupid. I stopped taking my medication—also stupid. I stopped eating." She made eye contact with him again. "I wanted to die, Carson, but I didn't want you to be close to me if it happened. I didn't want to hurt you because... I knew how much the death of someone you love hurt. I didn't want to hurt you."

Carson scooted over to her quickly as she finished her sentence, and she didn't move away from him. She welcomed his embrace. He hugged her to his chest, squeezing her tightly, truly realizing how fragile life was in that moment, that he could very well not have had that chance to hold her like he was.

His own tears began cascading down his cheeks as he considered the abominable thought of her life—of who she was, her very soul— being wasted. Gone forever. He buried his face into her hair that smelled how it always had to hide his tears from her father and the Judge. They were undoubtedly still watching and perhaps about to interrupt them because he was holding her to himself so firmly. Touching her at all was surely going to get him in trouble.

In that moment, though, as he inhaled the sweet vanilla in her hair, he didn't care what they thought, what they would say. He just wanted to hold Gina. Especially if it was for the last time.

"It would kill me if you died, Ginevieve," he told her. "There's no distance you could push me that it wouldn't hurt to find out you were gone forever."

He honestly didn't know what else to say. The information that Gina had suffered through so much mentally when she pushed him away clenched painfully at his heart. He remembered thinking something was wrong, but he never thought it was as bad as it had been.

Just as Carson predicted, Judge James and Mr. Blake walked back in. The Judge said, "Unhand each other," but it wasn't angry or even commanding. It was more sorrowful than anything else. Had they heard their conversation despite the whispering?

Carson let go of her and ducked his head to wipe the wetness from his face quickly. "I apologize," he said in a normal voice.

"Please don't do that. Don't apologize," said Gina, still whispering. Her face laid in her palms and the tears streamed over them too. She could not contain the emotion leaking out of her any longer. "I needed that from you. I really needed it. Thank you."

No one said anything. Carson wanted to hug her again, but it wasn't appropriate, and he had already been told to unhand her once.

Mr. Blake squatted down in front of Gina then. He touched her hair lovingly and asked, "Honey, why don't you go to bed? You've had a long day. You can give your final answer to the Judge tomorrow evening. C'mon." Gina stood up from the couch with her father's encouragement, and he led her down the hall from their sight.

The Judge turned to Carson. "Tim won't say anything about Margaret."

"Good," replied Carson, wiping the last of the tears from his face. "That's relieving to hear."

"No thanks to you. You're the one that got her into this mess."

Carson didn't reply. There was no argument to be made in his favor.

The Judge let out an exasperated puff of air. "Tim is adamant that Gina's going to pick you by tomorrow afternoon. And I must say, from what I've seen this evening..." He paused for a second, glancing back down the hall as Mr. Blake re-emerged. The Judge looked back at Carson. "I'll be surprised if she doesn't pick you. She loves you, and you obviously love her too. That just begs the question for me, though: What about my daughter, Carson? What was she to you? Because she loves you just as Gina loves you, and I can't be sure that you didn't take advantage of those feelings."

Mr. Blake butted in then, and Carson was grateful for the interruption. "It's twenty minutes until curfew. Perhaps both of you should head home." And so, both Carson and Judge James left the Blakes' that evening, with only twenty minutes to spare and no further words exchanged, just simply a parting glare from the Judge.

30

William Lach exhaled heavily as he closed the door to his empty living quarters.

"Forgive me, Margaret," he whispered to himself as he began walking toward his own bathroom and undressing, preparing for a long, hot shower. He wished he didn't have to act so crudely toward her, but she was a textbook-example of a wildcard—one he hadn't exactly been trained to handle.

His one and only purpose for being there was to protect her. If he screwed up, his commander would have his head. The strict man had promised William as much when he'd stationed him there and told him to stay close to the James girl. *By any means necessary*—those were his orders. William intended to carry them out as close to perfection as he could, but the girl wasn't making it easy on him.

And perhaps there was a better way of getting Margaret to submit to him and remain docile, but he wasn't an expert in psychology and had no idea how to make that happen besides creating fear inside her. Fear always worked, in his experience.

She needed to be afraid of disappointing him. She had to be if he was going to keep her safe. He wished it weren't that way—he honestly did—but there was no better option.

He thought Margaret to be a nice girl with a wild side, which wouldn't be cause for concern in the Kingdom of Soutas, the place he had called home for years despite their understandable prejudice against Matures. But in the Provinces—where the Matures ruled over the Immatures—Margaret's wild heart was dangerous and had to be controlled. She was unsafe as long as she allowed her heart to rule her.

Carson, on the other hand, was just as William expected him to be when he met him. A quiet man with no wild side about him whatsoever. Just like Derek Owens, in fact.

The commander had warned William about Derek and his intuition during the briefing before his mission commenced. "Stay away from him," he had told William. "He will, no doubt, find you suspicious. After long, he'll investigate. Steer clear of him if this happens. You will *not* be able to fool him."

And he was right. The moment Carson had been arrested, William noticed Derek giving him too wary of a look for him to be comfortable. So, he backed away from Officer Owens. Even treated him badly at work, as his superior. He wasn't sure if that was the right way to handle it, but what else could he do? He felt as if he was spiraling down, down, down, and any sense of control he had before had slipped from his grasp. The stress of that wore heavily on his shoulders, and a monster headache throbbed at his temples.

William stood in the hot shower for a long time thinking over everything. He was going to marry the James girl in just two days, and Carson Owens had a brand with the girl. Despite the bond between the two teenagers, they were surprisingly accepting of their supposed fate where the future held no significance for them as a couple. In fact, Carson seemed to be enamored by another girl entirely—which made William think he didn't actually love Margaret.

William supposed that was okay, though. The boy was only seventeen, and there were worse sins.

Faintly, a beep sounded in the next room. His stomach tossed. Quickly, he turned off the shower and wrapped a towel around himself. He hurriedly made his way to the nightstand by the bed.

He took a shabbily manufactured handheld device out of the first drawer. The tech had been hidden under a secret compartment William had installed. He clicked it on to see what message awaited him, his nerves wrecked from not hearing from the commander— toka, as was the man's title in the Soutan tongue—in nearly two months.

Report in, was all it read, the symbols foreign to the Provinces, though not to William. He had learned the language of the Forgotten Isle years ago, and though he didn't consider himself fluent like the natives, he knew enough to communicate effectively.

William sat down on the edge of the bed, still wrapped in a towel, and he spent the next ten minutes carefully typing up a detailed report over all the happenings and his solutions to the problems. He ended the report with a request for advice on how to handle the James girl.

He waited for a good thirty minutes before the tech beeped again with a new message. *Continue as you are. She is only a child and will obey you as long as you remain strict. Stay away from Owens family. They are not your responsibility. A friendly will soon arrive to watch over them. Remember: your main mission is Kristina Margaret James. Keep her safe, by any means necessary. Her life is worth more than yours.*

He sighed, disappointed in the answer though not surprised. *Aye, toka,* he typed in the Soutan tongue. *Tuxiish alhui vey.* And, what he said was true; he was ready to give his life.

After waiting five more minutes, another beep sounded from the tech. *Stay low and alert. Do not compromise your mission. Will contact for follow-up report in two weeks. Do not reply. Niu'herg.*

William slid the device back into the compartment in the drawer. *Niu'herg,* he thought solemnly, mulling over the wedding that was to take place soon. *Congratulations on your special occasion? Really?* The toka's joke did not amuse him even a little. He pinched the skin between his eyebrows, his head ducked.

William Lach did not want to marry the Duchess, and he didn't think his wife would approve of such drastic measures—though she would understand since she, too, owed the toka her life. As promised,

William would do everything in his power, by any means necessary, to ensure the safety of the James girl. His wife would understand.

"*Tuxiish alhui vey,*" he whispered out loud, repeating what he had told the toka, and he truly meant what he had said. He was ready to give his life for the forgotten countrymen's cause, for the Kingdom of Soutas. He just hoped it wouldn't come to that and Margaret would submit to the fear he evoked.

31

The toka clicked his tech off and shoved it in his satchel. The bandana around his mouth and nose threatened to slip off. He pulled the knot tighter behind his head. His skin, hair, and clothing had a layer of grime coated on it. He couldn't wait until he was home again. It had been more than three months since seeing his wife and daughter—and since taking a real shower.

He climbed the steep sand dune where one of his soldiers laid on his stomach at the top, binoculars held firmly to his eyes. He'd been on lookout duty for over three hours, and the sun was unforgiving.

William proved to be an adequate spy, as the toka knew he would, but he needed help as he had personally taken on more than he could handle—which he also knew he would do. William was an overachiever, and he was desperate for a pat on the head from the toka of the Soutan military forces. And, the toka assumed that if he did well enough, perhaps he would pat him on the head and tell him he was proud of the little monster he had rescued from certain death by execution all those years ago when the kid was just eighteen.

The good thing about William having a youthful appearance was that he passed as a much younger man more easily than most of his comrades. The other soldiers made fun of his "baby face," but the toka saw an opportunity that couldn't be wasted: the experience of a seasoned warrior in the body of a young, barely Matured man—

which, of course, was the lie. William was thirty years of age, and he was a very skilled warrior. One of the forgotten countrymen's best it had to offer, in fact.

The man at the top of the dune on lookout must have heard him coming and knew it was him. "There is no news, toka," he said, voice low.

Michael removed the binoculars when the toka laid down on his stomach next to him. He handed the binoculars over to him as he asked, "Are you sure it's nearly time?"

The toka squinted in the direction of Polaris from where he and his subordinate laid in the very outskirts of the Red Desert. He looked through the binoculars as he continued speaking, "Positive."

"It's just that you had said last month it could be another year before—"

"We can't wait another year," the toka snapped, removing the binoculars and glaring at the man.

Michael was quiet for a few moments before he finally stated, "You are worried about the Ritual."

The toka didn't respond.

Michael continued, placing his hand on the toka's shoulder, and speaking as a friend instead of a subordinate, "We know how to remove the Matures. You no longer have to worry about grabbing him before he turns eighteen."

The toka spit to the side. "Some of them don't wake up. Like you." He looked at Michael. "What if he's one of you? An Unwoken, I mean."

"What if your brother is one?"

He breathed out a single laugh. "Derek's a fighter. I know he is. They think they know him, but deep inside, where it matters..." He took his fist and beat his chest twice over his heart. "My brother is still there, and he would never allow a monster to live his life for him. But the boy... I can't say. I never met him."

"You have to have faith in the blood that runs through them both. They carry the Owens name, after all. Royalty."

Toka snarled. "Royalty. *Irwiiktu.*"

"It's not ridiculous," defended Michael. "You are the toka of the Gaalé Branch, commander of the Soutan military. By their own definition, your blood is royal."

He rolled his eyes. "I am only toka because my wife refused the position when her father passed. Many disapprove of me because I am not of the late toka's bloodline."

Michael shrugged. "Technically, neither is she."

"Enough talk." He quickly stood up, handing the binoculars back to Michael.

Michael stood with him, blinking his electric-blue Mature eyes against the ruddy sand that gathered on the tail of the sudden breeze. He used his fist and slammed it over the left side of his chest, and he bowed his head in respect.

The toka and Michael were quiet for a few long moments. Finally, he broke the news, though he assumed Michael already knew it, "I am sending your sister into the Province tonight."

Michael puckered his lips in thought. "Is Will needing backup?"

"Margaret James is taxing on him, apparently. He's having a hard time managing her." Toka crossed his arms over his chest. "While he watches over her, your sister will watch over my family."

Michael shrugged his shoulders. "As long as the two of them avoid each other, I'm sure Britt will prove herself to be an exceptional spy."

He ignored Michael's statement. He had already warned Britt to not speak to or even look in William's direction. He was hoping she would keep her hands to herself, and he wondered if he was making a mistake trusting her. "According to William, my brother married Kayla Pierce, and, besides the boy, they have an eleven-year-old daughter. She will be assigned to all four of them."

"Would you like me to brief her for you?" He rubbed his hands together, a sly smile playing on his lips.

"She is already briefed and ready to go. She will be heading in tonight and be settled into her position by morning. Her first day at her new job is tomorrow."

"You were able to get her a position so quickly?"

"I anticipated Margaret would give William some trouble. She's a James girl, after all. I had her go in and apply for the position weeks ago. I'm surprised she didn't tell you."

"She never tells me anything," said Michael, rolling his eyes. "So what job did she get?"

"Secretary to Judge James."

Michael laughed, and it was brimming with delight. "Oh, she's going to hate that."

The toka shrugged. "She doesn't have to like it. It gets her close to the Judge and his work. Plus, it's a better job considering the other option."

"Which was?"

"The school is in need of a custodian."

Michael's laugh was boisterous. "They'd weed her out quickly in that job! She can't even be bothered to clean her own home." He laughed again, wiping at his eyes, and sighed. Then he asked, tone much more serious, "Do I have time to pray with her?"

"Yes. She is packing to leave right now." Toka stuck out his hand and shook Michael's. "Give her a word for me. Keep a close eye on the boy. Let's hope he doesn't screw anything up for us. I pray he's nothing like me...or Kayla. Speaking of which, your sister should steer clear of that woman. Make her angry, and it's the very last thing you'll ever do."

"Sounds like you're speaking from experience."

He didn't respond. He simply reached up and scratched at the scar on the side of his cheek, recalling the last thing Kayla Pierce had ever said to him: '*Go to hell, Drew, and never come back.*' And then she threw a knife at him.

Kayla Pierce was the only person who had ever come that close to killing Drew Owens, and she was only sixteen at the time. And nine months pregnant, to top it off.

He was lucky to be alive.

PART 3

THE ANGEL
HE LOVED

32

The goddess was probably tired of hearing her repeat the same heartfelt plea for deliverance, but Gina Blake prayed it again anyway. Was it wrong to want a different life? A *better* life? A life where her family did not need to forgo something as basic as jelly on their biscuits just to afford medicine. Was that too much to ask?

Gina laid out the simple breakfast she had prepared for her still-slumbering family: eggs and plain biscuits made from scratch. Lilli Ann's stirring whines had Gina scurrying from the kitchen to the bedroom. The last thing she needed was a screaming, sick child. She didn't think her mind could hold up under any more pressure.

"Good morning, Annie," she cooed, picking the two-year old from her crib and holding her close. "Did you sleep well?"

Still half asleep, the child responded by snuggling into her and sighing deeply.

"You want more sleep?" Gina whispered as she gently bounced her baby sister back to sleep.

Am I just selfish?

Gina carried the child back to the kitchen, all the while humming gently and rocking Lilli Ann. Pausing before the sink, Gina stared out the window at the foggy morning. She loved her sister—and brothers—with every beat of her aching heart. But was it wrong to not want the burden of mothering them?

Once her brothers and father woke, they all enjoyed a rowdy breakfast with her brothers moaning the whole time about the lack of grape jelly. Soon, she thought, she would not have to go without grape jelly. Soon she would be able to afford such a luxury.

Curfew had been lifted for only an hour when a knock sounded at the door. Gina was elbow-deep in the warm dishwater at the sink. She looked over her shoulder at Asher and Sean coloring pictures at the table. "Boys," she called, "please answer the door."

The oldest, Sean, jumped up from the table. "I've got it, sis!" he yelled, as if she was hard of hearing.

Gina began drying her arms as she listened for who was at the door. A few seconds passed before the door creaked open and Sean shouted, "Carson!"

Her stomach tossed.

Asher crowed, "Carson?" as he jumped out of the chair he was squatted in and ran for the front door.

"Hey!" Carson's voice held a note of genuine affection. "Looky here. My two favorite littles." The boys giggled at something he did.

Gina's heart ached from his kindness toward them. Carson was always so good with her brothers. If she were honest with herself, she would admit that she missed him dearly and wanted no one but him. But after what he did with Margaret...

"Is your sister home?" he asked.

"Yup! C'mon!" they chirped.

Hurriedly, Gina unrolled her sleeves from her elbows and tugged on her white blouse, trying to make herself as presentable as possible. Her golden curls were loosely tied at the back of her neck with a blood-red ribbon to match her ankle-length pleated skirt. Her hair might not have been appropriate as defined by the rules, but at least she was dressed for the day. Although, she was missing her stockings and pumps, which, for half a second, she was acutely self-conscious about.

But it was only Carson. They had run barefoot together through the wheat fields behind the house multiple times in the past.

She spun around on her bare feet and strolled quickly from the kitchen to the foyer just as the boys were dragging Carson into the house, one boy hooked on each arm.

"Hi, Ginevieve." His voice was low, soft, delicate. Perhaps he thought he would break her further. He would be mistaken. She was shattered and there wasn't much more he could do to hurt her.

The boys jumped on Carson. "Will you take us to the park, Carson? Like you used to? Do you remember? You took us to the park a lot a long time ago." They tugged on him roughly as they wrestled for his attention.

"I remember," he told them, ruffling their hair. "But today I am busy. I'm sorry."

"Aw." Asher pouted.

Sean asked, "What do you need to do? Maybe we can help with your chores! It'll be faster, and then you can play with us at the park!"

"Yeah!" agreed Asher.

Carson chuckled and rubbed a knot on the child's blonde head. "I wish you could help me, but these are grown-up things that I need to do."

Sean crossed his arms over his chest. Bluntly, he said, "Oh yeah? I'm old enough to handle it!"

Gina sighed quietly. The poor child had inherited their father's personality. She glanced at Carson only to find him watching her.

"Well," Carson began, looking back down at Sean. "You could tell your sister to marry me. That's why I'm here, to ask her to be my wife."

A knot twisted in Gina's stomach, and her face flooded with heat. She wanted to run away, but both of the boys had turned to her and leaped at her, grabbing her skirt, demanding she agree to marry Carson.

She held up her hands to silence them but they wouldn't stop. "Enough!" she finally shouted. Immediately, the room became still. They were not used to hearing her yell. Pinching the skin between her eyebrows, she sighed. "Boys, please go do something else. I need to speak with Carson privately."

They ducked their heads and dragged their socked feet all the way to their room.

"Sorry," Carson said once they were gone. "I didn't mean to—"

"Please leave," she whispered, refusing to look at him. The heat in her face was still blazing. "I don't want you here."

That was a lie. She was unsure how she felt about him currently, but she was hyper-aware that, oddly and disappointingly, she wanted him there with her. If he was there with her, he couldn't be anywhere else. She liked that quite a bit.

He stepped up to her—so very close—and she was unsure why she didn't step away from him. She should step away. He grabbed her hand and held it gently in his own warm hand.

She liked him touching her. She really, really liked it.

"G," he whispered. His breath was warm on her face but not unpleasant. She refused to look at him despite the strong urge in her soul. "I beg you to reconsider. I realize I screwed everything up. This is my fault. I should've asked you for a clearer answer. I should've been here for you."

She shook her head and pulled her hand from his. "I told you to give me space, and you did. I guess I just assumed you knew I didn't mean forever."

"It was a misunderstanding."

She didn't reply.

"I acted like a jerk."

To that, she agreed, "Yes, you were."

They were both quiet again. She could feel her body pulling toward Carson's like a magnet. She would not give in. She took half a step back.

Carson also took half a step back. Perhaps he was afraid he had made her uncomfortable. "If you choose Bobby, I can respect your choice. But you should know, you will not be happy with him."

Finally, she met his eyes with her own. A prick of irritation gnawed at her, and it came through in her tone. "It is not your place to say who could make me happy, Carson."

Carson sighed but didn't look away from her. "You're right."

His eyes, milk chocolate discs floating in fresh milk, sparkled in the morning light. They were kind and beautiful and perfect—as usual. Her thoughts made her blush harder than she already was, and so she looked away from his stare to the floor.

He said, "Surely you know Bobby is not interested in women."

"Did he tell you that?"

He was quiet for a moment. "No," he admitted. "But I'm sure."

She shook her head. "You can't be sure without him admitting so himself. Besides, what makes you think that I am not relieved to have a husband that doesn't want to touch me?"

Carson was the only man she really wanted, and if she wasn't going to allow herself to have him, she didn't want to be with anyone else. A gay husband would be a blessing in disguise.

"I suppose," he sighed. "If that's what you want." He was quiet for a long moment before he continued. "I can make you happy. I know right now I cannot, but later, whether a few months or a few years, you'll be happy with me. But you will only be getting married once, and you're being forced to decide today who your husband will be. Please... Reconsider. Take a few moments and imagine your future with Bobby."

She paused and considered. She saw herself not unhappy, but perhaps not quite the version of happiness she would like. But at least she would not be unhappy.

Carson waited a few seconds while she thought before he said, "Now imagine your future married to me. Please try to imagine it after forgiveness has been given. After we have children together. Fifteen, twenty, thirty years from now. Try to imagine it."

Gina didn't have to try. She had been imagining their future together for years. But now the future she imagined was a bit bitter.

Several children—some blonde with green eyes like her, some with dark hair and dark eyes like Carson—would run around, playing and laughing. Her heart would burst with love simply watching them.

Carson would come home from work, kiss each child on the head, and go to kiss his wife. "How was your day?" he would ask. She would reply that it was fine, that the children kept her on her toes. He would kiss her again and tell her he loved her. All would seem well and perfect.

Until, of course, he would be late coming home one evening—maybe two or three evenings. Gina would find out Margaret would be back in town from her apprenticeship in the District with her mother. And it wouldn't be hard to figure out from there where he'd been spending his time after work. Her heart would rip to shreds.

Would he even do such a thing, though?

When she blushed and looked away from him a second time, Carson stepped closer to her again. He grabbed both her hands and squeezed once. "Are you thinking of it? What about children? You wanted several."

Her stomach knotted as her mind tossed at her imaginations of three or four children running around in their backyard, laughing and enjoying a carefree life. She had wanted several children, but that was before her mother died from childbirth. She still wanted kids, but she was terrified of giving birth. Not that she had a choice. Every able-bodied woman was required to give at least two children to the world in obedience with Anem's commandments.

She pulled her hands away and looked up at him, but she did not step back. She whispered to him, and he leaned down closer to her face, "I don't know what to do about my feelings for you, Carson. You have hurt me." Tears gathered in her eyes.

His face changed. Guilt mixed with sorrow painted him. He pulled her into his arms abruptly and squeezed her tightly, grabbing a handful of her hair and pressing her head into his chest. "I cannot apologize enough times to make it better. Yet... I am deeply sorry. I never meant to hurt you. You are my favorite person in this world, and that will never change."

"It might."

"It can't. Even marrying someone else and growing old with them, I can assure you that I will always love you more."

She rolled her eyes, though he couldn't see. "You're an idiot." But she didn't mean it, and her tone suggested the same.

He chuckled. "Perhaps. But I'm your idiot."

Mine. She leaned into him harder, so he held her tighter. *He's mine.*

She wanted to kiss him. But she also wanted him to stop touching her.

But she wanted to kiss him more.

Gina tilted her head up to look at him. He did not loosen his embrace. Not a second passed before he leaned down, a question in his eyes if he was overstepping or misreading her cues. He was not misreading.

She told herself to *pull away, pull away, pull away.* Her body did not want to, but she obeyed the inner voice.

"I love you," he whispered when she hesitated. "I always have, and I always will. I will never hurt you again. Choose me, Ginevieve. I will be the best husband. Faithful and loving. On my life and on the lives of our future children, I swear it."

She wanted nothing more than to say yes and kiss him, but the beautiful brand Carson had on his shoulder taunted her. It hid under his shirt like a hissing devil, screeching *'this should've been yours, but it isn't. He'll never be fully yours now!'*

When was the last time he touched the Duchess? When he was arrested? That was only the day before yesterday.

She yanked herself away from his comforting embrace. It hurt her heart, like the throbbing of a freshly jammed finger. She held her hands against her chest protectively, and subconsciously wrung them together. "No," she struggled to say, voice lost somewhere in her chest.

His eyes shifted. The pain of her rejection was hard for him to hide.

Gina felt a twinge of irritation return. How dare he feel hurt? He had no right.

"G—" he started.

"I said no," she affirmed, breathless, the words only a very soft whisper. She turned away from him and headed toward her bedroom.

As she grabbed the door to shut it, Carson startled her when he held out his hand to stop the white door from closing. She had not realized he had been right behind her.

"Carson!" she protested. "You are being inappropriate!"

"You didn't seem to mind a couple of moments ago when we nearly kissed. And what about that hug? If anyone saw us they'd say it was inappropriate. And, if you don't mind me reminding you of the past, it's not like I haven't ever been in your room alone with you before."

She snapped her mouth shut and clenched her jaw. She felt her face flush crimson with embarrassment. Worst of all, she couldn't argue with him. Still, it was her private room, and he had no right to be anywhere near it—especially if she told him to leave.

Carson continued, "What will it take for you to agree to marry me? I'm not talking about forgiveness right now. I'm asking for you to take baby steps in that direction. Because one day you will forgive me, but it'll be too late to agree to marriage by then."

Gina thought for a solid minute. Carson was very patient. He watched her face for any hint of possibility, hope dripping from him as sap drips from a tree.

At last, Gina knew what her condition would be if she were to marry Carson Owens. "If you can get the Judge to agree to relocate us out of this Province, I will agree to marry you."

He nodded quickly, not an ounce of hesitation. "I will talk to him as soon as I leave here." Then his eyebrows fell over his eyes. "But why do you want to move? What about your family?"

It would be hard to leave her family, but she would do it if that meant she'd get to marry Carson and ensure he'd never see Margaret again at the same time. She could always visit her family during holidays.

Bluntly, she told him the god-honest truth, "If I marry you and we stay here, I will always wonder if you're with her when you're not with me." It was all she had to say.

Guilt washed over his expression, flooding his eyes and softening his brow. He reached out to grab her hand, but she moved away from him. He whispered, "I will never see or speak or think of Margaret again. You have my word."

"Relocate," Gina repeated. "Or I won't marry you."

33

Carson rushed to the Courthouse after leaving the Blakes'. There wasn't much time. Gina had only until that evening to give her final decision. He thought it ridiculous that she felt forced to marry so young. She was only sixteen, and he was only seventeen. With the legal deadline to be married being twenty-two, he had thought he had a couple more years.

It was not uncommon for teenagers to marry after graduation, but it also was not considered normal either. Most waited until twenty or until the Judge picked them for someone else who needed to marry—like in Gina's case.

He strode up to the desk of the Judge's new secretary. The nameplate on her desk read *Britt Nelson*. "Hello," he addressed politely. "May I speak with the Judge, please? It's urgent."

She smiled at him, but she looked annoyed. "He's in a video conference. May I take a message?"

He paused for a moment and glanced at the Judge's office door. "When will it be over?"

She shrugged her shoulders and scratched an itch on her scalp covered in thick raven black hair pulled messily into a bun at the back of her head. "Who knows? It's with one of those High Elders from the District of Diphda." She waved her hand as she returned her attention to the newspaper in front of her.

"Must be important," Carson mumbled under his breath.

"Must be," she agreed, filing her nails casually as she read the paper. A few seconds passed before she paused and said, waving her nail file at him, a foreign accent slightly slipping through, though she seemed to catch it quickly, "Honey, you can stand at my desk all day if you like—and honestly you do not bother me if that is what you choose— or you can sit over there and wait."

"I apologize, Mrs. Nelson." Carson quickly made his way over to the seats several feet away from the woman's desk.

"It's just Britt," she corrected him, twirling her nail file expertly. "I'm not married, dear."

He was a bit confused about her statement. She was older than twenty-two, surely—maybe even thirty.

She must've sensed his confusion because she answered his unspoken question. "I'm a widow. Husband died a few years ago." She flipped through the newspaper. "It was a heart attack that killed the man." Carson thought maybe she didn't sound too upset about the death of her husband. "I'm not required to remarry until five years after his death. It's only been three, so I'm good another two years." She looked up at him and smiled. "He was awful. A bastard of a man. Terrible, really." And that was all she said to Carson regarding her late husband.

Carson was suddenly left wondering if it really was a heart attack that killed her awful, terrible, poor husband. He sensed something more sinister about Britt Nelson than was portrayed by the fair-complected woman. Or perhaps he was reading into it too much.

Five minutes passed, then ten, then fifteen. Carson tapped his boot anxiously on the tiled floor. How long could the meeting possibly last? He glanced over at the Judge's door for the hundredth time and caught Britt looking at him.

She smiled, eyes lingering. "You are more handsome than I thought you'd be, *haetho*." Her accent was strong on the last word, a name she called him.

He raised an eyebrow. "Excuse me?"

Her face was expressionless. She continued filing her nails, mumbling, "Calm down, Carson Owens. I am only joking."

She knows my name. He knew he had not told her his name.

"How'd you—" he started, but then his eyes caught and recognized his own face on the front page of the newspaper.

Of course, he thought pessimistically. They were going to broadcast Carson's sin for all of the Province to see. It was what the newspaper was for, mainly. The bigger the sin, the bigger the headline.

Carson's sin was only a side article on the front page—easily overlooked, yet still there in plain view for everyone to see and remember. The big picture and its matching headline was on a middle-aged man charged for assault and rape in the District of Diphda, sentenced to beheading by District's guillotine. Carson almost missed the two black Xs scribbled across the man's eyes on Miss Nelson's copy.

After she set it down several minutes later and turned her attention elsewhere, he hesitantly asked to see it.

Reading his own article caused a pit to form in his stomach. It was embarrassing having his picture printed but even more embarrassing was the article itself. *Man-whore,* it called him. *Sinful relations. Mysterious lover. Possible traveler. No woman has been found with a matching brand in Polaris. Judge orders search to expand to neighboring cities, though admits an oversight could be possible.* And then there was a sketch of his very own brand. They were not allowed to publish a picture of it, but no rule said they could not sketch it. Help us find his lover, the article encouraged its readers. *Check your wives and daughters for a brand like this.*

His stomach turned somersaults. To make it worse on his stomach, his thoughts turned to Gina. Had she seen this article? Had she realized how public they'd made his sin? Surely she knew. He couldn't imagine how much worse she would treat him if she felt embarrassed any more than she already was.

Bloody idiot. He prayed to Anem that Gina would forgive him for not only his sin, but for dragging her through such an embarrassing ordeal. Already she had been targeted for "random" checks three different times—that he knew of. All the while, Margaret hadn't been questioned once.

Everyone thought his lover was Gina—the angel that would never take a lover unwedded. Carson had unintentionally made her the main suspect of a crime she took no part in whatsoever. It'll be years before she forgives me. Of that he was despairingly sure. Still, he couldn't help the hope nudging him.

Finally, the door to the Judge's office opened, and the Judge stepped out. He handed Britt Nelson a stack of papers as he said, "File these, please, Miss Nelson." She opened her mouth to respond, but the Judge quickly said, "Please, for the love of the goddess, do not ask me if they are signed and dated. I know it's your first day, but I swear if you ask me one more time..." His sentence trailed as his threat fell short.

She made a face at him, and the disrespect surprised Carson. "Well, excuse me for doing my job." She sarcastically saluted him with two fingers. She was an odd woman, and definitely not from this Province. Her slight accent slip-up from earlier gave that much away. But Carson had no idea what accent it was or where she could have possibly come from. William was from the Province of Kaitos, but he had no detectable accent. Perhaps he was better at hiding it than Britt. Or perhaps she was from the District of Diphda, though her accent didn't remind him of any dialects from the island where the District was located.

Then again, he had never visited the District. There was no way for him to know all the different dialects from the other Provinces.

Judge James noticed Carson sitting in one of the seats once Miss Nelson took the files from him. "Carson," he said a bit sourly. "What is it?"

"May I speak privately with you?"

Out of the corner of his eye, Britt looked at him as if she were part of the conversation. Did she not care about the rules? She seemed to have no qualms with sticking her nose where it didn't belong.

The Judge was quiet for a whole second before saying, "No. I'm a very busy man, and you did not make an appointment." He turned and headed back into his office.

Carson hopped out of his seat and followed him. "Please!" he insisted. "It will only take a second. It's about Gina."

Huffing, Judge James spun to face him. "Believe it or not, I have no interest in listening to you whine about a girl."

"She wants to marry me!" he blurted. Remembering where he was—and who he was speaking to—he repeated calmly, "Gina said she'll marry me if you agree to relocate us out of this Province."

"Huh," Britt butted in. "Why's that, Owens boy? Is it because of the other girl? Isn't your lover a traveler? Why should this Gina girl care about another girl you'll never see again?"

Carson stared at her for a moment before he mustered the gall to lie directly. "Gina doesn't know who my *ex-lover* is, and that makes her uncomfortable."

"Ooh," said Britt, waving her fingers sarcastically. "Sorry, I mean your *ex-lover*." She smiled at him, but it felt insincere.

"Carson." Judge James redirected his attention. "As much as I would love to send Gina and especially you out of my city—and even better, the Province—the answer is no." He turned again and continued into his office.

Carson followed despite no invitation. "Why not?"

"Because I said so."

"That's not good enough!"

Judge James slammed his hand down on his desk. A vein popped out on his forehead as he clenched his jaw tightly, teeth grinding audibly. "Listen, kid, you need to learn sooner rather than later where your place is."

"Hear me out, please." Carson wouldn't give up. He couldn't. He was in too deep. "If you don't agree to relocate us, she won't marry me. Please understand... She's insecure."

"Of course she is. You destroyed any trust she had in you." He sighed and sat down in his chair. Carson took one of the leather chairs across from his desk despite obviously not being welcomed. The Judge continued, the bags under his eyes growing heavier by the minute, "I know this feels like a really big deal to you right now, but I promise, years down the line it will no longer matter. Perhaps it's better that Gina won't marry you. Your marriage may be a miserable one."

Carson shook his head. "It won't. I know it." He couldn't believe they wouldn't eventually be happy. Gina was everything he ever wanted and more. And he knew that once she forgave him, she would be happy, too.

"I'm not relocating you. That's final."

Carson was quiet for a few moments. "At least tell me why not."

The Judge sighed. "Fine. I met with one of the High Elders today over a video conference about you." He motioned to the slim computer.

Carson wondered what the video conference had to do with relocating him, and he felt a twinge of annoyance at the Judge for wasting his time.

"You see, there's only so much I can do. Some things I can't do without approval from the Celestial Court. You know there's a reason you haven't received your job assignment yet."

Carson's ears suddenly pricked with interest.

He continued, "Dr. Johnson is old, and he will be retiring in the next decade. We need new doctors to start training. You will be one of them."

"Doctor?" Carson was genuinely surprised. He assumed he'd be an officer like his father.

The Judge nodded. "Yes, a pediatrician, in fact, but your work would be more research related."

"But..." Carson paused for a second to consider his thoughts. "Don't doctors have to be High Class citizens?"

The Judge nodded once. "That's why I had to seek the Celestial Court's approval. They want me to promote you to a Class Seven."

His stomach knotted. "Promotion?" If he was promoted, he wouldn't be able to marry Gina.

"That is what I said. You have twenty days left as a Class Five." He waved his hand sarcastically. "Enjoy while you can."

Carson's mind raced. "But Gina's a Class Four."

The Judge's face didn't change. He looked as annoyed and impatient as he had been earlier. Dryly, he said, "She would also be promoted since she'd be your wife. That is, if she chooses you."

He jumped up. "That could work."

Judge James seemed uninterested in Carson's unexplained revelation. "Are you finally leaving my office?"

"Yes. Thank you for your time."

He left the Courthouse as quickly as he could, heading straight back to the Blakes'.

He rapped on the door, and it almost sounded frantic. Less than a minute passed before it swung open and Gina's father, Tim, stood before him smiling. "Well, well," he said. "If it isn't my future son-in-law! Come on in."

It was bizarre to Carson how supportive Mr. Blake was about his pursuit to marry Gina. But Mr. Blake had always seemed to like him. Carson was unsure if the man would have been angry at all if Gina had been his lover instead.

"Gina isn't here right now, but you are welcome to wait for her."

"Where did she go?" She knew Carson would be coming back eventually. At the very least, it could be assumed. Why would she up and leave?

Timothy glanced at Carson, hesitant. "She finished Margaret's wedding dress. Took it to her to try on."

"So she's at the James' house?"

He pursed his lips, pausing to assess Carson. "Yes."

"Mr. Blake," Carson began, sensing the middle-aged man's worry quite clearly. "I want you to know that what happened between me and Margaret wasn't that serious."

"I know." He nodded and shrugged. "I've been there myself, and I was already married."

Carson hit a hard pause on his thoughts and was suddenly very confused. He didn't say anything in response. He honestly didn't know what to say. Even his thoughts were mostly blank.

Mr. Blake answered the silent question weighing heavily in the air. "I was unfaithful to Emma when Gina was first born. It was one of her friends, to add salt to the wound. She didn't forgive me for about...eight, maybe ten, years."

"Who...?" He stopped himself short of an inappropriate question. He didn't want to overstep. But maybe he also didn't want to actually know the answer.

Mr. Blake chuckled. "You understand better than anyone else why I can't tell you who she was." Of course he couldn't. He would be exposing a woman who shared a brand with him. He was protecting her from public flogging, like how Carson was trying to protect Margaret from the same.

But Carson just wanted to know one thing. "It wasn't my mom though, right?" Kayla and Emma were friends, and Mr. Blake said it was one of Emma's friends.

Tim looked at him sourly. "No, of course not. Your father is my friend, and he's had to deal with enough betrayal for many lifetimes." Tim stiffened then. "Never mind," he said quickly. "I shouldn't have said that."

Carson opened his mouth to speak but Mr. Blake waved his hand. "I'm not going to answer any more questions you may have, so don't bother asking them." He motioned to the kitchen and then to the living room. "Help yourself to food and drink, and make yourself at home. I have to get back to work." Then he moseyed out the backdoor, mumbling incomprehensibly to himself.

What the actual hell?

What was he talking about when he said Derek had been through many lifetimes' worth of betrayal? Had his mother cheated on his father before? Multiple times, apparently? That didn't sound like Kayla Owens at all. She had a fiery soul, sure, but not an unfaithful one. She loved her husband very much—or so it had always seemed.

And Mr. Blake? He confessed himself that he had been unfaithful to Emma.

But he loved his wife. He loved her very much. Carson had always thought he wanted a relationship like Tim and Emma's. They loved each other, and it showed. Yet, he had broken his wife's heart.

That information changed how he saw Mr. Blake, unfortunately, but at least he had someone who understood him. There was a glaring difference, though. Carson would have never been unfaithful to Gina if they had been married. Honestly, the situation was entirely incomparable.

A toilet flushed near him, and a moment later Jedidiah came out of the bathroom connected to the living area. He flicked his just-washed hands everywhere to remove the water from them. "Hey, Carson," he said gleefully as he passed him, heading to the backdoor, not seemingly surprised to see Carson standing alone in the middle of the living room. "Gigi isn't here. She went to the Duchess' house. But she'll be back later."

Carson glanced around as if he'd find what he was searching for there in the empty living room. "Where's the baby?" It only barely dawned on him that he had not seen Lilli Ann at all that day.

"She took Annie with her." He waved at Carson as he opened the backdoor. "I have to go help my dad now, but you should go talk to her. Before she left, I heard her tell Dad she was hoping to speak with you soon." He smiled. "I know you did some bad things, but I think she'll forgive you in time. You make her happy." Then he left out the door.

Sure, Carson thought sourly, but he hoped the kid was right.

He glanced down the hallway at Gina's ajar bedroom door. The light streaming in from her window illuminated it. He could see from where he sat on the couch that the furniture in her room had been rearranged since the last time he'd been in there. It felt like yesterday, and yet it felt like ages ago.

Days after Emma died, his family had gone over to help with the newborn and other two babies as much as possible.

So many babies, Carson remembered thinking. How would Mr. Blake do it without his wife? Even with Gina's help, it would be hard. And it was hard. Excruciatingly hard for them. For her. But she never complained, that saint. She was a true angel.

A broken angel, even at fourteen. Her mother, having just passed, was not there to comfort her. Besides, there were three other babies to care for. Only Carson was there to be of any help to Gina, since his parents were helping with the other kids. So, they turned a blind eye—because it was easier, he imagined—and they allowed Carson and Gina to sit for hours in her room alone, with the door shut, nonetheless.

Of course, Carson never planned on doing anything inappropriate with Gina. She was hurting. He never even stopped to consider himself during that time.

But it happened: a kiss. He didn't plan for it to happen, truly. But then Gina didn't seem to mind too much once it was happening. She had kissed him back—more eagerly than he had imagined she would have. And, she had allowed him to touch her during the kiss. He recalled that her breasts were soft, like a downy pillow freshly stuffed. She hadn't stopped him either; he stopped himself.

Then everything had turned sour and spiraled out of his control.

She had felt guilty—which he understood completely and had apologized. But she couldn't handle the stress of the situation, he supposed. Not along with her mother's death, at least. So, she told him to leave her be. And, of course, he obliged.

Anything she wanted. *Anything*. He would make sure it was done.

His parents had still helped with the younger three children for many months following, but every time Carson went to help, Gina stayed away from him. It hurt his heart more than he cared to show. He didn't understand why at the time. And even now, he had a hard time wrapping his mind around her explanation.

Carson could have tried harder to talk with Gina, but she avoided him so fiercely. He felt unwanted, and that feeling caught painfully in his chest. Eventually he concluded that if that's what she wanted, then he would keep his distance. He had stopped going with his parents to the Blakes'. He didn't speak to her unless she spoke to him. After half a year or so, she still avoided him, and so he gave up. If she didn't want him, then so be it.

She said she had been struggling mentally. He could try to understand that. Depression wasn't something to take lightly. Perhaps she was just trying to help herself before helping their relationship.

And look at what you've done. You ruined everything.

Carson sat on the sofa for a few minutes more before he found himself heading toward the James' house. *What are you doing?* he scolded himself, yet he didn't slow down or turn around. *What could you possibly say to Gina with Margaret in the room?* And his imagination of all the possibilities caused him to slow his pace slightly.

He didn't want to hurt Margaret. He really didn't. But, in truth, he already had. She just wasn't aware of it yet.

He paused at the white fence in front of the two-story house. After a minute of back and forth arguing with himself, he finally started up the stepping stone pathway. His knock was light, and he immediately wished he had waited at Gina's house to speak with her.

Idiot.

His stomach flipped and twisted as the front door cracked open only a few inches. Half of Gina's face was visible, the other hiding behind the door.

"G—" he started.

"Are you crazy?" she hissed at him, and the venom in her words surprised him. "Of all the places you shouldn't be."

"I know." He tried to swallow, but his mouth had dried up. "I just really need to talk to you."

"Gigi! Gigi! Look!" It was the toddler, Lilli Ann.

Gina turned to her littlest sibling. "Lilli Ann!" She was not impressed with whatever she had done.

She shut the door in Carson's face with vigor. He stood there for a moment, hoping she would open the door again, but soon realized she had no plans to do so. He took a deep breath to steady his nerves and let himself in.

The entrance to the James' home was lavishly decorated with the most expensive materials available. A marble staircase was positioned only a few yards from the door, the upstairs winding away from view. A crystal chandelier loomed far above his head. There were tall archways outlined in extravagant molding leading to rooms on both his right and left. He had never been inside Margaret's home—with the exception of her bedroom, of course, but even then, he never placed a foot inside her room.

He could hear Lilli Ann giggling to his left, so he stepped to that room, nervous about what was about to unfold. He sent a quick prayer to Anem for there to be peace.

"Oh, it's just you." Margaret stood in the middle of the living room with her wedding gown on, pinned in certain places along the hem. Her auburn hair was pulled up loosely. Curiously, he wondered why she cradled her left arm. Was she hurt?

She smiled at him and said, "Hi."

"Hey, Margaret," he replied cautiously, glancing over at Gina who was removing a long piece of fabric from around Lilli Ann's neck as the child giggled at her.

"This isn't a scarf, Annie," she gently told the two-year-old. She exhaled, exacerbated, when Lilli Ann laughed at her in response.

Carson bent down next to the toddler. "Want to go play at the park?"

"Carson," Gina complained at the same time Lilli Ann screamed, "Yay! Park!"

Lilli Ann reached her arms out for Carson to pick her up, and as he complied with the two-year-old's wishes, he said quietly to Gina, "I don't mind. I'm happy to help you."

"Is everything okay?" questioned Margaret. She turned to face them.

Gina's face changed slowly and unsuccessfully. She was trying to put on a brave smile. She said to Margaret, "Of course. What could possibly be wrong?"

Margaret obviously wasn't buying it. "Uh-huh," she agreed sarcastically, then turned her attention to Carson. "Are you here to pick up the baby for her or what?"

He hesitated. "Yes," he said calmly, no emotion. "I heard she needed help. Thought I'd take the little one to the park to play for a while."

"That's kind of you," Margaret said.

"Yes," agreed Gina through her teeth. "How kind."

"So..." Carson paused, watching Gina. He could almost feel the fire from her anger. "Do you want me to take her? I don't have to. I just thought it would be nice."

Her eyebrows pulled down over her eyes, framing the fury blazing within. "That's fine," she eventually said, though he could tell it took a whole lot of effort to say it somewhat normally. "I will pick her up from your house around two."

"And then we can talk?"

Acidly, she replied as she turned away from him to attend to Margaret. "Oh, we will talk, you can bet on that."

His stomach somersaulted. He had never seen her angry like this, and it bothered his core that it was directed at him. Was it only because he had come over to the James' house? He wasn't there to see Margaret, if that's what she was thinking.

I hope she knows I came for her, not Maggie. He truly was done with Margaret, but only time could convince Gina of that truth.

34

"Sorry," Gina hissed as Margaret jerked her ankle away.

She wasn't angry with the Duchess, per se, but she had been in a bad mood since Carson picked up Lilli Ann—and for good reason. How dare he show up at the Duchess' house? How dare he? Even if he had been there to see her, he should have known better.

Of all places—

"Gina?" Margaret whispered cautiously, hesitant to address Gina in any way.

Gina took a deep breath and exhaled before replying, voice but a whisper, "Yes, my lady?"

"Did something happen between you and Carson?"

Did something happen? Is she serious?

Gina huffed and threaded her needle through the hem of the dress. "What gave it away, *princess*?" She regretted calling her that as soon as it left her mouth. Many called Margaret princess when referring to how spoiled she was. It was never a compliment.

Margaret jerked the skirt of the dress away, pulling the needle from Gina's hands in the process. It stayed stuck somewhere in the hem. "That's enough! What the hell, Gina? We're supposed to be friends."

Gina stood quickly. There were so, so, *so* many things she wanted to say, and she allowed herself to just say one of them. "*Friend* is a strong word, don't you think? You only care about yourself."

"Excuse me?" Margaret's eyebrows fell heavily over her eyes.

"You're selfish," added Gina.

"I have always been kind and generous to you! How dare you?"

"How dare *I*? How dare *you*? I know you know about me and Carson."

Margaret shook her head. "I have no idea what you're referring to."

Gina ground her teeth. "Give me a break, Margaret! You're trying to convince me that you're really that oblivious? Do you know how many times I've been stopped by officers due to *tips* that I could be his lover? Eight times! *Eight*. As if the first time wasn't invasive and embarrassing enough."

The Duchess was quiet for a long moment as she studied Gina's face. "Why does everyone assume it was you?" It was only a whisper, and her tone suggested she was akin to a sad, wounded animal.

Gina shook her head and laughed once. She motioned aimlessly to her surroundings. "Why do you think?"

Only a second passed before she asked, "The two of you were together? I know you don't have a brand, but...otherwise, I mean."

Gina was silent.

Margaret swore under her breath and looked at her left arm which she gripped tighter. "Were you two together while I was with him?"

Again, she didn't answer. She turned away from Margaret and began packing her sewing things. She didn't have anything else to add to the conversation. It was all pointless anyway. Nothing could be reversed.

"That doesn't sound like Carson," Margaret whispered. "Are you sure it wasn't a misunderstanding?"

Gina didn't reply. She didn't want to. She wanted Margaret to think there had been no misunderstanding between any of them. She wanted the Duchess to hate Carson. If she hated Carson, it was guaranteed they'd never be together again.

Her heart pinched in her chest. She was lying, even if only by omission, and lying was a sin.

Still, she pushed away the guilt and allowed her anger to rule supreme in her heart for the moment, knowing fully she would later regret it. But she *really* wanted Margaret to hate Carson.

"Why didn't you tell me?" asked Margaret softly, all anger diffused from her tone.

Gina shrugged, back turned to her friend. Was *friend* the right word anymore? Maybe they could never be true friends again, even if everything worked out well from here on out. "It wasn't exactly something we were announcing to the world, what with it being looked down upon."

A few moments passed in silence.

"How could he do that to you? Or to me?" Margaret whimpered, voice cracking slightly.

Is she crying? Seriously? Gina paused her criticizing thoughts. It dawned on her that Carson hadn't just hurt her. He had hurt Margaret too. Margaret James had truly loved Carson. Maybe as much as she loved him. That was why Margaret had suggested she marry him, because Margaret trusted that Gina would be a good wife to him. Margaret wanted him to have a good life, one she would never get the chance to live with him.

Margaret abruptly hugged Gina from behind, squeezing her tightly, pressing her cheek firmly against Gina's shoulder blade. "I'm so sorry," she whispered. "What a horrible thing to suffer through."

Gina thought perhaps she should tell Margaret the whole truth, but she physically couldn't. If she spoke, she would cry. Gina held her breath as long as she could, and as soon as she took a breath, tears choked her. She ducked her head and tried to stifle the hard sobs that violently exited her body with a cotton fabric cutting.

Margaret held her tighter. Several long minutes passed. Gina noticed Margaret crying too, only by the feeling of wetness where Margaret's face laid against her back. Other than that, she made no sound.

Finally, once Gina's sobs calmed a bit, Margaret whispered so quietly she barely made out what was said, "No wonder he always acted weird when I would mention you."

"You talked about me?" sniffled Gina. She wasn't sure how she felt about the two of them discussing her in private. Appalled felt most fitting.

"Of course," she whispered to Gina. "You're my friend. Best friend, honestly. I told him about that one time when you came over to teach me how to make an apple pie from scratch. Remember that?"

A giggle left Gina's mouth at the same time as a leftover sob. "Yes, I remember," she whispered back. "It was a mess."

"Never let me bake anything again."

Both girls giggled softly. Margaret finally let go of her dear friend, grabbed a small piece of cut fabric to be discarded, and she wiped snot running out of her nose. Her eyes were bloodshot, and when she sniffed, her nose sounded stuffy. She scooted across the carpeted floor to sit next to Gina, still in her unhemmed wedding dress. She wrapped her uninjured arm around her friend and pulled the girl to her. Gina allowed it, and it was comforting, despite being furious a few minutes prior.

She was glad she hadn't called her all of the names floating around in her head. Princess was thankfully the most forgiving one. "Sorry I called you a princess. And sorry I said you only care about yourself."

"Sorry I bound myself to your boyfriend." She made a gagging sound, as if she was disgusted. "I'm not that into him, by the way. Also, he's a bad kisser."

Gina knew that she was lying about not being into him, but she let it slide. Margaret was only trying to comfort her. Besides, she wasn't wrong about him being a bad kisser, but Gina didn't think the kiss she'd shared with him had been awful.

"You didn't give him any tips?" she joked, but it felt like it might have been out of place. "It was like kissing a wet rock with a tongue." An awkward flush reddened her face, and she regretted saying it the second it left her mouth.

But Margaret laughed loudly. "That's exactly what it's like!"

They laughed together, but it was still stiff with the awkward air between them.

Margaret added, "You forgive me, right? I didn't mean to ruin anything between the two of you. If I had known, I would've never gone near him."

"Yeah," whispered Gina. She sniffled. "That's the easy part though. Forgiving you, I mean. What do I do about Carson? I don't know how to forgive him."

She sighed but didn't miss a beat in her response. "I don't blame you. Didn't my dad give you five choices?"

"Yes."

"Who are the other four?"

"Bobby Collins, Scott Miller, Malcolm Perry, and David Adams."

"I don't know who Malcolm Perry is—"

"Me either."

"—but I do know the other three. I would say no to David. He's a real pervert. Bobby is kind; he is a good friend of mine."

"Carson said he's gay."

Margaret made a face of disapproval. "He wasn't gay when we kissed a few years ago." Gina was taken aback, but Margaret didn't seem bothered in the least. "Anyway, who cares? At least he'd be a kind husband." She quickly glossed over it, like it didn't matter that Bobby could be attracted to men—and maybe it didn't.

But maybe it did? Gina was confused.

Margaret added without a moment's lapse, "Plus, he's a better kisser than Carson, so bonus there." She nudged Gina with the elbow of her good arm and winked. It was all quite uncomfortable.

Margaret moved on to the next suitor she knew from the list. "Scott Miller is twenty. He's a mechanic. Works on the underground trains that travel the Wastelands and the Red Desert, as well as the city's tramcars. I have only had one conversation with him, but he seemed very kind and respectable. Plus, he's very handsome. Tall, dark hair, a bit tan, squared jaw, perfect nose. He has this super cute freckle under one of his eyes. And he's a Mature already, of course, so there's no chance he'll do that weird personality flip that sometimes happens after the Ritual."

Scott Miller sounded nice by Margaret's detailed physical description, but what about underneath all the beauty? Gina didn't know him. In her short time on this earth, she had quickly figured out that everyone had a dark shadow, no matter how handsome or beautiful they were. What was Scott Miller's shadow? Some were worse than others. Much, much worse.

Margaret released Gina from the embrace. She cringed and gripped her left arm at the sudden movement. "Still hurts like hell," she said through her tightly clenched teeth.

How was she supposed to hide her injury during her wedding? The dress would easily hide the brand, of course, but the pain couldn't be masked as easily. "What are you going to do about that?" asked Gina.

"Nothing," breathed Margaret. "Can't go to the doctor."

Gina's eyes widened. "They'll see your brand."

Tears cascaded from Margaret's eyes suddenly. She wiped them away ungracefully with the palm of her right hand. "What if it always hurts?" she whispered to Gina. "Forever?"

Gina didn't know what answer would comfort Margaret, so she just hugged her.

After calming down a few moments later, Margaret answered her own question, shrugging her right shoulder, careful of her left. "I'll just have to figure out how to live with the pain."

Gina said, "People will wonder what happened. What will you say?"

"I'll think of something."

"A lie?"

Margaret looked curiously at Gina. "Of course a lie. Gina, no one can know. I'll lose any respect in the District once my brand is discovered. I won't be able to be an Ambassador."

Gina fidgeted with her fingers in her lap. "Yeah, I understand."

Both girls were quiet for some time before Margaret stood from the floor and stated, "Let's go talk to Carson. Together."

Gina's stomach turned. She slowly stood as Margaret motioned her to help remove the wedding dress. She replied as she carefully removed the needle still stuck in the hem, "Why?"

"I have questions," answered Margaret without skipping a beat. "I have many questions, and now I really don't trust him to tell the truth. But if you're there, he can't lie."

Her stomach twisted. She didn't think Carson had been lying to either of them. Well, maybe to Margaret some, but maybe he hadn't been. Not intentionally. Maybe he had believed what he had said to both girls. She would like to give Carson the benefit of the doubt, but she was unsure if he deserved it.

Also, she hadn't been completely honest with Margaret either. "I don't know about that," she said sheepishly. "I would like to just leave it be."

Margaret helped Gina pack up her bag. "Perhaps you can let sleeping dogs lie, but I'm too nosey to do that." She stopped and turned to her friend, placing her right hand on her hip sassily. "My questions deserve answers. You disagree?"

"No—" Gina began, but Margaret cut her off.

"Then let's go."

35

Wind whistled down the dark, deserted alley. Derek slunk quickly down the shadowy path in pursuit of his target. He peeked around the corner, pressing himself into the wall as he watched the man stroll down the empty back-street.

What are you up to, Officer Lach?

Ever since William had called him by his brother's name, he had known the man was keeping some kind of secret. Derek knew in his gut that it had to do with his runaway twin brother, and his gut was never wrong.

He had suspected the chief officer had lied when he had said he was having lunch with his fiancé, what with all the checkpoints still erected in the bustling city. He hadn't intended to tail his superior, but when William had turned towards the outskirts and not in the direction of the James' home, Derek had been unable to suppress his urge to discover what the man was truly up to.

So, after about an hour of following from a distance, they had ended up in Oakdale Hollow.

William ducked into the back door of a flower shop, closed for renovation. Derek followed. He was thankful the door did not creak when he cracked it open to peek inside. Paint cans and wood boards littered the area. Cloth tarps had been laid on the floor of the shop to protect it from the hazards of renovating. The owners had covered the windows with the same tarp as on the floor. Light filtered in through the edges, but the room remained quite dim.

Derek searched for William. He had walked over to a corner of the room that was dark. A woman's voice spoke, but she didn't step out of the shadows. Derek strained his ears to listen. She said quietly, "You look like one of them." Her heavy accent was evident, but Derek couldn't quite place it. Was the woman from Kaitos? Perhaps Diphda? She definitely was not Denebian.

William's answer was low and matched the woman's tone. "That's the point." Did he have an accent, too? If so, it was much subtler than the woman's.

The woman was quiet for a beat. "I've missed you, vaakius," she whispered.

Vaakius? The hell is she saying?

Derek carefully removed his body camera from the clip on his chest and switched it on. He pointed it at the two individuals and waited. If he was going to get William to talk, he imagined he was going to have to blackmail the chief officer. And while that didn't necessarily sit well with Derek, he still smiled at the idea, because he was going to know more about William's knowledge on Drew soon. He could practically taste it.

"I've missed you too." He sighed and rubbed his eyes. "Listen, I am glad you are here to help me, but honestly, the boy and his family are not an issue," said William. "The kid's actually good. He's just made one bad decision and got caught."

"Same can be said of the James girl, no?" replied the unknown woman.

"She's a different story," he said, throwing his arms up as if surrendering. "She's hard-headed and difficult to control. I've had to take drastic measures to keep her in place. Look, I didn't tell you to meet me here to discuss the girl. I want to talk about you. This is your first day here, and the Judge is already asking me to look into where you're really from, because he doesn't believe you're from the District."

"It's harder than I thought it would be to control my accent."

William motioned wildly and generally to the space behind him. "How, Britt? You *are* from the District. You need to dig deep and bring that back to the surface. I know you've worked hard to bury all those memories but you have to if want to survive this. If you keep slipping up, they'll—"

"They'll what?" The woman stepped up to him, out of the shadows of the corner, pressing her chest against his. Derek was unsure if it was a romantic gesture or an intimidating one.

William didn't move away from her like Derek expected him to. The man simply sighed and said gently, "You're going to get yourself killed. I don't want that, Britt."

She reached up and touched his face. That, definitely, was a romantic gesture. "I will be safe," she said to him. Then, she took half a step back and looked him from head to toe thrice over. "Don't you dare touch that girl, Will."

William shook his head fervently, grabbing the woman he called Britt and pulling her back to him, their chests pressed together tightly, his hands on her backside. "You know I won't."

Britt smiled at him and tip-toed, hovering her lips over his. Derek considered looking away, but he didn't have a chance. Instead of kissing him like Derek assumed she was going to do, she grabbed him between his legs roughly and said, "I'm serious about not touching her."

William held her wrist that held his jewels and said to her, "So am I, vaakius. Let go of me, please." Derek thought his tone wasn't taking her grabbing him as seriously as he should. He almost sounded like he was trying not to laugh at her. She wasn't hurting him too badly, then, like she was threatening.

She smirked. "I don't want to."

"You must."

It took several seconds, but she finally released him, smiling. "It's nice to know you still like that."

William didn't respond to her comment and said instead, "I don't know why he sent you. It worries me, you being here among them. Be safe, okay?" He moved some of her black hair that had fallen from her high bun behind her ear. His fingers lingered there.

She relaxed slightly and nodded once, closing her eyes. "I promise I will be safe." Then she kissed his hand and said excitedly, "Toka said once this is all over, you and I can be discharged. Our debt will have been paid."

"So long as we don't screw up," he retorted.

"That's a given, obviously. You're missing my point."

He chuckled, leaned over to her and gave her cheek a small kiss. "I didn't miss anything. We'll build a small villa on the side of the mountain when he dismisses us. We will be away from the people, and we can finally die together of old age."

Her smile widened. "I'd like that, Will."

Derek was beyond confused. Was William planning on running away with this woman? To a place where mountains were, apparently. Except it didn't necessarily sound like they were planning on running away. Britt used the word debt—that they were currently paying one. So what did they owe, but more importantly, who did they owe? What—or who—is *toka*?

Derek continued filming, even when they surprised him by peeling off each other's clothing and proceeding to bind themselves together. When he glimpsed their backs, they already had matching brands—though the woman had three other brands in addition to the one she shared with William, while William only had the one in the middle of his back.

What the hell is going on here?

He didn't watch them love each other, but he definitely wasn't going to stop filming. The conversation William had with the woman was fine for blackmail, but fornication was even better.

He couldn't wait to approach William later about it. He became giddy just thinking about the look of horror that William would no doubt have on his face.

36

Margaret was in disbelief. She had been lied to by Carson and wanted to bury him alive. Yes, what he had done to Gina was horrible—worse, she could imagine, than what he did to her. But stars, did she want to bury him for lying to her.

He had said he loved her. He had held her as if it were true. He had said he wished to marry her. All the while he was planning a life with someone else? One of her best friends, nonetheless?

Anem better hold her back.

The two girls first went to Gina's home to drop off her sewing things. As Gina set her bag down in her room, Margaret asked her, "Do you know where he lives? Sorry, but I guess I just assumed you knew. If you don't, we'll have to find his address in the yellow pages. Do you have a copy of Polaris's Address Book here?"

Gina raised her eyebrows as she shut her bedroom door behind her, leaving. "You don't know where Carson lives?"

Margaret shrugged. "It never mattered. Do you?"

"Of course I do," she answered.

An expression crossed Gina's face, and though Margaret couldn't quite make out what it was, she was immediately defensive. She wanted to explain to Gina that it was better she did not know where he lived considering their illegal romantic history, but a door shutting in the back of the house and a man's hacking cough interrupted her thoughts.

Gina motioned for Margaret to come along as she started for the front door. "Dad," she called out. "Carson has Annie. I'm going over to pick her up."

Margaret was surprised at her honesty. She would've lied if it were her, especially concerning a boy.

Mr. Blake rounded the corner, covered in sweat and mud, holding a large glass of water. He was red from working hard. He nodded to Gina, "Okay." Then he noticed the Duchess, straightened, and said, "Good morning, my lady. Will you be accompanying my daughter to Carson's?"

"Yes," she answered with a small smile. "I thought after Gina picked up the baby that I could treat them to some pastries at the new patisserie in Uptown Polaris." She shrugged. "I thought it would be nice to spend some quality time with my friend before we both are married and too busy with our adult responsibilities."

His eyebrow raised in suspicion. It made her stomach toss.

Gina whispered to Margaret, "He knows about you and Carson."

Horror shot through Margaret like a bolt of lightning.

Timothy added, having heard Gina, "None of us want to see you in trouble with the law. If I may give you some advice—"

"I doubt she wants advice, Dad," interrupted his daughter.

He continued regardless, "Keep your distance from Carson. Gina doesn't need to worry about anything because she's innocent, and that's easy to prove, what with her not having a brand. But you have a brand which—"

"Dad!" complained Gina, turning away from him quickly, face reddening. She opened the front door. "We're leaving now. I'll be back with Lilli Ann in a few hours."

"Okay, darling. Have fun. Be safe." He tipped his sun hat toward both of the girls, and they quickly left the house.

As they started down the brick path to the cobblestone road,

Margaret hissed, "Why does your dad know about me and Carson?" She was horrified and felt utterly betrayed. "Did you tell him, Gina?"

Gina stopped at the chain-link gate and turned to her, wisps of her blonde hair flying wildly. "Of course not. He's very perceptive. He just...figured it out. Last night when your father came over."

Margaret paused to organize her thoughts. She whispered after a second, "Will he tell?" Her voice trembled.

"He has no desire to see you flogged and quite despises the idea of being a tattler." Gina crossed her arms, shoulders stiff, and rolled her eyes. "He was so quick to forgive Carson. Still wants me to marry him. He doesn't think anyone else will make me happy."

Margaret sighed, relieved. She was glad yet another person would keep her secret safe, but she hated that another person knew a thing at all about her brand.

They both began walking again, Gina leading the way. After a moment, Margaret whispered, "Happiness is overrated, you know. All I want is contentment. Peace. I think if Carson can give you—"

"Can we stop talking about it?" whispered Gina.

"Sure," she mumbled, though she didn't think Gina had the right to feel uncomfortable. It wasn't like she was the one that had a brand so many people were searching for.

Margaret didn't like that anyone knew. At any moment, any of them could decide to turn her over to the Correctional Lieutenant for whipping.

They hopped on a tramcar and rode it to the Moonlight Meadows subdivision only eight miles east. Margaret knew he lived in a Class Five neighborhood, but there were so many different Class Five neighborhoods all over the city. She was surprised he lived in one so close to the farming fields.

So close to Gina.

But she supposed it made sense that he lived there. Moonlight Meadows sort of bordered Oakdale Hollow; only some wooded area and a couple of pastures separated the two subdivisions. It made it safer and easier for him to sneak over to Margaret's during the dead of night since he didn't have to pass through neighborhood streets and yards.

They walked down to a dead-end circle drive. Every house they passed looked the same to Margaret: brick homes with cherry-red doors and gray slate roofs. White picket fences separated the street from the properties. Margaret didn't know any of the names painted or stamped on the white mailboxes.

Gina stopped abruptly in front of the house at the end of the circle drive. Margaret noticed the name *Owens* in bold black letters on the white mailbox.

So this is it. She examined the home as quickly as she could, but it looked just like all the others in the subdivision. The only subtle difference she could tell was the flowerbed under a large window. Bright yellow, orange, and lavender flowers bloomed brilliantly, tended to with love and care.

"I don't know about this," whispered Gina.

Margaret flicked her wrist, waving at her dismissively, as she tried to open the short gate to the property. She struggled with the stuck latch as she said to her friend, "It'll be okay. Promise." She shook the gate, frustrated. "Damn it," she muttered.

"Here." Gina reached over Margaret's hand, grabbed the gate itself and jimmied it at an angle. The latch popped open. How many times had she been here to learn that trick? "It's been broken for years," she explained, swinging the gate wide open.

Margaret felt a prick of jealousy in her heart that Gina knew so much about the Owens' stupid broken gate.

It was possible Carson wasn't even there since it was only one thirty in the afternoon, and Gina had told him she'd pick up Lilli Ann at two. They'd wait if need be.

As they walked up to the Owens' property, Gina stopped on the stone walkway, hesitating, wringing her hands. "Margaret," she whispered. "I really don't want to do this."

Margaret grabbed her friend's elbow to make sure she kept moving forward. "We have to."

"Why? It doesn't change anything."

"It does for me." She turned her head to Gina, pulling her up the porch steps. "Please. Allow me this closure. One conversation and then the three of us go our separate ways."

Gina glanced at the red door of the Owens' house. She whispered, "I guess."

Margaret hugged her gently and quickly released her half a second later, very different from the lingering embrace she gave her earlier. "Don't worry about anything. Out of all of us, you are the only one who has done nothing wrong. You should be the least anxious."

Gina made a nasally noise of disagreement, but Margaret ignored it and knocked on the door. Less than a minute passed before the door swung open, and Carson appeared.

His eyebrows furrowed over his eyes. "What are you doing here?" he asked Margaret, and she thought maybe his tone was rude—though she also thought she was looking for it to be so she could be angrier with him.

"The three of us need to talk," said Margaret stoically. She vowed to maintain her composure. He would not see her cry. "Privately."

He glanced at Gina, though she looked down at the stained wooden porch. "G?" he questioned, and Margaret thought his voice was softer when speaking to her.

Prick. She decided she hated him.

Gina looked up at him for a moment and nodded. That was all Carson needed. He opened the door and invited both girls inside with a simple motion of his hand. His hand that had held Margaret and touched her. He didn't have a brand with Gina, but had he touched her in a similar way with that same hand? Gina mentioned they had kissed. His lips had touched Margaret's and Gina's, and he didn't tell either of them of the other.

Bastard. She was making herself angrier the more she thought about his deception.

"Where's Annie?" was the first thing Gina asked when they crossed the threshold.

The foyer was painted a gorgeous robin's egg blue, and the decor hanging on the walls was of ivory coloring. Mrs. Owens—she assumed that was who decorated the home—had good taste.

"She is napping in the family room," answered Carson.

Gina had obviously been in the home before. She turned from them, strode straight through an archway and disappeared from sight. Carson motioned Margaret to follow, but Margaret motioned back for him to go first. He rolled his eyes at her and followed Gina.

The family room was also perfectly decorated. The same robin's egg blue from the foyer painted the walls. A few coordinating yellow and salmon-colored trinkets decorated the white shelf as well as the picture frames that hung on the wall across from it. Throw pillows of the same hues sat neatly on the white couch, intricate faux crystal beading stitched on the front. The decor was simple and minimalistic, yet pulled every aspect of the room together.

Gina quietly bent down next to the coffee table where a blanket had been thrown and mountains of pillows surrounded it.

"A pillow fort?" Margaret whispered.

"Yeah," Carson whispered back. "She was playing in it, and then just fell asleep."

"Where is your family?" she wondered.

"My parents are working."

"Don't you have a sister?"

He nodded, crossing his arms over his chest. "Cassandra. She's at her friend's house for the evening."

After Gina had checked on her sister, Carson suggested they all sit at the kitchen table. "If you are sure you actually want to talk," he added as they followed him to the kitchen, "we can sit in here."

"Just keep the knives away from me," Margaret sarcastically commented, nodding at the wood block full of different sized knives, ready for her picking.

Carson glanced at her, brow knotted. What was there to be confused about though? Surely he didn't think Gina wouldn't mention their relationship to her. If so, he was an idiot, and she would be surprised because she had thought highly of Carson Owens while in school. He had even tutored her in math the year before they graduated. Although only four of the sessions were over math. The others were on human anatomy—each other's anatomy, specifically. Requesting him to tutor her was how Margaret first got him to spend time with her.

The three of them sat at the small breakfast table in a little nook of the kitchen. The large windows they sat near illuminated the nook, and there was no need for any extra lighting, yet Carson flipped a light-switch anyway.

It was deathly silent for several seconds as they sat there together in a circle. Carson cleared his throat half a minute later and sat forward, fingers laced in front of him on the table. "What is this about?"

"You can't guess?" Margaret said quickly, not giving Gina a chance to respond.

He shrugged and looked down at his recently-trimmed thumbnail, picking at it with his other thumbnail. "I suppose I could. I would prefer the both of you just say what you want to say to me and get it over with."

Margaret looked to Gina to start, and Gina looked to Margaret. Margaret motioned for her to go first, but she shook her head no and looked down at her clenched hands laying on her lap. Her full lips were tightly pressed together. She wasn't ready.

Margaret sighed, looking back at Carson. "Gina told me that you two were romantic." The tears started forming, but Margaret shoved them away. *No, he will not see me cry. I would rather be flogged before he sees me cry over this.*

310

Carson nodded once, curtly. He stared at his laced fingers and glanced up for half a second at Gina before he said, "Yes."

It was quiet for a moment while Margaret thought of what to say next and how to say it. Even though she was glad he was being honest, she was so angry with his answer. "So... Why then? Were you not content with waiting for her? You needed to get off, and she wasn't going to give you anything, is that it?"

Carson's eyes shifted quickly from guilty to disgusted. "What? No, of course not. What—" he stumbled over his words for a second as he adjusted himself on his seat. "What are you talking about?"

Gina inhaled sharply, catching everyone's attention, and exhaled, sitting up straight. Margaret patiently waited to see if she was going to speak finally or not.

She was. "This was a mistake. I don't want to talk about this." She began to stand.

Margaret quickly grabbed her with her bad arm, forgetting it was injured at all. She yelped at the pain that pinched her nerves and pulled it to herself.

"Are you okay?" Carson reached for her, but he stopped short of touching her shoulder. He looked genuinely concerned. His big chocolate eyes scanned her for answers as he waited for her to speak.

Anem's burning stars, he's beautiful. She hated how attracted she was to him. And she hated that she liked how concerned he seemed.

"What happened, Margaret?"

Gina stood aside, watching Carson's reaction to his lover—ex-lover, that was. Their fling was over for good.

"It's nothing," she lied, gripping her arm and tugging it closer to her chest.

"Like hell it's nothing." He stood and looked at Gina. "Do you know what happened to her?"

Gina glanced at Margaret, who shook her head and silently begged her not to tell him the truth.

"Gina." Carson's voice was not soft and delicate like it had been toward her earlier. It was commanding. "What happened?"

She took a deep breath and looked him square in the eyes. And, bravely, she lied, "She fell down the stairs last night. She's very embarrassed about it."

His eyes narrowed suspiciously. "Why are you lying?"

She turned red and removed her gaze from his.

He stepped closer to her, but he wasn't angry. He looked upset, disappointed. Maybe even concerned. "G," he whispered to her, that delicate tone back in his voice. "Tell me what happened."

"Stop it, Carson," interrupted Margaret. She also stood from the table. "It's none of your business."

"Someone hurt you, and you're protecting them. You both are." He wasn't asking. He was quick. Smart. Although Margaret supposed it wouldn't take a genius to figure that part out. "Was it William?"

Margaret shook her head. "No. Leave it alone." She couldn't tell Carson what her father had done to her. She couldn't even tell Gina. They may say something, and Margaret didn't want her father getting into trouble—even if she was cross about what he'd done.

Carson's eyes narrowed again, at Margaret instead. "Fine." He motioned with his hands to her then Gina. "What else did you want to discuss? If you don't mind, Margaret, there is a conversation Gina and I need to have privately."

"No," whispered Gina. She stared at the tiled floor and shook her head quickly. "Whatever you want to say to me privately is a waste of time. I won't marry you, Carson. I've decided that much."

Carson was silent for a few heartbeats. He watched her carefully. Then, quietly he said, "But I spoke with the Judge, and—"

She said, "I'm sorry you wasted your morning. But I can't forgive you."

The silence that filled the house was sickening. Margaret didn't dare be the first to speak. She watched Carson carefully for any expression, but she saw nothing cross his face.

He finally spoke after a long minute had passed, "Judge James is going to promote me to a Class Seven so that I can be a doctor. He said that if you choose to marry me, you will be promoted too. You wouldn't have to worry about money ever again. And your family would be taken care of fully. I'd make sure of it."

Both girls stared at him, shocked. Being promoted was rare—very rare—and to have someone be promoted to the High Class was even rarer.

It dawned on Margaret the first thing he considered when realizing he'd be a High Class citizen soon wasn't that he finally had the legal ability to marry Margaret and try to get the engagement contract between William and her terminated. His only focus was giving Gina a good life. A better life than she could ever dream of otherwise.

He loved her. He might've even loved her more than he loved Margaret. And for some reason, that made sense. It hurt her to think about, but it did make sense. Margaret would probably love Gina more than herself too.

She should accept his proposal. But Margaret didn't think Gina should marry him because he loved her. She thought Gina should accept his offer because it was an amazing deal for her. She would never get this opportunity again.

"Gina," addressed Margaret, her tone hasty. "I understand how you feel about him right now, but you should marry him."

She wrinkled her nose, lips down turning. "For the money? Really, Margaret? I'm not desperately poor. I'm a Class Four, not One. You said Scott was a Class Six—"

Margaret shrugged. "Who cares about that? A doctor makes twice as much as a mechanic. Look, he'll never hurt you more than you've been hurt now, so that means no surprises, right? Bonus: You'll be rich because your husband is a Class Seven doctor. You'll be able to take care of your siblings with his money."

Gina was silent. Was she pondering the possibilities? She should. Hell, if Margaret were in her shoes, she wouldn't have hesitated.

Who cares if Carson's unfaithful? He is willing to take care of Gina and her family. I know she's angry, but come on. What's wrong with her?

Carson finally broke the silence. "You don't have to decide at this moment. Just think about it."

"But you do have to decide by the end of the day," added Margaret.

Finally, Gina spoke to Margaret, and she sounded irritated, "You told me not to marry him."

Carson's gaze snapped to Margaret. He opened his mouth to say something but then quickly thought better of it, and he shut his mouth.

"Look, I only said not to marry him because he was unfaithful to you, but—"

"Whoa, now. Hold on," butted in Carson, hands held up. "I have not been unfaithful to anyone."

Margaret stared at Carson so intensely that she thought perhaps she could bore holes through his skull. *How could he treat this so lightly? As if he did nothing wrong?*

Gina whispered, "I'm sorry, but I am still so upset."

He looked at her, and his eyes shifted to sorrow. Perhaps even guilt. If he felt guilty, then he did do something wrong. It wasn't up for debate. "Gina, I know I hurt you, but I did not betray you. I would never do that."

Margaret couldn't help herself as she asked, "How can you say you would never betray her when you, in fact, did?" She gestured manically at him and then herself. "And with me?! Her friend!"

He shook his head at both of them, taking a step back and steadying himself on the table. "Listen. Gina and I ended our relationship a year and a half ago. Then I was with you. And now you and I are no longer together, so I proposed marriage to Gina. How are the two of you able to make it so complicated?"

Wait. Margaret knew her and Carson were no longer together, but she didn't know Gina and Carson had ended things before she and Carson were ever together.

"I'm confused," whispered Margaret as she glanced to Gina, who was wringing her hands nervously and had a few tears running down her blushed cheeks. "Gina said you two were romantic."

"We were," confirmed Carson. "And then she told me to leave her alone. I did. And every time I tried to talk to her, she avoided me. She did that for nearly a year before I gave up. And then soon after that, you and I started talking."

She glanced at Gina, who was quite obviously embarrassed and shedding more tears.

"It's okay, Gina." She reached over with her right arm to pat her, but Gina stepped away, turned, and left the kitchen.

Why did she lie to me? Did she really think he would wait for her if she was avoiding him? If so, she has a naive view of boys. Boys are very impatient. And hardly any of them make it through school without having done something illegal with a girl, whether it marks their bodies or not. Margaret had more experience with impatient boys than she ever cared to admit to anyone, even Carson.

Carson and Margaret made eye contact then, and Margaret was suddenly reminded once again how incredibly beautiful he was. He said, "She says she never meant that we were not together."

"I understand," she whispered, glancing back to make sure Gina hadn't returned and could hear what she was going to say. "I would've assumed the same as you. She should've been more forthcoming."

"Her mom had just died."

"Still."

He shook his head, stood and left the room, following after Gina.

Margaret sat there for a few moments, chewing on her bottom lip. Did he disagree? She wanted to give them a couple of minutes to talk alone. They needed to speak privately, and she didn't mind it. But...

Carson's words repeated in her head over and over. *'How are the two of you able to make it so complicated?'* Perhaps he was right. They had complicated things when, to Carson, it was simple.

Yet, a couple of things came to Margaret's mind, starting with Gina not saying outright how she felt and what she expected from Carson. Then, Margaret and Carson bound themselves together despite the inevitable consequences they ignored at the time. One of those consequences being Gina's heartbreak.

It was not that it wasn't complicated. It unfortunately was complicated, and that really couldn't be argued, no matter how much Carson wished it to be different.

37

"**I** know you're angry," whispered Carson as he knelt by Gina where she sat on the floor next to the pillow fort. Lilli Ann was still sleeping soundly. Carson assumed she wanted to leave, but she didn't want to wake the little one either. "Please consider this opportunity Anem is handing to you, though."

Gina whipped her head toward him, eyes blazing. "Do not suggest this is the will of the goddess," she hissed low enough so it wouldn't wake the two-year-old. Her face was slowly crimsoning from her fury. "Anem did not will for you to lay with the Duchess, and Anem did not bless you for it either."

"I didn't say—"

"Enough, Carson."

Carson had never seen Gina as livid as she was in that moment.

Irritation bubbled inside of him. He was growing tired of apologizing. What had he truly done wrong to her? He would not admit to betraying her—because he hadn't. She needed to admit that all of this was partly her fault too. Sure, he sinned by binding himself to Margaret James. And of course, he regretted it. But he did not betray Gina. He honestly thought he and Gina would never be together.

He said quietly, "Why did you tell Margaret that I was unfaithful to you? You know that's not true."

She hesitated, then she rolled her eyes, which caused the tears welling in them to spill over. "I want her to hate you," she mumbled so lowly that Carson almost missed what she had said. "If she hates you, you will never be able to touch her again. I'm quite fond of that idea." She glared at him from the side of her eye.

He didn't know how to respond. What was he supposed to say? He couldn't tell her how he felt about it. It would sound harsh to tell her how childish that was, and it definitely wouldn't help his chances with her.

"It doesn't matter though," she whispered. Then, she said something that surprised Carson, and it took him a moment to process it. "My dad said I am not angry with you, you know. He said I'm angry with myself and am 'deflecting' that onto you." She made eye contact with him. "Maybe he's right. Maybe I hate myself for not communicating effectively with you."

He felt his hopes for her choosing him rise only slightly. *She may yet forgive me.* "Gina." He reached over and grabbed her clenched hand. She opened it a fraction to allow him to hold it.

But before he could say what he wanted, she added, "Or maybe you've embarrassed me, and that's why I'm so angry. Either could be true, I suppose."

He was quiet for a long while. He felt guilty that he embarrassed her, and he was sure the latter was probably truer than the former. But he truly had not intended on his actions affecting her in any way.

When he was sure she didn't have anything else to say, he whispered, squeezing her soft hand gently, "I love you, Gina. I always believed you were the one for me."

"And Margaret?"

He paused. "It's different." It felt like a half-truth, though. It wasn't much different. He did love Margaret. She was good to him. They had been good friends and decent lovers. If he couldn't marry Gina, he would be happy to have the chance to marry Margaret—if it were at all possible, which it wasn't.

Gina sighed and squeezed his hand back softly. *That's a good sign,* he thought. He was glad the conversation was ending on a positive note.

She said finally, "I love you, Carson, but I don't think I can marry you. Not now."

"Wha—what do you mean 'not now'?" *She said she loved me.* "Now is all you have, Gina. You have to decide by this evening. You don't get another chance."

"I'll be miserable. Every time I see that brand on your shoulder, I will be angry all over again. Do you really want a bitter wife?"

"Of course not," he whispered. He closed his eyes. Sorrow washed through him. "All I want is for you to be happy."

She nodded, gave him a small smile, and squeezed his hand once more before letting go. "Thanks for understanding," she whispered.

As she moved from the floor to the sofa to wait on Lilli Ann to rise from her slumber, he asked, "Does this mean you'll marry Bobby?"

She shrugged. "Maybe. Although I heard Scott Miller is a kind and handsome fellow. And he's already a Mature. That's a huge plus for me."

Carson nodded thoughtfully. Matures were less likely to be violent or break the rules and were generally a safer option. "Whomever you choose," he whispered, "may the two of you have a blessed marriage." And he meant every word. There was not an inkling inside of him that hoped for ruin in her relationship with anyone she chose. He prayed she would be happy all the days of her life.

May it be long and prosperous.

38

Nodding at the barista, William took the cup from the young man and gave him a coin as a tip. As he left the cafe, he took a swig of the bitter black coffee that often kept his vivid nightmares at bay. Images of Britt executed for treason haunted his dreams and plagued his thoughts. He couldn't shake the eeriness and fear that clutched at his soul.

Britt was a smart woman, but she was also quite reckless. How could Drew think it a good idea to send her, of all the drottnegs at his disposal, into Polaris? When he had told William he was sending a friendly to help out, he imagined it would be her brother Michael, the more cautious one of the two of them. But perhaps Michael was too valuable to their commander to put him in possible danger. He supposed Michael was his favorite drottneg soldier.

He hopped on a tramcar when it stopped for him. For the whole seven-and-a-half-minute ride back to the justice department, he drank the rest of his bitter coffee and prayed that Drew would make a move sooner rather than later. All William wanted was to go home with Britt. Sure, they were looked down upon and distrusted in Soutas because of what they were, but at least he had no secrets and they weren't committing treason there.

They were currently committing treason in the Province of Deneb. If they were found out to be working for runaways and withholding valuable information of the whereabouts of thousands of innocent humans, they would both be removed from their vessels. The human vessels they had learned to call their own would be executed, and their essence would be stored away in the District's cryobank until a cure was found for their real bodies. And then—if a cure was ever even found—who knows how they'd punish them for choosing humans over their own kind?

Traitors, is what they were. They had grown weary of jumping from one body to the next just to stay alive in hopes of finding a cure for their species. It was all in vain anyway, they believed. The goddess was not real; no matter how hard their prophets prayed, she would never answer. William was sure there was a god, but as far as he knew, that god was unknown and unnamed, and probably angry about his kind taking over the human's world and bodies.

He allowed himself to imagine living with Britt in a little villa they built themselves, back on the Forgotten Isle, on the side of the Gaalé mountain. They'd be able to grow old together, and they'd die together, in those bodies they'd stolen many years ago from unsuspecting humans.

It wasn't like they could return the bodies. The humans that used to own them were gone forever. Drew Owens had tried to rouse them by removing the very essence that was the drottneg William, but the bodies were what Drew called Unwokens. Empty vessels. That was why Britt, William, and Michael had been allowed to keep their bodies. Some humans did wake up, but not all of them. And Toka had no use for a comatose body. By allowing the demons to live, they owed the commander a large debt.

William was abruptly reminded of his upcoming wedding when the tramcar stopped for an elderly woman who greeted him and asked if he was getting nervous for the special day. "It's normal to be nervous to vow yourself to another in front of so many witnesses at the temple," she added.

He was annoyed at the reminder, but she meant no harm. He

tipped his uniform cap to her and smiled. "Not at all. I'm happy to marry such an honorable woman as the Duchess." *So many lies in that one sentence alone.*

He kept reminding himself of the benefits to marrying Margaret, but there was just one huge con he couldn't ignore. She was seventeen. A bloody child.

The idea was simple enough. Marry them young so they will have children young. The sooner they reproduce, the more children they are likely to have. Kids are stupid, and kids encouraged to have sexual relations are stupider. They get pregnant—over and over—and wonder how. But that was the very reason for encouraging them to marry young. The more children that are born, the more vessels that will be available for rent once aged to eighteen years and are finally ripe—*enough*—for the Ritual.

Once at the department, he set out to do his business as usual. The day was busy, but no one was murdered or whipped on his shift, so all in all, he was content with how the day turned out. Especially earlier that day, in that flower shop where he had spent an intimate moment with his wife. It had been many months since the two of them had even seen each other, let alone touched. He had missed how she felt in his arms and her skin against his, and though it had been severely irresponsible and risky of them to meet in that flower shop, he was glad he had the moment with her.

The door opened suddenly, startling William. Derek Owens stepped inside, a smirk on his face. He said sternly as the uniformed officer closed the door behind him, "You should knock, Officer Owens. It's inappro—"

"Oh, shut your trap." Derek sat in the chair across from William's desk. "You are going to answer my questions about Drew, and you aren't going to lie to me like you did yesterday."

William leaned forward, resting his elbows on his desk. Derek would not break his resolve. He had been trained for such situations. "What I said yesterday was not a lie. Honestly, yes, I was told about you having a twin brother, and yes, I was told his name. But that's it. You are looking for more information than I have to give you."

Derek, still smirking, handed William a computer chip. "Are you sure about that?"

"What's this?" Taking the chip, William curiously flipped it over, examining it.

Derek leaned forward. "Information." Then he sat back and motioned to William's small computer on the side of his desk. "Why don't you find out what *information* I have on you and your pretty girlfriend?"

William's stomach turned to stone. "Margaret? What did she do this time?"

Derek motioned to the computer again. "Only if Margaret has a diamond-shaped brand in the center of her back."

William tried not to be hasty or let his nerves show as he plugged the chip into the appropriate slot. It was a video file from one of their body cameras. He looked sidelong at Derek as he clicked on it. It was a dim video, and it was quite hard to see who was who or what was happening. What was there horrified him, and the stone that was his stomach dropped through the earth.

Derek had video footage of his conversation with Britt in the flower shop.

"You followed me." It was not a question.

"I knew something wasn't right with you. My gut is never wrong." He motioned to the video still playing. "Seems I was correct. Who is *toka*? What debt do you owe him? Are you planning on running away?"

William balled his fists. The video continued past their conversation and William's face grew hot. He quickly shut the video off, took out the chip with fumbling fingers, and broke it in half.

"That was just a copy," said Derek, voice emotionless.

William had figured as much, but he still had to get rid of it. "Destroy that footage."

"Answer my questions."

William paused for a long moment to gather his thoughts before taking a deep breath and saying calmly, "Really, Owens? Blackmail? You know that's illegal, right?" There was no way Derek Owens would out Britt, even if the man hated him. Derek was just not that type of person. The man was clearly desperate for answers about his brother's disappearance. William sat back and smirked.

The expression caused Derek's brows to twitch. "I see you aren't taking me seriously, Lach. Perhaps I should turn this over to the Judge then." Derek slipped a hand in his pocket and pulled out another chip, flashing it for him to see.

William started. How many copies had the bastard made?

"There," Derek said. "Now we're getting somewhere."

Forcing himself to stay calm, William held his smirk. "Don't fool yourself, Owens. We both know you're not that type of man."

"You really want to take that risk, Lach?"

For a moment, William ground his teeth and considered his options. He could gamble on Derek's honest nature and shrug off the threat. But with Britt in the video also... He could not take the risk. As long as that evidence existed, there was no telling who could get their hands on it. No, he could not take that risk.

He shut his eyes, cursing himself silently as he said, "Fine. You get three questions, and I want every copy of that video, including the original."

Derek lounged back in the navy fabric chair, resting his left ankle on his right knee. "You love that woman, don't you?"

He hesitated, but answered truthfully. There was no point in lying. "Yes."

"Yet she only just moved here last night."

"Two more questions, Owens."

Derek squinted. "You still don't seem to understand the situation you're in, Lach."

Clicking his tongue, William said, "I know her from before I moved here."

"Oh, is that so?" Derek said smugly. "I clearly recall you saying you moved here from Kaitos. She is from the District of Diphda. How could the two of you have known each other before? Unless, of course" —Derek shrugged— "both of you lied about where you are from."

William saw no point in lying at this point. "Our vessels were born and raised in those places."

Derek nodded, not surprised by the information. "There were reports in a rural town of Kaitos that a young man by the name of William Tatum went missing over a decade ago. He was eighteen. Only weeks after his Ritual."

William's heart skipped a beat. *He did research? Drew was right about Derek. He figured it out. I should have stayed away from him.*

"And there was a girl in the District that went missing at age twenty, along with her eighteen-year-old brother Michael. Her name was Britt Rogers." Derek rubbed his chin thoughtfully, though it was obvious to William that it was only for show. "Thing is, the picture they have on file of William Tatum bears an uncanny resemblance to you." He looked William square in the eye. "How old are you truly?"

It was quiet for several seconds. Derek was patient though. He didn't tap his foot or twiddle his thumbs. He just sat in that cheap fabric chair and stared a hole through William as he waited for an answer.

William sighed. "If you know all of that, then you know my age."

Derek grinned slightly, but he didn't answer. He sat up straight and stated, "I want to know what you and the girl were talking about. What are you planning? Who do you work for? How does it relate to Drew?"

"I said three questions, Owens," William said.

"Really, Lach?"

How did Derek truly expect him to answer that? Was it a test? Had his Ritual failed? Was he awake? "First tell me where your allegiance lies."

Derek's eyebrows furrowed. "What does that mean?"

William leaned forward, resting his elbows on the desk. "What is your name?"

The officer rolled his eyes. "What is this game you're playing?"

"No game. Tell me your given name."

He squinted at William, unsure. "I'll bite. My name is Derek Owens."

"Was that the name you were born with or the name you stole?"

Derek's eyes sparked with revelation. "Ah," he stated, "I see now." He paused. "You first."

William understood the hesitation. He felt it too. Neither could know if the other was going to turn them in to the law if they admitted the Ritual had failed. But if Derek's initial confusion meant anything... He smiled, taking the opening presented to him. "I was born William Tatum," he lied.

Excitement flickered in Derek's eyes. "So the Ritual failed on you too?"

"Too?" That was exactly what William wanted to be sure of. He had to admit a part of him was happy to hear it. *Drew will be pleased*.

Derek's jaw clenched. Clearly, he had not meant to say as much as he did, but it was out in the open now. No take backs.

William smiled at him. "Your brother will be happy to hear that. He was betting on you."

Derek was quiet for only a second. "It's true then? Drew's alive?"

William saw no harm in telling Derek the truth now. It was Derek Owens, after all—not one of William's kind, a drottneg. "Alive and thriving. He is our commander. Toka."

"What does that mean?"

"Toka means commander."

He waved his hand dismissively. "What do you mean by

commander? As if he has an army?" William nodded once, and he allowed Derek to take a few long pauses to process. Finally, Derek asked, "You work for him? You and Britt?"

"Yes."

"And why are you here? What's he planning?"

William opened a drawer and pulled out an atlas of their world. He pointed to the small island at the southwest corner.

"The Forgotten Isle?" Derek looked up from the map. "What about it?"

"There are humans there. Thousands. Drew wants to save his family from this house of horrors and take you to paradise." Derek's eyes slowly grew wider as William continued speaking, "You will be able to live out your life, happy and carefree, and your children will never have to go through the Ritual. That is what your brother wants. To save Carson and Cassandra from the Ritual." William added as an afterthought, motioning with his hands, "Oh, and Margaret too, but never mind her. That's a long story."

It was too much information. Derek sat back in the chair, eyes begging the gray rug for assistance in processing. After several long moments of silence, William asked, "You okay?"

Derek looked up at him from the rug. He didn't answer William immediately, but when he finally did, he grinned—small, tight—and said, "When do we leave?"

William returned the smile. He was relieved that Derek was taking it all so well. "I don't know," he answered. "I am here to keep an eye on Margaret and keep her out of trouble. Britt is here to watch out for Carson and Cassandra. Neither of us know when Drew plans on moving. It'll be before Carson turns eighteen, I imagine."

Derek shook his head and shrugged at the same time. "He only just turned seventeen a few months ago."

"I know."

Derek exhaled, as if annoyed. "Do you have ways of communicating with him?"

"Yes," he answered. "I'll tell him you said hello."

"Oh, stars, no." He seemed disgusted that William would suggest such a thing. "Do not do that."

"I have to tell him you know the plan."

Derek was pensively quiet for a moment before asking, "Wouldn't that only get you in trouble?"

William blew out a puff of air. "Yeah," he breathed. "I will be punished severely for disobeying direct orders." The image of building a villa with Britt after everything was over evaporated from his dreams. He would not be done paying off his debt when all of this was over after all.

"Then don't tell him," was Derek's response. "And when I see Drew again, I will not mention you or the woman. I will act surprised that he's alive." He leaned forward and pointed his finger at William. "But don't you be surprised when I bloody his nose and knock out his teeth."

William couldn't help chuckling. "Yeah, I imagine that's fair."

"You aren't going to ask why?"

"I know why. He is expecting you and Kayla to be angry. He even expects one of you—or both—to try to kill him. You won't be able to, of course. He has prepared for it. He will have bodyguards." William gestured to himself. "If I'm there, I'll be one of them."

Derek inhaled deeply and exhaled slowly. "I don't wish him dead," he whispered. "He is my brother. But I can't speak for my wife."

A moment of silence fell between the two men, but it was not uncomfortable. William assumed Derek was still processing everything he learned about his long-lost brother.

Finally, Derek said, "He is not Carson's father. I want to make that clear."

William shrugged. "It doesn't matter to me."

"It matters to me." He looked at William then, eyes intense. "I raised the boy. He is mine. Doesn't matter what his DNA says."

William shrugged a second time. "That sounds reasonable to me."

"Is he hoping to be his father?"

"I don't think so. He calls him *the boy* when speaking about him." There was a pause. "He's not looking to steal Kayla and Carson from you. He has a family of his own, Derek. He just wants to protect your kids."

Derek's eyebrows raised. "He found a woman willing to put up with him?"

William chuckled. "You'll understand when you meet her."

"And he has children?"

"You will meet them all soon enough."

Despite Derek's threat to beat Drew, William was sure by his questions and excitement alone that he was happy to hear his brother was alive. He wanted to know every detail of his brother's life he had missed.

A knock suddenly came at the door, startling both men. Derek reached across the desk and scooped up the broken pieces of the computer chip as William folded the atlas and stuffed it away.

"I want the footage, Derek," he rasped. "I've told you everything and more."

Derek simply slipped the broken pieces of the first chip into his pocket and proclaimed, "You may enter," to whomever was at the door. Then to William, he nodded and whispered, "Nice talking with you," and tipped his uniform cap to say goodbye. William was unsure if that meant he would destroy the video or not. He would have to trust Derek would do the right thing.

Margaret James was the last person either of them expected to walk through the door. William was frozen for a second and a half, confused. He watched Derek tip his hat toward the girl. She curtsied and asked the officer, "How do you do, Officer Owens?"

He said cheerfully, "Oh, I am having a wonderful day, my lady," and left the office with a slight skip in his step.

William shook off the surprise of seeing her as she said to Derek's back, "Glad to hear your day is much better than your son's."

But Derek ignored her and continued on his way.

William asked Margaret, "What is it you need?" He thought maybe she wanted something for the wedding last minute. He didn't care and was ready to tell her she could do whatever she wanted with the flowers, ribbons, lace, yada yada—whatever the hell weddings were made out of.

She shut the door softly and took a seat in front of his desk, indicating she wanted to have a real, actual, grownup, godforsaken talk. He sighed. *Oh, for the love of all things pure, may there be a god who'll have mercy and spare me from this wretched conversation.*

He sat down in his chair on the opposite side, gave a forced smile, and asked, "Is there something you'd like to discuss?"

She nodded, hesitated for a brief moment, then said bluntly, "I don't want to marry you."

The feeling was mutual, but he couldn't come right out and say that. He had to play his cards correctly with the teen girl.

When he didn't react immediately, she added, "I would like to terminate the contract and then marry Carson when the time is right."

William sat there for a moment—or five—staring at her. "You're insane," left his lips before he gave the words a bit more consideration.

Her face scrunched into one of irritation and annoyance. She tilted her chin up slightly and straightened her posture. "You can't stop me." She was lying, and she had to know that he definitely could stop her. She signed a contract with him, and the only way out was if he agreed to terminate said contract. Indeed, he very well could stop her.

"Margaret—"

"If you refuse, I'll tell my father about the stunt you pulled."

One of William's eyebrows quirked at the threat. *What is it with the blackmail today?* Though he knew what she'd say, he asked, "Stunt?"

"The bath." She didn't blink or take her eyes from his. She was completely unbothered by him, he realized.

Wild woman.

Feigning worry, he said, "I didn't touch you."

Her eyes narrowed. "You're sweating, Will."

He wasn't, but he ran the back of his hand across his forehead and swallowed loudly. It was good if she thought this made him nervous. If she was going to believe he'd willingly sign any termination form, she needed to think she had real blackmail on him.

Besides, he didn't want Judge James finding out about the bath incident.

He said, "Terminate the contract, though? To marry Carson?"

As composed as the politician she was born to be, she gave him a dispassionate nod.

"Have you lost your mind?" was his calculated response. "Your father won't approve."

"You don't know that."

"Don't be stupid, Margaret. Do I really need to remind you of Carson's social status? He's a Class Five. You know you can't marry a man from the Middle Class."

She rolled her eyes so hard William thought she may be able to see her incompletely developed frontal lobe.

What a childish thing to do, he sourly thought.

She jabbed her finger at him as she said firmly, "Actually, Father's promoting him to a Class Seven in twenty days. He's going to be a doctor." She looked proud. Very proud. And then, of course, the obnoxious teenager added, "So suck it, William. I'm not stupid." He wasn't even surprised by the words, nor offended, even though the rules were clear of its illegal vulgarity.

William looked down at the carpet for a moment to consider what gift he'd been given. And it wasn't just a gift for him. Someone upstairs saw it fit to bless Carson and Margaret too, apparently, despite their sin. "I see," he said, finally looking up and meeting her eyes. He would not argue with a plan from the heavens. "You have the opportunity to marry someone you love. I get it."

Her mouth twitched and a slight smile spread across her face, though she tried to pinch her lips together to make it smaller. "So, you'll sign the form to terminate the engagement?"

He fought a large toothy smile that wanted so badly to take over his face. The corners of his mouth twitched as he spoke. "I guess so," he downplayed.

She quickly, almost excitedly, pulled out a packet of papers from her bag and shoved them at him across the desk. "I marked all the places you need to sign."

Happily, he took his black pen from his shirt pocket. "Anything for true love," he said as he scribbled his mark on every page, trying not to seem too happy about the end of their engagement.

He was comfortable with ending the engagement only if she truly could marry Carson, because then she would be protected as ordered by the toka, and William could simply keep an eye on her from a distance. How much trouble could she really cause then?

But William tried not to get his hopes up. He was doubtful that the Judge would approve of the termination simply because there was no good reason they could explain to the public. And then if Margaret married Carson? She would be assumed to be his lover, and if anyone demanded she be checked, that was it for her. She would be publicly flogged and defamed.

He tried not to get his hopes up, because he knew that if he were the Judge, he would not approve.

39

"No," Judge James answered. He did not have to think twice about it. In fact, he honestly couldn't believe she had even suggested such a preposterous proposal. And two days before her wedding, no less!

"Father—"

He frowned, holding up his hand to silence the girl. Which was all she was. She was just a little girl. She was not in any place to make important decisions such as this. She was being stupid, thinking with her heart and not her brain. But he supposed that was usual of a seventeen-year-old. "I said no, and that's the end of it."

It was silent for a solid five seconds. William cleared his throat and shifted in his seat. Mark was already annoyed with whatever he was about to say. "If I may, Judge James—"

"I wish you wouldn't."

William ignored the interjection. "I don't see how it's a bad idea."

Surely he was joking.

"She has a brand with Carson," William continued, as if he needed reminding of his daughter's sin. "If she's ever stopped in the future for whatever reason, the officers will assume she has only one because of whoever she is married to. As long as they don't look too deeply into her brand, they'll never know that it matches Carson's current brand. But if she marries me, she will have two brands."

"Exactly!" Margaret jabbed her finger at William and nodded her head repeatedly. "And that makes it more dangerous for me. But since you'll be promoting Carson, doesn't it make the most sense for me to marry him?"

Mark glared at the pair over the rim of his spectacles. "And what am I supposed to tell people when they ask why your engagement was terminated?"

Margaret pursed her lips. She had clearly not considered that part. But of course the child had not. All she knew was she could finally marry Carson, so long as the wedding they'd been planning with William did not take place.

William said, having thought of an answer much quicker than Mark expected of the young man, "Tell them we both argue a lot, and that makes you uncomfortable. No father wants their daughter in a stressful and potentially toxic relationship."

He wasn't wrong, Mark supposed. He huffed and looked to his daughter. "And do you think people will ignore the oddity of an engagement to Carson Owens?"

"They won't think it's odd," she said. "Carson and I have been close friends for a year now. Bobby and Fiona would be able to vouch for that."

"Not good enough," the Judge said. "They will think you were his lover and—"

"They think Gina is his lover," she interrupted, tone chilling.

Was that resentment in his daughter's voice? Was she jealous that everyone who knew Carson thought he'd been with Gina and had not even considered her? The Judge thought of that as a blessing, but his daughter did not seem to agree.

"And I'm not suggesting Carson and I marry as soon as he's promoted. Perhaps in a year or two, once things settle."

Mark was quiet for a long moment. If she truly was willing to wait a couple of years, he was not unwilling to allow her to marry the Owens boy. He drummed his fingers on his mahogany desk and blew out a puff of air before he reminded her, "Gina may yet choose him. She has first—"

"She won't," interrupted Margaret, stating matter-of-factly. "She told me so. And Carson. We all discussed it a few hours ago. She said she was going to choose Scott Miller."

"Scott Miller, eh?" Mark rubbed a years-old ring stain from a cold drink he had on his desk. It took him a few more moments to consider, but finally he said, "If Gina does not choose Carson, and if you agree to wait a couple of years—"

"One or two," she said.

"A couple," he affirmed, voice strong and sharp, eyes warning. "At the very earliest."

Her eyes narrowed. "Fine."

He continued, "If you can agree to wait a couple of years, at the earliest, then I will grant you this request."

She smiled at him, fought a small dance in her seat, then jumped up and tackled him with a hug. He couldn't remember the last time they had embraced, and so he held her closely. It could easily be the last hug she ever offered him. He noticed as she squirmed that she was favoring her left arm, and that broke his heart into a hundred million pieces.

He hadn't meant to permanently damage her when he foolishly tried to remove her brand. He was gravely afraid he had, and he didn't know how to make that up to her. Perhaps giving her Carson as a husband would, in the end, be sufficient enough of an apology.

"I agree," she told him.

When his daughter released him from the sweet embrace, William handed him the termination form to sign. Both his and Margaret's initials and signatures already filled the document. He grabbed the wax and stamp from the drawer, and he placed his seal on the document, praying to Anem he wouldn't regret it.

40

"**M**oriah Ginevieve Blake."

Gina's stomach flipped at her father's flat tone and use of her full name. She turned her head slowly toward the entrance to the kitchen where he stood, wiping his calloused hands on a dirty work rag.

He was a burly man, broad-shouldered and muscly. Much, much bigger than her. She was like her mother—small-framed and petite. He had grayed exponentially since her mother's passing two years ago.

She dried her hands from washing dishes on the towel next to the sink. "Yes?" she said cautiously. She wasn't sure if she was in trouble or not, but whatever it was, he didn't look pleased.

"Why are you here?"

Confused, she answered, "I'm cleaning up after dinner."

"You know that's not what I meant. Don't you have an appointment?"

Oh. He was talking about her meeting with the Judge. "Judge James sent a message earlier that he'd come over to speak with me instead. Something came up; he had to cancel."

"Hmm." His eyebrows furrowed. "Wonder why."

Gina shrugged, turning back to the sink. She hoped he'd go away. She didn't want to talk about any of this with her father. She knew his opinion. He didn't have to keep reminding her.

"Did you get to speak with Carson?" And there it was.

His name simply spoken had the power to make her stomach bubble acid into her throat. She wondered if it would be that way for the rest of her life.

She inhaled deeply and exhaled. "Yes, I spoke with him."

"That's good." His tone was joyful. "Very good."

Gina sighed. She needed to break the bad news to her father. But why did she feel nervous?

She turned to him and said stiffly, "Dad, I can't marry him."

He pinched his lips together in thought for a moment, then pulled a chair out from under the table and motioned for her to sit next to him.

Great. He wants to have a talk.

She internally groaned, but took the seat anyway and waited patiently for him to start whatever long speech he had percolating in his head.

When he finally spoke, he avoided eye contact with her. Was he embarrassed? She wasn't sure she'd ever seen him embarrassed. "Honey," he began, "I would like to tell you a story. It's about a couple who were in love as schoolmates and were allowed to marry after they graduated. They had dreams of having a large family, and they vowed to teach their children the importance of love in a relationship. They waited a few years before having their first baby, a little girl they loved with all their heart. But, the man was still young and very stupid. And while he loved his wife, he missed her very much. His loneliness got the best of him."

"What do you mean? Did the wife go somewhere after giving birth?"

He shook his head. "No, but new babies take up so much energy and time."

That, Gina was familiar with, for the most part. She was the one that cared for Lilli Ann when her father could not. It was exhausting, and she hardly had time for anything else.

Her father continued his story, "You see, Anem had blessed the husband with a wife who loved him dearly, but he was blinded by his loneliness. And one day, he found himself in the bed of another, immediately ashamed of the sin he had committed."

Gina frowned. "That's horrible."

"He followed his flesh instead of Anem's commandments."

Gina wondered what her father was trying to teach her through this sad tale. "I'm sure she divorced him," she said. "He should be flogged, too."

He was quiet for several uncomfortable moments. Gina thought that maybe he disagreed with her statement. He finally said, still avoiding meeting her gaze, "He was thankful she didn't leave him and didn't report his infidelity."

Gina was appalled. "So he just...got away with it? He got away with destroying his family?"

"He was forgiven, but his wife did not forget about it. Their relationship took a long, long time to heal. But, praise the goddess, it *did* heal."

"Surely, if he loved his wife as much as you say he did, he would've controlled himself."

There was another long moment of silence. He glanced down at the table and then back at her. "I don't know," he breathed. "Now tell me something: do you think I loved your mother with all my heart?"

That was an easy one. "Yes, of course." A love like her parents' was rare. She had thought she'd found it with Carson, but she was wrong. She was very wrong. She would never have love like that.

"My love for her grew every single day I spent with her, and I learned to appreciate her more as the years passed. I am grateful she forgave me for the sin I committed, or else I wouldn't have had such a blessed life with so many children that I love dearly."

What? Gina was quiet as she processed his words. "The husband in your story was you?"

Her father? He couldn't have... He *wouldn't* have betrayed her

338

mother. He was a good man. A faithful husband to Emma Blake. And her mother loved her father very much. She not only said it many times, but she showed her love for him. There was no way he had ever hurt her like that.

He gave her a small nod to confirm and posed a question: "Was what I did worse than what Carson did?"

She didn't reply.

He reworded, "If you and Carson were married and you had just had a baby, and he came home and admitted to you that he bound himself to your friend, would that be worse than what he has *actually* done?"

Her face grew red, but not from embarrassment. Anger flooded her. Fury, even. She said fiercely, "If I marry him, the likelihood of that exact thing happening is high."

"I disagree. If he loves you—and he does—he will remain faithful to you. Do you know why?"

She dared roll her eyes. She grumbled, "Why?" and crossed her arms tightly over her chest.

"Because he didn't actually betray you. The two of you have not been close for some time, and that's more than understandable. Since your mother's passing, it's been hard for you to balance all your responsibilities." He reached over and patted her cheek lovingly. "I'm proud of you for all you've overcome, Gigi. And of all the men on that list, Carson Owens is *truly* the only one who will be as proud of you as I am, and who will care for you as I do. What other boys were here for you—every single bloody day? Who helped with your chores, listened while you cried, sat with you when you grieved? Who was it that was always here for you, until you told him to give you space?"

Hot tears welled in her eyes. They flowed down her face like a stream. "You don't understand."

"Yes, honey, I do—"

"No, you don't. He loves her, Dad. He actually, really loves her."

He was quiet, expressionless, and unblinking. Finally, he said,

"Even if that's true, why does it matter? He wants to be with you. He chose *you*."

Was he implying that it didn't matter that he loved another woman? She shook her head and looked down at her lap. "I've already decided to marry Scott Miller," she whispered.

"Who the hell's that?"

"I haven't met him yet."

"You're going to choose a stranger over the man you love?"

She sighed, rolling her eyes. "I'm sorry to disappoint you, Dad. I really am. Perhaps Mom was a better person than me, but I just cannot forgive him."

He was quiet for only a second. Then he whispered, "Can I tell you more of the story? Details?"

She hesitated. She didn't like that she knew what he already told her. But what did the details matter now? She already knew her father was an adulterer. "I suppose that's up to you."

He paused for several beats to consider how to start. Finally, he began, "The day it happened, I immediately came home. Your mother was rocking you to sleep. You were only a month old, maybe two. I waited until she laid you down in your crib to confess my sin to her. But it didn't matter whether she had been holding you or not. She yelled so loudly, you woke up anyway.

"So, there I was, right there" —he pointed across the hall toward the family room— "begging Emma to forgive me. All the while, she was screaming at me, and you were in the other room crying. She, of course, attended to you as soon as she realized you were hollering. But she was still so very angry. She wouldn't let me near her for months, and she didn't speak a word to me for weeks. I swear, during those days, by the way she looked at me sometimes, she probably thought about killing me. One night I woke up with her standing over me. I remember asking her if she was okay. She just spit on me and walked away."

Gina wished she had said no to the details. She couldn't imagine her mother ever behaving in such an abominable way. It was as if she didn't know her mother at all. The Emma Blake she knew was loving and sweet. In fact, Gina couldn't remember her ever even raising her voice.

Her father continued, "She finally decided, for your sake, that she wanted us to at least get along. She didn't want you to grow up watching your parents hate each other and thinking that was okay. She wanted you to believe in love, even if the love you saw was fake."

"Fake?" *No, no, no. My mom loved my dad.* Gina shook her head fiercely and covered her ears. "Dad, I can't hear that she didn't really love you. I can't. That's a lie."

Gently, he removed her hands from her ears and whispered, "We loved each other very much, Gigi. Our love was not a lie. My point is, it was hard—very hard—and it took a long time for her to love me again."

Both of them were quiet as they sat at the table, the setting sun causing the room to grow dimmer and dimmer.

Her father added, "You do not hate him, Gigi. Trust me. I know what a woman full of hate looks like. You are not full of hate. You are sad, and maybe a little mad. But you don't hate him, because you know that what he did had nothing to do with you."

"Isn't that the problem, though? It should've been no one else."

"I understand, but you are not his wife. You were focusing on healing yourself. He moved on. Now that he knows you are ready for a relationship, he has been right here with you. Am I wrong?"

He wasn't wrong... But he wasn't right either.

Suddenly, there was a knock on the door. It was soft but loud enough for them to hear it from the kitchen table. Gina was thankful the muted knock did not wake the young ones. She really didn't want to fight with them about going back to bed. Not tonight.

Both Gina and Tim answered the door. Judge James tilted a fedora he hardly wore toward them as a hello. The reason for the hat was probably to protect his head from the gentle rain that pelted off him.

He glanced at his watch before any words were exchanged. "Sorry about today, Gina. Things came up about Margaret's engagement that are now resolved. We have about five minutes at the latest, and then we have to head to your suitor's home for him to sign the contract. Gina, darling," he motioned to the girl with butterflies swarming in her abdomen, "I hope you've made up your mind. If not, I'll have to choose for you."

She hesitated, looked to her father who was of no help to her nerves, then nodded at the Judge. "Yes, sir. I have decided."

"Please," Timothy gestured inside the home he built with Emma— the wife he had been unfaithful to. "Come in from this weather, Mark."

"Greatest thanks," he mumbled as he crossed into the foyer. He turned to Gina, not removing his coat and hat. He didn't want to waste a moment. "So?" he asked. "Whose name shall I pen on the contract?"

She wrung her hands, and took a full second to consider all she knew about the world, about her father's past, about Carson's past, about the pains of life in general. She hated the life she'd been dealt. She really, really hated it. It was cruel, and she didn't feel like she deserved such pain.

The Judge cleared his throat to remind her of how short of time they had.

She exhaled roughly, to clear her lungs and her brain of the fog attempting to envelop her. She just wanted to go to bed.

"I'll marry Carson," was her whisper, and she was surprised to see the Judge frown deeply and *humph*, as if it mattered to him.

"Popular choice," the Judge grumbled, and she was confused what that meant. "Now, let's go see him and finish this up."

41

"Margaret had to hurry. She only had thirty-three minutes until curfew.

She ran up the cobblestone path to the Owens' home and knocked on the door rapidly. She wished she hadn't have knocked so aggressively as to alarm them. She simply didn't have much time, and she didn't want to wait until the next day to tell Carson the good news.

The door swung open seconds later, and Mr. Owens, who did indeed look alarmed, met her gaze. "Duchess," he said, almost a bit relieved. "You should not be here."

Nice to see you too, Mr. Owens. "I need to speak with Carson."

He glanced down the street, left and right. No one was out currently though. "I don't know if it's a good idea for you to be seen around Carson, especially a couple of days before your wedding."

Right. She had forgotten Derek Owens knew she was Carson's lover. "Yes, I realize that this puts me at risk, but please, let me speak to him. I am not marrying William. My father agreed to terminate our engagement so I could marry Carson in a couple of years after he's been promoted and the drama of our sin has settled."

Derek's eyes widened slightly. He glanced behind him and kept the door tightly pulled. She was not welcome, obviously. He turned his head back to her and whispered, "Listen, Duchess, save yourself the embarrassment and go home. You'll find out why soon enough." And then he closed the door in her face. She blinked a few times, frozen on their porch. She had not expected to be denied access to Carson.

Catching a tramcar just before it left its stop, she headed to the uppermost part of the city, where she lived in Oakdale Hollow along with a few other Class Sevens and Eights.

She envisioned Carson running the back part, through the pastures and wooded area, to see her. It was a shorter distance than the tramcar took. She wished she could take that unmarked path, but without Carson to guide her, she would surely get lost.

But what had Derek Owens meant by not embarrassing herself? He had said she'd find out soon enough. Though it ate away at her not knowing, she supposed there was nothing she could do but wait. She settled that she'd visit the Owens' residence in the morning and try to speak with Carson then.

42

Carson shifted on the couch. Next to him, Gina sat as still as a statue, hands laced in her lap, eyes on the gray carpet. An entire foot of space separated them, though the distance between them felt much greater.

"Who was at the door?" Kayla asked Derek.

His father fiddled with the watch on his wrist as he said, "Patrick's son found my watch in the road. He was returning it."

"Huh," said Kayla. "I hadn't noticed you missing it."

"Me either." He cleared his throat. "Everyone needs to be going home soon, so shall we wrap this up?"

Timothy Blake clapped his hands softly once. "I agree. I have to go make sure Jedidiah has managed to keep the three young'uns alive for the last half hour. Let's get this thing signed."

Carson was still in shock that Gina ultimately chose him. Only a few hours prior she had seemed so sure that she would not marry him. *I wonder what changed between then and now,* he thought, but he didn't care to ever know the answer. He was going to marry Gina Blake, and that was more than good enough for him.

"Okay." The Judge finished penning a few details onto the engagement contract as he spoke. "Carson, you're first." He handed the document to him. "We don't have time for you to read the whole thing, so I'll just tell you what it basically says. Once both of you sign this, you are both bound by your word to marry each other on the date listed in the document." He tapped the page with his finger to indicate where. "She has to be married by tomorrow evening, so the date is the eleventh."

"Obviously," muttered Carson, but he didn't mean it to be rude.

Judge James either didn't hear him or was ignoring him. "The only way to break this contract is if both of you sign a termination form, which I also have to approve. Pretty much, it all goes through me."

"Where do we sign?" asked Gina as she leaned closer to look at the document. She fidgeted with her skirt and worried her lip between her teeth. Was she anxious? Carson didn't blame her. The whole ordeal was nerve-wracking, considering the conversation between them earlier alone.

The Judge indicated where to sign, and Carson didn't hesitate to jot down his name on the dotted line. He handed the contract to Gina, and she, too, did not hesitate to scribble her name where designated.

"I need a few initials as well," Judge James said, grabbing the document and flipping pages. He gestured to the yellow highlighted boxes on the page. "These are the rules. They aren't hard rules to follow since you should be following them anyway. No abuse—verbal or otherwise. No disrespect. No public flirting. Start practicing commitment to each other. No kissing, no hugging, no relations— which includes any kind of sexual conduct until you're married."

The Judge gave Carson a wry side glance, the implications of which Carson did not appreciate in the least.

He continued his spiel, "You are both to consider each other an extension of your own selves. Gina will be able to speak on Carson's behalf, and vice versa. Premarital counseling is typically required by law, but since this is not a typical situation, that section has been revised. I will require two years of mandatory marriage counseling beginning no later than the twentieth day of this month. Have I been clear?"

The two teenagers gave a lackluster nod. Carson, personally, thought marriage counseling was a great idea, even if he wasn't looking forward to it all that much. But he would do whatever it took to mend the shattered relationship between him and his soon-to-be wife.

Wife. He tried not to let a small smile slip onto his lips. *Thank you, Anem. I do not deserve this blessing.*

"Questions?" Judge James asked. He was already beginning to gather his things, and the two had not even initialed the boxed sections.

"No," replied Carson.

Gina agreed with a shake of her head, pen ready in her hand. His heart weighed heavily at the sight of the dark circles under her eyes and the droopiness of her eyelids. Had she ever looked as tired and miserable as she did now?

They both took turns initialing each box. JCO/MGB, over and over and over again until all the yellow highlighted boxes were filled with their markings. Judge James practically snatched the document from their hands, quickly skimmed the pages to make sure everything was filled out, nodded and said, "Perfect." He pointed at Gina and then Carson. "The two of you will meet me tomorrow at the Courthouse at six-thirty in the morning."

"Six-thirty," said Kayla, surprised. "That's only thirty minutes after curfew is lifted."

The Judge shrugged. "I go to work every morning as soon as the curfew is lifted. Gives me a couple of hours to finish up some extra work before my appointments start piling up." He looked back to the engaged couple. "Six-thirty sharp. If you can be there by six-twenty, even better."

"Six-twenty is good with me," muttered Gina.

Carson whispered, "I can make it there by then."

The Judge pulled his coat on and placed his charcoal gray fedora on his head. "Now, if you'll excuse me, my daughter is home without supervision. Ginevieve, Tim... I suggest you two head home soon as well."

Mr. Blake stood from the chair he had been so comfortably lounging in, groaning with the movement. "Yes, we should go."

Carson stood when Gina did. "G," he whispered. "You won't regret this, I swear it. I'll—"

She didn't look at him, but she replied feverishly as she snatched up her tattered cloak and scarf, her tone vexed, "I didn't do this to please you or because I felt sorry for you." She met his gaze then, and her eyes were flames of unmitigated hostility. "Perhaps you deserve a bitter wife."

43

Judge James called out as he walked through the front door of his home, "Margaret!"

"I'm home!" she called back to him. From her bedroom, he assumed.

"Come here," he ordered his daughter. Then added sternly a few moments later when he didn't hear her door open, "Now, Kristina Margaret!"

"Give me a minute!" she yelled back at him. "I just got out of the shower!"

He was patient for two more minutes. Finally, she skipped into the living area where he had sat to take off his laced shoes. "Welcome home," she said, smiling.

He motioned to one of the two white fabric sofas they owned. "Sit. I have something to tell you."

She plopped herself down. She was already dressed for bed and her medium length hair was wet from washing. The tips of her hair had yet to dry, and they dampened her nightgown where they touched it. Her smile was genuine and showed no signs of faltering. Certainly, he was not looking forward to breaking the bad news to her.

"I know you were at the Owens' home less than an hour ago. Derek Owens told me as I was leaving."

She shifted on the white cushion of the sofa, avoiding eye contact with him. She grumbled, "You were there?"

"Yes, I was, but why were you there?"

Slowly, protectively, she crossed her arms over her chest. "I was just going to tell Carson about the termination—"

"No need," Mark interrupted. He didn't mean for it to sound so harsh.

Confused, she remarked, "Why? Does he already know?"

Oh, my sweet child. How I don't want to be the one telling you this. "No. He signed an engagement contract with Gina Blake this evening. Before seven in the morning, they will be married."

Margaret didn't move a muscle. She stared blankly at him as if she hadn't understood the words he'd spoken. He allowed her a full minute to process. "But... you agreed to let *me* marry him. You said—"

"I said," he started, "that if Gina didn't choose him, I would allow you two to marry in a couple of years. I am not—"

"I know you said that," she interrupted. "It's just..." She looked away from him. His heart broke when he saw the tears swelling in her eyes. She kept a stoic face though. Mark gave his daughter more time to compose herself. It took only half a minute before she said, voice wavering only slightly, "Gina said she would not marry him. She was very clear."

Mark blew out his breath and looked down at his socked feet as he said, "I don't know what to tell you, darling. She signed a contract with him."

She ducked her head, face crimsoning. If she was embarrassed now, Mark couldn't imagine how much worse it would have been if Derek Owens had not lied about who had been at the door. He would have to thank him for considering his daughter's feelings later.

Mark pulled one of the several documents from his case. He waved it as he spoke, "You can still marry William. I haven't filed the termination form yet."

She was silent and refused to grace him with even a glance.

He added, "That is if you want. If we can help it, I'd like you to grow up a little more before marrying." She crossed her arms tighter across her chest. "But I know you don't care what makes me happy." There was a long pause. "You'll meet someone else."

She finally spoke, and her statement was painfully young and naive, "There is no one else."

He exhaled some frustration building. *Teenagers are so bloody difficult.* "I know you feel like you can't love anyone else, but you will." To himself mostly, he grumbled, "As long as I can keep your mother from making your marriage political."

She stood up, quite aggressively, fists clenched, and marched out of the room. Her bedroom door slammed a few moments later.

Mark groaned as he laid back into the recliner he'd been sitting in. What was he going to do with his daughter?

"She's just like her mother," he grumbled. He recalled many headbutts between himself and Amaia, one recently being about Margaret marrying a boy from the District. She'd been irritated when Mark had convinced Margaret to sign a contract with William instead but accepted it more gracefully than he expected. He expected her to throw one long tantrum for the rest of their lives, and when she simply didn't speak another word about it, he'd been surprised. But perhaps her vengeance was coming for him.

Probably the only thing that kept them from fighting so much was her job. As an Ambassador, she was off in the District most of the time. But she was supposed to be arriving early in the morning to attend Margaret's wedding.

He rubbed his forehead roughly. *She's going to be upset that I agreed to terminate her engagement. Or maybe she'll be ecstatic for Margaret to marry that Diphdan boy.* He was already rolling his eyes at every possible thing he could imagine leaving Amaia's mouth.

44

Tossing and turning atop her fresh white sheets, Margaret seethed with disdain. She considered she might boil over soon and do something reckless, yet she dismissed the thought of caution as quickly as it came to her.

Gina had lied. Gina had lied to her face.

Margaret tossed herself onto her back, and her arm pinched in protest. She ignored it, grinding her teeth as she mulled over Gina's deception.

I hate her, she seethed. They had been friends—or so she had thought. *Friends don't deceive each other. I was honest*, she thought. *I did not hurt her knowingly. She didn't have to lie to me.*

Gina had been adamant that she would not marry Carson. And being the stupidly trusting friend that she was, she had believed Gina. Believed her, and had gone as far as making plans to marry Carson instead. Even her ex-fiancé and father were okay with it. It had seemed like a perfect plan, one sent to her by the goddess herself.

So what the hell was Gina doing screwing it all up?

She knew I could have Carson if she didn't pick him. Skank! She did this on purpose.

Margaret threw the covers off herself so brutally they flew completely from the bed. She jumped out, fueled by her rage, and pulled her burgundy cloak over her white nightgown. A small voice in the corner of her mind whispered to get back in bed and let it go. If that voice had a face, she'd probably punch it.

It took her a while to figure out the way through the back pastures and woods. She followed certain stars as Carson once taught her—though he cautioned her to never find herself in such a predicament, yet there she was, roaming the woods at night alone, simmering with fury. The stars helped guide her to the most southern district of Polaris. The outskirts, where the houses were spaced out quite far from each other and each family owned plenty of land they tilled with their own hands. These were the Denebian farmers.

Margaret couldn't walk the street; she feared being seen by an insomniac peering out their window. Stealth was a skill that she had not acquired, but she took her time and watched carefully. She steered clear of yards with dogs in them and would take a long way around to avoid catching their attention. All in all, she made it to the Blakes' home without sounding any alarms—which she was quite proud of.

She had only visited Gina's once prior to earlier that day when they dropped off her things before heading over to speak with Carson together. Gina had wanted to try some new cake recipe she thought Margaret would like and invited her over to taste the sugar-glazed goodness. For a Class Four, Gina knew how to make mediocre ingredients taste spectacular. But that was many moons ago. Their friendship was much simpler back then when neither of the girls were verbally honest about their mutual feelings for Carson Owens.

After several minutes of trying to recall Gina's exact room location and counting the windows down the side of the house, she hoped the one she settled on was indeed Gina's. To avoid waking the person inside if it was not Gina, Margaret cracked open the window to peek inside.

Back turned to the window, Gina laid peacefully in her bed. Her silky blonde hair was long, the natural curls falling beautifully over the pillow behind her.

Stars. Her thought was a hiss. *Even her hair is gorgeous.*

She noticed red-handled scissors on the desk across the room. She was wickedly pleased with the image of Gina's blonde hair falling to the ground in mounds. It wasn't like Margaret would be permanently damaging her.

Hair grows back.

Gina shifted in the bed. Margaret froze, half of her body inside the room. She stayed still, but Gina moved again, rolling over onto her back. Then Gina raised her head and looked directly at Margaret.

The blonde girl bolted upright once she registered someone was there. She didn't scream despite her mouth opening to let one loose. Her voice seemed lost altogether. Her almond-shaped eyes were wide and full of terror for a moment and a half. Gina's terror-induced breathing began to calm after a few seconds, and she squinted her eyes to see the looming figure better. The only light was from the moon, and that provided very little.

"Maggie?" she guessed, whispering. She reached over to her battery-operated lamp and switched it on. The warm light filled the room with a soft yellow glow. "You frightened me."

Margaret finished pulling herself into Gina's room and shut the window behind her. The golden locks cascading over Gina's shoulders infuriated Margaret further.

Carson's going to love her hair. She could easily see him combing his fingers through it, golden as sunshine and silky as a satin blouse. He would wrap her curls around his fingers tightly as he'd nuzzle into her neck to kiss her. She would giggle in that sweet and shy way she always did, and he'd grip her tighter to himself.

Her jaw clenched.

"Why are you here?" asked Gina, still whispering. "You're so far away from home. Did you walk the whole way?"

As Gina pretended to be concerned about the Duchess's safety, Margaret took a seat on an ottoman in the corner next to a small bookshelf. She surveyed some of the books there. Most were required school readings, but a few were tattered old things. Collectables, perhaps. Heirlooms. One was titled *Foundations of Mental Health Care*. Emma Blake had been a nurse, so Gina must have kept it from that time.

Gina stepped out of bed. Her nightgown was similar to the one Margaret wore under her cloak, except instead of white, Gina's was mauve. It had been cut shorter—to her mid-thigh—and hemmed, which surprised Margaret considering how prude Gina was.

Perhaps she had made herself something nice to wear for Carson tomorrow night with the extra fabric cut from the bottom. There would be more than enough material for a skimpy outfit or two.

The thought only fueled Margaret's anger. She looked at the red-handled scissors again.

"Maggie?" whispered Gina. She hesitated at the edge of the bed. "Are you okay? Did you want to talk? Is it about your wedding?"

"Not mine," Margaret finally answered, and her words were flat—much less angry than she thought they'd be on her tongue. They definitely did not portray the fire churning inside her heart. "Yours."

"Oh," said Gina, nodding once and glancing out the window Margaret had slipped in through. "Your dad told you, then. That's good. I didn't want it to shock you."

Margaret pulled a teal, fabric-covered book off the shelf, one she didn't recognize as a school reading. It was the most tattered book of them all. The title's letters were in gold and read *Anem's Great Plan for Us: A Guide for Couples on Childbearing*. She opened it to the worn and discolored title page. A notecard was stuck inside.

Gina said as Margaret pulled out the note and examined it, "I know I said I wouldn't marry him. But I thought about what you said. It would be good for me and my family. Also, I learned new things today that I cannot unfortunately unlearn, and that was what ultimately helped me make my decision. Are you displeased? I thought this was what you wanted, Margaret."

Margaret hardly heard her. She was too busy fuming over what she saw on the scrap of paper placed between the pages. It was a message

355

addressed to the annoyingly beautiful blonde pauper:

Gina,

This was my mother's mother's mother's book. Mom tossed it into the bin (as you know, she's still very bitter), but I pulled it from the trash. I know we are many years away from marriage, but I think it's never too early to prepare.

Oh! Congratulations on finding out you'll be a big sister again! Anem smiles down on your parents for going above and beyond what she has called of her servants. The gift of children will not go unrewarded, as the Star Scrolls say.

Save this book. We can read it together one day, when we are ready to have our own children. Hopefully we will be just as blessed as your parents.

Carson

In the top right corner, the note was dated back three years. Carson was fourteen when he wrote that note and gave his pretty little girlfriend such a particular book on childbearing. What fourteen-year-old boy would consider such things? In the Duchess's experience, fourteen-year-old boys only thought about satisfying themselves and asking the girls to help them with it. Margaret had known Carson was not like the majority of them, but apparently Carson's mind held more mysteries than she truly realized.

He had been planning a family with Ginevieve Blake.

Margaret snapped the book shut and the loud crack of it startled Gina. The girl hastily put her finger over her mouth to shush her while looking at her bedroom door and back to the Duchess. "Quiet," breathed Gina, as lowly as her voice could possibly go. "Jed's room is right across from mine, and he's a light sleeper."

"Oh, what do you care?" hissed Margaret. "You probably would love for me to get caught, tied to that damn post, and flogged in front of the whole Province."

Eyebrows furrowed and eyes questioning, Gina's perfect pink lips formed a silent question: *What?*

Margaret rolled her eyes and stood. She showed the notecard to Gina. "How many notes and letters has he written you?"

Gina took the note but didn't look at it. "I'm unsure of the approximate amount." As Gina spoke, Margaret set the book down on the desk and grabbed the red-handled scissors. "Why does it matter? Are you angry?" Gina glanced down at the scissors. She quickly put the note in the drawer of her nightstand and stood protectively in front of it as though Margaret would destroy it otherwise.

For reasons unknown, that irritated Margaret more. Shifting from one foot to the other, Gina added in a formal tone suddenly converted from her lax one, "Forgive me, my lady. I was only doing as I was told."

Margaret approached slowly. "Turn around."

Tears fell from the girl's winsome green eyes as she shook her head and stepped away. She gripped her hair tightly, knuckles white.

Margaret grinned. Gina knew her hair was beautiful, and that was exactly why she would take it from her. "Turn around," Margaret said through her teeth.

"Please," begged Gina, voice caught in her throat. Her face reddened with dread as she continued to plead quietly.

Ignoring the pain in her left arm, Margaret grabbed Gina's nightgown and tugged it hard enough to move her a couple of inches forward. "I am your Duchess," she spat as Gina stumbled into her. "If I say to turn around, what should you do?"

Gina ducked her head, and she shakily turned her back to the Duchess. She placed her hand over her mouth just as a soft whimper escaped her lips. She was still trying not to alert anyone else in the house to Margaret's presence.

"Release your hair."

Hesitantly, she obeyed.

Margaret tugged at her hair quite hard. Gina muffled another whimper. She twisted her hair into a thick rope, snipping a few escaped curls in the process. Bit by bit, she sawed through Gina's hair. A mountain of the long golden hair laid on the ground at their feet, silky and shining.

Satisfied with how hideous her hack-job looked, Margaret threw the scissors onto the bed. As she opened the window, she paused and turned back to Gina, one last thing she wanted to say to the girl lingering in her head.

Gina laid over her bed, clutching her sheets against her mouth as she sobbed. Before leaving, Margaret leaned down by Gina's ear. "Bitch," she hissed. Now satisfied, she stood, smirked at the mound of hair on the floor, and then began climbing out of the window.

"I'm sorry if I hurt you," whimpered Gina before she had completely exited the room.

Margaret stared at her friend, her beautiful golden hair now butchered so brutally, and guilt crept into her heart for what she had done.

The girl sniffled as she bent down, picked up a chunk of her hair and held it against her chest. Looking up through her black eyelashes, all sorrow was abruptly replaced by a fury that could chill hell itself to its fiery bones.

"But at least I'm not a slut who seduced a good man away from the woman he loved and gave him back to her once I was satisfied," Gina spat. "At least I didn't insist she marry him for monetary gain if not love, and then turn around, *change my mind and blame her*." The latter part of her statement she hissed through clenched teeth, and the venom in her words surprised Margaret. Gina added in a breathless wisp of emotions as angry-hot tears streamed down her face, "At least I'm not *that* bitch."

Margaret's remorse vanished like dew in summer heat, and she said calmly to the lock-less girl, "Jump off a sea cliff. No one will miss a poor girl like you for very long."

She slipped out of her room completely and left the window open.

As she walked away, the window slammed shut. Margaret's heart jumped and skin crawled. She hurried home, not as careful in her journey as she was the first time. She was hyper-aware that Gina could very well report her. Probably would. She was angry enough to, at least. Hell, Margaret had chopped off her hair!

What have I done?

Margaret laid in bed for the next three hours, listening carefully for any sounds of officers coming to arrest her. She prayed Gina did not and would not tell anyone what had happened, though she knew she didn't deserve her mercy.

She dozed into a restless slumber and dreamed of a young girl jumping off one of the cliffs by the Glassy Sea—falling, falling, falling to her death on the rocks weathered by the waves far below. And the cliff wailed in sorrow for the loss of life. And the fish bellowed their grievance. And the people of Deneb lamented, crying out in the streets, "Our beloved child is gone!"

Gone. Gone. Gone.

45

Carson's alarm blared at four forty-five in the morning. He had placed it across the room so that he would be forced to drag himself out of the warm bed to turn it off. He exhaled heavily as he clicked the off button.

While he showered, he realized he didn't feel excited about getting married. It wasn't that he wasn't happy Gina chose him—because of course he was happy about that—but it wasn't like he was all that thrilled for the two of them to be marrying so young. Neither of them had ever thought they would be getting married before their eighteenth birthdays, at the earliest. They had both always talked about marrying after their Rituals, when they'd be Matures and considered developed enough to start their own household.

But the marriage was necessary. She didn't have a choice, so neither did he. And that sucked. He was glad there was no wedding, at least. If Gina wanted one later, he supposed that would be fine. But right now, only days after being flogged for extramarital relations, he wasn't ready nor in the mood to be the center of attention again. The flogging was still fresh in people's minds, as were the scabs on his back.

He supposed even though they would be married, they did not need to be together for a while. In fact, he planned on taking it slow with Gina. She was delicate, and she deserved time to believe in love again—to believe in him again. He would make sure she was always comfortable and never felt pressured. He would get to know her all over again. He simply wanted her to be and feel safe. Their home would be a place of peace for her. To that, he vowed.

Timothy Blake's account of his past surfaced in Carson's mind then. He was still quite surprised by the unsettling knowledge of Mr. Blake's actions. He couldn't understand why the man would do such a thing. Why couldn't he stop for even a moment to consider Emma, his hapless wife, who had only just given birth? Birth was the work of the goddess, and Mr. Blake had been unappreciative of his wife's dedication to Anem. Carson concluded that he and young Timothy would not have been good friends if his morality had been so dubious.

He wondered if Gina knew of her parents' past struggles. She would hate knowing, since the only memories she wanted of her mother were happy ones. Carson would not mention to Gina any of what Mr. Blake had said to him. Her mother had been a happy woman in front of the children, and Gina deserved to remember her that way—not as a wife who'd been scorned.

Derek, Kayla, and Casey were eating breakfast at the table when Carson finally emerged, fully dressed and ready to go. They, too, appeared ready, and it was only five-thirty.

He'd be a husband in less than an hour.

"Don't you look handsome," his mother commented. "You even put on a tie."

"Of course he did," grumbled Casey. She sounded tired. "He's getting married. You have to wear a tie when you get married."

"I didn't wear a tie," remarked their father, reaching over with his fork to steal a bite of Casey's waffle. She swatted at his hand, and he chuckled.

"Oh, yeah," said Kayla as she handed Carson a full plate: Scrambled eggs, two slices of thick bacon, and blueberry waffles with maple syrup. "I vaguely remember being annoyed at how casual you were dressed."

Casey seemed quite surprised. "How did that go? I bet the Prophet wasn't happy with it, showing up to the temple in casual-wear. For your wedding, too."

"They didn't get married in the temple," said Carson without thinking. He knew about his parents having been in the same situation as he and Gina currently were in, but he had not realized that Casey didn't know.

Casey's eyebrows furrowed as she stuffed her mouth with a huge bite of her waffle. "Wha—?" she barely managed to say around the food.

Kayla explained, "I was sixteen, like Gina."

Casey looked from her to Derek, still obviously confused. Derek said to Kayla, "She's old enough to know," before looking back at Casey. "I was seventeen, like Carson. Your mother was part of a verbally abusive family, and she had secretly requested the Judge at the time to get her out of that house. His solution was marriage."

Casey swallowed the food. "Did you two pick each other?"

So his sister was just going to ignore the part about their mother growing up in an abusive home? Perhaps she knew more than he thought. Maybe since they didn't see or speak to any extended family, she figured—as Carson had many years ago—that their parents came from bad families.

Or maybe she just didn't care.

Casey continued. "My teacher said that about forty-three percent of cases are arranged by the Judge." It was a good question, one Carson had never considered. His parents seemed to love each other, so he had always assumed they had chosen each other.

"No," answered their mother, picking at the few bites of egg left on her plate. "The late Judge Stern—may his soul rest in Anem's embrace—assigned your father to marry me. He wasn't very happy about it at first." She gave her husband a coy smile and winked. "He thought I talked too much."

He smiled back, chuckled and said, "I was seventeen and barely knew you. We'd had maybe two conversations. And by conversations, I mean you talked and I listened."

"At least you thought I was pretty." She tilted her cheek to him flirtatiously.

He leaned over to her and kissed it. He replied amorously, "I thought you were beautiful. Honestly," he shrugged at Casey, "it's why I didn't complain."

Carson rolled his eyes at the two of them. "That's a horrible reason to just accept an arrangement."

Derek looked at him for a whole second, then gestured to his breakfast. "Not hungry? Are you nervous or what?"

Carson poked at the eggs. "I guess so. I don't really want to do this today."

Kayla set her fork down on her plate. "Get married?"

Derek added onto her question, "It's not ideal—trust me, I know—but at least you love this girl and you both chose each other." He motioned to Casey. "Apparently you're part of the fifty-seven percent that gets to choose." He made a fist and gently touched Carson's shoulder. It was awkward. "Good for you, son."

He was right. Carson needed to make the best out of it.

"After we get back, we need to rearrange and organize your room," said his mother. "Make space for Gina's things."

Though he knew she'd have to move in with them—namely him—his stomach still formed a pit in it at the thought of them sharing a room.

He replied quietly, "If she wants."

"Well, she doesn't really have a choice. Married couples have to live in the same house. And Immatures cannot purchase their own home. You know that."

His father nodded in agreement and added, "It's either she moves in here or you move in there. Isn't the whole point of her getting married now to get her away from the farm?"

Carson rubbed his eyes roughly and sighed, "Yeah, it is. But she doesn't have to share a room with me if she doesn't want to. I don't want her to feel uncomfortable."

"She can stay with me," said Casey excitedly. She bounced a couple of times in her chair, looking at their mother for approval.

Kayla said to her, "We will give her the choice. Carson's right; the last thing we want is for her to feel uncomfortable."

A loud banging on the door startled everyone at the table.

"What in Anem's—" Derek stood from the table. Curfew was still in effect. No one should be out at this time.

Curiosity got the best of the three others at the table. They followed Derek to the door and peeked over his shoulder as he opened it. Two officers in uniform stood there, hands on their utility belts. "Officer Owens," the fat one addressed. "You are needed to assist in a search party."

"Search party?" Derek questioned. "Who's missing?"

"Eight Immature girls and two Mature men."

Carson's eyebrows shot up. That was ten people missing. All in one night. And people hardly ever went missing in Polaris.

How strange.

"Okay, I will be there as soon as I can. In the meantime, get William to approve—"

"Chief Officer Lach is one of the missing," informed the officer who had yet to say a word. It was quiet for a long moment. The same officer added, "Judge James said all orders are to come from you. You are acting chief."

Derek inhaled and exhaled, processing the information. "All right then," he accepted. "Involve the northern, southern, eastern, and western precincts. I want every officer in the city on the clock. Split into groups and search each victim's home for any clues of struggle. Rally volunteers too. Have them meet in the city's square at eight. We'll need as many eyes as we can get to search the wooded areas, fields, pastures, and the beaches. If nothing comes up, we'll have to get out the wings and search the Red Desert and Wastelands."

"You think they are runaways? That it was planned?" The fat officer sounded skeptical.

Derek shrugged. "This was obviously planned, but whether it was by those missing or by someone else entirely doesn't matter right now. Assume nothing and assume everything. Do you have a list of who all is missing?"

They nodded, and the fat officer ripped a piece of paper from the small notebook in his hand, having prepared ahead for such a question.

Derek scanned the names. Carson thought he spent a lot of time looking over the piece of paper. He cursed under his breath suddenly then asked the two officers, "Is this list accurate?"

"Yes, sir," they chimed.

"Are you *positive*?" Derek didn't seem happy with their first answer.

They glanced at each other but answered timely with the skinnier officer saying, "Yes, sir. We've already taken statements from the different family members."

Derek cursed again.

"What is it?" Carson couldn't stand the suspense anymore. If his father knew someone on that list, it was possible Carson did too.

He glanced back at Carson for only half a second, then said to the officers, "I will be at the station as soon as possible. Don't wait for me. Start investigating the homes of the missing kids first." They nodded their understanding and left as Derek closed the door.

He turned to Carson and hesitated briefly, but he ultimately offered the paper to him. "Gina is one of the missing girls."

ACKNOWLEDGEMENTS

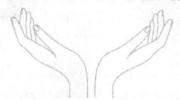

There are so many people over the last thirteen years or so this story has been in my heart to thank. Starting from the beginning, and the most important, I thank God for laying this oppression-to-freedom story on my heart and keeping it there all these years.

My parents, Guy and Kimberly, have always been so supportive of my writing and my strive to make it a career. I recall them reading the first chapter I wrote. It was in Carson's viewpoint, in first person, and I had next-to-no writing experience. Not once did they make me feel like it was cringe, even when, in fact, it very much was.

My sister and developmental editor, Jayci, who helped me figure out some major issues in the story and exponentially aided me in improving my own skill in writing prose.

My husband and best friend in the whole freaking world, Chris, who believes I can do anything I put my mind to and is an amazing father to our beautiful children.

All others who have been there for me in big ways and in small, I want to thank with all my heart: Braedon, Taylor, Rhonda, Vanessa, Devyn P. Guerra, Elisabeth Wheatley, Tracey Barski, and Xyvah Okoye. Whether you helped with beta reading, brainstorming, listened to me rant over writing struggles, or was simply a friend I knew I could talk to about anything—thank you so much for all you've done for me, for this book, and for simply being in my life.